MURDER ON THE SET

"Sedra Stone's dead? How?" Polly gasped. "What happened? An accident? Did Dorothy's house finally fall on her?"

"It's all over the news," Tim said as he reached for the television remote control. He pushed the power button. The plasma screen mounted over the fireplace at the foot of Polly's bed filled with an image of a reporter in the field who was covering the story from the scene.

"What we *can* report at this time is that her chauffeur found the body of the star at approximately midnight. She was discovered in the swimming pool on the high school location set of her new movie. She apparently fell from the ten-meter diving platform."

"Drowning," Polly shivered. "A horrible way to go."

"The pool was . . . empty," the reporter said, as if he'd heard Polly and corrected her presumption. "But according to Detective Archer of the Santa Clarita Police Department, they can't rule out the possibility of foul play . . ."

Books by R. T. Jordan

REMAINS TO BE SCENE

FINAL CURTAIN

Published by Kensington Publishing Corporation

REMAINS TO BE SCENE

A Polly Pepper Mystery

R. T. Jordan

KENSINGTON BOOKS
http://www.kensingtonbooks.com

KENSINGTON BOOKS are published by

Kensington Publishing Corp.
850 Third Avenue
New York, NY 10022

All Kensington titles, imprints, and distributed lines are available at special quantity discounts for bulk purchases for sales promotion, premiums, fund-raising, educational, or institutional use.

Special book excerpts or customized printings can also be created to fit specific needs. For details, write or phone the office of the Kensington Special Sales Manager: Attn. Special Sales Department. Kensington Publishing Corp., 850 Third Avenue, New York, NY, 10022. Phone: 1-800-221-2647.

Kensington and the K logo Reg. U.S. Pat. & TM Off.

ISBN-13: 978-0-7582-1281-8
ISBN-10: 0-7582-1281-X

First Kensington Hardcover Printing: February 2007
First Kensington Mass Market Paperback Printing: January 2008
10 9 8 7 6 5 4 3 2 1

Printed in the United States of America

For Robin Blakely
(With love and gratitude)

Acknowledgments

I sort of pinch myself with wonder every time I get to publicly thank my amazing editor at Kensington, Mr. John Scognamiglio. Thanks for another book, John! Also, my agent Joelle Delbourgo gets a standing ovation for welcoming me into her illustrious fold. A special note of gratitude to Dorris Halsey, who gave my novel its fun title, and to my fellow Kensington author Laura Levine—who writes the wildly hilarious Jaine Austen mystery series—thank you for telling me that you liked this book and for writing such an awesome and bubbly blurb for the jacket of the hardcover edition! Kevin Howell, I could never thank you enough. Julia Oliver, the same goes for you, too.

To Muriel Pollia, Ph.D.: There is no separation between us. You promised. To William Relling, Jr.: You were wrong. You *did* make a difference. Mr. Billy Barnes—you're an awesome and talented man.

"Murder is always a mistake—one should never do anything one cannot talk about after dinner."
—Oscar Wilde

"One must never set up a murder. They must happen unexpectedly, as in life."
—Alfred Hitchcock

Prologue

"There's no business like show business, eh? What a load!" said veteran actress Trixie Wilder as she opened the door and stepped inside her dressing room trailer on the movie location of Sterling Studios' new musical, *Detention Rules!* "Damn starlets," she added, as her hand automatically met the switch plate on the wall just inside the entry. But in that nanosecond between flipping on the light switch and the flooding of illumination via overhead fluorescent tubes, the sound of something moving in the deep black maw of the trailer made her heart skip a beat. Her concern was instantly quelled by the sight of her tabby, Patches, racing unusually fast to greet her. Trixie took a deep breath of relief and closed the door behind her.

"There's a pretty bay-be! Yes, indeed!" Trixie squealed as she lovingly scooped the cat into her arms and rocked her like a newborn. They affectionately nuzzled noses. "Mommy's finally home from a big ol' bad day at Black Rock. Yes, she is! Yes, she is!"

Preoccupied with cuddling Patches and listening to the animal's contented purr, Trixie moved into the room toward the sofa—and abruptly tripped. She dropped the cat, but was able to break her own fall by tumbling forward onto the soft upholstered cushion of the sofa.

"What the hell?" she cried, irritated and confused. When she righted herself and was assured that she hadn't twisted an ankle or injured a wrist, she looked back and discovered a red brick on the floor in the center of the room. "What the hell's that thing doing . . . ?" She looked around, then returned her attention to her pet and profusely apologized for scaring the critter.

Trixie Wilder was nobody of any serious consequence in Hollywood. At her advanced age she wasn't anyone about whom editors at *People* magazine ever thought to devote even an inch of column space. If one of the gossip queens at *The National Peeper* referenced her in a story, it was always a piece profiling someone else. Trixie had long ago accepted the fact that she would never become a headline news subject.

She was a recognizable face from her steady appearances in bit parts for half a century, but she wasn't even the caliber of celebrity who would show up on the old "Hollywood Squares" television game show with the likes of Rose Marie. Indeed, aside from a couple of minor recurring roles on sitcoms, she was seldom more than a day player in feature films. But she'd worked with practically every legend from the golden age of motion pictures . . . if only to deliver a wiseacre line to Roz Russell or Jimmy Stewart.

"Ahh," she sighed, sitting down at her vanity. She took off her shoes and rubbed her sore feet. "Honey, I think I'm finally too old for this grueling work," she said to the cat. She began to remove her makeup. "If I don't retire soon that little no-talent upstart Dana Pointer—or someone like her—is bound to be the death of me. I can see malice in her eyes whenever I deliver my lines."

Trixie squeezed a dollop of Vaseline Intensive Care lotion

into the palm of her hand and slathered her face. "Can I help it if I'm a better actor? Sheesh!" She gave another heavy sigh.

Draping a kerchief over her head of short gray hair, which was matted from being trapped under a wig for fourteen hours, Trixie tied the ends of the scarf under her chin. She looked at herself in the mirror and groaned at the sight of her Grandma Moses face. "Maybe in my next lifetime . . ." she said wistfully. "Okay, kiddo. Let's blow this joint. I've TiVO'd 'Project Runway.' Let's get home and see what Heidi Klum's up to."

As Trixie reached for her purse, she sensed a subtle transfer of weight at the other end of the aluminum trailer. She stood perfectly still and held her breath. She scanned the room for a weapon with which to defend herself against a possible attacker. The only item readily at hand was a half-full carafe of coffee left over from breakfast. She automatically grabbed hold of it by the handle.

"I'm calling security," Trixie called out for the benefit of anyone who might be in the trailer. With her free hand she reached into her purse and retrieved her cell phone. She'd seen enough slasher films to know that it was a cardinal rule *never* to venture down into darkness alone to investigate peculiar sounds. "Hell, I don't even know the number for security," she whispered, as she opened the lid to her phone and moved backward toward the front door. She decided to dial nine–one–one, but to save the last digit until she was certain that there was an actual emergency. She looked down at the keypad and squinted at the tiny numbers. She found the #9 and could hear a soft tone as she pushed the button. She pushed the #1 and momentarily took her eyes off the LED display when she was distracted by the sense that someone was walking out from the shadowy end of the trailer. Just as she looked up, a reflexive jolt of adrenalin shot through her body and she gasped.

"Jeez Louise!" Trixie said, panting and holding her cell close to her rapidly heaving chest. "What the hell are *you* doing in here? You should know better than to scare an old woman." Trixie was at once startled and relieved to discover who had been hiding in the bathroom. But her ease quickly turned to anger. "If you're trying to give me a heart attack, you practically succeeded!" she said. Then a thought dawned on her. "Oh, I get it. This is about our earlier discussion. You can save your breath. Take it up with the director, 'cause I'm not leaving this show under any circum . . ."

In an instant, Trixie was pushed to the floor. The glass carafe flew out of her hand and splashed coffee all over her clothes and the carpet. Her cell phone dropped from her other hand. And her head hit the brick on the floor. Patches hissed and leaped onto the sofa.

Then the trailer became deadly silent. The lights were turned off, the door to the trailer opened and was locked from the inside, then closed.

And the world continued to revolve—despite the sudden and unexpected departure from the planet of an old Hollywood actress—one whom no one would miss. One who would finally have her name in a featured news headline.

Chapter 1

"I want a job like Marg Helgenberger's," Polly Pepper pouted as she sat reading *The National Peeper* at the poolside patio breakfast table on the sprawling grounds of her Bel Air mansion. While sipping a Bloody Mary through a crystal straw engraved with her initials, she read and agreed with the lead article. The opinion of the writer—that Marg had a very cool career on "CSI"—made her envious. Polly sniffed. "I can do Marg's job in my sleep! Don't we solve those damn murder cases before anyone, including that sexy Gil Grissom?"

Polly recounted a recent scenario from her favorite television series. "Hell, as soon as the bride-to-be slept with the male stripper from her bachelorette party it was obvious that the jealous fiancé asphyxiated the stud. It didn't take a forensic expert to figure out that all those Ziploc bags filled with the bits and pieces of the corpse could be traced back to said fiancé!" She then turned the page and began reading about a mass grave of family pets exhumed on Reba McEntire's estate.

Wrapped in a pink silk monogrammed robe, with her

dyed red hair and most of her famous face shrouded behind a curtain of paisley scarf, Polly looked up from her paper and absently peered over the rims of her designer sunglasses. She blinked with annoyance and then stared at her handsome but disheveled son, Tim. He was seated opposite her, wearing shorts and a nearly diaphanous T-shirt that was threadbare after years of use. Polly supposed it was his adult version of a security blanket.

Tim clutched a coffee mug with both hands holding tightly, as if it might escape. His body was hunched over Doonesbury in the *Los Angeles Times*.

Without question, Tim was the light in Polly's life. Bright, talented, articulate, popular, and every inch the sum total of a good gene pool and private physical fitness trainers, Tim was pretty much the perfect son. As for a career—that was spotty; however, nobody in Beverly Hills was a better party planner than Tim. He was meticulous, and his theme soirees made Polly equally famous as a revered hostess. But at ten o'clock in the morning it was still too early for him to make coherent conversation. Until his infusion of caffeine, grunts were the extent of his ability to communicate.

Polly's eyes darted from Tim to their maid, Placenta, who, in the starched white uniform that she loathed wearing, was well into her daily chores, scooping out purple bougainvillea petals from the koi pond. To Polly, Placenta was an oddity because she was more interested in the lives of ordinary people than what she called the "superficial set dressing of Hollywood." Placenta occupied her time and mind with what she considered to be more significant cultural events, such as the bits of fingers that litigious patrons of fast food restaurants slipped into their soups and chilies. She was bored by Polly's discussions of the mercurial whims of ancient celebrities, most of whom were presumed by the general public to be dead anyway.

This morning, neither Polly's only offspring nor her servant seemed to pay any attention to what she had to say. It occurred to Polly that practically anyone else of a certain age on the planet, if provided the opportunity of being seated at Polly Pepper's breakfast table, would have hung on her every word, gesture, and puff of cigarette smoke.

Polly cleared her throat, raised her voice half an octave, and continued her rant. "It says that the 'CSI' writers and producers have tons of technical help to keep the audience constantly guessing. Heck, we usually know in the first two or three scenes! We should have our own show. 'CSI: Holly-wood.'"

Without looking up from the comic strip panels, Tim yawned, and in a groggy voice he forced out a sentence almost in monotone. "A whole series about stars who have gone missing from the tube since before the turn of the millennium—like you," he said, then took another gulp of coffee.

Tim's sarcasm buffeted Polly like an unexpected bad review. "I'm iconic!" Polly huffed. Her memory flashed on the tough but fulfilling life she'd once known as an international television superstar. For a time, she was the biggest. The highest paid. The most honored. The most beloved. An entire room in Pepper Plantation, her famous home, overflowed with Emmys, People's Choice, and nearly every other show-biz award—a testimony to her stature in Hollywood. Like Bette or Cher or Barbra, Polly's first name alone was all the identification anyone needed in order to know about whom one was speaking. Only a Maori Aborigine or a Gen-Xer might be excused from knowing that Polly Pepper was a goddess from the golden age of television's musical/comedy variety hours.

With a singing voice just slightly less raspy than Rod Stewart's, and dancing aptitude limited to a soft shoe, Polly had hit the talent jackpot with brilliant comic timing that turned ordinarily lame chicken jokes into labor-inducing convulsions. She parlayed her minimal talent into stardom and her own wedge of cement on the Hollywood Walk of Fame. With her trademark feet-on-the-ground personality, viewers, if asked, would describe Polly as "a real live person."

Two decades had passed, however, since her hit variety series, "The Polly Pepper Playhouse," disappeared from the airwaves. Another decade has flown by since the network pulled the plug on her attempted comeback in the critically skewered sitcom aptly titled, "PP!" And more recently her big-budget Broadway-bound musical bio of Typhoid Mary was pronounced D.O.A. in N.Y.C. (although a dance remix of the show's best song, "Bacteria," became a hit at clubs). Her career now was reduced to playing Mame or Dolly each summer in what she euphemistically refers to as her "Mortgage Tours." After three decades in show business, Polly Pepper's luster was fading faster than Scott Peterson's virginity in San Quentin.

Tim, usually sensitive to his mother's vulnerability, and now realizing that his attempt at levity so early in the day had been unkind, mumbled to his mother, "Honey, you'll always be a star, and I know that you'll get another series. The Young Turks who run this town just haven't caught on to how much the general public loves you, and wants you back in their living rooms," he said.

"You think I still have some market value?" Polly asked.

"Like Vicoden," Tim insisted.

Still, Tim's smart-aleck remark had magnified what Polly had been feeling for too long—that she was a relic, like something once treasured but now stashed away in an attic and forgotten. For the past several years she and her analyst had tried to justify her diminished position in the hierarchy of Hollywood by deciding that a "has been" was better than a "never was," and that after her many years of hard work and self-sacrifice, she was entitled to an extended hiatus. But her ego was too big to accept anonymity for more than the tick of the second hand on her Cartier wristwatch.

The truth was that she missed those exhausting years when she was forced to be out of bed by 5:00 A.M. The chauffeured car would take her to the television studio, and by seven she was meeting with her producer and writers and reading the script of the comedy sketch routines for the week's show. By ten, she would be in the rehearsal hall with her choreographer learning a dance number with Robert Goulet, Betty White, or Benji. The afternoons were reserved for meetings with the network suits, lunch with a *TV Guide* reporter, or working with her personal assistant to respond to the thousands of letters that arrived in bulk each week.

Those letters were indispensable to Polly. Most important, they confirmed the public's adoration of her, and they were used as a barometer of what her fans liked and disliked about each week's guests, sketches, and the selection of musical material. Second, the mail was used as a prop on the program. In a novel and always hysterically funny way to open each week's hour of comedy and music, Polly would call for the house lights to be turned up—the better to emphasize her accessibility. She would then sit in a wingback chair that was placed at the foot of the stage, beside a coffee table on which sat a large fish bowl filled with mail. She then invited a volunteer member of the studio audience to hold the fishbowl while Polly closed her eyes, turned her head, and reached inside. She removed what was presumed to be an arbitrarily selected envelope.

Polly would slip a pair of reading glasses on, open the envelope, clear her throat, and read aloud the message. The questions were always intentionally provocative inquiries about Polly's personal life or peculiar problems that required her sage but amusing advice.

Of course, this was a scripted and well-rehearsed gimmick. Polly and her staff of writers selected and embellished the lamest missives. It was clear to Polly from the content of the semi-literate mail that she was a darling among gun-hording trailer-dwellers, rather than the class of sophisti-cated PBS-supporting left-wing liberals to which she aspired.

The staff writers on "The Polly Pepper Playhouse" com-posed Polly's supposedly extemporaneous sidesplitting re-sponses. A typical recitation at the top of the show's one-hour broadcast would find Polly in a serious ladylike de-meanor, opening an envelope and reading, "'Dear Polly, do you sleep in the nude?'" Polly grimaced in a way that made audiences roar with laughter and anticipation of her response. She blushed on cue and feigned embarrassment. Then, with a wink of an eye, looking straight into the camera she asked in a sultry voice, "Am I alone?" The audience nearly busted a collective hernia with Polly's seemingly spontaneous and naughty wit. The phrase, "Am I alone?" quickly made it into the vernacular of pop culture.

Or, "'Dear Polly. You're such a common and down-to-earth star with lots of ex-husbands (that same wide-eyed look of unease crossing her face) and lots of Emmy Awards, too. What's the difference between your ex-husbands and your Emmy Awards?'" Without missing a beat Polly replied, "The difference, my darling, sweet, invading-my-privacy fan, is that if my ex-husbands were all in a car that drove off a cliff, I'd feel terrible if my Emmys were in the trunk!

"Thank you, everybody," she would declare and quickly stand up as if putting an end to the public humiliation. "To-night we have a fabulous show for you. Don Adams is here! (Applause.) The Captain and Tenille are here! (Applause.) Jack Klugman is dropping by! (Applause.) Our regulars, Arnie Levin, Tommy Milkwood, the lovely and talented Laura Crawford! (Applause.) And of course the Polly Pepper Prancers! We'll be right back after these messages from our sponsors and station identification. Don't you dare go away!"

But the audiences did go away—eventually. Now, Polly's

glory days of hard work, discipline, and #1 Nielsen ratings had morphed into a star's worst fear—looks of vague recognition and whispers between strangers who ask, "Didn't she used to be . . . ?"

Slowly slipping back to reality, Polly exhaled loudly as she refocused on her present life and turned the page of *The Peeper*. Her eyes focused on a picture of Lindsay Lohan, which set her off on another rant. "Good God," Polly winced. "Look at those bazongas! Who did that tramp have to kill to get into all those Disney movies? Remind me to call her up and ask to recommend a hit man. Although it's probably her mother."

Polly noisily sucked up the last of her Bloody Mary, then impatiently wiggled the glass high above her head. "Oh, Placenta, darling," she cooed.

Placenta dumped soggy bougainvillea petals into a trashcan and wiped her hands on her apron. She marched up to the table and snatched the glass out of Polly's grasp. "Don't exhaust yourself," she sniped. "And if you're thinking of killing off young movie stars for a role, skip Lindsay or that Duff girl. Try being age appropriate for once. Think Faye Dunaway."

"Does anybody even remember her?" Polly scowled.

"Whatever. But you're never getting a Nicole Kidman hand-me-down, honey, no matter how hard you cry, or how young you think prosthetic makeup can fool the gullible public into believing you are."

Tim, finally emerging from his semi-catatonic state, looked up from the newspaper and said, "There's only one actor on the planet who Polly Pepper wouldn't mind being poured into an urn and sealed away forever in a vault at Forest Lawn."

"Polly Pepper would never wish ill upon a fellow thespian," the star said. "It says so on my official Web site. Or in that otherwise horrid unauthorized biography."

Setting down his coffee mug, Tim prodded, "I suppose the *initials* Sedra Stone no longer mean anything to you?"

Polly sat perfectly still—as one who isn't sure whether to laugh or cry is wont to do.

Placenta, dumping a can of V-8 into a tumbler and measuring in a couple of fingers of vodka, some Worcestershire sauce, lime juice, and a celery stalk, looked at Tim as if he were crazy to bring up the taboo subject of Sedra Stone. She braced herself with a surreptitious slug from Polly's Bloody Mary before moving to the table and tentatively placing the glass before her mistress.

Polly gave Tim a cold stare, then dipped her straw into the drink and took a long pull that drained half the glass. She smacked her lips in satisfaction, and said, "Tim darling. Just because Sedra Stone stole your semi-daddy . . ."

"And your second pathetic excuse for a husband, too," Placenta added before quickly walking from the patio through the open French doors leading to the kitchen.

". . . doesn't mean I hold the slightest grudge against her," Polly continued. "We all do what we have to do to succeed and survive in this crummy town. I certainly wouldn't trade all the combined Oscars on Hilary Swank and Meryl Streep's mantles for Sedra's mucky Karma."

Sedra Stone was Polly Pepper's biggest rival in Hollywood. Also a legend from 1980s television, she was the antithesis of Polly Pepper. Her long-running primetime soap opera "Monarchy" gave Sedra fame, fortune, and an identity that, all these years later, was still synonymous with a steely disposition, mastery at manipulation, and an acid tongue that could sizzle through an umbilical cord. On screen she usually played an emasculating CEO who would lie, cheat, embezzle, murder, and have sex with half a dozen board members from competing corporations before lunch. She would then move on to seducing hard-bodied and equally unscrupulous male office assistants who were younger by more than half her years before the Swiss weenies were served at cocktail hour.

She was equally malevolent offscreen. At the height of her fame, even naïve young school kids who didn't get the joke would giggle and repeat, "What's the difference between Sedra Stone and the *Titanic*? More men went down on Sedra Stone. Tee-hee."

Polly wagged a finger. "No, Tim darling," she said. "When it comes to failed and scandalous Hollywood marriages, I've learned a lot from dear Debbie and Liz. Anyway, Sedra's rat droppings in this town. She can't get arrested."

"Except for that time she took a swing at that hunky Beverly Hills traffic cop when he forced her to take a Breathalyzer," Tim chuckled.

"Mark my words, dear heart," Polly continued, "directors would surely come to me before they would ever think to hire Sedra. On the other hand . . . ," Polly thought for a moment. "This town could actually do without that Trixie Wilder and her ilk."

"One less character actor might make way for a star to get her face back on screen," Tim agreed.

"At this stage, I wouldn't mind having Trixie's career," Polly said.

"At least she's got one," Tim said.

"You can have it," Placenta said, overhearing the banter as she hurried from the house into the bright warm morning.

Tim interrupted. "Trixie Wilder? She's not even a star," he said. "Oh, she was fun on that Bob Newhart thing years ago, but that's so far in the past it doesn't even appear on 'Nick at Nite.' She does character bits. People recognize her from commercials and cameos, but they don't even know her name."

"Trixie takes anything that comes along, so she'll never stop working," Polly lamented.

"One day she'll be dead and she'll still play the role of the corpse that the coroner pulls out of a morgue refrigerator, when someone comes to identify what's left of a serial killer's victim," Tim laughed.

"She's in rehearsals," Placenta said, panting, and trying to get a word in edgewise. "She's got herself a toe tag."

"Ach! Trixie's as ancient as Lauren Bacall," Polly said. "But let's face it, character types last well past a star's shelf life. Speaking of Miss Bacall," Polly changed the subject and glared at Tim, "How did *she* rate a Kennedy Center Honor? And she's not even on life support. Yet. So there goes that stupid theory about the Grim Reaper stalking old stars who finally get some renewed recognition. Back to Trixie. You think that nobody knows her? Well, she's mentioned in *The Peeper*!"

"Yes, about Trixie . . ." Placenta said.

Polly picked up the paper again and thumbed back several pages. "Here it is," Polly said. "'Although it's hardly anyone's idea of an old-fashioned Judy and Mickey musical, Sterling Studios is banking on Dana Pointer and Missie Miller to make *Detention Rules!* next summer's box office blockbuster. And despite the fact that music video director Adam Berg is no John Hughes, there's little doubt that audiences will flock to the theater to see Dana and Missie mixing it up with sexy Jack Wesley, who plays—well, Sexy—with a capital Take-Your-Clothes-Off-Fast-And-Don't-Open-Your-Mouth. *With golden girl Trixie Wilder in the cast, too*, maybe these pretty Hollywood screen teens will learn a trick(sie) or two about propriety and professionalism.'"

Placenta put her hands on her hips and said, "Poor Trixie, having to put up with that crowd in her final hours."

"Poor?" Polly barked. "I should be so poor! While she's cashing in with back-to-back films, I've got to kill myself for eight shows a week in Kansas City this summer!"

"Trixie's cashing in all right," Placenta said. "She bought the farm!"

Polly and Tim both gave their maid quizzical looks.

"Trixie Wilder's gone," Placenta announced. "Dead. Stiff. Ready for planting. Possibly rubbed out by some maniacal diva like you, or one of your friends who were dropped off in that space ship that couldn't rush back fast enough to whatever galaxy you all come from."

"Murdered?" Polly gasped. There was a hint of intrigue in her voice.

"Katie Couric said maybe," Placenta reported. "If you'd listen to real news instead of reading that *Peeper* trash. . . . Katie explained that Trixie was found last night, dead in her trailer on the location of that movie you were just reading about. Katie said something about a trauma to the head and that the police are investigating and can't rule out foul play."

For a fraction of an instant, Polly's showbiz survival instincts surfaced as she thought, "Have they recast her role?"

"Make a donation in Trixie's name to the Motion Picture Retirement Home," Tim suggested.

"To absolve you of your self-centered thoughts that Trixie's misfortune is an opportunity for you," Placenta said.

Polly upbraided her servant with her eyes.

"Don't play innocent with me, Your Highness," Placenta said. "I see through you as plainly as all those mediums on TV see dead folk."

Chapter 2

Happy Hour (otherwise known as Lush Hour) began at five o'clock at Pepper Plantation. As usual, Polly, Tim, and Placenta were lounging in the Great Room of the mansion, dividing their time and attention between killing off another bottle of Veuve, and nibbling on Placenta's salmon tortilla appetizers. But tonight was different. Instead of their ritual of ferreting out killers on The Mystery Channel, they were surfing through "Larry King Live," "Access Hollywood," and the "ABC Nightly News." Trixie Wilder, a minor acquaintance of Polly's, was the lead story on every local and national network news broadcast. She had become a teaser to lure viewers away from the ubiquitous reruns of "Friends."

Although the coroner had yet to determine the specific cause of Trixie's demise, journalists were playing up the angle of possible foul play—mainly because Hollywood hadn't enjoyed a celebrity murder scandal in at least a week. If there was an upside to Trixie's death, it was that she had an actor's perfect timing. Her final bow took place during a slow cycle when movie and recording stars' DUIs, rapes, drug charges, child molestations, shoplifting arrests, and other sure-fire attention-grabbing debaucheries were temporarily off the court dockets. For the first time in her long if unremarkable career, Trixie was a household name.

A lot more people than Tim had originally imagined they knew who Trixie Wilder was. After a day of being bombarded with biographical highlights on CNN and "Anderson Cooper 360," Tim could recite the ups and downs of Trixie's entire life story. As a noncontract day player at all of the Hollywood studios during the 1940s, 1950s, and 1960s, she had appeared in dozens of feature films and shorts. Her stock in trade was playing a wiseacre nurse to Ray Miland, or the tough-as-nails housekeeper for Doris Day, or a spinster librarian dispensing one line of life-altering advice to a depressed Bette Davis. Although she never came close to playing a leading role, zealous film buffs today could tick off Trixie's list of credits in an instant.

Now that Trixie Wilder was suddenly a name worth talking about, the world tuned in to what the producers at "Larry King Live" had hastily pasted together as a special edition of the program.

With Jayne Meadows and Nanette Fabray as guests, they sat opposite their host's suspenders and chattered about the almost maniacal dedication to the craft of acting that Trixie had always displayed. According to the two magpies, whose recall of facts was dubious at best, Trixie's work ethic was so sacred to her that she never married or had children who might have interfered with her vocation. Instead, they claimed, she devoted her time and energy to the masochistic endeavor of auditioning, and accepting whatever minor film or stage roles she could find. She was often nothing more than atmosphere on the platform of a train station. Her image personified the idea of the true artist, alone in her room, with only a cat for company. (Although Trixie actually lived comfortably in a high-rise condo in Century City.)

With little relevant information to offer in the way of personal anecdotes about Trixie, Jayne and Nanette instead tried to recall what the really big stars of their day had said about the character actress. That she was "special." That her comedy was "unique." That she "had an unusual face that transfixed audiences." It was obvious to Larry King (and his audience) that neither guest really knew their subject very well—if at all—but they wouldn't miss the opportunity to be seen on national television and remind viewers that they themselves were still breathing—if through badly reconstructed noses.

"Is it true that Trixie was alone in the world? That her only living relative is a grand niece who's shackled to a cinderblock cell wall somewhere in a Costa Rica prison for smuggling drugs?" Larry asked Jayne and Nanette. Both women shrugged their shoulders. Then, raising her voice to be heard over Nanette, who was saying, "When I was starring in *The Bandwagon* with Fred Astaire . . ." Jayne plowed ahead and said, "When Steve and I were playing Vegas, this ghastly thing happened when . . ."

"Let's take a call," Larry interrupted, his voice pleading to be rescued by anyone in Chillicothe.

Polly switched the channel to "Access Hollywood," and marveled that anyone could be as unctuous as Billy Bush. "There must be millions of vacuous viewers who consider him inordinately sexy," she said, mainly for Tim's benefit. "I mean I can understand the reaction. But I for one certainly do not get the message of his being."

"We're on the same page," Tim said, evading his mother's bait for an argument about who was hot and who was not. It was an ongoing game between the two. Most of the time they agreed. Yes, for Hugh Jackman. Yes, for Colin Firth. Yes, for Mark Harmon. No, for Vin Diesel. Yes for Jon Stewart.

Placenta said, "Billy reminds me of the first ex–Mr. Polly Pepper. From whom Timmy gets his best genes."

"Sure, slurp down my expensive champagne and cleave this loveless, thrice-divorced legend down to the marrow in her bones by mentioning that louse," Polly whined. After a moment and several more sips from her own glass of bubbly she conceded, "You're right, of course, and that's precisely why I loathe BB. Every man I've ever loved—except Timmy here—has been as artificial as that plastic fichus you never dust in the breakfast nook," she said. "But Mr. Number One was a hottie, all right. He was definitely catnip to me. Still, I can't bear Bush."

On television, peacock Billy continued with his gleaming if insincere smile. "It was precisely Trixie's lack of glamour that made her popular with movie-going audiences of all ages," he said, trying to appear like an analytical film historian, as if the thoughts and words he was speaking were his own. "She was common, and one of the few women in Hollywood who never dated Howard Hughes, Clark Gable, or Bogey," he said. "However, we did uncover this snapshot. It's Trixie on a night out with Regis Philbin."

A faded photograph from the 1970s appeared on the television screen. In the image, Trixie was apparently seated in a restaurant's red leather banquette. She was wearing a plaid sweater accented with a string of pearls around her neck. Holding a glass of red wine in one hand, the look she was blasting at Regis was one of utter boredom.

"I know how she feels," Polly said, reading Trixie's body language. "Regis tried to date me once, and . . ."

". . . And if you'd only known how stinking rich he was going to be, you'd have said, *yes* . . ." Tim completed her thought. It was a story he and Placenta had heard as far back as they could remember.

When the television camera returned to Billy's smirking face, he said, "That's an exclusive, folks. It proves that Trixie did have a life outside of a soundstage."

For the remainder of the program, "Access Hollywood"

was stuck making do with showing archival film footage as filler between commercials for Clairol hair-coloring products, and repeated showings of a video taken earlier in the day of Liza Minnelli wiping away a tear and sniveling, "I'm just glad that Mama's not here. This would kill her!"

As the champagne loosened Tim's tongue, and after watching so many black and white clips from Trixie's early films, he stated the obvious. "God, she looked as old in the 1940s as she did in the twenty-first century," he said.

Polly, comfortably seated in a leather wingback chair, her feet resting on an ottoman and facing the large television screen, agreed. "That's the beauty of being a homely girl," she said, taking another sip of champagne. "We never fade."

"We," was the well-placed cue for Tim to contradict his mother's self-deprecation. He'd been through this a million times and had learned how to assuage her self-conscious fears—real or imagined. "You'd never have gotten a guy like Dad if you were unattractive," Tim said with all the warmth and sincerity of an automated voice menu. "He chose you when he could have had a whole stable of starlets," Tim allowed.

"And did. Which is why we divorced," Polly reminded him, pulling an accent pillow out from behind her back and tossing it at Tim. "Trixie may have been a grinning walrus from day one," she said, "but she made lemonade out of her life. That's what we actors do, dear. I mean look at Owen Wilson's broken nose and tiny pouting mouth and wrinkled lips, but by sheer force of personality he became a leading man." She then switched the channel again.

Another news anchor on Channel 2 speculated that because Trixie had been working on a closed set, if she in fact met with foul play, it would have had to be an inside job. "Is that right, Tiffany?"

The screen filled with a honey-blond reporter who could

have been a swimsuit model. She was standing at the crime scene with strips of yellow police tape as a backdrop to her story. She said, "That's right, Kevin. The stars in Hollywood aren't twinkling so brightly tonight."

"Yes, we are," Polly talked back to the screen.

Tiffany the reporter continued. "Potentially hundreds of people—film crews and celebrities alike—may become suspects in this all-too-real reality show called, 'How Did I Die?'" The reporter was doing her best to sound as though crime was a novelty in Tinseltown. "Party princesses throughout Beverly Hills may be shaking in their Pradas until this alleged killing is solved. Now, back to you in the studio," she said, projecting a straight face that told viewers she honestly believed that the story she just reported was the most important event shaking the planet.

"They're making this up as they go along," Polly groaned, then added, "Who did you say is in the cast of *Detention Rules!*?"

"It's been repeated all day long," Tim said, slightly annoyed. He reiterated that Dana Pointer had first become known for posing semi-nude on a billboard that advertised the sex appeal of drinking Johnny Walker Red. Missie Miller, who had cut a CD with the church choir at Harvard, had unexpectedly hit the top of the Christian record charts with the solo portion of "Jesus Is the Answer (So Hit the Nail on the Head)." Both girls were summoned to Hollywood as a result of their small notoriety—then started making movies.

Polly considered all the gossip she'd ever heard or read about the two teen stars—and the massive retouching required of their publicity photos. It was no secret that Dana was notoriously unprofessional. They called her "an alumna of the Shannen Doherty Charm School."

Missie, on the other hand, was considered a Julie Andrews knockoff for her sweetness, wit, vocal pipes, and for still living at home and caring for her semi-blind and widowed mother.

Where Dana was a self-absorbed, club-hopping, paparazzi-bashing, bulimic, nymphomaniac who openly hated Missie's guts, her co-star was a straight-A Harvard freshman majoring in biochemistry, who had a patent pending for a pill that if tested by Merck might lead to a cure for halitosis. In her spare time, she was the guest first chair violin with the Boston Youth Symphony Orchestra.

In Dana's spare time, she appeared in court as the corespondent in divorce suits.

"And the male lead?" Polly asked. "Jack Wesley," she answered herself. "They've all got reputations."

"Ooh, Mr. Jack 'Sexy' Wesley," Placenta said, "Lord knows he's got the body of a lean grease monkey. But he's got Charles Manson eyes. They're completely dead. No depth. But hell, when you've got shoulders, abs, biceps, and pecs like what he showed in that underpants billboard ad, nothing else matters."

Polly thought about the trio of teen celebrities for a long moment, trying to find a common denominator other than their youth, sex-appeal, and appearing in a movie together. "Sometimes so-called good girls like Missie can't resist a bad boy like Jack," Polly said, as if she knew from first-hand experience. "Perhaps the two girls were fighting over the affections of Jack, and maybe Trixie was a third wheel who got in the way," she said, making up a story that, considering the blank stares of Tim and Placenta, was as farfetched as Britney Spears remaining married for more than half a minute. "Trust me, I'm as intuitive as Jessica Fletcher," Polly said. "One of those girls was involved in Trixie's death."

Switching back to "Larry King Live," Tim said, "God help us if this is the kind of media circus we have to look forward to on the day you drop dead, Mother." He pointed the remote at the television set and clicked to another station—only to find mascara-smudged Liza unhinged again.

Polly said, "I'm not afraid to die. It happens to the best of us. But when it's my time, I expect rioting on Hollywood Boulevard and preemption of 'Desperate Housewives.' Make a note of that for my publicist and attorney," she instructed Placenta. "And swear to me that the coverage of my eventual demise will be more tasteful than this déclassé spectacle." Polly grabbed the remote from Tim and again switched channels. "I don't want Larry scraping the bottom of his e-mail list for media whores who don't really give a damn about me. I'm not inviting Jayne to my memorial service," she said. "And dear God, don't let me get screwed like Mother Teresa and Prince Ranier. Rotten timing to go out at the same time as Princess Di, or the Pope!"

Evenings at home, sharing a volley of conversation like this with her two best friends, and knocking off a couple of bottles of midpriced champagne, always gave Polly a glow and a sense of peace. Despite all the dreary talk of death, Polly was actually happy tonight. She looked around the vast room and counted her blessings, as well as her Emmy Awards, several of which were used as decorative bookends on the floor-to-ceiling shelves that dominated one wall.

Placenta kept these intimate evenings running smoothly with one chilled bottle of Veuve Clicquot following another, until it was time to serve dinner. Tonight, however, no one in the family was interested in dining. Although the news of the day had become tiresome, Polly and Tim, and Placenta, too, kept a close watch on the television for the latest developments, just in case it was revealed that they personally knew whoever was eventually accused of "allegedly" murdering Trixie Wilder.

"One down, two to go," Placenta said, a reference to the theory that stars drop dead in series of threes. "Any bets on

who's next?" Placenta asked. "Big points if it's someone
young and totally unexpected, like Sophia Bush."

"I was so close when I put Siegfried and Roy on my list,"
Polly said, "proving that I have decent intuition. Perhaps it
hasn't been honed to perfection, but if you'll remember, Bob
Hope was another name I felt strongly about—for years."

Suddenly the telephone rang in the distance. Placenta set
her champagne flute on the oval glass-top coffee table that
separated twin Tahitian cotton upholstered sofas in the center of the vast room. She was used to stopping whatever activity she was involved in to answer a telephone. Polly
placed outgoing calls only. She refused to answer incoming
ones.

Still, the ring tone made Polly perk up. "It's a little late for
the press to be calling me for a quote," she said to Tim, pretending to be miffed. "What should I tell 'em about Trixie?
One appearance on 'The Polly Pepper Playhouse' does not
an intimate relationship make. But I always sent Christmas
cards."

"All actors are liars," Tim said. "Just say that you spoke to
Trixie yesterday morning, and you're completely shocked by
what's happened since then."

Returning to the great room with the cordless phone in
her hand, Placenta walked over to Polly and said, "Put your
intuition to the test and guess who's calling."

Polly playfully put the tips of her index fingers to her
temples. "Um, it's Ed McMahon . . . he's bringing the Prize
Patrol over for drinks, but they're lost in Benedict Canyon."

"Almost." Placenta handed her the phone. "It's your agent."

For a moment the only sounds in the room were the
voices issuing from the television's speakers. Polly, Tim, and
Placenta looked at each other with confusion. It was highly
unusual for J. J. to be calling—at any hour.

"How'd he get my number?" Polly joked, as she accepted

the phone from her maid. She pressed the talk button. In a tone of voice that she generally reserved for her money-grabbing second cousin in Des Moines who invented outrageous scenarios about health issues, or biblical invasions of flying insects that required biblical-sized checks from Polly to help eradicate, she said, "Hello, J. J. What level of Dante's Hell are you calling from, dear? Still married to Jackie? Right, Vickie. Still under IRS investigation for fraud? Still running an agency?"

Tim and Placenta pretended to give Polly privacy and returned to watching CNN. They each picked up their drinks and although they feigned interest in the news, they cocked their respective ears to eavesdrop on Polly's conversation. Intermittently they gave each other furtive looks that plainly said, "J. J. Norton only calls when a commission check has to be countersigned."

Polly was clearly talking to J. J. about Trixie. She said, "Yes, it's a terrible tragedy. Of course I adored her. We all did. Yeah, so much talent wasted. Yada, yada. Get to the point."

Then there was a long stretch of silence. Polly was obviously paying close attention to what was being said by her agent. The cessation of Polly's voice caused Tim and Placenta to turn around and look at her with curiosity.

Noticing Tim and Placenta's attention, Polly drifted away from the center of the room and took a seat on the piano bench in the corner. She was slowly nodding her head in agreement with whatever J. J. was telling her. Finally, she responded. "Well, it's rather short notice," she said. "Yes, of course there was no way of knowing. By all means, tell them I'll consider it. We'll chat in the A.M., when you have more info. Love to Jackie. Vickie? Whatever."

Polly pushed the disconnect button on the telephone and laid the handset on the piano lid. She looked dazed as she raised herself up. Deep in thought she slowly crossed the room and retrieved her champagne flute. With Tim and Placenta staring at her, she finally spoke. "I'm up for Catharine. Trixie's role."

Tim and Placenta were stunned into dropped-jaw silence.

"One of the producers got the DVD boxed set of *The Best of the Polly Pepper Playhouse Comedy Sketches* for his twenty-fifth birthday, and he thought I might be good. *Might* be good? What a putz."

Tim was suddenly uncorked with excitement. "It's what you sort of wished for this morning," he said.

"Sort of?" Placenta jeered. "The gears in your head were exposed."

"Don't worry about those other two stars in the film," Tim smiled and hugged his mother. "They may be the leads, but you'll be the star. Guaranteed."

"*Other* stars?" Polly said, feigning offense.

Polly took a long swallow of champagne, held out her flute for a refill from anyone, and made a face. "It's hardly a done deal," she said. "They're auditioning a number of actresses. You know what an idiot agent J. J. is. Chances are he'll price me out of the job. It's happened before. I'm not getting my hopes up."

Tim raised his glass and proposed a toast. "To the legendary Polly Pepper, and her triumphant return to the silver screen! Of course you'll get the job! It's got your name written all over it. Probably always had, but Trixie got in the way and the ghost of Euripides had to make some adjustments. Not good for Trixie's health, but as a trouper she'd be the first to say, 'That's showbiz!'"

Placenta raised her glass, too. "Cheers," she said. "J. J.'s a lousy agent, but he wouldn't call unless a job for you was dropped in his lap. He'll take all the credit, and the commission, of course. But you can probably start packing!"

"Oscar! Oscar! Oscar!" Tim chanted. "You'll be noticed again." Then, shifting his thoughts, he tentatively asked,

"What else did J. J. have to say about this producer, other than he's twenty-five and smart enough to recognize your value to his project?"

Polly shot a lascivious smile at her son, and tickled him under his chin. "Leave it to me, sweetie. You'll get an introduction."

Chapter 3

B y the time Polly tottered to her chair at the patio breakfast table the next morning, Placenta had already placed
the *Los Angeles Times* morning edition over the vacant
eyes of Paris Hilton on the cover of *The National Peeper*.
For the first few moments of her day Polly's undivided attention was on her Bloody Mary. After sucking up her breakfast, she adjusted her shades, lit a Merit cigarette with her
BIC, and gazed around her property. Polly admired the
artistry of the landscape gardeners who maintained Pepper
Plantation as if they were manicuring the grounds at a Disney resort.

The yard was immaculately groomed, and the men who
Tim hired for the chores were an exhibition for Polly to appreciate as well. The workers, all shirtless and in the bloom
of Antonio Banderas-hood (pre-Melanie), were out in force,
scattered about the property, mowing the grass, planting an-
nuals, and vacuuming the swimming pool. Slight irritation
crossed Polly's face when she couldn't spot Hector, the inordinately seductive, perspiration-glistening Latino foreman
who was usually on site. "Bummer," she thought, mentally

calculating the hours of practice she'd completed with her Spanish 101 Berlitz CDs. She hoped to soon begin conjugating verbs with *Señor El es muy guapo*—as Tim, too, referred to Hector. She aimed to give him instructions with as much fluency as Tim. "*Como se dice* . . . prune this bush?" she often rehearsed, spying on him from behind the louvered shutters in her bedroom.

A bee interrupted her reverie about Hector by lighting on the newspaper and crawling over the headlines.

Polly looked down. The headline beamed up. Polly screeched, "Mother of God! Was I in a coma?"

The Los Angeles Times was adamant: TRIXIE TRAGEDY RULED ACCIDENTAL.

"Anticlimactic, eh?" Placenta said as she came out from the house, placed a basket of warm bran muffins on the table before Polly, and shooed away the bee.

Polly was incredulous. "A few hours ago the police were investigating a probable homicide," she said. "Now, Trixie's just any old dead woman."

"The media turned that poor dear's death into an all points bulletin Amber Alert for a maniac who never existed," Placenta clucked. "It didn't take Kinsey Milhone to figure out that the media was milking this nonstory for all the juicy gossip it could squeeze from a stone cold corpse."

Polly picked up the paper and scanned the front-page story. "Stroke followed by heart attack," she read aloud. "Collapsed. Fractured her skull on a brick lying on the floor. Case closed. See page E12 for memorial service details." She slapped the newspaper down on the table and picked up her glass for another sip of her BM. "A brick," she snorted. "Murder would have been the perfect coda to Trixie's dreary life. Even minor celebrities win instant immortality if they die under any circumstance that might hatch a lame conspiracy theory."

Tim emerged from the house. Hearing the tail end of his

mother's comment, he sort of asked, "Wha?," then plopped himself into a chair at the table. Placenta poured Tim's coffee and retreated into the house for the plastic tub of I Can't Believe It's Not Butter. Tim locked his lips over the rim of the mug and noisily slurped up his cure-all. After a long moment waiting for the caffeine to kick-start his engine, he flipped the newspaper pages to Doonesbury then made an effort to ask, "News 'bout Trix?"

"Too upsetting," Polly said, as if closing the subject.

"There's something worse than her *death*?" Tim said, then came to a quick conclusion. "Plain ol' final grain of sand slipping through the egg timer of life, eh?" he said knowingly.

"Where are the Hollywood deaths of yore?" Polly bemoaned. "The entertaining ones, like Jayne Mansfield. Or Bob Crane."

"Or Mama Cass," Tim said, and reached for a muffin.

"Vic Morrow," Polly continued. "John Landis's personal Cuisinart sliced and diced him into Kibbles 'n Bits."

"Marvin Gaye," Tim added. "Target practice for his old man."

"Sonny Bono," Polly quickly jumped in. "What sort of idiot hits a tree while skiing?" she mused. "Or did the tree hit him? See, a conspiracy theory!"

"John Denver," Tim said sadly, missing one of his favorite singers. "Musta been on a Rocky Mountain high 'cause nobody leaves the ground without fuel in his private airplane."

"Marie Curie," Polly trumped Tim. "Of all people, she should have known that exposure to that radiation stuff couldn't be good for her health!"

"Isadora Duncan? Rather chic, but an embarrassing way to be remembered!" Tim said. He crossed his eyes and shoved his tongue out the side of his mouth, mimicking strangulation.

Placenta walked back out onto the patio. "This should

cheer you up," she said, holding a large manila envelope in her hand. "Just arrived via messenger."

Polly's eyes widened with excitement as she grabbed the package from Placenta and completely forgot about Trixie and famous dead people. "It's from Sterling Studios!" She immediately saw the address label with the SS logo (which had undergone a radical design change when the Anti-Defamation League pressured the studio to modify the twin lightning bolts that had long been the company's trademark), and eagerly ripped open the sealed flap. She withdrew a three-hole punched script that was fastened together with brass brads. Polly held it up for Tim and Placenta to see.

"*Detention Rules!*" Polly declared triumphantly as she read the title. "A Screenplay by Ben Tyler." She frowned. "Remind me to Google that name," she said, then started flipping through the pages searching for a character named Catharine. With each page of the script that Polly scanned she seemed to become more frustrated. Then, three quarters of the way into the text, her face beamed with a wide smile. "Catharine! There you are, you little career-saving vixen!"

"Read it aloud," Tim implored.

"Cold? And out of context? Never! Not to this tough audience," Polly said. Then her lips began to move in silent unison with her eyes. But as she continued reading to herself, her smile faded. She turned a page then flipped back to the previous page, as if checking to see if she'd missed some vital information. Polly began to bite her mother-of-pearl–lacquered thumbnail as doubt crept across her face.

Placenta quipped, "You were expecting Neil Simon?"

Polly ignored her maid and leafed through the last quarter of the screenplay. She counted the few pages on which Catharine had lines of dialogue. Then, in a daze, she closed the script and placed it on the table. She stared blankly past Tim.

Judging by his mother's imitation of a zombie, Tim knew

that Polly was disappointed and ticked off. He picked up the script and began looking for the character name, typed in bold letters. "You'll make a wonderful Catharine. Whoever she is," he said, still searching for her dialogue.

Polly looked up, reached for her glass, and drained what remained of her Bloody Mary. Then, in a crescendo of anger she snapped, "Catharine's a goddamned freaking *grand-mother*, that's who Catharine is! The role is nothing more than a frigid old biddy who gives rotten lonely hearts advice to *sextavert* Dana Pointer!"

Placenta anticipated Polly's need for a drink refill and deftly removed the glass tumbler from the table. As she headed for the poolside bar she wickedly sang out, "Will you still need me, will you still feed me, when I'm sixty-four."

Tim looked up from the screenplay and agreed with Polly. "Yeah, there aren't many lines. It's a Trixie Wilder role, through and through."

Polly was crestfallen. "I don't know whether to feel insulted that my name came up as a replacement for Trixie in the first place for this piece of crap movie, or to be furious with J. J. for leading that pisher producer to think I'd consider such an insignificant role."

Placenta returned to the table with Polly's Bloody Mary. As she set the glass down on the table she said, "I think you should at least read the entire script before rejecting it outright. It might be a good part after all."

"Might be good for Michele Lee," Polly scowled and picked up her glass. "Michele still looks decent, but she's a hell of a lot older than she lets on." Polly picked up the tumbler, but immediately set it down—on top of the script cover. Condensation from the glass began to bleed a ring on the paper. "I'd rather die and move to Florida than play a loveable, blue-haired—*Republican*!"

Except for the sound of a leaf blower at the far end of the property, and the gentle ping of wind chimes colliding in a slight breeze that issued through the gazebo, there was silence around the table. Tim and Placenta both felt pangs of sorrow for Polly. It didn't take an empath to know that she was deeply disappointed by the turn of events.

In a somber voice, Polly whispered, "This is every Christmas morning of my childhood, when all that was under the aluminum tree was a box of new underwear, wrapped up as a present."

"Perhaps if they rewrote the part so that Grandma Catharine has an affair with Jack Wesley . . . ," Tim joked, trying to ease the tension.

"It's worth discussing with J. J. and the producer," Placenta agreed, lifting Polly's glass off of the script cover. "Take the screenplay into your office and read it from beginning to end. It can't be that bad if it's being filmed by a major studio," Placenta said.

Tim agreed. "Mom," he said, "Sterling's sinking a gazillion dollars into this project, so there's gotta be something of value here. Plus, strong actors in small roles often get noticed by the critics . . . and the Academy. Hell, Judi Dench was only on screen for a lousy eight minutes and she nabbed an Oscar for *Shakespeare in Love*."

Polly slowly nodded her head in agreement. "*Meet the Fockers* was rubbish, but it was a megahit. Gave ol' Babs a leg up again."

As Tim and Placenta continued agreeing about the possibility that the screenplay had potential, they hardly noticed that Polly had raised herself up and out of her chair and was retreating into the house. Before she reached the door, she tightened the belt around her robe, then turned and said, "Spank me for being such an ingrate. I may be aged out, but I'm still a star. My charity work does not include making Dana Pointer and Missie Miller look as though they're the next Meryl Streep and Joan Cusack. I covered for Laura Crawford all those years on my TV show. 'The lovely and talented Laura Crawford,' I used to say and audiences never caught on that I use 'lovely and talented' as a euphemism for anyone I actually loathe. I'm going to make-up and then pay a visit to J. J. *The 'lovely and talented,' J. J."*

On any other day the forty-five-minute traffic-congested drive from Pepper Plantation in Bel Air to J. J.'s office in the old Playboy building on Sunset Boulevard in Los Angeles would have irritated Polly as a waste of valuable time. This morning, however, as she sat behind the maple steering wheel of her Park Ward Rolls-Royce, Polly gently braked at yellow traffic lights, maintained the legal speed limit, and felt no imperious need to curse at inconsiderate and impatient drivers of less ostentatious cars.

Upon arrival at the building that housed her agent's headquarters, Polly eased her classic vehicle into the subterranean garage and stopped before the valet attendant. She alighted from the Rolls, and with a gracious nod and a cheerful smile Polly appeared to be as benign and serene as a New Year's Day Pasadena Tournament of Roses Parade queen perched on her float of turnip seeds and rhododendron petals. When Polly breezed into the building's marbled lobby, she greeted the inflexible security guard with a disarming smile and recall of his first name. One of Polly's greatest talents was her ability to enchant. She used her wiles effortlessly and charmed the guard into allowing her to pass to the elevator without first signing the guest book or announcing her presence to J. J.'s office assistant.

Polly postured a star's not-a-care-in-the-world persona as she entered the elevator and turned once again to face the guard, whose countenance had morphed from Mike Wallace granite to Van Johnson affable. Polly pushed the button for the penthouse and before the doors closed she once again radiated a generous smile at the guard and gave a wink of her eye, and a wiggly finger wave good-bye. Now, alone in the car as it moved with its hydraulics, pulleys, and weights up through the shaft in the center of the building, Polly took a deep breath—and prepared for battle.

Moments later, when the elevator doors parted, Polly stepped out of the car and into the museum-quiet foyer of Jason James Norton and Associates Theatrical Agency. The heels of her shoes clicked on the polished and bleached hardwood floor as she strode with confidence halfway to the receptionist's desk. Polly quickly assessed the age of the young man who presented the company image, and intuitively presumed that although she had once been the agency's star client, and a floor-to-ceiling black and white photo of her still dominated the wall behind the desk, she couldn't expect to be groveled to.

Then, in a burst of aggressive but joyous enthusiasm, meant to position herself as the dominant force in the room, Polly called out in her most theatrical voice, "I'm *he–er!*" With a gleaming smile and the hands-on-hips, head tilted skyward pose that she usually reserved for the paparazzi along a red carpet, Polly achieved the desired result: immediate attention. The sentry at the desk looked up from his computer monitor and was taken aback by the presence of a glamorous woman his mother's age dressed to the nines and sparkling as if she were entering a cocktail party given in her honor.

Polly continued her advance into the room. When she reached the desk and got a closer look at the swarthy, beard-stubbled face of the young man she thought, *J. J. and Tim have the same taste in sweets.* "Honey," she smiled, veering off toward the frosted glass doors that led to the executive offices, "Don't bother to announce me. I know my way. I'll just tippy-toe in and surprise J. J. It's his birthday." She lied.

"Wait!" the receptionist said, and stood up from his chair.

Polly stopped. "Not to worry," she said, evading her rival's obligation to keep the unwanted within the quarantine-like confines of the closed-circuit-TV–monitored reception area. "I know how much J. J. hates to make a fuss about these things. But this is a big one. Guess the number that precedes the zero! It's too horrid!" She winked conspiratorially. "You can score major kiss-ass points by bringing him a cruller with a single candle when you get his mocha frappuccino. Oh, and darling, since it's a special occasion, and God knows we all have to fake liking the boss, have the Starbucks counter man add coconut syrup, whipped cream, and chocolate sauce. Don't forget the little coconut flakes sprinkled on top! J. J. can worry about his diabetes tomorrow. So shush. Not a word about me. I adore surprises. Don't you?"

Polly switched her famous smile up from Sylvania fluorescent to Times Square neon, then turned and continued to walk toward the doors. "Just buzz me in, dear heart," she called over her shoulder as she reached for the handle.

"But you . . . !" she heard the sergeant at Checkpoint Charley cry, which again stopped Polly in her tracks. With her back to the receptionist, she rolled her eyes and pursed her lips, preparing for a verbal spar. "Not to worry," she sang out, still holding on to the door handle and trying hard not to turn around and pummel the kid. "If ol' J. J.'s not in I'll just leave his little prezy on his chair."

"You're not . . . ," the young man started to speak but Polly interrupted him.

". . . Exactly expected?" Polly said completing his sentence. "I know, sweetums, but this is a special occasion. My little diversion will only take a sec. Be a love and push the little buzzer thingee to unlatch the door," she said, an edge creeping into her voice.

". . . Polly Pepper?" the receptionist finished his own sentence. It was more a statement of open-mouthed wonder than a question.

Suddenly Polly felt as if Homeland Security had just cleared her through Customs despite finding a Ziploc bag filled with enriched uranium in her purse. She straightened her posture, turned around, and for the first time since Placenta had handed her the script for *Detention Rules!*" she produced a genuine smile. "I'm so ashamed," she said. "I should have properly introduced myself." Polly walked back to the receptionist. "Don't you just hate it when living legends think we're above common manners?" She reached out her hand. "I'm Polly Pepper. Of course. And you are?"

"Michael," the young man said. He was grinning with excitement, as he accepted Polly's hand and gave it a quick shake.

Polly recognized a fan when she met one. But, she thought, *Michael is too young to have seen the original broadcasts of my shows.* She also suspected that anyone bright enough to know her name must, by virtue of a gene reserved for her favorite ten percent of the planet's population, sing in the choir with Tim.

"We studied you in college," Michael said with pride.

"An anthropology major?" Polly joked, trying not to appear irritated that she was suddenly being made to feel like something viewed under the magnified lens of a microscope.

"We examined your complete oeuvre," Michael said.

Polly blinked. "Only my gynecologist is supposed to have that much fun," she laughed.

Michael looked askance at Polly, not getting her joke. He recovered. "You were a required subject," he said, trying to explain. "'Icons: Critical Thinking and the Myth of the Value of Celebrity in Global Society.' AFI."

"Myth?" Polly repeated, awkwardly.

"I got so hooked on you and your work that I even bought bootleg 16 mm prints of the horror movies you made in Mexico. You were the best in *Crawling Eyeball II: The Vision Returns!*"

Polly emitted a giggle of self-satisfaction. "Mary Kay Place and I had a scream making that one," she said. Polly was so completely charmed by Michael's attention that she temporarily forgot the reason for her visit to her agent's office. "Film school," she said, finally making the connection to the AFI. "Perhaps your thesis script—you did have to write one, didn't you—has a role that requires my talents?" she cooed. "I'm not one of those horrid golden calves who only accepts material submitted through my agent."

"J. J. would fire me. We're not even supposed to talk to clients," Michael said, looking around to ensure that no one was watching. "But I guess it's not like you're Diana Ross, or someone."

"Or someone," Polly repeated. "Oh, screw J. J. And Diana," she declared. "Until this morning, he hasn't sent me anything to read in over a year!" Polly caught herself slipping into J. J. bashing mode. "I mean, there's so little material out there for a star of a certain age."

"For a star with a certain comic brilliance, you mean," Michael corrected.

"You're such a transparent toady," Polly said with a lascivious smile. "You'll go far." She wanted to wrap her arms around his youthful body and physically express her appreciation for his obvious intelligence and sophisticated taste. Then Polly looked at Michael and pouted. "How can a young man of your elevated sensibilities be working as a mere receptionist?" she said.

"A college degree doesn't mean anything in Hollywood," Michael said. "Here it's all about nepotism, and who you put out for. But you know all that."

"There are exceptions," Polly said, eliminating herself from Michael's generalization.

"I'm paying my dues," Michael added. "J. J.'s promised to give me a hand."

Polly stopped herself from making the obvious comment.

"By the way," Michael added, "I think you would have been awesome in *Detention Rules!*"

Polly continued smiling for an awkward moment. "Would have been? I haven't exactly made up my mind yet about the role," she said, suddenly feeling uneasy. "Perhaps with a bit of a rewrite," she said. "But I'm such a wuss. And J. J.'ll probably talk me into doing the damn thing before I have a chance to discuss changes with the producer."

Michael stepped backward several paces to the desk and blindly reached behind himself until his fingers connected with the morning's edition of *Daily Variety*. He brought forth the paper, and without saying a word he held it up for Polly to examine.

STONE GETS DETENTION

Polly squinted at the banner headline. The words meant nothing to her. "Stone gets Detention," she read aloud. "So? Stone gets . . . *Detention*," she read again. Then, as if finally getting the punchline to a joke, Polly snatched the paper out of Michael's hand and looked more closely at the article. One name, repeated several times, jumped off the page: Sedra Stone. Sedra Stone. Sedra Stone.

"Sedra Stone got *my* role? I'll kill her!" Polly said. As her anger set in, her wrath poured out and was reflected in the escalating volume of her voice. "I swear I'll absolutely slap that minor talent, scene-stealing, home-wrecking, wicked bitch of the west into an early grave. And where the hell is that lousy J. J.?" she snarled.

The last thing that Polly remembered before driving down Sunset Boulevard was the security guard from the building's lobby forcibly dragging her out of the reception area of J. J. Norton and Associates Talent Agency.

Chapter 4

Polly's Rolls-Royce slowly glided along serpentine Stone Canyon Road until it reached the ornate monogrammed black wrought-iron dual swing gates that secured Pepper Plantation. Reaching for her electronic door opener clipped to the sun visor of the front passenger seat, Polly pressed the button and waited for the entryway to clear. She then languidly drove onto her estate and gradually made her way down the cobblestone lane. She rolled the car under the shelter of the front portico, where, between the pillars and porch, she parked, turned off the ignition—and sat in dazed silence.

For a few numb minutes Polly replayed in her head the scene of hysteria that had unfolded in J. J.'s reception area. She felt embarrassed and stupid for allowing Sedra Stone to once again trump her life and make her feel inadequate. Then, with great effort, Polly opened the car door and stepped into the warm afternoon.

Although there were only two granite steps up to her front entrance doors, Polly ascended them as slowly as if she had exhausted all her energy running a marathon while simultaneously fighting the bird flu. When she reached the massive Gothic double doors, she pushed the keypad on the security alarm system and waited for the release sound made by the deadbolt disengaging. With a torpid nudge, she urged the left door open.

Stepping into the foyer and lethargically closing the door with her hip, she leaned her back against one massive panel to rest for a moment. Polly heaved a heavy sigh, grateful to be home at last. She was safely away from the harsh world of professionally impotent Hollywood agents, duplicitous has-been TV icons, and inordinately young and inexperienced film stars who wouldn't recognize a decent script if it were written by Dorothy Parker, typed by Robert Benchley, and handed to them by Nancy Meyers.

At Pepper Plantation, cocktail carts stocked with a variety of liquor bottles were in nearly every room. But for the good stuff, the Bombay Sapphire London Dry, Polly had to raid the kitchen freezer. She automatically headed in that direction. Prescription meds, however, were stored in her bedroom suite. As this inconvenience occurred to her Polly changed course and moved instead toward what was affectionately referred to as the "Scarlett O'Hara Memorial Staircase." She decided that a couple of antidepressants and a champagne chaser would be the best temporary antidote for her misery. With as much exertion as she employed entering the house, she now depended on the banister to help her tired body ascend to the second floor of the mansion.

At last on the landing, Polly stepped out of her high-heel shoes and abandoned them in the corridor. She felt a vague sense of guilt that Placenta would have to pick up her mess, but her contrition was fleeting. "'Maid' is your job description," she heard herself say, as she slogged barefoot down the long carpeted hallway toward her room in the east wing of the house.

Along the way she began to pass a gallery of framed oil portraits and memorabilia. They were mostly visual images of herself, and represented various phases of her career, and particularly memorable characters she played on her television show. Although the art had been hanging in the same location for years, Polly seldom paid any attention to the artifacts unless there was a houseguest (especially her mother) with a nose she wanted to rub into the sweet smell of her international success; however, today she was drawn to review the displays.

She stopped in front of a large, ornately framed illustration of herself dressed in a white, starched nurse's uniform, and wearing a cap emblazoned with a red cross that was dripping blood. "Bedpan Bertha," she said to herself, remembering the countless times she practically killed her audiences when she played the role of the klutzy R.N. The artist had depicted her with a goofy freckle-face bucktoothed grin, Marty Feldman bug eyes, and stretching a latex glove over an exaggeratedly large hand.

In every Bedpan Bertha sketch, nitwit Bertha confused doctors' orders on a patient's chart. The unprepared and unlucky sick person (played by such guest stars as Burt Reynolds, Liberace, and Gavin MacLeod) endured extensive body examination procedures that should only be performed by master plumbers on hair clogged drains. The AMA blamed the "Bedpan Bertha" sketches for a sharp decrease in elective surgeries, whereas the network rewarded her ratings with a bigger promotional budget for the show.

Polly stared at herself as Bertha for a long moment, and then glanced to the right and found another classic character captured on canvas. "Madame Zody," she whispered and couldn't prevent a small smile from spreading across her lips.

Dressed in a colorful caftan that was embedded with rhinestones and beads in patterns of stars, crescent moons, hexagrams, and dollar signs, Polly, as Madame Zody, wore the same maniacal grin as Bertha, and had a distorted Picasso-like third eye smudged in the middle of her forehead. In the palm of one hand she clutched a cracked crystal ball. In her other hand she held a Ouija board.

Polly's memory reached back twenty years and fused to-gether a dozen episodes of her show starring such popular guests as Roddy McDowall, Bill Bixby, Anne Francis, and the Muppets. At one time or another during the run of "The Polly Pepper Playhouse" every star of the day had entered Madame's fortune-telling emporium. The predictable sce-narios of each "Madame Zody" sketch found the guest star terror-stricken as he received the dire warning of a long journey—to the sand dunes of the Gobi desert where he would be stalked by something ominously called the Mon-golian Death Worm. Another seeker of things yet to pass was destined to be snatched up by Hydralike aliens. In the worst of all fates, however, a predicted hell was to be stuck for eternity in an elevator with Paul Anka singing "You're Hav-ing My Baby."

Polly began to look at the other cherished images along the wall of the long corridor. Among the Hershfeld carica-tures, the photos from state dinners at the White House auto-graphed by several presidents (for whom she hadn't voted, but wouldn't say *no* to a party), she discovered a forgotten treasure. Half hidden behind a floral arrangement centered on a hall table was a framed handwritten note from Lucille Ball. Polly gently pushed aside the petals of a Casablanca Lily and read the fading message. "What's good for Polly is good for the planet. L.B."

Polly stared at the message for a long moment, recalling how frightened and excited she had been the day when her idol, the week's special guest, arrived for rehearsal. She re-membered that during lunch break, Lucy had pulled her aside and offered words of advice. "If a sketch like this one isn't working, make the writers work all night to change it," she had said, "Grab their cojones and squeeze 'em tight, sweetie!"

Polly took Lucy's advice. She delegated to her then producer/husband, Tim senior, the nasty business of torturing her writers until they came up with the famous "Miss Midas" sketch. In that popular series of routines, Polly portrayed the bored wife of a billionaire who thinks it might be a hoot to switch places for a day with her servants. The role reversals all end with dire yet comical consequences for Miss Midas, of course. But those with whom she traded places realized their own potential and ended up accomplishing something that made them rich, too.

Now, all these years later, Polly thought about Lucy's counsel and the handwritten note she'd received from Miss Ball following the taping of the show. Polly suddenly realized that although she no longer had the equivalent of a bad cop/husband to do her bidding she still didn't have to take crap from anybody, especially her agent.

"Damn right, 'What's good for Polly is good for the planet,'" she quoted aloud, and then turned and walked with renewed purpose to her bedroom. There, she removed her clothes, drew a hot bubble bath, turned on a CD with the calm voice of Deepak Chopra telling her that she had the power to fulfill her desires, and withdrew a bottle of Veuve from her bedroom wine cooler. She popped the cork, poured a flute, checked out her still slim and supple body in the bathroom mirror and raised her glass. "To Lucy!" she said. "To Trixie, too! But most of all to Polly Pepper!" she declared. "You guys are gone, but I'm still here!"

Polly took a long slug of champagne and savored the cold effervescence as it frothed over her tongue. She forgot about the Xanax as she stepped into her bath, glass in hand, and submerged herself up to her neck in lilac scented suds. She took a deep breath, sighed in blissful satisfaction and made another toast. "To Sedra Stone," she said. "Break a leg, honey. Or a hip. While you're stuck in a few frames of a film that'll have Roger Ebert sharpening his tongue for new ways to slash a bad performance, Madame Zody foresees a more important career change—for Polly Pepper—somewhere."

Polly drained her glass and placed it on the bath caddy that held her seaweed therapy oils, moisturizing syrups, and other bottles of antioxidant products, the labels of which boasted ancient secrets for maintaining soft virginal skin. She laid her head back on the built-in cushioned headrest of the tub and let the alcohol flow through her bloodstream. As her anxiety poured out into the warm, womblike bath, her eyelids became heavy and she fell asleep.

At precisely five o'clock, Tim and Placenta looked up from the television and their heated argument over who murdered the publishing heiress in the evening's old rerun episode of "Matlock," as Polly, dressed in bright red drawstring pants and a kaleidoscopic floral silk jacket with cuff sleeves, shoulder pads, and a belt tied in front, made an elegant entrance into the Great Room of Pepper Plantation. "The romance writer did it," Polly said without seeing more than a few frames from the show. Time for champys," she sang out, striding toward the ice bucket.

"Miss Punctual," Tim said as he turned off the television and happily poured a flute of bubbly and handed it to his mother. "Sit down and tell us every little detail," he insisted, like a best girlfriend sharing secrets during a sleepover. "Dish about the flick! When do you start shooting? Need me to approve your wardrobe? Saw some divine Dolce at Neiman's. Ferretti and Cavalli, too," he teased.

Polly ignored her son's questions as she accepted the glass from him. She cleared her throat and said, "I have an announcement. I'm throwing a party!"

Tim and Placenta looked at each other and nodded mutual approval.

After a small sip of her Veuve, Polly continued. "Timmy, my most precious and brilliant party planner slash co-host, it must be bigger and splashier and more decadent than the Nuclear Winter theme you did so brilliantly for the second Bush inauguration party we gave for all our friends on Homeland Security's list of enemy combatants."

"Mass extinction of humankind is sorta hard to top," Tim smiled hesitantly, suspicious of Polly's sudden interest in entertaining.

With a nod and an earnest look, Polly said, "But maybe this time we do something like. . . ." She thought for a moment. ". . . Like extraterrestrial colonization of Hollywood and enslavement of petty vain stars, egomaniacal non-entity B celebrities, agents, managers, and publicists."

Stone-faced, Placenta said, "You didn't get the job."

Polly leaned down to Placenta and gave her a peck on the cheek. She then turned to Tim and offered the same expression of affection. "I know how supportive you've both been about me taking over Trixie's role, but I've decided against accepting the part," Polly said. "J. J. and I had a mind-altering exchange this morning. It occurred to me that another actress of a certain age would be more appropriate for the role. Somebody like Kathy Bates—she doesn't show up on screen much these days. Or, Swoosie Kurtz. There's a goodie. I also suggested Sedra Stone."

"Sedra Stone?" Tim repeated. "Why would you be magnanimous to the woman who keeps ruining your life?"

Polly became defensive. "I'm not being in the least bit charitable; not by any stretch." She feigned indignance. "Catharine's a crappy part in a crappy movie and Sedra will be crappy playing her. It's perfect. Anyway, it was practically your idea," she added. "You accused me of wanting something vile to happen to Sedra, which I didn't, and don't—and now it has. She has to work with those two opportunistic Hollywood whores."

Placenta eyed Polly suspiciously. "Why a party?" she asked. "You're celebrating what, the fact that you can't get a job?"

"As a matter of fact," Polly said, "that's exactly what I'm doing. When you're out of work, throw a party! Invite everybody in the biz. It reminds them that you're still alive. Some of my best gigs have come after a fabulous soiree." She turned to Tim. "That's why you've got to pull all the stops out for this one, hon!"

Tim nodded his head. "Show the world that you don't need to work, and that's when more work comes along, eh? I'll start brainstorming," Tim said, sinking comfortably into the sofa next to Placenta. "What's our time frame?"

Polly raised her glass high above her head. "Yesterday," she said. "Not a moment to waste. I want to invite the entire cast and crew of *Detention Rules!* before they resume shooting next week!"

"Whoa!" Tim shot back. "Impossible! I couldn't even get decent cater waiters without at least two weeks' notice. Remember how long it took to plan our *Titanic* party? That chunk of glacier in the swimming pool didn't just slide out of Ann Coulter's veins. It took three months to arrange shipment from Alaska! And don't forget the penguins."

"Those damned penguins," Polly said testily. "They were guaranteed to be alive on arrival. I'm still mortified about having to explain to PETA what their stiff little bodies were doing in the deep freezer chest under the frozen pizzas."

Placenta said, "You were too cheap to pay hush money to that petty wait staff person who ratted on you."

Tim was adamant. "If you're serious about a last- minute party, we only have time for a plain and simple cocktail crush," he said. "Look, I can arrange for a really chic evening here at the house with a tent and a small chamber orchestra. But on such short notice for entertainment we'll be lucky if we can hire the Amazing Kreskin. Although maybe he can tell us where you left your sanity."

"No, no, no," Polly protested. "You can wave your magic fairy wand and do absolutely miraculous things for parties. You're a pro. Those Queer Eye guys would have lasted longer if they'd had you on their dream team."

Placenta spoke up. "Polly, your parties are legendary. You can't lower your standards for the sake of trying to prove something to beastly Sedra Stone."

"Polly Pepper has nothing to prove." Polly faked astonishment at the implied suggestion that Sedra Stone was at the root of her plans. "I'm only thinking of myself, as usual, and my stalled career. I need a little lift, and a party is the solution. Black tie will be fine," she said to Tim, relieving him of the burden of having to devise an elaborate theme worthy of Donald Trump's overproduced birthday celebrations.

Chapter 5

Evening arrived and for the second night in a row, dinner at Pepper Plantation was cancelled—due to lack of appetites following another stomach-churning telephone call from J. J.

"Aneurysm, anyone?" Placenta deadpanned, before announcing that Polly's agent was on the line. "Says that Someone owes *Someone* an apology," she said, handing the handset to Polly.

Polly Pepper rolled her eyes and reluctantly accepted the telephone. Broadcasting a phony smile through the microphone she cheerfully said, "Twice in as many days, eh, J. J.? Going for a personal best? Jeeze Louise!" Polly shook her head and shot a look of exasperation at Tim.

"I can't talk long, J. J., Madonna and little Lourdes are due here any minute," Polly lied, and paused for a moment listening to J. J.'s comment. "I do too know her! We go way back. Long before Sean. And *Sex*. The book, I mean. She's in town doing the talk show circuit. Promoting the latest reinvention of her career—wife, mother, mistress of the manor in England, and children's book author. Title? Um . . ."

Polly was temporarily stumped. "*The Little Virgin Who Could*? *Humpty Dumped Me*? Beats me. Probably a collection of nursery rhymes all of which begin, 'There once was a man from Nantucket.'"

An expression of annoyance crossed Polly's face. She couldn't bear it when she was trying to be clever and the joke soared over someone's head. As Polly half listened to what J. J. had to say, she tapped her toe, pursed her lips, and made a *wrap it up* gesture with her free hand. She raised a finger to attract Tim's attention and pointed to her empty champagne flute. Polly mimed knocking back a drink, then looked to Placenta and force-whispered an accusation. "Never answer the phone during Lush Hour!"

Returning her attention to J. J., she listened for half a minute then held the phone with both hands and pretended to choke the device. "J. J.!" she said, her frustration racing toward meltdown. "J. J.! I'm not interested in a voiceover role for a toenail fungus infection commercial. But you owe me big time, mister. At least find me a job as a judge on one of those freaky bottom-of-the-barrel reality shows—'Who Wants to Marry a Bankrupt Former Child Star Turned Death Row Inmate.'"

J. J. apparently took her seriously because Polly spat, "I'm not an idiot, J. J. I just played one on TV." Polly looked at Tim and swirled an index finger in the air next to her temple.

"Fungus infections aside, just explain to me about Catharine, and why I wasn't even allowed to audition!"

The retort wasn't lost on Tim and Placenta, both of whom blatantly eavesdropped on the conversation. They looked at each other in bewilderment.

"And now," Polly continued, "because of my snake pit scene in your lobby, Thesmokinggun.com is probably boasting that Polly Pepper deserves a big fat nomination for The Russell Crowe Tantrum of the Week Award! My hard-earned reputation as the Gandhi of Hollywood is definitely in the crapper."

Polly became aware that Tim and Placenta were scrutinizing her every word and decided to end the call. "Oh, drats," she said. "We'll have to chat about this later. That Lourdes thug is pitching pebbles at my Rolls. Obviously, Mrs. Kabbalah Blah-blah didn't pass on her Material Girl genes to her offspring."

But J. J. said something that made her give him another fraction of her life. "An unlikely story," she said. "Speed things up here, J. J.," Polly said, "I've got a cake or something in the oven." She called out, "Lourdes, darling, that's Lalique. Put it down and play 'Find the Doggy Bone' with Mommy's sparkly lavaliere instead, dear. She can afford breakage better than I can."

Polly, an actor to her marrow, nearly believed her own fiction. "Sorry, J. J. Have to dash. Gotta throw these guests out of my house." Then she unexpectedly smiled. "A party?" Her face just as quickly folded. "Missie Miller's," she said with an edge of scorn in her voice. "Yes, Little Mary Sunshine, indeed. Fax me the details." And then Polly pressed the release button on the telephone and set the handset down on the glass coffee table. "That man is so full of hot air he should be tethered to a stake so he won't drift away in a breeze," she said, reaching for her champagne.

Evading the questioning stares from Tim and Placenta, Polly tried to side step what she knew was about to turn into a sequel to the Spanish Inquisition. She forged ahead under the full-throttle pretense that J. J.'s call had been purely social.

"The usual nonsense," Polly said, intentionally ignoring Tim and Placenta's unspoken questions. "A lot of smoke up my tushie about how much he respects my talents, that my best work is ahead of me, and he loves my new hair color. Yada, yada. Oh, and he said that a pharmaceutical behemoth wants me to pitch a pill that cures something so gross that they have to animate the TV ads to prevent viewers from up-chucking their Lean Cuisines on their dinner trays. I've obviously graduated to Jane Powell's rejects," she grimaced.

"He takes me for a fool," she chattered on autopilot. "J. J. claimed that the reason I didn't get to read for the role was because Sedra had already . . . um. . . . If you ask me, Sedra deserves . . . , er. . . ."

Polly realized she'd blathered herself into a corner and exposed her disgrace. She clamped a hand over her mouth.

"Mother, what happened?" Tim asked, leaning closer to her on the sofa.

Placenta, with maternal compassion added, "You didn't voluntarily turn that job down, did you?"

A disconsolate Polly looked dolefully at her maid and friend and said, "Now look at who has the sharp intuition." And then, with what began as a quiver of her lower jaw and rapid blinking of her eyelids, Polly began to tremble and cry. The combination of an exhausting and humiliating day, J. J.'s badly timed call, the weight of her own subterfuge—and the champagne—conspired to make her feel as vulnerable as an orphan in a Dickens novel. "You were right," Polly admitted, squinting at Placenta through a blurred veil of stinging tears. "You called it correctly the first time you suggested that I didn't get the job. I just couldn't admit my failure to you two."

Rivulets of watery black mascara found wrinkle paths from the corners of Polly's eyes and streaked down the side of her nose and cheeks. She made a soft sniffle, and then she gave a sigh of defeat. "I've become my worst fear—an old-timer.

"The truth is, when I arrived at J. J.'s office this morning, I planned to tell him to take the job and shove it at Mitzi Gaynor. But then I learned that it wasn't mine to blow off. It never was. The lovely and talented Sedra Stone had already seduced whoever makes the casting decisions."

Tim and Placenta were stunned. They offered nonverbal coos of sympathy and disbelief. Tim reached over and enveloped his mother in his protective arms, while Placenta patted a comforting hand on her knee. "I don't understand," Tim said. "Yesterday J. J. insisted that they wanted you to read for the part. I figured it was just a formality."

"I don't understand either," Polly said. "But it was in this morning's *Daily Variety*. Sedra Stone beat me again."

Tim asked, "Did J. J. explain why he led you to believe that Catharine was pretty much your role?"

Polly shrugged. "He may have tried to, but I cut him off," she said. "I don't care anymore. I want to forget the whole thing and simply move on. Perhaps Sedra's a bigger name than mine, after all."

Tim disagreed. "You're a living legend. Sedra Stone can't touch your status."

Placenta harrumphed, "I don't understand why Sedra, or anyone, cares about this measly Catharine role in the first place. Are all these people dense? With a few exceptions, musicals are as dead as Rob Schneider's movie career. And that's a blessing. I mean about Rob Schneider's movie post-mortem," she explained.

Polly sighed. "This role has become important—at least for me. Playing Catharine would be no great shakes, but if I'm not even wanted for one lousy minute of screen time, then where's the hope for higher profile Blythe Danner-like parts?"

Placenta said, "Someone ought to finally teach Sedra a lesson. Furthermore, you shouldn't be associated with such a schmuck as J. J. It only reflects poorly on Polly Pepper's image."

Polly took a deep breath. "J. J.'s mendacious and mean

and stubborn and can be all smiley-faced and giggly while he's grinding his knee into somebody's groin. Which is completely fine as long as he's doing so on behalf of getting me a job. But that describes every other agent in this town. If I dumped him I'd just be making a lateral move, no matter who reps me."

For a while the air in the room was filled only with the mellow sounds of Carly Simon singing romantic standards from the CD player. Finally, Tim shifted his weight on the sofa and said, "Did I hear you say, 'party,' as in an invitation to a social gathering?"

Polly waved away the idea. "Some little thing that Missie Miller's throwing on Saturday," she said. "Probably BYOB. A combination memorial service for Trixie, and a pep rally for the troops before they return to battle on the set of *Detention Rules!* There go my plans for a party here! I don't think I'll be in the mood."

"That would be a first," Placenta said, giving her mistress a playful nudge. "I've never known you to miss a party, except fundraisers where you have to dole out coin. *Infectiouschronichosis* will continue to be a scourge on the planet as along as you're invited to make a contribution for its eradication."

Tim slapped his knee and triumphantly said, "You're definitely going to Missie's party. We all are. It may be the only occasion we'll have to be in the same room with Sedra and the two twits. We've got to find out how she weaseled the role away from you. With the three of us working the room independently, we're bound to connect with loose lips."

A glint came into Polly's eyes and she looked at Tim with animated excitement. "You're so right, my dear Dr. Watson. We'll all sparkle and show 'em how real Hollywood royalty behaves. I've always had a special knack for making people putty in my hands. Strangers tell me their most intimate secrets."

"Columbo raised stupid to an art form to solve mysteries," Tim said. "Jonathan and Jennifer Hart used their money and sophistication. With your genuine stardom as a cover, you'll be the best damn amateur sleuth since . . . since . . . Bubbles Yablonsky," Tim said, picking a name out from a mystery novel he'd recently read.

Polly looked into Tim's green eyes. "Um . . . better not cancel the cattle herd for your Running with the Bulls in Pamplona theme for our own party. Depending upon what we uncover at Missie's, I may want to position a few select guests in the middle of the stampede!"

Chapter 6

Missie Miller lived in Fryman Canyon, a bucolic and expensive pocket of Los Angeles real estate. The area's narrow meandering streets, carved deep into the canyon, boasted an eclectic collection of homes set on large parcels of wooded land and exuded all the rustic charm of rural Connecticut.

It was evening in late June, and summer sunlight remained at 8:00. As Tim gently guided his mother's Rolls-Royce over a rutted lane that rambled past a Tudor-style estate, a French chateau, and a classic Colonial America-style house, Polly and Placenta kept their eyes open for Missie's address. "We'll never find it in this maze," Polly whined from her place in the backseat. "She gave us dumb directions!"

"The numbers are still going up," Placenta observed, shushing Polly. "If we get lost you can play Donner Party and drink the hostess's gift. Anyway, it's gotta be the next driveway."

And it was. Tim was the first to see the large numerals

burned into an oval weathered wood sign that was hung by a rusted chain over the property entrance between two oak trees. He turned left and eased the car down an unpaved stretch that was so narrow that bush branches on either side grazed the car.

"My paint!" Polly cringed and added, "I'll kill if there is so much as a scratch."

They came to a semi-circular drive in front of one of the least pretentious homes in the canyon. It was a modest American Georgian-style house, painted white, but in need of a fresh coat of Sherwin-Williams. Blue shutters flanked either side of the multi-paned, double-hung windows on the first and second stories. An American flag hung limp on a pole bracket mounted on the front of the house. "Enchanting," Tim said, admiring the old world style of the residence as he brought the car to a stop. He switched off the ignition and unbuckled his seatbelt, then opened the door.

Before stepping outside, however, he heard Polly cry, "This can't be the right house, dear. It's too puny for someone who's in *The National Peeper* every week. And there aren't any other cars. Where are the guests? What about a security detail? Is this Missie person too cheap to protect me out here in the boonies?"

"This is the address on the fax," Tim said. "Perhaps we're the first to arrive. And I didn't notice any street gangs hanging around the fountains at the replica of Versailles on the corner."

"Security?" Placenta pooh-poohed. "In this neighborhood you'll be lucky to be shot by paparazzi lurking behind the garbage cans. Although you could use the exposure."

In that moment, the front door of the house opened and a beaming Missie Miller, wearing casual black Capri pants and a man's Oxford cloth white dress shirt untucked and opened at the collar and down three buttons, stepped outside. A black Labrador ambled close by her side. "Welcome," she called out, and advanced to the car from which Polly was emerging.

"Remember our mission," Tim admonished his troops in a whisper. "Just for tonight you *love* Missie Miller and Dana Pointer *and* Sedra Stone. You're committed to putting on your most precious Polly Pepper sweet-as-pie pose. You too, Placenta," Tim implored. "We're Audrey Hepburn, Annette Funicello, and Tom Hanks all rolled into one loveable package, casually gathering information."

"You found us!" Missie said, arriving at the car. She unconsciously brushed shiny shoulder-length black tresses away from her face.

"Only by divine intervention," Polly stage whispered to Placenta.

If Missie overheard Polly's remark she gave no indication. Instead, she offered a hand as Polly and Placenta eased themselves out of the car. "It's a great pleasure to meet you, Miss Pepper," Missie said, with a warmth and dignity that was at once deeply sincere yet not obsequious. "And you must be Tim, the famous Beverly Hills party planner," she said leaning in to brush a kiss on his cheek. "I've read all about you in *The Peeper*. Yeah. I admit it. I read that rag just like everybody else. And you're Placenta," she said knowingly, also bestowing a kiss to Placenta's cheek. "The whole family," she smiled. In that moment Missie had disarmed them all.

"And this is Luca," Missie said, introducing her dog. "She's rather old, but very docile. I love her to bits." After a moment of tousling Luca's well-groomed coat and patting her head, and babbling lovey-dovey baby talk to the animal, Missie's attention returned to her guests. "Please, come inside," she said.

As Polly, Tim, and Placenta followed Missie and Luca down a short flagstone path, they each exchanged looks of surprise, delight, and relief at their warm reception. Then they stepped through the open doorway and into the front entrance hall.

"You have such a lovely home, dear," Polly cooed as she looked around and noticed the hardwood floor, a polished mahogany hall table set against the wall, and a tall faux Wedgwood ceramic urn used as a holder for umbrellas and walking sticks. A collection of four cameos grouped together in small old-fashioned oval frames added a Colonial touch to the entryway.

"I'm afraid the Chippendale's a fake," Missie said modestly, nodding at the antique table. "However, it's of the period. And the primitive is an authentic Zoto," she said, pointing to a small rectangular oil painting.

Missie ushered her guests into the cavernous living room which was accented with wide crown moldings, and decorated in chintz fabrics, floral print wall paper, and a baby grand piano beside a bay window that looked out over the grassy backyard and swimming pool. A wood-burning fireplace dominated the right side of the room, and expensive coffee table books with glossy color covers featuring formal English gardens, portrait paintings by Sergeant, and modern architecture seemed to be stacked everywhere. Missie implored them to make themselves comfortable.

"If the fire gets too warm, let me know," she said. "I realize it's summer, but evenings get so nippy here in the canyon. A welcoming fire reminds me and Luca of home. Nibbles are on the table. More on the way." She pointed to trays of Brie, crackers, and dips. "I'll be back in a moment with some champers. I know that's your favorite," she said to Polly and embraced the trio with her radiant smile.

While Tim and Placenta each took seats on the sofa facing the fireplace and sampled the hors d'oeuvres, Polly walked about the room, admiring the curios. She examined the numerous small tables on which were displayed photographs in expensive silver frames as well as cheap wooden ones. A built-in bookcase contained an enormous selection of contemporary and classic novels, and more framed pictures. It was one of the coziest settings in which Polly had ever recalled finding herself. "French country shabby," she said approvingly.

As Polly was admiring another colorful primitive painting that was hung over the fireplace mantle, Missie returned to the living room. "Miss Pepper, Tim, Placenta," she addressed the group, "I'd like to introduce you to my darling mother."

Standing beside Missie was the farthest thing from anyone's idea of a sweet little old mother. Instead the woman was a sturdy, steel gray-haired matron immaculately dressed, but seemingly uncomfortable in a mandarin collar Chinese motif silk blouse and black slacks. Her eyes were hidden behind large black plastic glasses that wrapped around the side of her face. "Everybody, please meet Elizabeth."

The trio erupted with friendly overlapping greetings.

"Mom," Missie said, "I'd like to introduce you to your favorite star."

As Polly smiled, waiting to play the role of the humble and unworthy superstar, Elizabeth snapped, "Gloria Swanson's dead."

Everyone but Missie giggled at the unexpected response. "As a matter of fact, that's true," Missie said trying to conceal her embarrassment. "But I meant your favorite *living* star is here."

"All the good ones are gone," Elizabeth grumbled.

The old woman was obviously in a sullen mood and in need of a laxative or a stronger dose of whatever pills she popped to keep her out of a sanitarium.

"Not all of them, Mother," Missie said, her patience beginning to fray.

Elizabeth shot back, "For crying out loud, you'd better

give me a hint. I can't see more than a blur, so I can't imagine who you think will impress me." She castigated her daughter as though they were the only ones in the room.

Missie stumbled nervously with her words. "Um, remember, I said that the famous Polly Pepper was coming to the house? She's graced us with her presence, Mom. This is Miss Pepper."

In a husky voice that matched her severe look, Elizabeth dramatically clutched her hands to her chest and sighed loudly. "I'll be damned," she said. "I guess this is supposed to be the happiest day of my life."

"As a matter of fact, Mom really was your biggest fan," Missie acknowledged.

Polly melted, although the past tense of Missie's affirmation wasn't lost on her.

"I liked you in that Palmolive dish washing detergent commercial you did oh-so many years ago. Before my situation," Elizabeth conceded, expressing a tad more sincerity and obliquely referring to her near blindness.

Polly thought for a moment. "Dish detergent?" she said. She turned to Tim and asked, "When did I ever . . . ?"

Elizabeth stepped on Polly's attempted recall of her early career. "Don't be modest. I bought the damn soap because of you. Although I can't say the stuff gobbled up grease the way you promised. But I sparked to you and your television show," she said. "Now I remember."

Again Polly pretended to be overjoyed, if a bit dubious, and offered a plastic smile. She was about to repeat her stock comment about how much she missed the years of being on television each week, when Elizabeth interrupted. "Whatever happened to your cute brother?"

"Brother?" Polly said, looking to Tim and Placenta for guidance.

Missie playfully hugged her mother and said, "Um, Mom, Miss Pepper doesn't have a brother."

"Of course she does," Elizabeth spat and wriggled away from her daughter's embrace.

"Actually, I'm an only child," Polly concurred. "Alas."

"Listen," Elizabeth charged, "I remember quite clearly. "One of you was a little bit country. And the other was a little bit rock and roll. *Alas*." She mimicked Polly's affected language.

Tim caught on. "You're thinking of Donnie and Marie Osmond. Way different generations. Although Polly's got a lot of big teeth too. And a huge overbite. Go ahead and put your hands on her face. See for yourself," he urged.

Polly's eyes grew wide with the fear of a stranger's fingertips tracing her every line and pore. She automatically took a nearly imperceptible step backward.

Missie added, "Easy mistake to make, Mom. Polly and the Osmonds both had musical variety shows. All that singing and dancing and special guests each week. Plus you were seeing double at that time. But this is Miss Pepper. From 'The Polly Pepper Playhouse.' We watched her every Friday night when I was a kid."

Elizabeth reluctantly gave in.

For the sake of ingratiating herself into Missie's life, Polly pretended to be genuinely touched by the old woman's greeting. "Oh, dear Elizabeth," she said, "you've made my day. I'm so delighted to meet you, and your lovely daughter, too. I actually worked once with your favorite star Gloria Swanson. A true legend."

"Robbed of her Oscar!"

"I completely agree," Polly said. "*Sunset Boulevard* is one of my all-time favorite classic films."

"No, for *Gone with the Wind*," Elizabeth corrected.

Missie shook her head and gave a shrug to the group that said, "I give up." Then she suggested that Polly take a seat in a comfortable plush chair adjacent to Tim and Placenta on the couch.

"I need my drink now," Elizabeth said.

"I was waylaid from the champagne," Missie apologized to her guests, as she assisted her mother into another chair. "I think we're all a little desperate right about now. I'll just be a sec." And then she left the room again and headed back down the hall toward the kitchen.

In the quiet that immediately followed, the guests became aware of the barely audible voice of Billie Holiday singing, "I Gotta Right to Sing the Blues," through hidden speakers. But just as they all began to settle in and adjust their ears to the distinctive plaintive vocals, they were startled by a blood-curdling scream blasting like a tsunami warming siren from the far end of the house and reaching into the living room. Elizabeth didn't flinch, but Tim and the others immediately stood up ready to rescue Missie from Freddie Krueger. "Never mind," Elizabeth said. "It's just the little Drama Queen having her hourly breakdown. Miss Congeniality, my ass."

Tim tentatively sat back down onto the sofa and exchanged looks of confusion with the others. The room returned to semi-quiet with Lady Day singing, "Good Morning, Heartache." To ease the tension, Tim cleared his throat and directed an innocuous comment to the old woman. "Mrs. Miller," he said, "you have a great house. Have you lived here very long?"

Silence filled the space until finally, the old woman turned and asked, "You're not speaking to me, are you?"

Tim chuckled. "I was just saying . . ."

"My name's not Miller. It's Stembourg," Elizabeth said. "Missie changed her name. We decided that Stembourg sounded too much like a science fiction creature. Like her daddy."

Polly spoke up. "Early in my career it was suggested that I change my name, too," she said, trying her best to insinuate herself into the conversation. "But I like the alliteration. And I'm fairly common anyway, so I just kept ol' Polly Pepper. I think it's served me well. Don't you?"

"To answer your question about residency in this house," Elizabeth said to Tim, ignoring Polly and her self-deprecating assessment of her career, "we've lived here for going on a year. We moved from our home in Massachusetts so that Missie could become a star. There, she was a big fish in a little pond. Had a scholarship to Harvard, and a violin chair with the Boston Symphony. She made a hit record there, too, but this is where the movies are. She's going to be huge."

"Harvard?" Polly was impressed. "But education is over-rated, don't you think so, Elizabeth?" Polly said. "Especially when everything anyone needs to learn about life is in the movies." She was trying desperately to connect with the woman. "Surely you wouldn't have preferred that Missie stay in that dreary old school when fame and fortune were beckoning."

Elizabeth blanched, "Harvard was a surefire ticket to a Kennedy," she said. She quickly calmed down. "But Hollywood could mean an Orlando Bloom or George Clooney. Here is where make believe becomes reality. Missie's living proof. She's a triple threat. Can't sing. Can't dance. Can't act. But she's got a look that's popular for the moment. I've gotta cash in while I can! If I could just convince her to join Scientology, she might even get a contract with Tom the next time he's available. Then she'd be made!"

Missie returned to the room just in time to hear her mother's comments. "Elizabeth's my most ardent supporter," she said with an edge of sarcasm in her voice. "At least you didn't tell them that my chest is flatter than Debra Messing's," she said to her mother. Addressing her guests she said, "I'm in a few hit movies—they call me a star, which I know I'm not—and Mother makes sure that none of the studio publicity hype goes to my head. How did I get so lucky?" She rolled her eyes.

"You're turning out to be just like that beastly Dana Pointer you hang out with," Elizabeth complained.

"We don't 'hang out,' Mother. We're colleagues," Missie politely corrected. Then, as she offered Polly the first flute of champagne she said, "I suppose mothers always worry about their kids, don't they Miss Pepper?" Missy said, making Polly the center of attention again. "I know that what Mom is saying is simply an expression of deep love and devotion for me. Or so my analyst keeps trying to convince me, at three hundred per."

Polly agreed. "Absolutely, my dear," she said, determined to stick to Tim's script that demanded she maintain dignity at all costs. "I can tell that Elizabeth is as proud of you as I am of my Timmy." She lied. "I dread the day he leaves home. But I have to prepare for the moment he meets Mr. Right. Or when he decides that living in a twenty-seven room mansion in Bel Air on a pastoral estate complete with an Olympic size pool, his own Beemer, as well as an allowance and a no limit expense account at Barney's, is no longer a turn-on."

Tim shot Polly a look of mortification.

"'Someday he'll come along, the man I love,'" Missie sang, as she passed the tray of champagne flutes to Placenta and winked at Tim. She then set a flute down on a glass-top table beside her mother's chair. "But I have no illusions about this business," she continued her examination of her own celebrity. "I'm simply the flavor of the week. I accept that. Eventually we all make the 'Dead or Alive?' quiz."

Then, standing in the center of the room facing her guests and holding a glass of champagne, Missie proposed a toast. "To this happy occasion when Mother and I finally have the opportunity to play host to our favorite star, Miss Polly Pepper."

Polly smiled as broadly as she would for Barbara Walters. Tim, Placenta, and Elizabeth raised their glasses.

"Please, my dear," Polly said, working on her humble act, "I'm a great admirer of your work, too. And call me Polly. We're practically old friends. I offer a toast to you and your career, which is sure to shine bright for many more weeks . . . er, years . . . to come!"

Tim cringed at his mother's overplaying her role.

Everybody in the room took a sip from their glasses and expressed satisfaction. "Please help yourselves to the hors d'oeuvres, too," Missie encouraged, pointing to the trays of pate, mini quiches, a bowl of humus, and another basket of toasted pita bread chips.

"Darling," Polly addressed Missie, after half of the champagne in her glass had been consumed, "I'm so sorry if we're early for your party. I hope we didn't throw you off."

"Everybody else is late," Missie said. "As a matter of fact, it's not much of a party, per se. Nothing like the storied affairs from Pepper Plantation. Hint, hint. I'd love an invitation some time. I'm just having a few people in from the show before we have go back to work on Monday. But I wanted to include you because I thought it might be our only opportunity to meet in person, since things didn't work out with Trixie Wilder's role, bless her soul. I'd rather spend the evening with just the five of us than with the prickly group I've invited."

"Someday I'd like to hear the details of what actually happened with that role," Polly said as discreetly as possible. "My lovely and talented agent, J. J. told me so little."

"Isn't J. J. adorable?" Missie gushed. "I think it's so rad that we share the same agent!"

"Yes. 'Rad,'" Polly tried to smile. "Not that it matters, but really, why didn't I at least get to read for the part?"

"Simple," Missie offered. "Although everyone agreed that you were perfect for the role, damn Dana has casting approval, and she's a big fan of 'Monarchy.' It's rerun all the time and she wanted Sedra. Nothing personal," she added.

Polly took a deep breath trying hard not to show her hurt feelings. "Just as J. J. said," Polly lied, addressing Tim and

Placenta, letting them know that she was in control and maintaining her poise.

"I still don't want that tramp Dana Pointer in our house," Elizabeth said. "The fans you're gaining expect you to be the good girl. Hanging out with Dana will blow your façade!"

Missie ignored her mother's outburst and sat against the upholstered arm of Polly's chair. "Quite honestly," Missie said, placing a hand on Polly's forearm, "I really wanted you in the movie. I'm terrified of returning to the set. I adored Trixie Wilder—the one time we met. She was a sweet old lady. But I haven't heard anything nice about her replacement, Sedra Stone. I thought that if we did a social thing with her here at the house, she might take it easy on me—the new girl. They say she's a director-eating dragon."

Polly looked up at Missie, and her smile masked how peeved she was. "She and I have bitched and fought with each other over silly things like, oh, let's say—adultery with my husbands," Polly said.

Placenta suddenly choked on a cracker and a dollop of thick humus, while Tim, too, coughed loudly when he accidentally swallowed a sip of champagne that went down the wrong pipe.

Polly continued, "Quality people like Carol Burnett and Mary Tyler Moore have sworn they'd never work with Sedra again. Dear Angie Lansbury is too gracious to make any public comment on their feud. And I think poor Renee lost her sight for several hours after stumbling upon the frightening scene of Sedra in the sack with her hubby Kenny." Polly paused for a moment and beamed a brilliant smile before adding, "But that doesn't mean you two won't get along."

Then, as an added word of caution Polly said, "But don't let her know who you're sleeping with or he'll soon be kissing *her* instead of your lips!"

Suddenly, with the shattering effect of a firecracker blasting through the silence of a church, a voice refracted in the atmosphere of the room. "Christ, what an act!" All eyes in the room immediately found Sedra Stone leaning against the arched entry into the living room with her arms folded across her ample chest. Dana Pointer was by her side. "Carol, Mary, Angie, and Renee?" Sedra scoffed. "Are those the only stars you can pull out from under your gray roots to insult me? Sticks and stones may break my bones—or in Trixie Wilder's case, her fragile little skull—but the names of old celebrities whom I loathe anyway will never hurt me." She laughed evilly. "We let ourselves in. Hope you don't mind, *Prissy.*"

As Polly struggled to maintain her promised grace and composure, Missie stood up and smiled brightly. "Miss Stone!" she called enthusiastically. "You found us! Welcome to our little home!" She turned to her mother. "Look who's here, Mum. It's your favorite star!"

Polly looked at Tim who looked at Placenta who looked back at Polly. "As you said," Polly reminded Elizabeth. "All the good ones are gone."

Chapter 7

Polly reached over and swiped Placenta's champagne glass from out of her hand and with one long swallow she drained the flute. "It's only my fourth," she snapped, before Placenta could object and pass judgment. "It's medicinal. Tim said that I could . . ."

Placenta glowered. "Tim said, 'Audrey Hepburn!'"

Remembering her pledge, Polly reeled herself in. Proving her commitment to their covert operation, she turned and looked at Sedra Stone across the room. She called out, "Congratulations on the film role, my dear. I trust you'll make your *line* a memorable one."

Sedra looked over at Polly and abandoned her conversation with Missie. She casually pushed herself away from the archway, arrogance beaming from her phony smile as she walked the short distance to where Polly was seated. Then, looking down her imperious nose at her rival she smiled and said, "It only takes one good line, *dear*. We all remember, *When Harry Met Sally.*" Sedra imitated Estelle Reiner's "'I'll have what she's having.' However, this darling girl,

Dana, has arranged for Trixie's . . . er, *my* role to be embellished—just a tad."

Dana, who, like a devoted puppy, had tagged along beside
Sedra, didn't bother to greet Polly or the others officially.
She simply picked up the thread of the conversation and
huffed, "A tad? I got you pivotal."

Sedra nodded in self-satisfaction. "How do you like them
egg rolls, Mr. Goldstone?" she bragged to Polly.

At first glance Dana was nearly a Sedra Stone clone.
They were dressed in similar V-neck halter top cocktail
dresses with matching rhinestone belts. Dana continued
boasting of her generosity. "No one would have believed that
I'd have a grandmother as ancient as that Trixie Whatshername. If my dimwitted agent had told me sooner that that
old spinster had been hired, I'd have fired her bony ass before she'd placed an orthopedic shoe on the set and wasted
all our time. The important thing is that she did leave."

"If not of her own volition," Polly said.

"If there's one thing Sedra's taught me," Dana plodded
on, "it's that almost nobody in this business knows a rat's ass
about what they're doing.

"If I don't take control of my projects, I'm screwed. The
part of Catharine actually works now that she's younger and
gets to have a sex life, like normal people. Trixie did me—
and herself—a favor by dropping dead. She was in the way."

Hidden underneath Polly's mask of Max Factor base make-
up #12, her face drained of its color as she simmered in the
truth that not only was Dana as crass and self-absorbed as
the tabloids depicted her, but it seemed that she'd become
Sedra's protégé. It wasn't enough for Sedra to have copped
the role that Polly wanted, but she also coerced Dana into
turning it into far more than just a one-scene day player's job.

"A favor," Polly said. "Yes, Trixie was a great one for
doing good deeds. But as she drew her last breath I doubt

that she was thinking only of saving your little film and career, dear." Polly made the sign of the cross.

"Dana was being facetious," Sedra cracked. "I'm sure that she was as shocked and upset by the tragedy as everyone else."

Polly was aching to tell Dana in graphic detail where she could put her facetious comments and her big budget movie. Instead she demurely said, "You're blessed to have a Hollywood guru, my dear. Surely, Sedra's the right mentor to help you navigate through the perilous mine field of this treacherous industry. Almost like a wise stage mother. Or rather a stage *grand*mother."

Tim, anticipating the possibility of a public altercation, left his place on the sofa and protectively sidled up to Polly. He sat on the arm of her chair, poured what remained in his own champagne glass into hers, and politely reintroduced himself to Sedra. He was surprised that she seemed genuinely pleased to see him again.

"Darling," she oozed, and leaned down to kiss him on both cheeks. With his heart-melting charm, Tim turned to Dana Pointer. He extended his hand. "I saw you in *Bummer*," he said.

For the first time since arriving at Missie's home, a smile crossed Dana's lips. As she shook Tim's hand her brown eyes made an obvious tour of his handsome and dimpled face, wide shoulders and the cut of his shirt, which she surmised covered a muscled torso. "Cool," she said, pleased with his remark. She involuntarily gave her hair a seductive flip. "I like to meet my fans, especially when they're . . ."—she raised an eyebrow and lowered her voice—". . . studs. What did you say your name was?"

Sedra interrupted. "Isn't he adorable? This is my little Timmy."

"Yours?" Dana marveled.

"It's not what you think. Unfortunately. No, I just married a couple of his fathers," Sedra corrected Dana's impression.

"But I've practically watched him grow up to be . . . well look at him." Sedra nudged Dana in the shoulder. "How deep can a cleft in the chin go before it's obscene?" She looked him over with the same amount of lust as had Dana.

Polly was completely disgusted by Sedra—a woman her own age making it clear that she wouldn't mind a wrestling match with Tim. "Apparently it's true that the sins of the father are often visited upon the son," she spat. "You being the sin, of course."

Sedra ignored the barb and continued her introduction to Dana. "Tim is Polly Pepper's son, and pretty famous in his own right. He's a marvelous and wildly creative party planner. I should have known that you two would hit it off. You're obviously from similar stock. Er, I mean you're about the same age."

Dana made a nonverbal sound that indicated her overall approval of Tim. "Polly Pepper," she repeated, trying to recall where she'd heard the name. "Your mother, eh? A famous actress, right?"

Tim maintained eye contact with Dana as she began digging a hole for herself.

"I think I remember," Dana said vaguely, a fog lifting. "Someone said that Polly Pepper wanted Trixie Wilder's role in my film," Dana said. "Tell your mother that I'm really sorry if she got her wires crossed, but at this stage in my career I need to be surrounded by important names. Kate Hudson. Kate Beckinsale. Kate Winslet."

"Kate Moss. Cate Blanchett. Kate Mulgrew, Kate Jackson, Mary-Kate Olsen," Tim added to the ridiculously long list of Hollywood actresses named Kate.

For a fraction of a moment, Dana look perturbed, as if she were being mocked. Then she softened. "I'm sure your mom understands. Rejection's part of the game."

Tim nodded. "A game," he said. With his smile firmly plastered to his face, he turned to Polly and said, "You understand, don't you . . . *Mother*?"

Dana had the sense to allow a look of humiliation to play across her face. She looked at Polly. "I didn't recognize you," she said. But rather than apologize directly to Polly she snapped at Sedra. "Thanks for letting me go on like an idiot," she said, her voice rising. "You must get turned on by watching me imitate you as a bitch?"

Placenta cackled softly from the sidelines as the three women began to spar. Even Missie's mother had been drawn to what every Hollywood gossip monger yearned for—a cat fight between two rival stars and an heir apparent to their diva crown. This time, however, Missie entered the fray and the claws of the trio of tigresses temporarily retracted. "No blood on the furniture, please girls," she smiled with her patented good nature. Then, pleading with Dana she said, "Let's treat Miss Pepper with all the respect due a woman of her tremendous accomplishments."

Polly smiled up at her hostess and with a hint of condescension in her voice said, "Not to worry, dear. At this stage in my charmed life and brilliant career, I hardly have any ego about these minor nuisances."

"Now I'm a nuisance!" Dana said, her eyes shooting daggers at Sedra. "You're supposed to be helping me. Isn't that our deal?"

With as much graciousness as she could muster, Polly leaned forward in her chair, smiled and placed a hand on Dana's arm. "I may have thought about the role for a teensy fraction of an instant," she said. "But I'm really too busy being inducted into the Television Hall of Fame to take on any new commitments just now. But I promise to attend a screening of *Detention's Fools*, and lead the applause when it's released."

"*Detention* Rules!" Dana corrected.

"Dana doesn't have a drink," Sedra observed. "And Tim, you're empty. Since Missie's not making the rounds, why don't you two scoodle off and find another bottle. And bring one back for me. And one for your mother, too. Polly and I have much to prattle about."

Missie looked embarrassed. "Things have gotten a little out of hand," she apologized. "It seems everybody I invited decided to invite somebody else."

Dana took another look at Tim and regained her smile. "My date's supposed to be here any minute," she said. "Where the hell is that Jack Wesley? Until he arrives we're gonna scout for the party favors and whatever Missie and her mother have thrown together. Even I know to hire caterers," she hissed to Missie.

"I was only expecting a few . . ."

"Save your acting for the camera," Dana huffed. Then, turning to Sedra, she ordered, "Keep an eye out for Jack. So help me, if he bails on this so-called party . . ." Then she took a parting look at Polly. "I saw you on 'Inside the Actors Studio' once," she said, as if it were a compliment. Then, morphing back into vixen, she grazed Tim's cheek with her hand. "Come keep me company," she said.

As Tim rose to follow Dana he admonished his mother and Sedra. "I'm leaving Placenta here as both referee and bouncer. Trust me, if you two get into a brawl she can easily take you down. Simultaneously."

As Dana plowed through the room she reached behind her to take hold of Tim's hand. Two dozen more guests had arrived and the house was becoming choked in noise. The duo wended their way through cliques of unknown actors who, desperate for the slightest bit of reflected glory from a working film star, called out to Dana and tried to get her attention. She ignored them all and heard more than one person snigger that she was merely a flash in the pan and a first-class bitch. "Thinks she's Jennifer Aniston, for crying out loud," said one guest to another.

Finally entering the hallway between the living room and the kitchen, Dana and Tim walked down the hallway until they came to the small formal dining room, into which Dana pulled Tim. "I was here for dinner a couple of weeks ago. I know that Missie's mother keeps the good hooch in the hutch," Dana said letting go of Tim's hand and heading straight for the liquor. "Here we go," she said, opening a door in the bottom of the cabinet and withdrawing a bottle of Chivas Regal. "Hand me a glass," she said in a tone that was more a command than a request. "Behind you."

Dana had already opened the whiskey bottle and was waiting impatiently as Tim turned around and discovered a highly polished mahogany buffet on which crystal rocks glasses were arranged upside down on a silver tray. He lifted one and handed it to her. She filled the glass more than half way. "How about you, mister sexy?" she asked, still holding the bottle, expecting Tim to join her for a drink.

"Can't mix my alcohol," Tim said. "But I'd kill for another glass of champagne."

Dana took a large swallow of her Chivas. "The wino keeps gallons in the fridge," she said, cocking her head toward a swinging door. Dana smiled and allowed her eyes to take another grand tour of Tim's physique. Then she reached out to Tim's shirt and with one hand maneuvered another button from its hole, exposing the cleft between his strong pecs. "Mmm. Hurry back," she purred. "I need more than a stiff drink."

Tim walked backward, pushing through the swinging door and entering the kitchen. There, he took a long moment to recover from Dana's aggressive attempt at entrapment, then looked around the room. It was a small kitchen. In fact it was more of a galley in desperate need of renovation and upgrades. Many of the white tiles on the countertops were chipped, and the grout was gray and cruddy. The cupboards were midcentury faux country and coated with layer after layer of heavy robin's egg blue paint. The lighting was a sallow yellow. The windowsill above the sink was crammed with plastic prescription medication bottles. He surreptitiously examined the labels: Tegretol. Eskalith. Xanax. All were prescribed by a Dr. Richards for Elizabeth Stembourg.

Tim stored the information in his memory with the intent of Googling the medication names and cross-referencing the symptoms for which they were prescribed. Then, as promised, when he opened the refrigerator door, it was practically a warehouse for Mum's and Piper Heidsieck. He withdrew a chilled bottle and reluctantly returned to Dana in the dining room.

"She's got quite a stash in there," Tim agreed as he caught Dana swallowing the remains of what he presumed was a refill of whiskey.

"You'd self-medicate too if you had only minimal talent and that albatross of a mother hanging around your neck constantly pushing you to be a star while confirming the worst fears about your insecurities," Dana said. "I kinda—but not really—feel sorry for Missie. But thank God for psych drugs! She and her mom are both total whackos without their meds. And don't let Mama's blindness crap fool you. She's like all stage mothers—a natural born killer." Dana refreshed her glass again and slowly circled Tim like a shark around surfers, ready to feast on a *Leg McMuffin*.

To divide his attention, Tim ripped the leaded foil wrapper from the champagne bottle and untwisted the wire bonnet that secured the cork. He gently eased the stopper out of the bottleneck and smiled at the sound of a light pop. He then poured the bubbly into another rocks glass. "Cheers," he said, raising his glass to Dana's.

Dana took another long pull of her whiskey and stood before Tim. As she reached out and passed yet another of his shirt buttons through its loop, she touched his flesh with a long, manicured index finger and said, "I need a strong man in my life. I'm tired of sissy actors."

Tim took a swig of cold champagne and immediately changed the subject. "Um, back to work on Monday, eh," he said sidestepping her overture. "Got your lines down?"

Dana snort laughed, as if she'd just heard a stupid question. "That wuss of a screenwriter is still hammering out the notes I gave him before our forced hiatus. I swear, every little shit in this town claims to be an actor or a writer—or both. I have yet to meet one so-called writer who can follow simple instructions, for Christ sake." Dana was beginning to slur her words. "How 'bout we go upstairs. Missie's bed?"

Tim shuddered. "This place is getting crazy crowded," he made excuses. "People are probably going in and out of that room. Plus, if Missie or Jack finds us . . ."

Unbuttoning her own blouse, Dana said, "It would kill Sedra if she found us," she laughed. "She can't bear that I get all the men she likes. They used to howl at her door every night. Now they howl under my window. She resents my youth."

"And then you'd have to find a new co-star," Tim chided. "Anyway, you really want to be with Jack. He seems like a very nice guy. We've met at a couple of parties."

"Ach! Screw Jack," Dana said. "He's not really into . . ." She stopped herself. "I just want to get this freakin' movie over with, and bury these misfits." Then, for a moment, Dana appeared to lose focus. She returned to her earlier thoughts about the power she wielded on the set of *Detention Rules!* "Sedra says she'll help me handle the writer. And the director. And the producer." She began to snigger. "And the costume designer. And the composer." Dana seemed to think she was being funny. "I'll take care of a few people. Just as Sedra did on *Monarchy.*

"Sedra was a pretty big star in her day. I'm giving her a chance to make a comeback," Dana said. "Two decades is a long time to be out of the public's eye. Heck, she hasn't really worked since before I was born."

"Cheers to you!" Tim said raising his glass. "Sedra's a star. At least in gay drag clubs."

Dana laughed out loud. "I can totally see that," she said. Then, smiling conspiratorially, Dana whispered, "Tell you a secret. Sedra wasn't the first choice for Trixie's role. Hell no. She wasn't even the second or third or tenth. Nope. Not at all. I wanted Cher to play my grandmother. But Cher said *no*. Then I demanded that lady on that old show, 'Raymond.'"

"Doris Roberts?" Tim said. "She would've been great."

"Hell yeah, she would have been great. But she said, 'No-way Jose.' Then I had a fight with the producer 'cause he wouldn't even contact Sandra Bullock or Angelina Jolie. Said he wouldn't insult 'em. Sheesh, what a jerk. He insulted me by making me feel less of a star than those old women. Sedra and I have plans to bite his butt, too. But he finally got me Sedra. Which was totally my idea 'cause she's been writing me letters for a couple of years. Said she could tell that I came from a long line of talent. Said she was a fan and wanted to know me better. No line of talent, trust me. My parents are boobs who believe in the resurrection of Elvis. Anyway, I'm adopted."

"Maybe it's time you produced and directed your own films," Tim said. "You've had two back-to-back blockbusters. I'll bet if you asked politely, the studio would say, 'You go girl! Make us buckets of dough!'"

Dana was suddenly a bit more alert. "I wouldn't even have to be polite," she said. "I'm not as dumb as people think. Even Sedra treats me as though I've got mostly air between my ears. Thinks she's teaching me about life." She rambled, realizing that she was offering too much information, but was unable to stop her wagging tongue.

Tim said, "Don't let Sedra suck too much of your power. You can do very well without her help. I don't believe that anybody thinks you're dumb."

"Well, my producer's too dumb to think I'm dumber," Dana giggled.

"You were smart enough to think of Sedra Stone for the role of Catharine and to build it up with more dialogue," Tim said.

"Smart. Not dumb," Dana parroted Tim, and nodded her head in a wobble. "I would have thought of Sedra eventually, if she hadn't thought of herself first. Matter of fact, Sedra's dumber 'cause she wanted that stupid role when it only had one line. Said she wanted to be close to me. Oh, not like a lez or anything. Said she felt maternal pride . . . even though we'd only e-mailed each other."

"Now her character has pages of dialogue," Tim said. "She was damn smart to find another meal ticket. But I can tell that you see through her. She's always been transparent to me, too, and to anyone with an ounce of intuition."

Suddenly feeling vulnerable, Dana pulled her blouse closed and fumbled with the buttons. "I should be directing my own work," she repeated Tim's ludicrous suggestion as if she'd just thought of it herself. "And what's this about your mother and a Hall of Fame? She's not like someone that important, is she?"

Tim slowly nodded his head. "Used to be," he said. "Did you ever hear of Carol Burnett?"

Dana shrugged.

"When Polly Pepper—Mom—was working on television, she was a bigger name."

Dana looked around, unable to find her whiskey glass, which was immediately in front of her. For a long moment she sat and starred at the paisley wallpaper, which only helped to make her dizzy. Then, in a defeated voice born from too much alcohol, and way too many surprises, she said, "I think I knew that. I don't feel so great."

Dana folded her arms on the table and laid her head down. She instantly fell asleep.

Tim smiled when he looked at the scene—the mean girl undone by her own gluttony. He took another sip of champagne, buttoned his shirt, then picked up the champagne bottle and left the room.

As he made his way back through the house a sea of twentysomethings were drinking and dancing. (Billie Holiday had been replaced on the CD carousel by Beyoncé). He caught sight of Sedra and Jack Weasley seated side by side on the piano bench, engaged in an animated conversation. As he got closer he heard fragments of their discussion above the din. Sedra was saying, ". . . She's dead . . . Missie too . . . Have to be discreet . . . So deserve their fate . . ."

And Jack was saying something that included, ". . . Bloody hell! Don't get me involved . . ."

Just as Tim thought he was going to hear words that would connect into a full-fledged thought, Polly and Placenta were at his side. "Let's blow," Polly said. "I can't bear these people. But I've gathered enough dish to make Billy Bush's hair turn Anderson Cooper gray!"

"I'll send her a note in the ay-em," Polly said, not bothering to say a proper good-bye to her hostess. She led Tim and Placenta through a crush of party crashers and out the front door. Finally ensconced in the car, silence filled the space as they made their way down the narrow lane and out onto the serene streets of Fryman Canyon. As Tim guided the vehicle onto Laurel Canyon and up toward serpentine Mulholland

Drive, Polly yawned. It had been a long day and a seemingly endless evening. Their thoughts were all bottlenecked somewhere between their brains and their tongues, and letting one word escape felt risky. But by the time they reached the crest of the Hollywood Hills, one by one they began to volunteer comments on the party.

"Cute house," Tim said, finding something positive to say.

Polly agreed. "Missie has lovely instincts for interior decorating," she said. "Her mother seems to have adapted well to her near blindness. Did you notice how easily she found the champagne flute that—if I'm not mistaken, Missie intentionally placed at the far edge of the table beside her chair? It was practically balancing and waiting for the slightest vibration to fall."

"Missie seems very attentive toward Elizabeth," Placenta said. "But what was that banshee scream from the kitchen?"

"And it was fun to meet Dana Pointer," Tim said. "We had quite a chat—before she passed out. She wants to take over Hollywood." He took his eyes off the road for a second and looked at his passengers in the rearview mirror.

"Now there's a troublemaker," Polly quickly added. "She came right out and said she was glad that Trixie Wilder was dead!"

"She's a pit bull, alright," Placenta said. "It doesn't surprise me one bit that she and Sedra are so close. Birds of a feather."

Their barbed comments began to overlap. "Perhaps Missie and Dana have bloodstained hands," Polly said.

"Sees a shrink 'cause she hates her mother," Placenta said.

"Mom's on a ton of meds. The kitchen looks like Rush Limbaugh's personal pharmacy," Tim said.

Polly denounced Missie as a social climber, while Placenta dismissed Elizabeth's near blindness as an attention grabber, and Tim expressed skepticism over Dana's bluster that she had the power to have a role rewritten expressly for Sedra.

By the time they arrived back at Pepper Plantation, they were no longer tired. What they wanted to do was continue to tear apart the young people who were now running Hollywood, and to contemplate the fireworks that awaited the cast and crew on Monday when Dana Pointer, Missie Miller, and Sedra Stone showed up for work.

Chapter 8

Monday morning arrived with clear California skies, mild summer temperatures, and an ominous rumbling of the earth beneath the *Detention Rules!* film location at Gary High School in Santa Clarita, California. The good will and enthusiasm that had accompanied the cast and crew on their return to work was short-lived from the moment Sedra Stone's hired stretch limo rolled into the parking lot and the diva emerged.

Behind dark sunglasses, and dressed in a suit of black, Sedra's couture business attire seemed to broadcast her grim aura as she walked with an air of superiority toward the school's gymnasium. As she reached for the door handle, however, Duane, the chubby, red cheeked and cheerful uniformed security guard, dutifully intercepted her and politely asked if he could be of service. A big mistake.

"You know how it is, ma'am," Duane tried to joke. "Although I'll bet that you're probably a big, important, famous rich person, 'cause you sure look and act like it, if your name's not on the list you'd have to prove to be the Virgin Mary before I could allow you onto a Dana Pointer film set."

He chuckled good-naturedly. His harmless form of levity usually disarmed even the most arrogant personal publicist or film producer. "It takes divine intervention from the omnipotent one herself to reach her inner sanctum." He rolled his eyes as if to say, "Get her!"

Sedra removed her sunglasses and with a steely gaze instantly transformed Duane into a wiggly mold of Jell-O. "Sedra Stone hasn't been a virgin since age ten," she said with a tongue that had decapitated more heads than the French guillotine. "And the only Mary I see is *you*."

Duane's eyes watered and his cheeks turned a deeper shade of cherry. He had "issues" when it came to women—especially women who emasculated what little was left in his nearly depleted Y chromosome pool. Duane swiftly made a call to the production assistant. "Someone named Sedra Stone's not on the list," he panicked. After another ego-shredding attack from the PA, he added Sedra's name to a column on his clipboard then groveled an exaggerated apology for not knowing who she was. He chased his servility with a silent wish that Sedra would be sucked into a black hole—along with the PA, his mother, his landlady, and every girl who never sat with him in the cafeteria in high school.

Sedra dismissed Duane without further acknowledgment of the fat boy's existence, and entered the building.

Most people mask their insecurities when they begin a new job, and only reveal their true natures incrementally over time. Sedra, however, made it clear from the start that she didn't give a damn whether anybody liked her or not. As far as she was concerned she was a star, and that meant behaving like royalty. With a bearing of entitlement, she stood just inside the gymnasium doorway expecting to be retrieved. And she was. Almost instantly another production assistant arrived and escorted her to a luxury dressing room trailer.

En route, Sedra reeled off a list of food items she wanted delivered to her, pronto: A case of Cristal, a platter of foie gras, and a box of Twinings peppermint teabags. "And a proper nameplate, for Pete's sake," Sedra said when they arrived at her Star Waggon and she ripped from the door a strip of masking tape with her name printed in black Sharpie.

"The production wraps in five days, Miss Stone," the unflappable and impossible to impress PA said. "You won't be around long enough to enjoy the engraving." The PA opened the door to Sedra's trailer and stepped aside, allowing the star to enter first. She handed Sedra a folio containing the cell phone contact numbers for each of the cast and filmmakers. "In case you need to reach anyone," the PA explained. "Someone will be along shortly to take you over to wardrobe. Oh, and there's the laptop you requested," she said, pointing to the latest model iMac notebook sitting on the coffee table. Then the PA left the trailer with a curt, "Ciao."

Sedra removed her black suit jacket and laid it on the back of a chair. She settled in. Feeling quite satisfied with her life at the moment, she examined her accommodations and nodded approval at the accouterments: a flat-screen plasma television, video and DVD equipment, a stereo system, wet bar, microwave oven, and sleeper sofa. As she had only worked sporadically since the end of her television series, she was inwardly thrilled by the way she was being treated. She moved to the computer and pushed the power button. The tinny announcement sound that issued from the speakers reminded Sedra of a cyber orchestra tuning up before a concert. She then retrieved a floppy disk from within her purse and pushed it into the disk drive. She clicked on the disk icon and a document filled the screen. Sedra scrolled to the bottom and began to read aloud. Then she typed:

INTERIOR: DRESSING ROOM TRAILER ON MOTION PICTURE SET LOCATION.

Director Adam Berg, having heard about the old star's grand entrance tantrum, decided it prudent to pay an early morning courtesy visit to Sedra. He would apologize for the mistake and any inconvenience the security guard may have caused her. Surely, he thought, this gesture would make an ally of the woman referred to as "The Tetanus of Television."

As a Broadway dance choreographer turned director of music videos, Adam Berg was used to handling difficult personalities. He had survived Betty Buckley in New York, Lil' Kim's street thug entourage in Brooklyn, and even Joss Stone's bombastic management and publicity team in the UK. Although he wasn't naïve enough to expect feature film directing to be a walk in the park, he thought he had the creative and diplomatic skills to handle Hollywood. Wrong.

From the moment he knocked on Sedra's trailer door and popped his head in to wish her well, his already waking nightmare of working on *Detention Rules!* was ratcheted up to the power of ten. In Sedra Stone he found the subject for behind-the-scenes showbiz horror stories to repeat at cocktail parties.

Adam smiled brightly as he stepped inside Sedra's trailer with his ubiquitous assistant Judith Long following behind him. His British accent clipped through the air as he introduced himself. "I was a huge fan of 'Monarchy,'" Adam lied, having been in Pampers when the show first aired, and he held out his hand in vain for her to shake.

Sedra looked up and barely acknowledged the filmmaker's presence. She offered a tight obliging half smile as she closed the computer notebook.

"You'll excel in the role of Catharine," Adam continued, feeling an instant dislike for the woman who emitted a palpable caustic vibration. "Dana has keen instincts," he continued. "I admit that I sort of fought her all the way on the script changes she demanded . . . er, requested. But I confess she was spot-on about making her grandmother less apple pie and more toxic medical science waste dump."

Sedra gave him a weak smile.

"The new dialogue is smashing and funny as all hell," the director enthused. "Don't you think so? Can't wait to hear you deliver those wacky lines."

"I've read better lines painted on the street," Sedra deadpanned.

Adam laughed out loud until he suddenly realized that Sedra wasn't smiling and that her remarks were not meant to be a joke. He took a deep breath and settled into an uncomfortable snicker. He looked over his shoulder at his assistant who was of little use to him outside his bed. And now, when he needed her loyalty he found that rather than coming to his rescue she pretended to be searching for something within a stack of papers on her clipboard.

"Lines on the street," Adam repeated and smiled nervously. "Very funny. You should do stand up at The Improv," he faked another laugh. He cleared his throat and simply said. "Indeed. Well."

The trailer was suddenly plunged into torpid silence.

"Um, is there something you'd like to discuss with me?" Adam eventually continued. "Perhaps you think the script needs to be tweaked? Although we begin shooting in twenty minutes, if there's anything . . ."

Tweak this, Sedra said to herself as she imagined being in bed with Adam. He may have been the person in charge, but that didn't mean he couldn't also be a playmate. Her eyes made an obvious tour of the twenty-something-year-old director. From the logo on his *Detention Rules!* baseball cap to his tight Coldplay T-shirt, through which he boasted a torso of gym-packed muscles, down to his baggy blue jeans and Adidas tennis shoes, Sedra approved of his appearance.

Then she looked at the director's assistant who stared defiantly back at her; one gold-digging, man-hungry woman to another. Unspoken rules of engagement—in which there are no rules—were instantly established. Individually, both women were secure in the trust that in any showdown, she alone would be the victor. One held the seductive power of youth. The other held the equally magnetic sexual power of cunning and experience.

"I try to run an amiable set," Adam continued. "I want my cast and crew to be content. Simply let me know if you need or want . . ."

"Never mind," Sedra interrupted, picking up her script and finally turning on a camera-ready smile. "I'm really delighted to be in your debut feature."

Adam grinned and Sedra shot another look at his assistant that said, "Score one for the visiting team, honey."

Then Sedra returned her attention to Adam. "Don't worry your sexy English muffins," she cooed. "At least you're not pretending to be creating art. *Detention Rules!* will be a lovely teen date movie. The audience won't be paying any attention to Sedra Stone, or to your wide angles, master shots, editing, or musical score. They'll only be thinking about screwing after the end credits crawl. It's a fact of life."

Adam had only known Sedra Stone for a total of two and a half minutes, yet he already wanted to be rid of her. "I'm not worried about the success of my film," Adam assured Sedra. "Your presence on screen will elevate the genre."

"Shall we report to wardrobe?" Sedra finally said, exuding warmth that seemed to come over her as unexpectedly as light after a power failure. She continued, "I feel like being on the strong arm of the man in charge." She and the assistant exchanged last looks of forewarning.

"You're from England?" Sedra asked, as she followed Adam out of her trailer and intentionally missed the step and fell into his rescuing embrace.

"Nah. Jersey City," Adam said, helping Sedra to steady herself.

"I would have believed Brit, or Aussie."

"You, too."

"Affectation," Adam's assistant muttered loud enough for the star to turn around and give her a withering stare.

Meanwhile, in makeup trailer #1, Dana Pointer was being powdered and sprayed and tweezed and creamed. Next door, in makeup trailer #2, Missie Miller was undergoing the same treatment, but with an added spritz. Both were trying to memorize lines from the new pages of script dialogue. As a result of Dana's insistence that Sedra's role be expanded and rewritten, they were scrambling to forget their original lines and learn the new material.

One of the major changes in the script had Catharine advising her granddaughter on how to deal with best friends who steal their lovers. In the back story, Catharine is far from the best source of advice for taking care of jilted lovers because she's recently been released from prison and is on parole after being jailed for twenty years for what she did to Grampa Tommy when she caught him having an affair with her closest friend. The jury in her trial had quickly convicted Catharine based on her lack of remorse, and her on-the-record Martha Stewart-like remark that "Cuisinarts can be as practical in the bedroom as they are in the kitchen." (In the original script, Catharine tries to comfort Dana's broken heart with a cup of Chamomile tea and a Duncan-Hines double Dutch chocolate fudge brownie fresh from her oven.)

Twelve days before, the principal cast had filmed the old breakdown scene so many times that the assistant director lost count of the number of takes. With each new number on the clapboard, Dana had found something to criticize in the other performers' work, and insisted they shoot it again and again.

Eventually, late in the evening, and far into IATSE union overtime pay for the crew, Dana again halted the action and shouted, "Cut! Cut! Cut!" She glared at the director and ranted, "Why are you doing this to me? Why aren't you directing these cretins? This Trixie person is forgetting her lines!" She turned and poked a finger into Trixie's chest and warned, "This is the last picture you'll ever make old-timer. I'll personally see to it." She then pivoted and pointed to Missie and Jack. "She's hogging the scene, and he's gotta put his shirt back on otherwise the audience won't be looking at me! And, hello, but his character would never go for the so-called good girl. He wants to have sex with me . . . er, my character! Why am I the only one who gets this? Why must everything depend on me?"

Silence had fallen over the school gymnasium-turned-soundstage as the cast and crew held their respective breaths. They were too amused by the egomaniacal actress trying to castrate Adam Berg. The producer, too, had simply stopped in his tracks and stared at Dana as though she were a cat coughing up a fur ball onto a brand new expensive silk shirt, a sight at which he could not avoid gaping in horror.

Many among the seasoned crew had worked with real talent—Jon Voight, Meryl Streep, and Cliff Robertson—and knew how generous true stars could be. They were artists who thought only of the work and a job well done, who had nothing to prove and thus had no need to show off their power by obliterating those around them. On the other hand, the same grips and stagehands had also worked on movies with Whoopie Goldberg, Lindsay Lohan, and Rob Schneider. All would attest that, like Dana, they were nothing more than insecure despots who should be on their knees thanking the gods for having squeezed fame and fortune from beneath the thin layer of their minor talents.

During Dana's diatribe, director Berg decided he'd had enough for one day. It was ten forty-five and he gave the assistant director the sign to clear the set for the night. He sent his weary cast and crew home with a reminder that the morning call time was six o'clock.

Dana stormed off the set and disappeared into the night. Missie was last seen heading toward her trailer. Jack threatened to telephone his agent to report how intolerable the working environment had become. A dejected Trixie, after being publicly humiliated, scuttled to her trailer—and died.

"That was then. This is now," Dana sighed smugly, sitting in her make-up chair and remembering that night when she proved that she wielded enough star power to close down the production. She now tried to concentrate on her lines and fought misgivings about making Sedra's role larger. She read the pages aloud while under a hair dryer. "I'm still the school slut," she smiled with satisfaction as she read the scene and turned the page. "Everybody loves a tramp, and I'm really no different than any other teen who needs to satisfy her raging hormones. *Insert song.*" She realized that she'd read the stage direction and then crossed out the two words with her red pen.

Suddenly, even from under the hood of the noisy hair dryer, Dana could hear Missie Miller scream from the trailer next door. "No way! My part's been chopped all to hell!" The voice of Missie was clear. "Someone's gonna die! Dana!" she screamed. "I swear I'm gonna kill you and Sedra, too!

Just then, the ring tone of Dana's cell phone played the first bars of the television theme music to "Tales from the Crypt." Dana looked at her phone and found Missie's name and number on the caller ID. She smiled and let the call go to voice mail. Looking at the makeup artist, Dana said, "Wait'll she finds out that the writer has made her character pregnant . . . with twins!"

Chapter 9

"Take twenty-seven." The voice of the bleary-eyed assistant director was as somnambulant as a caller in a Bingo parlor. The morning, which had begun with a varnish of euphoria and camaraderie over the cast and crew, had evaporated into an afternoon of Armageddon, starting at the top with the stars, and quickly funneling all the way down the food chain to the craft service workers. Now it was dusk, and although director Berg and his principal players had been working the entire day, they had yet to commit one scene from the *Detention Rules!* script to film.

With stand-ins doing all but speaking the lines of dialogue, the pivotal scene in the movie had been blocked and reblocked, and the lighting was set and reset, per the whims of Sedra telling Dana what she—not director Berg—thought was best. Now, the cameras were ready to roll again, but when the cast was called from their respective trailers to report to the set only Missie Miller and Jack Wesley showed up. Sedra sent word via production assistants that she and Dana were unhappy with the director of photography's camera angles, as well as the costume designer's wardrobe. Most especially, they were disgusted with the ludicrous dialogue they were required to recite. "This guy's writing for Lynn Redgrave, not for a teen like Dana, for Christ sake!" Sedra told the PA. Therefore, in solidarity, until changes were made, she and Dana would be too ill to work.

Adam Berg, known for being a safe harbor in a storm, finally snapped. He called his producer, who called Dana and Sedra's agent, J. J. Norton, who telephoned Sedra Stone in her trailer and screamed, "Get your finally working ass onto that set. Has been!"

Within minutes the older star and the younger star were back together in the school's gymnasium. Dana, however, was just as petulant as she had been before J. J.'s call. Out-for-blood, she angrily attacked the director with a mother-lode of venom. She insisted that the screenwriter be summoned to fix the script again.

"We don't have time," Adam Berg began to calmly debate the issue. "You'll follow my direction and stand on your marks. Then you'll speak the lines as written. Or else . . ."

With an imperious look Dana stepped forward. Her body language dared him to continue.

"Or else I'll be forced to bring you up on SAG charges," Berg accepted her challenge.

Dana looked at Sedra, who gave her a quick nod as if to prompt her to rehearsed action. Furious that she had been publicly upbraided in the condescending tone in which Berg was dismissing her, Dana dug in her heels. Standing before the entire cast and crew she took aim. "Okay, Mr. Big Shot first-time feature film director," she sneered. "Right now, in front of all these people, tell me who is your star?"

A deafening silence fell on the set, but Berg did not flinch. "Well?" Dana provoked him further, trying to bully Berg into a fight. "Whose name is above the title of this film?"

Missie stepped forward. "Excuse me," she interrupted, "but my name is next to yours. Stop wasting Mr. Berg's and everybody else's precious time."

Dana ignored her costar and continued her diatribe against the director. "Who can't you do without at this late stage in the production?" Dana folded her arms across her chest. "Does the crew have to reset the lights again? Damn right they do. Do you have to reblock the scene to show off my best side? Without question. Does the costume witch have to find something more suitable for Sedra Stone to wear? Until you answer *yes* to all of the above, Sedra says we'll be in our trailers." And then she linked arms with Sedra and turned to leave the set.

The usually unflappable Adam Berg was now nearly apoplectic. He stood in dumbfounded anger and watched the two actresses retreat. Then he mimicked Dana loudly enough for her and everybody else to clearly hear. "'Sedra says, 'go fetch.' Sedra says, 'roll over and play *dead*.' Sedra says . . ."

Dana and Sedra both stopped at the door and turned around. "Is that some sort of threat?" Dana asked, feigning amusement.

"A prophecy," Adam smiled evilly.

"Kiss my prophetic butt," Dana said, mocking Adam's baneful smile. Then she pushed open the door and began to leave. When Sedra did not move Dana whined, "Let's go!"

"Um, you run along, dear," Sedra encouraged. "I'll be with you shortly."

In a huff, Dana was gone.

Berg shook his head. "It was bad enough with the great and powerful Dana Pointer trying to run my set by herself," he said to the rest of the cast and crew. "Now she's got a master manipulator teaching her how to fine tune her diva skills." He cocked his head toward Sedra.

"She has a lot to learn," Sedra said apologetically. "Now,

if you'll simply consider a few changes to the script here and there. . . ." She stopped herself. "No, you're in charge, and I'm simply a little cog in your big creative wheel. I certainly didn't mean to overstep my bounds. I apologize." Sedra hung her head in shame. "While you're resetting the lights, I'll be in my trailer," Sedra said before exiting the building.

The delays in filming had been mounting even before Trixie's death; however, director Berg was biting his nails and trying to figure out a way to replace the aging star Sedra Stone. But he was boxed in. How, he asked himself, could he replace Sedra this late in the production? Polly Pepper immediately came to mind. She had made it clear, however, that she was otherwise engaged. Even if he managed to get rid of Sedra through a buy-out of her contract, Dana still had casting approval. It was a no-win situation. Adam Berg was defeated. He had no choice but to make the changes demanded by his teen star and her nefarious mentor.

Missie sidled up to Adam and casually patted him on the back. "You could always have them electrocuted," she whispered and smiled at Adam and his assistant. Missie pointed to the floor. "Gee. With all these cables and wires and voltage boxes, there's a tragic accident waiting to happen. I'm kidding, of course." Under her breath she added, "Sort of."

"Trust me. I've considered that—and a dozen other possible scenarios," Berg smiled conspiratorially. He sighed. "Those two no talent bitches aren't worth facing LAPD homicide charges for and ending my career. Of course when the film is ready for release we'll all do the press junket publicity stuff and tell 'Access Hollywood' how much we loved working with each other."

"I know the drill," Missie laughed. "We'll smile and say that Dana's a generous and talented actor. And that Sedra's nothing like her reptilian reputation. She's a saint and we can't wait to work with her again."

Adam and Missie shared a snicker. "That's the business of show," Berg said.

"And people buy all the lies we sell," Missie agreed. "Dana and Sedra will get what they deserve," she said. "It's karma. And you'll have the pleasure of watching their careers die."

Director Berg faced his young star. "You're the only human being on this production," he said. "As a special prize, you should be dating Jack Wesley. He's really a nice kid. And he's going to be the next Matt Damon."

Missie blushed. "He's definitely nice looking," she said.

"He's got a killer bod!" Judith pointed out, trying to ease Missie away from her meal ticket.

Missie looked at Judith. "But I'm not his type. He's with. . . . Never mind. Plus I think Sedra has her delusional sights on him. When I was coming to the set I saw him leaving her trailer and buttoning his shirt."

"Good grief," Berg sighed. "Next thing you know, she'll be teaching him how to castrate a director."

Just then, the assistant director called out, "Stand-ins! On set, please!" Activity on the set went into overdrive as the technicians began to reset the lighting and reblock the scene with the stand-ins substituting for the actors. "I'd better help out," Judith said, and left to join the crew.

Berg returned his attention to Missie. "This'll take at least an hour to set up. How about a drink in my trailer?"

Missie deftly deflected his advances. "I'm afraid of your cute girlfriend," she chuckled. "She looks as though she could beat up Sedra—and would actually like to." Missie caught herself. "Oh, but in a totally feminine kind of self-defense way, naturally."

Berg laughed. "She's a bigger man than I am. Take a rain check?"

* * *

Never far from the set, Sedra Stone's stand-in Lauren Gaul appeared prepared to start all over again working with the director of photography and camera crew to reset the scene. Lauren, who was also an actress—when she could find work—had a lengthy resume of motion picture credits as a stand-in. A woman of fifty-five, she had worked with such legends as Jessica Tandy, Katharine Hepburn, Judi Dench, and, most recently, Trixie Wilder. Now she was Sedra Stone's stand-in, although the star had never acknowledged her presence. *Typical diva*, Lauren thought and shrugged her shoulders in resignation. On motion picture sets, as in any profession, there is a hierarchy of queen bees and drones. Stand-ins are among the worker bees. They're just above background extras, but they are below the acting talent. And there is an unspoken law that they never associate with the stars for whom they are standing in, unless the star speaks first. Still, Lauren felt that she was just as good, if not better, than Sedra Stone, with whom she had a past association.

Although Lauren was usually employed on feature films, she had also worked on television programs. In fact, although Sedra would never remember—and Lauren couldn't bring it up—early in her career she had been a stand-in on "Monarchy." However, her assignment on that show was short lived. While filming the pilot episode, one of the production assistants informed her that her services were no longer required. "Miss Stone said to beat it."

"But why?" Lauren had pleaded, as tears welled in her eyes.

Although the production assistant was as tough as frozen Styrofoam, she felt a moment of pity. She shook her head and said, "Listen, honey, an insecure star like Sedra Stone doesn't want a stand-in who's younger and prettier than she is. Them there are the breaks. Sorry."

Those were the exact words. Lauren had never forgotten

them and never forgiven Sedra's vanity and cruelty. She had been unceremoniously dismissed from a job she desperately needed, and was depressed and out of work for three months afterward.

It had been Lauren's fate to work in the industry not as a player, but ostensibly as a piece of equipment. Serving as a facsimile of the star on the set, a stand-in saves the actor and the production a lot of time by simply standing still as the DOP set the lights for the scene.

In addition to being cooperative and taking direction well, Lauren had to be the same height and have the same hair color as the actor for whom she was assigned. On some jobs, if the star was particularly lazy, Lauren actually got to film the long shot scenes, or stand-in for overhead shots, or shots from behind. The fun part of her job was when she was asked to run the star's lines with the other actors until the cameras were actually rolling and the real star was ready to emerge from the chrysalis of her trailer dressing room to shoot the scene.

Although she had once been an ambitious young actress herself, Lauren had eventually accepted the fact that her bread and butter came from merely being nothing more than a member of the crew. She did all of the off-camera work with the other actors, but as soon as the star was ready to face the lens, Lauren stepped back into the nothingness and anonymity of being behind-the-scenes. Yes, the work was steady, and she could earn more than a thousand dollars a week for her services, but a part of her was still bitter and resentful that she wasn't a working actor. It sucked. But it paid the rent.

Lauren spent the next hour along with the other stand-ins being moved from one spot on the set to another. She stood patiently still while the DOP checked his light meter, and another assistant placed colored tape next to her feet on the floor to mark the spot where Sedra Stone would eventually stand. All the while she was thinking; *After all these years, I'm still a stand-in. And I'm a better actor than Sedra Stone could ever hope to be.*

When the new camera blocking was done, Lauren left the set and continued her off-time habit of exploring whatever location she was on. In this case, the school campus. As a new state-of-the-art institution, Gary High School had an Olympic-size swimming pool and Lauren discovered it boasted a ten-meter diving platform. Although the water had been drained, she strolled around the perimeter of the pit and inhaled the scent of chlorine.

By the time the screenwriter reluctantly altered several lines of his script, as Dana had commanded, and the cinematographer reset the lighting, and the new blocking had been worked out, and the caterers had fed the cast and crew, it was nearly nine o'clock at night. Director Adam Berg summoned his principals, and sarcastically asked if they were finally satisfied with the dialogue changes, the costumes, the lighting, and the overtime penalty pay that the technicians would be receiving as a result of having to work fifteen hours straight. In a gentle voice he said, "Let's try this once again, shall we?" Then he sat in the director's chair and let the assistant director call, "Take twenty-eight. Action."

Three minutes later, Berg's quiet and mocking voice said, "That was lovely. Thank you. We'll print it." Continuing to speak as though to a classroom of children, Berg said, "How good of you all to spend twelve hours rehearsing that one-hundred-thirty second scene, and committing to film the extraordinary new dialogue of Mr. Ben Tyler.

"A special note of thanks to our luminous star, Dana Pointer," Berg said looking directly at her. "It was absolutely delightful not to hear her whiny voice deviate from the lines on the page or complain that Jack or Missie or Sedra was giving her hives. I'll try to squeeze another thirty seconds of film out of her tomorrow." He rose from his chair and indolently walked out of the gymnasium. The cast dispersed as well, while the technicians and assistants packed up their gear, anxious to get home to their families.

It was dark outside the school building, as Dana, Missie, Sedra, and Jack walked toward their respective trailers. Laughing, Dana said, "I think we showed that bum who's boss, didn't we?"

Sedra smiled. "You were far from professional today, dear," she said. "If I were Mr. Adam Berg, I'd probably never work with you again."

Dana was dumbfounded. "You're the one who insisted that a bitch has to mark her territory!"

"You're not a dog." Sedra's voice was calm. "You must pay closer attention to how *I* behave. I push a little, and then I pull back. Today I showed how I care deeply about my character and the film project, and that I was ultimately willing to be the director's piece of clay."

Dana turned on her. "You told me, 'Give ulcers, don't get them.'"

"Darling, you're giving me an ulcer," Sedra deadpanned. "Now go to your trailer and think about how to make things up to Adam Berg in the morning." She added "Ta," as she split away from the group and went to her own trailer.

"Don't 'ta' me," Dana spat at Sedra. "We have an agreement."

"From what I witnessed today, you're succeeding beautifully on your own," Sedra said. Then she opened the door to her trailer and stepped inside. Before closing the door she added, "Stop by before you leave for the night. I've got a few important things I want to say to you." Then she disappeared into her Star Waggon.

Dana was at once furious and embarrassed. "Missie," she hissed, "that bitch made me look like a freak today. The way I behaved . . . I mean it was all her doing! Sedra told me to break the director's back, that it was the only way to show who was in charge."

Missie continued walking toward her trailer. Finally she said, "Sedra's right. You don't need her help. You've been difficult since day one of this shoot. You're so insecure that you think you need to bully people to get your way. Keep it up and you'll be renting movies instead of starring in them."

Dana was speechless with rage. Then she turned to Jack. "Let's get out of here. I need a drink."

"Nah, I'd better not," Jack said. "I'm exhausted. We have to be bright-eyed and bushy-tailed first thing. And it's a long drive back to Studio City. Maybe another time."

Dana huffed in protest. "Fine," she said, spitting the word out as though they tasted of Listerine. "And I won't bother to ask you, little Miss Brown Nose the Director. You've probably gotta get your dear old mama home."

"As a matter of fact, I do. She's been stuck in here all day," Missie said, as she arrived at her trailer. "Jack's right. Have to be all perky for work in just a few more hours. Try to have a pleasant night." She then opened the door and disappeared inside.

Dana and Jack fanned out and headed toward their respective dressing rooms. Before closing their doors however, they both took another long look at the other. "Goodnight," Jack called. But Dana simply slammed her door.

It was a quiet summer night. Little more than the sound of trailer doors opening and closing could be heard until a hostile argument broke out in Sedra's trailer. The ruckus could be heard throughout the school campus. One after another, the cast slipped out of their mobile homes forming an audience of eavesdroppers for the melee. Soon most of the assemblage tired of the disturbance and found their way to the parking lot and their respective cars.

By the time security came around to turn off the lights in each trailer, the Santa Clarita location was deadly quiet again.

Chapter 10

Various telephone ring tones issued from a dozen extensions throughout Pepper Plantation and fractured the early morning tranquility. Placenta, diligently marinating salmon for the evening meal, was startled. She automatically glanced at the clock on the face of the microwave oven. It was only 7:00 A.M. Friends—with the exception of Helen Reddy, who never caught on to the time difference between Australia and California—knew better than to call before the mistress of the manor was finally out of bed. Everybody knew that was seldom earlier then ten.

The number displayed on the telephone caller ID readout was unfamiliar to Placenta. With slight trepidation, she gingerly picked up the receiver. She answered in the secret code of cautious celebrity households everywhere: "Dialysis Clinic," she said.

Within moments, Placenta was racing up the Scarlett O'Hara Memorial Staircase two steps at a time and sprinting down the second floor hallway. She didn't bother to knock on Polly's bedroom door. She barged into her private chamber and stood over Polly for a moment. Then, "Polly! Wake up. Polly!" she demanded.

With her black silk sleep mask askew on her face, Polly drowsily flailed her arms like a rag doll and tried to push Placenta away. "Wha?" she groaned as if she were in the middle of a nightmare. "'Nother hour, please?" Polly halfway opened the one eye not hidden by her shade and squinted at the digital alarm clock on her nightstand. "Are you kidding me?" she bellowed. "The coyotes are still scavenging for cats at this hour!"

The combination of the telephone ringing at a relatively early time of the morning, and the distant sound of Placenta's voice wafting back down the hallway, mixed with Polly's equally obstreperous complaints, wrested Tim from a luxurious dream. All that remained in his foggy memory was a vague image of sharing a compartment on a train to Paris with Olympic gymnastics legend Bart Conner. "Damn. I think I was his personal masseur!" Tim whined, his dream interrupted before he'd had an opportunity to give the gold medallist a rubdown.

He pushed away his top sheet and comforter and reluctantly slipped out of bed. Wearing his ubiquitous boxers and T-shirt, Tim finger-combed his hair, adjusted his manhood, and shuffled barefoot down the corridor and into his mother's boudoir. "Wass up?" he asked, fighting for consciousness and bracing himself in preparation for upsetting news.

Placenta sat on the edge of Polly's bed. She shook her head and looked from Tim to Polly. "I've got terrible news," she said. "You're not going to believe it." She leaned over and reached into the top drawer of Polly's nightstand and retrieved a bottle of Valium. "Here," she said, twisting open the child-proof cap and shaking out a blue tablet into her palm, "you'll need this."

Polly was now fully alert and waved away the pill. Tim had crawled into bed with his mother and put a strong and

protective arm around her shoulder for mutual support in anticipation of news that either the universe was about to implode,
or that France-hating Congress had banned the importation
of *Taittinger 1995 Comtes de Champagne Blanc de Blanc*.
In terms of catastrophe, both possibilities would be equally
disastrous to life at Pepper Plantation.

Placenta made the sign of the cross, and held Polly's
hand. "It's terrible," she said again, preparing to deliver the
news. "The *L.A. Times* just called."

Polly's eyes widened and she stifled a grin in anticipation
of seeing her name in the paper.

"They wanted a statement," Placenta said.

"For that they can go to the bank," Polly said. Then she
became serious, knowing that unpleasant news was about to
be delivered.

Placenta continued. "There's been another incident on the
set of that movie you were supposed to do. This time . . . I can
hardly bring myself to say it. This time . . ."

"Sedra Stone's keeping Trixie Wilder company," Polly
said.

Placenta gasped, "Damn, you're good! How is it you can
always beat Jessica Fletcher to the killer even before the
body shows up, but you can't figure out that Thursday is my
payday?"

"What? I didn't know anything!" Polly gasped. "What are
you talking about? I was kidding! Sedra's a corpse? I was
joking!"

"You were subconsciously hoping," Tim added.

Polly began to hyperventilate. When she finally caught
her breath, she was dazed and confused. She repeated,
"Sedra Stone's dead? How? What happened? An accident?
Did Dorothy's house finally fall on her?"

Polly and Tim both competed to ask questions for which
Placenta had no answers.

"It's all over the news," Placenta said, as she reached for

the television remote control that was still on the bed where Polly had left it before falling asleep the night before. She pushed the power button. The plasma screen mounted over the fireplace at the foot of Polly's bed filled with an image of a reporter in the field who was covering the story from the scene. She was saying, ". . . Back to you in the studio."

"Damn it," Placenta yelled at the screen, and switched to channel seven. This time, Tim's favorite reporter, sexpot Lowell Lodge, was beginning his coverage.

". . . Stone. What we *can* report at this time is that her chauffeur found the body of the star of the popular 1980s primetime television soap 'Monarchy,' at approximately midnight. She was discovered in the swimming pool on the high school location set of her new movie. She apparently fell from the ten meter diving platform."

"Drowning," Polly shivered. "A horrible way to go."

"The pool was . . . empty," the reporter said, as if he'd heard Polly and corrected her presumption. "Police are investigating this as an accident. But according to Detective Archer of the Santa Clarita Police Department, they can't rule out the possibility of foul play."

The screen smash cut to a prerecorded interview with Detective Archer. "All I can tell you is that although the death of Miss Stone appears to be an accident, the investigation is ongoing. That's all I know for now. Thank you."

"He's a cutie," Polly said of Detective Archer, obviously paying more attention to what the man looked liked than the substance of what he had said.

Video images of the pool cordoned off with yellow police barricade tape appeared on the screen. The camera panned up to the diving platform. "It must've been an accident," Placenta said. "Sedra wouldn't take crap from a cold-blooded killer. Hell, she could stare down a gang of thugs led by Ann Coulter and Karl Rove. Nothing scared her."

"Except wrinkles," Tim said.

"I vote for killer," Polly added. "She couldn't swim, unless it was upstream to spawn after mating with someone's husband or boyfriend."

"You're right," Tim said. "I never saw her put so much as a toe in the Jacuzzi during the summer that I spent at Dad's place with her."

The reporter continued. "This is the second tragedy to strike the Sterling Studios production of the new Dana Pointer and Missie Miller musical, *Detention Rules!* As you may recall, just twelve days ago, another Hollywood celebrity, Trixie Wilder, suffered a stroke and died while filming at this very location. In fact, Sedra Stone had replaced Wilder in the same role."

The camera returned to the morning newscast's anchorman who feigned incredulity. "They die in threes, don't they, Lowell?" he said to the field reporter. "Celebrities, I mean. One. Two. Three. Do police have any idea who will be next?"

Reporter Lowell Lodge professionally controlled a need to roll his eyes at the vapid anchorman's ridiculous question. Instead, in all his Anderson Cooper earnestness he said, "Dan, it isn't yet clear what Sedra Stone was doing at this indoor venue, which is primarily used for swimming and diving competitions. And it hasn't been established that she was alone at the time of the tragedy."

"Is there any indication as to why Sedra Stone was swimming at night?" the anchor asked, unable to ad lib a sensible question.

The reporter subtly corrected the anchor. "Sedra Stone wasn't swimming, Dan. As previously reported, the pool was empty," he said. "We've learned that the facility had been drained only yesterday for routine maintenance and resurfacing. One of the many mysteries in this case is why Sedra Stone remained at the film location long after the cast and crew had been dismissed for the day. We're awaiting further details from the Los Angeles County Coroner's Office as to the exact cause of death."

Then he signed off. "Reporting live from Santa Clarita, this is Lowell Lodge. Now back to you in the studio, Dan."

The camera returned to a wide two-shot of the male anchor and his pretty but equally vacuous female co-anchor, presenting what they hoped were reasonably somber expressions. The camera switched to a close up of the anchor who solemnly reiterated, "Legendary television star Sedra Stone. Dead at sixty-two."

"She's history," the perky co-anchor added without thinking of her unfortunate *double entendre*. Then, as if someone in the control booth had flipped a toggle labeled "lively and fun" and sent a jolt of electricity into the co-anchor's chair, she beamed and said, "Let's check in with Helen Rodriquez for a look at your traffic commute. God, I'd rather be *dead* than stuck on the 405 Freeway this morning. Tell us about it, Helen."

Placenta switched off the television. Seated on the bed beside Polly and Tim she silently tried to think of the right words.

Polly's thoughts had turned to the day she received a telephone call from *The National Peeper*, asking her to confirm that her husband, Tim senior, was divorcing her for siren Sedra. "Let me check," Polly said at the time. Holding her hand over the telephone mouthpiece she yelled out from where she was reading a script in the den, "Hey! You! Mr. Hanger-On! Are you leaving me?" There was no answer. Her husband had climbed out the window and scampered off into Sedra's arms without so much as a confrontation with Polly. Although he'd already met with attorneys to discuss spousal support—for him.

Tim flashed on a memory of the year after his parents' divorce when he spent a summer with his father and Sedra. A precocious boy of ten, whose favorite old movie was *The Women*, he insisted on calling Sedra, "Auntie Crystal." Not only did Tim think that Sedra sort of resembled Joan Crawford, but one afternoon he discovered her sucking face with the shirtless and muscled pool boy. In Tim's young mind this was not unlike Crawford's sinister character Crystal Allen who rips off other women's rich husbands. He knew that his father was being cuckolded, and Tim spent the rest of the summer spying on Sedra and getting an accelerated lesson in the facts of life. He wasn't trying to lay claim to any evidence of her infidelity to his father, rather, he was intrigued by how she so easily seduced men and he wanted to follow her example.

Placenta recalled having to comfort Polly after Sedra made headlines by flaunting her acquisition of husband number two of America's favorite television musical/comedy variety show comedienne. For months, Polly was a zombie. Thanks to Placenta's loving care, she never missed a rehearsal or publicity event. It was possible that Placenta hated Sedra Stone even more than Polly. Still, now that Sedra was in the news as literally a bag of broken bones, Placenta felt sorry for her.

The telephone rang for the second time that morning, breaking the reverie in Polly's bedchamber. This time, Placenta recognized the number on the caller ID display. "Are you in for your agent?" Placenta asked before picking up the receiver.

Polly shrugged, too consumed with lethargy and thoughts of Sedra to care about much else. She decided that the least she could do was express her condolences for J. J.'s loss of another client. She reached out and accepted the cordless handset from Placenta. "This is Polly," she said.

After an exchange of only a few syllables of shock and sympathy between Polly and J. J., she said, "Never! What am I, a third runner up, for crying out loud? This is not high school where I had to tolerate being the last one picked for the softball team. Anyway, that set's jinxed. I wouldn't set foot in a place with so many dead celebrity spirits hanging around! With my luck Jayne Mansfield's there with Dick Kallman!"

After a short pause that suggested intrigue she asked, "How much did you say? Single card billing? Immediately below Dana and Missie? You actually got them to agree to the use of the words 'iconic legend' before my name? Hmm."

Polly exchanged looks with Tim and Placenta. She mimed knocking back a drink to indicate it was time for breakfast, which sent Placenta to the bedroom bar for a chilled bottle of champagne. After another moment of Polly nodding her head and making the type of agreeable sounds that she usually reserved for expressing approval over the glistening body of a beach Adonis, she simply said, "Send over the new script. I'll let you know by Lush Hour." Then she hung up the phone.

For a brief moment, Polly's mind wandered as she stared into nothingness, picturing her professional comeback. It was only when Tim said, "We're shadowing you on the set—for protection," that Polly smiled and acknowledged that she had been offered the role of Catharine. Again.

"I'm trying very hard to be sad for Sedra," Polly finally said as she accepted a mimosa from Placenta and took a long first sip. "But I can't. Even now, she's trumped me in the fame department. She'll be a freakin' legend long after you dispose of my ashes because she died in a hideous way. They'll probably rename that goddamned school pool in memory of her. And you can bet that hordes of demented fans will create a myth to surround her memory. They'll be making yearly pilgrimages to throw roses from the diving platform. Books will be written about her and people will forget what a shrew she really was. There's still no love lost between us, even though I wouldn't have wished her fate on anybody."

Placenta poured a flute for Tim and one for herself, and refilled Polly's glass. "Well, let's have a combination invocation and toast," she said, raising her glass. "Lord, have mercy on Sedra Stone's shriveled soul . . . and cheers to Polly Pepper and her well-deserved return to the screen."

Polly added, "Lord, don't judge me for once wishing that Sedra go to hell. I didn't really mean it. Not much anyway. And, as 'The Good Book' says, 'Make hay while the sun shines.' I'm just thankful it wasn't me—or someone I liked—cracking that cement."

Chapter 11

"Was there an apocalypse and I missed the CNN report?" Polly said as she surveyed the dismal Los Angeles bedroom community of Santa Clarita from the backseat of her Rolls. Tim was chauffeuring her and Placenta to the first day of work on *Detention Rules!* As they passed over rutted streets that ran beside decrepit stuccoed apartment complexes splashed in multihues of bile, and graffiti defaced empty strip malls, she turned to Placenta. "You say I don't get out enough. Do you blame me? This is downtown Baghdad—on a good day! I'll spend my time in Bel Air, or the *Cote d'Azur*, thank you very much."

Placenta agreed. "If ever a place screamed for an armada of bulldozers . . ." she said. "I'll never again complain about where we live, or those tasteless tour buses jamming the street outside Pepper Plantation. J. J. better have negotiated for mileage, per diem, and gasoline, too. Check out those prices!" She pointed to a Chevron filling station sign. "You almost can't afford to go to work!"

"Talk about social elitist snobs," Tim chided. "Not everybody can afford to live as we do, ya know. I'm sure the locals have other things to enjoy here—like sex and drugs."

Finally, after a full hour of driving, Tim found Chaparral Vista Street. He turned right and glided the Rolls up a hill and onto the Gary High School campus. He pulled into the circular driveway and stopped beside a smiling piggy-faced security guard who cradled a clipboard in his arm.

Tim pushed the power button on the armrest of his door and the passenger-side window slipped down. "Morning," he said, cheerfully smiling back at the sentry.

Ever since security guard Duane Dunham's altercation with Sedra Stone, he had become cautious and paranoid of people who drove about in ostentatious cars. Nonetheless, he continued smiling and peered at Tim. *Sexy and rich*, he thought.

"Polly Pepper is reporting for duty," Tim said.

Duane's doughy white face became whiter. He suddenly lost focus and, for a moment, he thought he was going to faint. "Polly Pepper?" he asked, checking his clipboard and the list of expected visitors. Duane was an ardent fan of Polly's; however, her name was not on the call sheet and no one had warned him that she was coming to the set. Beads of perspiration began to form on his milky white forehead as he feared another celebrity tongue-lashing. He tentatively said, "With all due respect, sir and ma'am, may I ask ya'll to park over there, while I get a pass for you?" He pointed to a spot between a Jaguar and a Mazeratti, in a row of cars that cost more than the combined treasuries of a dozen Third World countries.

Suddenly the rear passenger side smoked glass window of the Rolls was slowly and ominously lowered. Duane automatically stepped backward onto the curb. Experience had taught him that a serrated tentacle would likely reach out from the maw and slap his chubby cheek. Instead, the familiar face of his favorite old star Polly Pepper was framed as though she were staring at him from a TV screen. To Duane's great relief and excitement, she leaned forward and reached out. "Lovely to meet you . . . Duane," she said, surreptitiously diverting her eyes to his name badge and back to his large brown eyes. "I'm Polly Pepper. I guess we'll be seeing a lot of each other during the next week."

Starstruck, but filled with a combination of awe and trepidation, Duane took a step closer to the car. He made contact with Polly's hand and literally shivered. "It's an honor to meet you, Miss Pepper," he said with wonder, the sycophant emerging. He looked around to see if anyone was watching him. Then he whispered, "I'll risk getting into trouble but I have to say this: I'm your biggest fan." He nearly squealed the last word.

Polly laughed heartily. "Trouble? Honey, you'll be in deep doo-doo if you don't sit with me when we break for lunch today!"

That was enough to do the trick. In the campfire of life, Duane melted like the big fat marshmallow that he was.

Polly Pepper had been Duane's favorite star for as far back as he could remember. He had been a weird kid whose parents barely tolerated him sitting for hours in their garage in Haverhill, Indiana, memorizing Polly's television sketch routines. Although the height of her fame occurred at just about the time Duane was born, at age twelve he discovered Polly on a television retrospective and instantly fell in love.

As hobbies, some kids collect baseball cards, or jars of spiders. Duane collected Polly Pepper memorabilia. He spent a small fortune for a Polly Pepper doll (dressed by Bob Mackie) that was advertised in *Reader's Digest*. He also owned a bootlegged copy of the limited edition two-disc CD set of Polly's best-known songs including "For New Kate." (Religious conservatives spoke the title quickly, running the words together to make their point about the lack of morals in Hollywood).

Duane also possessed a Polly Pepper Playhouse coffee mug, as well as copies of half the complete set of her fan club monthly newsletters. He even had a rare Polly Pepper wristwatch (albeit permanently stopped) with the star's freckled face and toothy grin under the plastic faux crystal. He was most proud of his latest acquisition: the boxed DVD set of the first two seasons of "The Polly Pepper Playhouse" (with hours of commentary by Polly and the cast as well as outtakes and bloopers).

To say that Duane was a fan was an understatement, and he wasn't about to keep a legend cooling her heels simply because someone forgot to enter her name on a list or to leave an identification badge. As far as he was concerned, if one didn't know who Polly Pepper was—they'd been locked away all their life.

"Miss Pepper, he said, "you and your guests certainly don't have to wait. Park wherever it's convenient for you." In the back of his mind he knew he could be given a demerit for not strictly enforcing the closed set rules, but he didn't care. "I'll call the PA and tell her to meet you by the gymnasium door." He pointed to where Polly would be greeted. "She'll escort you to your trailer."

"It's lovely to be made to feel welcome on my first day on the job," Polly called back to Duane. As Tim slightly accelerated and rolled the car away from the guard to the parking slot, Polly said, "Such a sweet young man."

Placenta added, "That boy's gotta get off The Jim Belushi Diet!"

By the time Polly, Tim, and Placenta walked from the car to the meeting place that Duane had indicated, an imperious young woman with a noisy walkie-talkie greeted them and introduced herself as Iris, one of the production assistants.

She looked with disapproval at Tim and Placenta. "This is a closed set. Visitors aren't permitted, unless expressly permitted by Dana Pointer and Missie Miller," she said.

Polly responded casually. "Nonsense, Virus. Tim and Placenta aren't visitors . . ."

"Iris," the PA corrected the pronunciation of her name.

". . . they're my 'posse,' my 'Turtles.' If you know who I mean. They'll be at my side steadfastly," she said, making it clear that she would be easy to get along with, as long as there was no interference with her way of doing things. "Simply instruct security to print out name badges for Tim *Pepper* and Placenta *Bartlett*. A pretty lariat to hang around their necks would be lovely too. Thank you, dear. Oh, and make Tim's rainbow-colored. Placenta's too. We're a proud PFLAG family, you know. You're a dear," she said as if her wish was a command.

Following Iris around to the back of the school gymnasium building, Polly finally stopped and cooed, "Oh, this must be our lovely trailer," she stood in front of a Star Waggon with her name printed on a strip of masking tape. She turned to the PA. "Isis, you're a doll. Many thanks for your assistance. I think we can handle things from here."

"I-*ris*. Not I-*sis*," the PA muttered as she handed Polly a manila envelope with a cast and crew contact list.

"So sorry, dear. I shouldn't get those two mixed up with *you*," Polly said. "One or the other was a goddess of fertility, wasn't she?"

Iris raised an eyebrow.

Then Polly smiled as she opened the door to her trailer and stepped inside. Tim and Placenta followed.

Before closing the door Polly called back to the PA, "Just give me a holler before I'm required in wardrobe, would you? That's a dear. Ta."

As Iris shook her head and turned away, Polly called out again. "One more thing, hon—was this Sedra Stone's trailer?"

Iris nodded. "And Trixie Wilder's before her. Not to worry. Woolite spray and a lot of scrubbing got most of the blood out of the carpet." With a smirk of satisfaction she added, "I hope you last longer than the previous occupants. Watch out for stray bricks, and don't swim for an hour after eating," she chuckled and then walked away.

Polly closed the door and complained, "She reminds me of that obnoxious Vicki Lawrence I had to work with for a nightmare week."

"Shudder," Placenta said, mocking Polly.

In the sanctuary of the trailer, the trio began admiring the deluxe accommodations. Then, out of morbid curiosity, they scrutinized the carpet for signs of Trixie's dried up blood. Iris was right. The carpets were immaculate. And so Polly, Tim, and Placenta ravenously peered into the small refrigerator in the minibar. They filled three glasses with guava juice, grabbed bags of mini pretzels for a light breakfast, and then settled into their home away from home.

As Tim toyed with the television remote and surfed for reruns of "Seinfeld," Placenta opened a copy of the *Detention Rules!* script that she found wedged between the cushions of the couch. Written on the cover was the name "Miss Stone." The name "Miss Wilder" had been scratched out. She scanned the pages looking for Polly's dialogue. On page ninety-eight she found the first reference to the Catharine character, along with handwritten notes scribbled in pencil all over the page. Lines of dialogue were also crossed out. She looked at the front cover again for the screenwriter's name. "I guess someone wasn't too wild for this Ben Tyler guy's screenplay," Placenta tsk-tsked.

Polly took a seat on the couch beside her maid and looked over at the page. She slowly deciphered the nearly illegible scrawl. "That's Sedra's handwriting, all right," Polly said. She read aloud in a halting voice. "'Ridiculous! Insipid! *Blind* to comedy! *Killing* me!'"

Placenta added, "Sedra must have been really ticked." She pointed to the words blind and killing. "She underlined 'em in red ink."

"A bit of an exaggeration," Polly said. "Although I admit she was right about the dialogue being insipid. The new draft that I read last night has much more punch and zest. Whodathunk that Sedra had any insight into storytelling for the movies. Or maybe she was just throwing her weight around."

As Polly and Placenta considered the possibilities of Sedra's temperament there was a knock on the door. "It's Adam Berg," the director called in his affected accent. "Just want to welcome you aboard, Miss Pepper."

Polly quickly stood up and opened the trailer door to the bright morning sunshine. She looked down at the director and with her famous wide mouth she presented him and his assistant with a radiant smile. Then, in her trademark voice—which was Shirley Temple revved up on Red Bull and espresso beans—she practically screeched, "You're so young! And handsome, too! Come and meet the family!"

Adam was sincerely thrilled to be working with Polly Pepper. Although he was only vaguely familiar with the body of work that had made Polly a legend, he knew her reputation as a gifted comedienne, as well as a professional and dedicated team player, and one who easily got along with her colleagues. Adam sensed that he was finally about to get a reprieve from the torture of trying to handle the parade of clashing egos that had dominated his film set since the beginning of production.

Polly introduced Tim and Placenta, each of whom gave Adam and his assistant a friendly handshake. *Yes*, the director thought, *perhaps my nightmare is over. Polly Pepper will easily fit in and maybe even teach Missie and Dana a thing or two about behaving like decent stars*. He welcomed them all, and thanked Polly for stepping in to save the day. "You know our two leads, so I'm sure you'll all get along famously," he said. "I'm hopeful that we'll complete principal photography by the weekend and finally have a well-deserved wrap party. Now then, Miss Pepper . . ."

"Please, call me Polly," the legend insisted.

Adam smiled. "Polly. Okay, we're setting up for your first scene, so I've got to get you over to wardrobe. Do you know your lines, or do you need some rehearsal time?"

"Working in television made me a quick study," Polly said. "Just remind me which scene we're doing first."

Adam's assistant handed him a dog-eared copy of the screenplay and he flipped to nearly the back of the script. "This is the scene in which you give Dana Pointer's character your grandmotherly advice . . ."

Polly feigned hurt pride. "Grandmother, indeed," she said. "Are you sure I'm the right age for this role?"

Adam smiled and continued, ". . . about how to overcome her broken heart. Dana's been dumped by Jack Wesley's character, who's now sleeping with Missie Miller's character, and Dana is both suicidal and murderous. She's plotting revenge. We'll do the 'Rip Him a New One' production number after they reset the lights."

"Right," Polly said, remembering the scene. "This is where I coax away her rusty razorblade and homemade pipe bomb. I adore the new speech about not being so plebeian as to open her veins in a tub with a mere drugstore brand of bubble bath—hold out for raspberry aromatherapy suds! And no WMDs in Missy's school locker, please! Very nice. I'm sure we'll nail the scene on the first take."

Berg sighed as if to say, *From your lips to Missie and Dana's pierced ears!* "That would be awesome," he said. "But remember, these girls don't have your experience, or your discipline. If I can just get this one scene shot by the end of the day, it'll be a water-into-wine miracle."

Polly pooh-poohed Adam's concerns. "I'm sure we'll do a fine job. Now, where do you have the costume department set up? I'd better get my famous fanny in gear."

"I'm heading that way. Stella, the costumer, is expecting you. Shall we?" he said, initiating the entire group to depart together.

As they stepped out of the trailer, Polly said in a solemn tone, "I'm so very sorry for your loss of Sedra Stone. I know what a blow it must have been to you and the cast and crew. And losing Trixie, too. At least they died while doing what they loved—working on a film. That's the way I'd want to go." Polly instantly checked herself. "But not on this movie!" she sniped. "I'm far from ready for that final fade to black!"

Placenta closed the trailer door and followed several paces behind the others. As the group continued walking, Adam acknowledged that the tragedies had indeed adversely affected the production, not just in terms of the financial cost of running behind schedule, but the human cost of losing members of the film family. "It's affected morale, of course," he said. "And it doesn't help that police investigators are all over the place. I had to get the CEO of Sterling Studios to call in a few favors from the LAPD in order to keep the production from closing again after Sedra's death. It's imperative that we finish by Friday."

As the group approached the makeshift location wardrobe department, which was a long six-axle freight trailer truck set high off the ground on a temporary foundation of cinder blocks, Adam addressed the subject of the police investigation. "Speaking of Sedra's horrible death," he began, "detectives are still hammering away at everyone."

Polly said confidently, "I'm hardly one they'd want to chat with."

Adam continued, "Regardless of who you are or where you were at the time of the incident, this one detective . . . Archer . . . will probably corner you for a statement."

"Archer," Polly thought for a moment. "I love his news conferences. Strikes an imposing figure, don't you think so?"

"That's him," Adam said. "He and his team are interviewing everyone from Missie and Dana on down to the grips, gaffers, extras, and stand-ins. Even the cleaning crew is being grilled."

"They'll soon confirm that Sedra's death was indeed murder," Polly prophesized. "Hell, I would have killed her ages ago—if I weren't such a sissy. I had plenty of motive way back when."

Director Berg was intrigued. "Polly Pepper wouldn't harm a fly," he chuckled.

"Common houseflies, no," Polly said. "They're a nuisance, but as a rule they don't destroy homes. However, Sedra was one big ol' Mike Tyson-sized fly. I could have swatted her into the next dozen or so lifetimes on her karmic wheel—if I'd really wanted to. But that's water under the bridge. I had nothing to gain by seeing Sedra dead now. Oh wait," she said. "Actually, I did get her job, didn't I? Ha!" She laughed uncomfortably.

Adam Berg concurred. "If it makes any difference, I totally disagree and am sure that Sedra's death was just a horrible accident. Maybe she was sleepwalking in the pool house building." He stopped for a moment. "Oh, that's an idea," Berg continued. "Maybe she was chasing booty."

Polly said, "Speaking of such, how are the girls handling this latest crisis?"

Berg rolled his eyes. "What crisis? For their lack of interest you'd think Sedra was merely that housefly. Squash the damn thing and move on."

"I'm sure they're mourning in their own way," Polly said.

"You'd hardly know it," Berg said. "But, life goes on. Or in this case, their party goes on."

"Dana, too?" Polly pressed the director. "She and Sedra seemed to be close allies."

"Actually, she has changed," Berg paused. "She's not as obstreperous as she used to be. I'm chalking it up to all the mercy sex she's having with the DOP in her trailer," the director said. "They're not very discreet. Everybody knows what's going on between scene changes."

Polly laughed. "Puppy love. Isn't that cute."

And then they were climbing the metal steps to the open tailgate of the wardrobe trailer. "I'll just leave you in Stella's capable hands," Adam said as he introduced Polly to the costumer. Then he turned to leave. "See you on the set," he called back. "And again, it's a pleasure to have you with us."

He said good-bye to the group and stepped out of the trailer to where Tim, and his assistant Judith, were becoming fast friends. "You two take a tour," Berg suggested, glad for a break from his increasingly annoying lover/assistant.

In the midst of rack upon rack of hundreds of items of clothing all jammed together like a dry cleaner's inventory, Polly smiled warmly at Stella, and introduced Placenta. "And what divine creation have you selected for me to wear in this important scene?" she asked.

Stella had no problem locating a specific garment on a coat hanger and shrouded in plastic with a tag that said, *Catharine, Scene #73.* "You can change in there," she said, handing the costume to Polly and pointing to a drawn curtain, behind which was a makeshift dressing room.

Stella offered Placenta a cup of coffee and found a chipped mug with the film title, "Psycho IV: The Beginning." She handed it to Placenta then refilled her own mug.

After much zipping and unzipping, and buttoning and tying, Polly drew back the curtain and stepped out wearing an inordinately ugly gingham housedress. She handed Stella the coat hanger and said, "Honey, we've gotta talk."

Stella held up her hands to remove herself from accountability. "I didn't design the damn thing. I just hang these cheap threads on actors," she said.

Polly waved away Stella's defense. "I mean we're practically old girlfriends already. Let's dish about Dana and Missie and Sedra and Jack . . . and why are the police still hanging around this place when it's obvious that Sedra Stone's death was accidental. I'm tired of getting my dirt secondhand from *The National Peeper*."

For a moment, Stella looked at Polly and Placenta with suspicion. Then she gave in with a smile and whispered, "I've gotta tell you, I was a huge fan of your show. Remember the sketch in which you and Henry Winkler started a sexual enlightenment seminar . . . for Jehovah's Witnesses?"

The three women burst into the laughter of co-conspirators. "Oh the pranks we got away with on that show!" Polly said. "We had our share of intrigue, too," she added. "Hell, I guess every show has its skeletons. Just like *Detention Rules!*"

"Hon, I could tell you stories that would curl the hair under your arms," Stella said. "Of all the shows I've worked on, this one has the vilest group of egomaniacal, self-absorbed narcissists. I'm surprised that only two of 'em have been done in. What makes you so sure that Sedra's death was accidental? Or Trixie Wilder's, for that matter?"

"Not accidents?" Polly said, as if the idea had never occurred to her.

"I have my theories," Stella said, just as Iris the PA arrived and said it was time to report to the set.

Chapter 12

Although Tim had spent more time in childhood playing with set props on a sound stage than in a nursery with a *Sponge Bob Swap and Bop*, he never tired of being in the midst of a busy film or television production. He compared the swirl of activity with a colony of unionized ants. Hundreds of workers scurried about performing seemingly mundane duties for one collective purpose—to make rich producers richer.

Judith enjoyed film locations, too, mainly because it brought her into contact with some of the most renowned people on the planet. As far as she was concerned there was no better place to find her Holy Grail—marriage to a wealthy actor, filmmaker, or studio executive. Until she could snag a Spielberg, Weinstein, or Bruckheimer, however, she knew that she had to earn a living, and being a lackey to a movie director (with sex benefits on the side) certainly beat toiling in a bank teller's cage, or analyzing actuarial tables at an insurance company. The perks were considerable too: free travel and meals, and T-shirts with the film's title emblazoned across the chest. But never mind the journey. For Judith it was all about the destination.

Determined to make a positive impression on Tim, primarily because his lineage connected him at zero degrees of separation to the rich and famous, she played docent and escorted him around the school campus-turned movie location. She walked him to the main points of interest.

Playacting the role of a tour guide to Hollywood celebrity homes, she cupped her hands to her mouth to make the distorted sound of one speaking into a crackly old microphone. She announced in a deep voice, "Welcome to the super-duper deluxe and expensive journey to the hellholes of Hollywood."

Tim shook his head and couldn't control a bemused smile.

"Keep your hands and feet inside the tram as we approach the luxury dressing room trailer of the infamous Dana Pointer. For those of you onboard who are over the age of twelve, or who have an IQ higher than Walt Disney's frozen brain, and would therefore have no clue who or what a Dana Pointer is, I'll explain. Think Helen Hunt—but without a trace of that star's talent. We're talking about the teen star of not one, but *two* box office blockbusters: *Road Kill* and the Sterling Studios' animated feature, *Oxy the Moron*."

Stepping closer to the trailer, Judith continued, "We're in luck today, my friends. The Star Waggon is *occupado*, and rockin' in rhythm to 'Push Push in the Bush.' Which in English, translates to Dana Pointer is in the sack trying to make whoopee with none other than hunky Jack Wesley! Accent on *trying*."

Tim feigned naiveté. He whispered, "Dana and Jack are . . ."

Judith smiled but continued speaking in her loud tour guide voice. "Doing it? I said, 'trying.' "

Had the music inside been any less loud Judith could have been heard, which frankly didn't faze her in the least.

Tim raised his eyebrows. "Can't blame Dana," he smiled. "I mean Jack's one of the hottest studs in Hollywood right now. What's keeping him from becoming a break-out star?"

" 'Cause he's not sleeping with the right people," Judith said, now speaking in her normal voice. "He even gave Sedra Stone a toss. She's hardly in a position to help her own career, let alone his. Unless he's going for a Demi Moore/ Ashton Kutcher Oedipus sort of fling. Though he'd much prefer Ashton."

"Who wouldn't?" Tim said, aware that he just outed himself to Judith. "But, um, I imagine that doesn't surprise you," he said.

"Oh, please," Judith said, as if she were offended by a stupid question. "Does anybody care about that stuff anymore? It's a cliché, but you're too cute to be straight. I knew it from the moment I laid eyes on you—and you laid eyes on Adam."

"His biceps gave me away, eh?" Tim laughed.

"Nah. You've mastered discreet," Judith said. "But my gaydar is more acute than the homing device on a scud missile. Jack's the one with the seriously damaged poker face. But I'll keep his boring little secret—from Dana and the press."

"Dana's no dummy. She must have figured it out," Tim said.

"Trust me, she *is* a dummy," Judith said. "The fact that she's also making it with the director of photography speaks volumes about her unfulfilled needs. As a matter of fact, Jack's making it with the DOP, too. Ha!"

Tim and Judith shared a laugh. "Morals are for people with a conscience," Judith said. "In this town, that part of the brain rots faster than any post-'Seinfeld' sitcom starring Jason Alexander. Here, people play by their own rules and live by hedonist's standards. Heck, I've worked as an assistant on dozens of features and television movies. I could make a fortune selling gossip. Kate Beckinsale, this. Bill Murray, that. So much to write home about. But I'm saving everyone's peccadilloes for my memory box."

"Or bank account?" Tim added. "Is there anything that goes on around here that you don't know about?"

"Nope. I've got eyes in the back of my head. I have to know what's going on, if I'm ever going to parlay this subservient job into a permanent place on the arm of a red-carpet hotshot," Judith said.

"Then tell me what happened the night of Sedra Stone's death?" Tim asked.

Evading the question, Judith again returned to her tour guide persona. She spoke into her hands, "Ladies and germs, prepare for the crème de la crème macabre Grave Line Tour. Follow me, and we'll duck past the police barricade. You'll see how the mighty can fall—literally."

"Ewww!" Tim whined.

"Not to worry, folks. They've pretty much scraped up everything that used to be the star of 'Monarchy.'"

Judith and Tim entered the unlocked building that housed the swimming pool and diving platforms. As they walked around the side of the empty blue cement pit, and looked up at the place from which Sedra had dropped to her death, they simultaneously quivered at the horrible thought of the star's fate.

Tim finally said, "Dana's a bitch. And a slut. And she'll do almost anything to be a star. But I'll never believe she had anything to do with Sedra's death. Although I also don't believe it was an accident."

"Yeah?" Judith said.

Tim sighed. "I'm inclined to think Sedra was murdered."

"Inclined?" Judith mocked.

"Can you think of anyone with a motive?" Tim asked.

"Dozens on this movie alone," Judith said. "And she was only here for a day!"

"Plays well with others," Tim said with sarcasm.

"Hell, I hated her guts, too," Judith admitted. "There was something absolutely toxic about her. She actually challenged me for Adam. At her age! But Adam's so not worth killing someone over. He's hardly the hottest pistol in the sack. Screws like an actor, if you get my drift."

"Sedra had tons of people who disliked her," Tim agreed. "But she disliked them as well."

"Even your friend, Placenta, seemed to have a grudge."

"Placenta's top of the line. She loathed Sedra out of loyalty to Polly and me. She was there to help pick up the pieces after Sedra practically shattered Mom's life, or at least her self-esteem—twice."

"Still, if that detective Archer knew of her disdain and your mom's past history with Sedra, he'd add both of their names to his list of suspects," Judith said.

"They'd be at the bottom of a very long list," Tim said. "Are there actual suspects? Is this detective investigating a homicide?"

"What do you think?" Judith challenged. "Everyone is considered guilty until proven innocent."

"So many motives, but so few clues," Tim said.

"Who says there aren't any clues?"

Tim shrugged. "Six o'clock news."

"You have to ask, what was Sedra Stone doing on the ten meter diving platform above an empty swimming pool," Judith said.

"Alone, late at night," Tim added.

"Again with the assumptions. Who knows for sure that she was alone?"

"Maybe it was a suicide," Tim suggested.

"Celebrities who commit suicide leave notes to be published in tabloids like *The Peeper*," Judith said. "They want their last words to be scrutinized by biographers and the insatiably curious public. No note. And no discernable reason to be depressed since she was finally working again."

Judith cocked her head toward the metal stairs leading to the diving platform, suggesting they climb up for a better view. "Let's check it out," she said.

Tim hesitated. He looked up at the platform that seemed to nearly touch the ceiling. He could feel a rush of vertigo. "Um, I think I'm probably leaving footprints or something," he said, and stepped back onto the ground. Then, from the distance they heard the assistant director's voice booming over a bullhorn. "Quiet on the set, please!"

Tim looked at Judith. "Let's go and catch the fireworks," he said, glad for the reprieve.

Judith paused for a moment, weighing what to do. Finally, with a tone of resignation, she said, "Okay. Tour's over. Everybody clear out."

They scrambled out of the building and easily evaded the Santa Clarita Police Department's one-man patrol detail, an officer who was more interested in seeing live movie stars than guarding a dead one's accident scene.

As Tim followed Judith into the gymnasium, he said, "Remind me to ask you again about the night of Sedra's death."

"You sound like Detective Archer," she said and pointed to a place behind the cameras and lighting equipment. "You'll have a good view from there. I'd better check in with Adam before he files a missing persons report on me. Wouldn't want him to think he might have another dead body on the set. Three's a crowd."

They smiled at each other and Judith stepped away.

In a moment, Placenta sidled up to Tim and for the next hour they were both riveted to the activity in front of the cameras and behind the scenes.

Polly Pepper was sensational in her role as Catharine. She

elevated the dialogue, and appeared to be having the time of her life. She delivered her lines with warmth and comedy, as well as a touch of pathos. In so doing, her professionalism intimidated both Dana and Missie, making them fumble their lines and miss their cues. Thus, the scene required five takes. But finally, in what director Berg considered meteoric time for getting the performances he wanted, he called out "Cut! Print! Very nice, people!" Applause erupted, which on a jaded film set is practically unheard of. Polly humbly bowed and accepted the accolade, while Dana and Missie looked peeved and flounced out of the gymnasium.

"Back in one hour please, Miss Pointer and Miss Miller," the assistant director called out over his bullhorn.

Polly spotted Tim and Placenta. In a moment, the three were reunited and Polly begged for them to please tell the truth. "Was I really okay? I was so damn nervous."

They reassured her that she was magnificent and had shined far brighter than any of the other actors. "You should think about doing this for a living," Tim joked. "You're actually quite good."

Polly gave him a warm smile and said, "I'm starved! Let me change then we'll join Adam for lunch."

At that moment, director Berg came up to the trio. "Marvelous! Well done!" He looked at Polly. "If we'd had you in the role from the beginning we would have wrapped weeks ago," he said.

Polly played her humble card. "It was your insightful direction that brought the emotions out of me. You're a great director. You must know that. I'm going to tell all my friends that if they want a good performance ripped from their guts, they have only two choices. Hitchcock or you. Whoever isn't dead gets the job! Ha-ha!" she trilled.

Berg smiled and silently agreed with Polly's assessment of his talents. "Ready for lunch?" he asked. "Chef's got a special meal in honor of your first day. We'll eat in my trailer."

From the corner of Tim's eye he caught the peripheral image of a balloon-shaped object bouncing across the gymnasium floor. It was Duane the security guard. Tim elbowed his mother. "You promised your big fan that you'd break bread with him today," he said and nodded toward Duane.

"Oh, damn, did I?" She vaguely remembered and intentionally did not look his way. "Ask him to take a rain check for tomorrow. He adores me. He'll understand that something unexpected came up."

"No way," Tim insisted. "If you're bailing on that poor lost soul, I'm not going to be the one who breaks his heart."

Polly looked at Tim. "There are some people I can always count on in my hours of need," she said. "Unfortunately, you're not one of them." She turned to Placenta. "Tell the sweetheart that I have to meet up with the director for notes about the next scene. I'll catch him later."

"Although lying is actually part of my job description— article twelve, paragraph three—I refuse to hurt that boy's feelings," Placenta said, hands on hips. "Plus, after what Sedra did to him—and what happened to Sedra afterward— not that there's proof of any connection, I'm not taking any chances."

"For Pete's sake, are there no perks for being a star anymore?" Polly snapped.

Berg stepped in. "No *problema*. We can do lunch tomorrow. It's way cool."

Polly sighed in resignation. "And I'm *way* disappointed. Keeping my fans happy is a full-time job. Being a legend is all work and no play."

"I know that you suffer terribly," Tim mocked.

The director smiled and gave Polly a wink of his eye. "Whenever you can tear yourself away from your legions of admirers, there's another fan in my trailer who'd enjoy spending some time with you."

Polly blushed, as she looked Adam in the eye before he

turned and walked away. "He's so adorable!" she said to Tim and Placenta. "I'm imagining his lips against mine. I can see him taking off his shirt and letting me touch his strong chest and arms and . . ."

"Stop teasing me, Mother!" Tim chided.

Polly fumed. "Damn, he's hot!"

And then Duane was upon them. He smiled broadly and said, "It's lunchtime, Miss Pepper. That is, of course, unless you have something important to do."

Polly turned to Duane. "As a matter of fact, I do." She stopped for dramatic effect as Duane's face caved in like a fallen soufflé. "But nothing's more important than *our* date!" Polly enthused, dragging her index finger under his third chin and giving Duane a reason to live another day. "Give me ten to change my costume, then call for me at my trailer," Polly said. She watched as Duane wobbled off doing what was probably the roly-poly equivalent of a tap dance.

Tim and Placenta both smiled proudly at Polly. When they passed by the stand-in, Lauren Gaul, Polly turned to her and said, "You're my stand-in. Lauren, isn't it? How do you do?" She reached out for a handshake. "I just want to thank you for helping to make my job so much easier."

Lauren was taken aback. Never in all the years of her working in the industry had a star ever thanked her for the work she did on their behalf. She became an instant Polly Pepper fan.

"Another chocolate shake and a plate of fries?" Placenta said to Duane, offering a third helping of lunch.

"Maybe just this once," Duane said, playing the fat person's game of trying to convince a thin person that his weight was a genetic fact of life, rather than an overeating control issue. As he gladly accepted the food, Duane said,

"I'm probably eating so much 'cause I'm nervous about actually meeting my favorite star."

By now Polly had started to like Duane. He seemed genuine in his adoration for her and her career. All true fans have a gift for absorbing minutia about their star of choice. Duane had the capacity to recount the guest list of every "Polly Pepper Playhouse" episode. He could also recite in perfect order the titles of the songs that Polly and her guests had sung each week. Polly was fascinated by his encyclopedic store of information about her. "You should have been a fact checker on that horrid biography of me that came out last year," she said.

"*The Pepper Principle*," Duane said with a sneer. "Dialogue Press. December. Four hundred ninety-eight pages. Clip job. No new interviews. Terrible! Curiously, I can't reduce fractions or tick off the names of the countries that border Australia, but when it comes to certain celebrities, I could get a Ph.D. in trivia about their lives," Duane admitted proudly. "But I can only focus on the nice ones . . . like you, Miss Pepper. I have no retention for facts about the evil ones like that deservedly dead Sedra Stone." Duane's voice suddenly turned cold and distant. "I hope she was as scared of blue cement ruining her last face lift, as she made those around her afraid of her tongue."

Duane stopped midshovel of a fistful of French fries. "Sorry. I forgot that she was someone you knew. And I wouldn't really wish her fate on anyone. Not even my mother. Or Iris. That bitch."

"We're a bit resentful, aren't we?" Placenta whispered to Tim, who rolled his eyes in agreement.

"Rest her soul, I wasn't a fan of Sedra's either," Polly said. "But whatever did that poor excuse for an icon do to make you dislike her so?"

Duane revealed the story of his altercation with Sedra,

and how Iris the PA had made him feel stupid, and insisted that he send Sedra a bottle of her favorite champagne otherwise he could kiss his job good-bye. "I couldn't afford to buy the champagne, so it's lucky she died before I had to take out a loan," Duane said. "I didn't mean it was 'lucky' for her to die," Duane backpedaled. "But her ending up the way she did saved me a hundred seventy-five dollars!"

Tim joked, "One dead legend . . . priceless. For everything else there's MasterCard."

Polly suddenly felt uneasy. She remembered the line in a crime novel she'd read in which the character she suspected all along—an introverted computer nerd—finally confessed to a killing spree. During the penultimate courtroom scene, when asked what all of his victims had in common, the character replied, "They made me feel stupid."

"Well dear," Polly said, standing up to signal the end of the repast, "it's been lovely, but now it's time for my nappy. We must do this again!"

Duane smiled. "If I can do anything for you while you're working . . . anything at all . . . you can count on me," he said holding out his hand for Polly to shake.

She accepted his damp paw. "Oh, dear me, I can't think of a thing right now. But I'll certainly give a holler if something pops up." Duane wasn't moving fast enough as she tried to scoot him out the door. As added incentive, Polly added, "Keep your ears open to any gossip about Sedra's death. You know how I love my slander and defamation of character to come from a reliable source . . . before the tabloids get hold of it and subvert the juiciest parts out of fear of lawsuits!"

Duane smiled knowingly. "The things I could reveal . . . but we're not allowed to tattle about what goes on during our shifts. But . . ." He hesitated for a moment. "But you're Polly Pepper. I completely trust you to keep a secret."

"Of course you can!" Polly insisted. "You know that Discretion is my middle name. That's what the D stands for!"

"Your middle initial is P, for Patricia," Duane corrected.

"Naturally, dear," Polly said. "I was simply testing you."

"I'll find some fun stuff to chat about for the next time we meet."

"Goodie," Polly said and closed the door. She turned to Tim and Placenta. "That kid's got a lot of pent up hostility."

"If anyone had a misguided reason to knock off Sedra, I'll wager he's a perfect suspect," Tim said.

"So many perfect suspects to chose from," said a confident baritone. All eyes turned toward the voice at the trailer door. "I'm Detective Archer. Mind if I intrude for a moment?"

Detective Archer entered the trailer without waiting for a formal invitation.

Polly raised an approving eyebrow. *Assertive, yet polite*, she thought to herself. Her heart beat faster as she assessed him with her eyes. *Full head of hair. Body height proportionate to weight. Wide shoulders. Decent suit.* Her gaze drifted to his left hand. *No ring*, she thought as she calculated his approximate age. *Damn. If only I were two decades younger.*

An aura of importance radiates from celebrities. The instant that Detective Archer stepped into the trailer and looked at Polly, he knew from the vibrations in the room that she was the star from whom he was supposed to obtain a statement. He couldn't help being intrigued by her wide smile. He speculated about her age, too. He decided that regardless of her years, Polly Pepper was an interesting woman. Detective Archer smiled warmly and extended his right hand to shake Polly's.

"Your timing couldn't be better," Polly beamed as seductively as she knew how. She held his hand a moment longer than necessary. She then gently, yet forcefully, made Placenta move over on the sofa and motioned for Detective Archer to take a seat. "Forgive my manners," she lamented

as Archer settled in. "This is my family. Tim, and Placenta. I
suppose you're here to talk about Sedra Stone. Yes? Of
course we're happy to cooperate any way we can. Dear, dear
Sedra. Her killer must be apprehended and brought to justice."

Archer nodded his head and withdrew a microcassette
tape recorder from the vest pocket of his suit jacket and
placed it on the coffee table. "Mind if I use this?" he asked.
"I've got a terrible memory, and I can never read my own
notes."

Still happily taking mental snapshots of her interrogator,
Polly agreed to be recorded. "It's not like we need a lawyer
or anything," she laughed. "Or do we?"

Detective Archer smiled and his eyes once again met
Polly's. "Ma'am, I'm sure that a lovely woman such as yourself has better things to do than to run around knocking off
other famous people. And no doubt you have an airtight alibi
for the time of Ms. Stone's death. You were probably at some
fancy party with your—husband? Em, boyfriend?"

Polly blushed. "Husband? Boyfriend?" Polly adopted a
demure posture. "My last romance said he'd call when he returned from a business trip to Chicago. As that was more
than five years ago, I don't expect him home anytime soon."

Archer sighed. "He's not worth issuing an APB for. Using
my highly trained detective skills, I'd say that you'll soon be
swept off your feet again. Your new man will know how
lucky he is."

Tim and Placenta looked at Polly and watched as she
morphed into a schoolgirl with her first crush on a boy.

Archer cleared his throat and returned to the moment.
"Em, now then," he said. "You said that Ms. Stone's killer
must be brought to justice. What makes you think that her
death wasn't an accident?"

Polly was abruptly and unhappily snatched from her romantic reverie. "Dear Detective, the only thing more shock-

ing than Sedra's death is that it took so long for someone to do the deed. I'm sure that your little tape recorder is filled with many other people on this film location saying exactly the same thing. Fortunately, I do have an alibi for that evening. We were all at home TiVOing 'American Idol.'"

To herself, Polly was thinking, *Why can't I have a good-looking alibi like you?*

Chapter 13

As Polly Pepper's Rolls-Royce retraced the forty-mile stretch of clogged highway from Santa Clarita back to Bel Air, the star and her troupe were exhausted but uplifted after a day of being once again fawned over like a queen and her consorts. Such a long dull drive in the rear seat of her car would typically bore Polly more than the daily sports report, and put her in the mood to pop a cork from a bottle of bubbly. This evening, however, she was on an emotional high and she decided she could hold out for Lush Hour until after a relaxing bubble bath at home.

As the sun was setting over the Pacific Ocean, Tim finally glided the car onto the grounds of Pepper Plantation. They passed through the open iron gate portal and eased down the cobblestone lane. Tim parked the car beneath the porte-cochere and the trio happily stepped from the vehicle and marched up to the front doors.

As they entered the house, Polly moved swiftly toward the staircase and ascended toward her bedroom.

Placenta griped, "Y'all are on your own to forage for eats tonight. I'll be damned if I'll do anything more taxing than let my fingers do the walking over Wolfgang's private number. I've got a date with my pillow. Per chance to dream . . . of all those hunky set builders who I spied hammering away this afternoon. Take your pick. They're all variations on a theme of Viggo Mortensen!"

"A rhapsody," Tim agreed.

Placenta's blank gaze indicated that her memory had shifted into reverse and she was deep in visual thought for a particularly rugged and muscled laborer posing in shorts, scuffed work boots, and a flesh-revealing tank top. She made an exaggerated sound of swooning. "Never expected to see such a variety of tattoos, long sun-bleached hair, and earrings on straight men. And such tight abs, too! Lordy, the sight actually seared my eyes!"

Tim teased, "A teensy flute of champers before beddy-bye should help speed you along on the Fantasyland Express. C'mon. I'm throwing an impromptu post–first-day-on-the-job party for Polly." As he headed down the hallway toward the kitchen Tim added, "You can go brain dead for Viggo's sexier brothers after a nice, lethal dose of fizzy hooch. We'll assemble in Polly's powder room while she soaks away the stress of her selling her soul to be captured on film, and a grueling tête-à-tête with that police detective she seemed to like so much."

"Polly devoured every nauseating nanosecond of the flatfoot's attention," Placenta quipped.

Polly had reached the second floor balustrade of the Scarlett O'Hara Memorial Staircase and called down, "*Tout suite* with the bubbly. Mummy's got cottonmouth. By the way, what did you think of that nice Detective Archer?"

Tim smiled at Placenta.

"Wasn't he just a wee bit cute?" Polly yelled from the distance. "In an off-beat Michael Chiklis-with-hair sort of way?" She didn't wait for a response as she turned and walked down the corridor to her bedroom.

Tim looked at Placenta and shook his head. "'A wee bit cute,'" she says. "Ha! Next she'll be insisting that Tony Soprano makes her swoon. She's nuts!"

Placenta said, "Polly requires lots of attention. You know how she likes to be interviewed . . . even if it's by The Grand Inquisitor of the Santa Clarita Police Department."

"Yeah," Tim said. "I've gotta cut her some slack." Then he pushed the master switch to turn lights on throughout the house and wistfully said, "I actually feel sorry for her. She hasn't had a date since the twentieth century. I really should encourage her fantasies. Detective Archer's actually a catch, I think."

As the two moved through the living room toward the kitchen Placenta said, "Her taste in men has improved with age. She's not oblivious to physical appearance, but she realizes that life isn't only about sex."

Placenta harrumphed and followed Tim into the vast designer kitchen. There, she opened the refrigerated wine closet and withdrew a bottle of Dom while Tim collected Waterford from the crystal cabinet. He removed three flutes and placed them on a silver tray. Working in tandem, Placenta picked up a cut glass ice bucket and held it as Tim scooped in cubes from the freezer. He then planted the dark green bottle into the bed of ice and draped a starched and folded white linen table napkin as a blanket over the bottle and bucket.

"Brie?" Placenta asked and removed a wedge from the refrigerator without waiting for a reply. She unwrapped the cellophane and placed the cheese on a granite platter with a serving knife.

Tim opened a box of Carr's crackers and deftly arranged them in a semi-circle on either side of the soft wedge then garnished with a small bunch of Concord grapes. Without need for words, they performed this ritual and then headed up the staircase to Polly's bedroom.

Arriving in the grand suite, Tim yelled through the bathroom door, "Are you decently sudsed?"

"You've seen a naked legend before!" Polly called back.

"Mark Wahlberg you're not," Tim said.

"I'm under a suitable froth," Polly conceded. "Redi-Whipped! The water jets are pulsating at all the right spots. Heaven!"

The door was ajar and Placenta pushed it open all the way with the toe of her shoe. She cautiously carried in the tray of crystal flutes, while Tim followed behind with the champagne bucket. As he entered the room he announced, "Your reward for a job well done today."

"Took you long enough," Polly snipped, playfully splashing around in the tub. "I'd like a ducky."

Polly's spa-like bathroom was cavernous. In addition to the airbath, rainshower, and sauna, the room was decorated with an antique marble-top sideboard on which Polly maintained a collection of skin softening lotions and intoxicating perfumes and scented candles. An overgrown philodendron in the center of the sideboard, the tendrils from which spread out over the length of the stone surface and hung down each side, dominated the piece of furniture. Placenta cleared away a space for the tray of glasses, as Tim placed the ice bucket on the marble top. He then returned to Polly's bedroom to retrieve the platter of Brie and crackers that had been temporarily set on her bed comforter.

Returning to the steam-filled bathroom he attended to the champagne bottle, pulling off the leaded foil that covered the cork and set it aside. He untwisted the wire, which secured the stopper, then casually abandoned the bottle for the mere seconds it took to drop the foil and wire into the trashcan. But that moment was long enough to wreak havoc as the pressure from inside the bottle was too great, and an explosive pop sent the cork blasting like a cherry bomb and ricocheting off the vanity mirror and landing in the tub.

"Jesus, Joseph, and Mary!" Polly swore, startled out of her mind and cowering under a meringue of suds. Her heart beat like a bird caught in a cat's jaw. "The neighbors'll be calling nine–one–one, or Homeland Security!"

"The good stuff's not supposed to make more than a burp," Tim said, looking at the bottle as if it might taste more like iodine than champagne.

"A burp?" Polly scolded. "That was a mortar rocket loud enough to make Christianne Amanpour duck and cover! In the right hands, a champagne cork could be a weapon!"

Tim lifted a bath towel from a hook and dropped it over a puddle that had frothed out of the bottle and foamed onto the tile floor. "What a waste!" he said, and began pouring what remained into three flutes.

Tim handed a glass to Polly and then to Placenta, before taking his own and raising it to offer a toast. "Who says that stars never go to the bathroom," he joked, looking around and thinking how fans would have a coronary if they ever had the opportunity to visit with Polly in her own bathroom. "To Polly Pepper, and an Oscar-caliber job today!" he declared.

"Cheers!" Polly agreed and took her first sip.

Placenta and Tim both pulled wing back chairs over the tile floor and set them beside the tub. "This is living," Placenta sighed, putting her feet up on the side of the tub. For a long moment afterward there was only the muted sound of Streisand singing through the household music system, and the gurgling water rushing through the bathtub jets churning the water into whitecaps.

"Yeah," Tim agreed, "Punishment for whoever killed Sedra—surely it *was* murder—should be to have their Jacuzzi tub taken away."

"I'd die without this refuge," Polly agreed, draining her glass and holding out a sudsy arm with her glass flute for a refill. "How did Martha Stewart survive in prison! And of course it *was* murder. Sedra's death, I mean. Not that domestic diva phony having to do hard time. I already have my suspicions about the perp."

"The perp?" Tim imitated his mother mimicking a trite line from every 1970s television cop show. He poured another round of drinks. "So, you're smitten with Detective Archer, are you?" he smirked. "What's the attraction? Other than the fact that he's a man without a wedding ring—and at least twenty years younger than you."

"Need there be more?" Polly sniffed. "Anyway, I'm far from smitten. Just because I have 20/20 vision when it comes to romance . . ."

"You're as blind as I am when it comes to recognizing a flirt," Tim corrected.

". . . and can see that he looks healthy enough. That doesn't mean I'm thinking about him stepping into the bath with me. At least not while you two are in the house to spoil the fun," she joked. "And what about you and that Judith friend?" she addressed Tim. "She was plastered all over you like an immigrant in search of a green card."

"My virginity—and inheritance from you—are safe," Tim said. "Anyway, she's looking for a Harvey Weinstein or a Michael Eisner. Wants to be the trophy wife."

"Too butch. She'll never get more than a Disney Studios marketing executive." Polly leaned back in the tub and groaned with satisfaction. "And by the way, you're not getting a dime in my will. It all goes to the Monks of the Order of Saint Someone Or Other. They make embroidered tea towels for sale at Bloomingdales."

"You've given up deep sea tortoise sanctuaries?" Tim chided.

Polly ignored her son. "Frankly, I confess that I was *slightly* enamored of the good detective," Polly said. "Anything wrong with that? I may be 'of an age,' but I refuse to sacrifice good looks and brains for a man with nothing more than a sense of humor. Randy—Detective Archer—told the most amusing story about the LAPD's so-called *P* File. Okay, so he has a sense of humor, too. He said there's a vault full of pictures of naked male movie stars and their . . . well, let's just say their Wee Willy Winkies. They apparently got 'em from a raid on Shari Draper's office."

"Scary Shari," Tim recognized the name. "That moronic Sterling Studios publicity exec who screwed up your last movie marketing campaign."

"Detective Archer said that Willem Dafoe's is the *most* impressive!" Polly said. "He promised to show me. You don't think that means he's gay, do you?"

"Dafoe or Archer?" Tim quipped and was reprimanded with a withering stare from Polly. "Don't ask me if he's gay or straight," he said in self-defense. "I never get it right. It's all that metrosexual stuff. But if it means anything, my antenna failed to pick up the slightest vibration around your policeman. Perhaps like you, he simply has good vision, and can appreciate—or envy—another guy's God-given gifts."

"Such talk while on official business!" Placenta interjected.

"You know how it is," Polly said, "people end up telling me their most intimate secrets. They feel that I'm trustworthy, and of course I'm a clam when it comes to keeping a secret. But I liked Archer's sort of veiled attempt to hide his fascination for me."

"Any chance he was interested in a different body? A dead one?" Placenta said. "He may have been using you to get more information about Sedra."

"I knew he was a fan from the get-go," Polly continued. "He just couldn't bring himself to drop his professional demeanor."

Placenta restrained an "Oh brother" comment. "If he were such a fan, why was he practically interrogating you?" she asked.

"Just getting his facts straight," Polly said, slightly perturbed. "Sure, he wants to solve a case and get some personal recognition in the papers, but all work and no play. . . . I came right out and told him that Sedra had a gazillion enemies and that I didn't buy her death as accidental. He agreed."

"No-brainer," Placenta said.

"Anyone on your personal list of potential killers?" Tim asked as he yawned and closed his eyes, settling comfortably into the leather-upholstered chair.

Polly, too, had closed her eyes, enjoying the womblike warmth and serenity of the tub. "Potential killers?" she mumbled. "Only every waiter in town. Sedra stiffed 'em all," she said. "And every housekeeper she ever set her dogs on. And the wives and or girlfriends—or boyfriends—of the men she slept with. Add the revolving door of directors on 'Monarchy,' who became alcoholic drug addicts because she had a knack for emasculating their already tiny manhoods. As I've said before, the list is endless."

Placenta, nearly asleep in her chair managed to say, "I vote for someone the police don't suspect. Like Charlize Theron. Or maybe one of the girls. It was so obvious that they wanted you out of the way once you started stealing the scene today."

Polly giggled, "That was fun, wasn't it? I love it when I make people squirrelly with envy of my innate gifts. It's the A student in me. Poor darlings. They rode into Dodge on looks alone. They'll leave as a contestant on 'Snorkeling with the Stars.'"

Tim poured himself another glass of champagne. "What about the possibility that The Bluebird of Happiness— Missie Miller—is the evildoer?" Tim asked. "I think there's more going on behind her brown eyes than most people notice. She's inordinately eager to get this movie finished."

"Of course there's more going on with her. She's an

egghead," Placenta reminded. "Harvard brain—which I don't really believe. Musical prodigy—so we're told. I didn't see any sheet music on her piano."

"Remember that offstage meltdown at her party?" Polly said. "She's probably Betty White on the outside, and Sue Ann Nivens on steroids on the inside. Honestly, no one's as sweet as she pretends to be. Except me."

Placenta agreed. "God knows even I put on a great big smile in front of some people. Every week when you grudgingly hand over my paycheck. You don't wanna know what I'm actually thinking."

Polly flecked soapy water at Placenta with the back of her hand. "And I smile whenever you cook up that Tahitian dish that tastes the way I imagine pureed Purina Puppy Chow would taste."

"It is pureed Purina Puppy Chow!" Placenta snapped.

"A recipe for salmonella poisoning, if you ask me," Polly retorted.

Placenta ignored her and the trio settled down and resumed their languorous activity of drinking, listening to music, and playing Grand Jury, indicting everyone in Hollywood for the murder of Sedra Stone.

Streisand's voice over the central stereo gave way to Tony Bennett singing about wanting to be around to pick up the pieces of a former lover's broken heart. It was the sort of "I told you so" song with which every jilted lover identified. It started Polly thinking about the vindictive nature of romance gone sour. "D'ya think it's true that Jack Wesley was having an affair with Sedra? Perhaps he dumped her. And maybe she felt used and abused and decided to be mean about it—as she was wont to be. And he decided to get rid of her before she could rat him out to the tabloids?" Polly said. "Nobody dumps Sedra Stone, etcetera."

Tim had been on the brink of falling asleep in his chair, but his mother's comment brought him back to full consciousness. "Hate to burst your bubble, but Sedra wasn't exactly Jack's type. Want me to spell it out in graphic detail?"

"Oh please!" Polly said as if to an idiot. "That's old news, at least to everyone who isn't Jack. We all know that it's the worst kept secret in town. As Dorothy Parker quipped, 'Scratch the surface of any actor, and you'll find an actress.' But then, Sedra always liked a challenge. And hey, sex is sex. With Jack's looks and libido, he's bound to spread himself around with X and Y chromosomes."

Suddenly, in a change of subject, Polly whined, "My goddamn bubbles are disappearing. Everybody out. I'll be down in the Great Room shortly." As she began to break through the water and to stand up in the tub, Tim and Placenta stood and averted their eyes from the view of Polly plastered with remnants of suds. They began to leave the boudoir.

"Don't forget the champagne and cheese," Polly said, wrapping a large plush white towel around her torso. "Scat!" she said as they hauled away the treats. But before they closed the door, Polly added, "I'll figure out who the killer is and explain it all to you in a few minutes."

A short while later, when Polly joined Tim and Placenta downstairs, she was wearing silk pajamas and a monogrammed bathrobe. It was nearly bedtime for all, but she wanted to crack the case before hitting the sack. "Who's the least likely person—besides me—to have knocked off Sedra?" Polly said. "Isn't it always the shy ones like Duane, that namby-pamby guard? Or how about that screenwriter guy, Ben Tyler. The word from Adam Berg is that the writer was royally pissed off at Sedra because she embarrassed him in front of the entire cast and crew. Sedra said that his script wasn't worth shredding and that she'd already tossed her pages of dialogue in the school's pool. Or how about the wardrobe mistress?"

"What's her motive?" Tim asked sarcastically. "Sedra doesn't like polyester blends?"

Polly said, "I had a little *conver-say-she-oney* with Miss Threads this morning. Spilled her guts about how pooped she is of demanding celebrities, and that Sedra was among the more difficult. Didn't have nice things to report about Dana, or Missie for that matter. Said that these days, even the stand-ins were becoming troublesome because they're all envious that they're not the star. Said that my stand-in, Lauren Gaul, wanted to be dressed precisely as Sedra for each scene. The way she now dresses like me. After twenty-five years of pesky actors, Stella's ready to pack it in and become a real estate agent in Antarctica."

Then the telephone rang and the trio abruptly stopped their banter. The answering machine engaged and a voice came through the speaker. "Um. Er. Adam Berg here," the director began to ramble. "Sorry to be the guy to tell you this, and over a mechanical device no less, but . . . um, er . . . the Channel 2 news just reported that um, Sedra Stone's death was, um . . . murder. Geez. They've charged Dana Pointer. Damn. I was only four days away from wrap. This sucks. We're outta work—again. That little pisher is ruining my career. All our careers. That arrogant Detective Archer couldn't have waited four more freakin' days! As I said, this sucks."

In the background the trio at Pepper Plantation could hear the voice of Dana Pointer over a television news program pleading, "I'm innocent! I'm innocent! I swear it! For Christ sake! L'me go, you moron!"

Chapter 14

Tim quickly grabbed the television remote control and turned on the monitor. He found a local news broadcast that was recapping their top story. "Screen teen Dana Pointer, star of the box office hit *Bummer*, among other films, has been charged at her home in Benedict Canyon for allegedly murdering TV legend Sedra Stone."

With the surliest visual image of Dana that the station could find to accompany the story, the news anchor continued reading from a teleprompter. "As well-known for her offscreen temper tantrums as her onscreen bad girl roles, Dana Pointer was taken into custody this evening shortly after returning home from the location shoot of her new film, *Detention Rules!* According to her publicist, Pointer is innocent of the charge and will sue the quote 'Lyin' bastards of the LAPD' for false arrest."

The anchor made an involuntary and ever-so-slight smirk. "Moving on to sports, we turn now to Buck Jones," he said. "How about those Lakers! Wouldn't you love to murder their coach?"

Tim muted the sound of the television and simply stared

at his mother. After a long silence, he said, "I'm stunned. I really thought that Dana was too obvious to be the killer. Frankly, I thought they'd come to the conclusion that Sedra's death was an accident."

"An accident waiting to happen!" Placenta said. "The only thing about this mess that surprises me is that Sedra didn't meet her end years ago."

Polly stood up and moved to the champagne bucket. The bottle was empty and upside down in the icy meltwater, like something drowned face down in a pond. For the first time in ages, Polly didn't ask that someone else fetch another bottle. Instead, she lifted out the empty one, which dripped melt water all over the coffee table, and walked to the door leading out of the Great Room. She left Tim and Placenta staring at the door after her departure.

Now alone in the vast room, with only the silent images on the plasma television screen to intrude on their thoughts, the two looked at each other for a long moment. Tim shrugged. Placenta shook her head in agreement and said, "The one I feel most sorry for is Polly. I mean, Sedra's dead and there's nothing we can do about that. But your mama's an innocent party. They'll shut down production and her career is back in the crapper. It's not fair."

Tim nodded like a bobblehead toy. "She can't catch a break. It's easier to become a star than to remain a working actor. When this all sinks in she's going to be totally devastated."

At that moment, Polly appeared. She stood motionless for a moment, between Tim and Placenta, trying to find the right thoughts to express her feelings.

When it was obvious that words were failing Polly, Tim stood up and raised his glass. "I think I know what you'd like to say, Mom," he said softly. "We all knew Sedra Stone, and although she wasn't exactly a friend, we respected her talents. Well, not her talents necessarily because let's face it, she was more like Ally Sheedy than Meryl Streep. But, she was unique. Sure she was vulgar, and at times—most times—nasty and hateful, and a lot of people didn't understand her. But she carved a niche for herself in pop culture, and that's certainly to be commended. There are a lot of fans who'll miss her. And they'll be very pissed off at Dana Pointer for prematurely ending an icon's career. We send Sedra's soul our best thoughts and prayers."

Tim lowered his glass to his lips and took a sip of the cold golden potion. Placenta and Polly followed his lead and savored their drinks as if it was the first of the evening.

Placenta said, "That was lovely, Tim. I know that's what your mama would have said had she not been so choked up." Placenta looked over at Polly who had still not uttered a word since returning to the room. She reached out for Polly's hand. "Sit down, hon. It's okay to express your emotions and to say what's on your mind. You're among family." Placenta had a great gift for comforting others during a time of grief. She had nursed Tim through more than a few broken hearts, and now her protective and mothering traits came into full force again. "Tell us what you're feeling, sweetheart," she said, patting Polly's forearm.

Polly looked into Placenta's kind eyes. She turned to Tim and forced a tight smile. Finally, she cleared her throat and said, "There might be a slight problem."

Tim took hold of Polly's hand and said, "Don't worry, Mom. You'll get another job. This isn't the end of the world. For Dana, maybe. And Sedra for sure. But not for you. Plus, your name'll be in all the papers. I'll bet this triggers a ton of publicity."

Polly heaved a cryptic sigh.

Placenta took a closer examination of Polly's face. "I've seen this look on you before," she said, her compassion wan-ing. "Like the time you taped that mean-spirited comedy sketch parodying Mary Higgins Clark, and the day before it aired *Redbook* came on the stands with an article she'd written about how she considered you a national treasure as well as her favorite star. Remember how you freaked and made the network destroy that bit of film, then splice in a replacement segment from a portion of an old program with Steve and Eydie—and that was in black and white! So what's up this time?"

Polly looked away, avoiding eye contact. She looked at the ceiling. Then she looked at her Emmy Awards on the bookshelf. She glanced at the grandfather clock.

"Mother," Tim said, "this question may sound like a non-sequiter, but I'd like you to tell us again how much you like Detective Archer. You think he's pretty nifty, don't you. 'Cute' you said. So how much did you try to impress him? How helpful were you to his investigation? You're hardly one to keep your opinions to yourself, so what did the rich and famous celebrity tell the impressionable fan about her theories regarding a certain person of interest in the case?"

Tim and Placenta leaned in close to Polly. With four eyes boring into her soul, Polly made a loud swallowing sound. She stood up and walked to the floor-to-ceiling bookshelves and touched one of her People's Choice awards. Finally she turned and said, "I might have . . . probably not, but I *might* . . . somewhere along the line . . . have repeated stuff that's common knowledge."

"Common knowledge?" Tim repeated.

"Only that Sedra had tons of enemies," Polly said.

"Such as Duane the security guard," Placenta encouraged.

"Right," Polly agreed.

"And . . ." Tim pursued the line of questioning.

"Um, Stella the costumer," Polly added. "Oh, and Adam's assistant Judith."

"And the screenwriter, Ben Whatshisname," Tim said.

"What about Lauren the stand-in?" Placenta said, shaking her head in disbelief.

Tim prompted his mother again.

"And . . . oh, I don't know, I think maybe I alluded to something about Missie and Jack and . . . Detective Archer may have jumped to the conclusion that Dana Pointer was capable of not only stepping over bodies, but creating the bodies in the first place. That's all," Polly said. "Nothing terribly tragic."

Placenta said, "If the detective jumped to conclusions, you pushed him. What did you say to make him leap? Pretend you're under oath, 'cause baby, something tells me you're going to be a star again."

Polly's dour expression turned to a wan smile.

"A star witness in a murder trial, is what I mean," Placenta said sternly.

"I don't remember, what I said. Not exactly, anyway." Polly clammed up.

"Mother, if you used your influence as Hollywood royalty to get Dana arrested . . . What if she's innocent?"

"So, a jury'll decide," Polly said. "Like getting signatures for a ballot measure. Then you let the public vote."

Tim was practically apoplectic. "Juries aren't always fair, Mother! They don't necessarily care what the verdict is. They just wanted to go home. That's what juries are like!"

"But Dana's a celebrity," Polly debated. "You can't compare some boring federal income tax evasion trial with a juicy Hollywood murder mystery, can you?"

"A jury actually acquitted O.J.," Tim reminded, to which Polly grimaced.

Placenta took center stage. "Polly," she began, "Tim and I have pulled you out of enough scrapes to make us honorary caped crusaders. But if you influenced the detective into casting Dana in the role of killer, and she's not, I don't know how we're going to get you out of this mess."

"I'm going to bed now, 'cause I've had way too much champagne, and way too much bad news for one day," Polly said.

Placenta demanded, "First thing tomorrow we have got to find out if Dana is really guilty, or if you've just ruined a young girl's career."

"Her career would have been over after this movie anyway," Polly sniped.

Placenta continued. "Tomorrow . . . you . . . the legendary Polly Pepper . . . are going to come down off your high horse of celebrity and mingle with the plebes and find out if Dana is guilty or not."

"I'm not going to interfere with the police investigation," Polly said adamantly.

"You already have," Tim said. "So maybe Dana is a cold-blooded killer. But maybe she's not. We have to find out. Otherwise, your karma is screwed for the rest of eternity."

The next morning, when Polly arrived at the patio breakfast table, she was perturbed to find that the only items on the glass top were a scattering of bougainvillea petals. There was no place setting and no ashtray, and her badly needed Bloody Mary wasn't waiting for her. In fact, there wasn't any sound coming from the kitchen, and it appeared that Placenta wasn't around. Polly steadied herself with a hand on the back of a wrought-iron chair and looked around the back yard of her estate. She squinted at her wristwatch, then complained aloud, "Where's Hector today? And most importantly, where's my breakfast?"

Polly tottered back into the house and entered the kitchen. She noticed that coffee was brewing and the dishwasher was going through its rinse cycle. The morning edition of the *L.A. Times* was on the island in the center of the room, but appeared not to have been opened. She looked around then called out Placenta's name. There was no response. Polly called again and moved from the kitchen down the hallway toward the Great Room. She called for Placenta again, but was greeted with silence. Then, as she passed the Scarlet O'Hara Memorial Staircase, she saw Tim and Placenta coming down the steps. Again she looked at her watch.

"It's not even ten o'clock," she said, addressing Tim. "You're up and dressed rather early, aren't you?"

When Tim and Placenta reached the foot of the staircase, they both gave Polly a look that said, *Don't you remember what day this is?*

Tim carried a yellow legal note pad and the three-ring binder that the production assistant had given Polly, which contained contact information for the entire cast and crew of *Detention Rules!* "We've gotta get started," Tim said.

Polly looked slightly confused and exasperated. "I thought the production was shut down indefinitely."

"You're not working on set," Placenta said. "You're visiting Dana in jail today."

Polly heaved a heavy sigh of irritation. "The girl hasn't even been arraigned. I doubt that the police would let me in to see a criminal before she's faced the judge. Anyway, I want breakfast, and it'll take me hours to put myself together."

Placenta put her hands on her hips and said, "Mr. Coffee's ready, and I'll make toast after you've showered and made up. You've got thirty minutes. As for seeing Dana, put on your most endearing Polly Pepper persona and you can get yourself in anywhere. It's time that you used your celebrity for something better than getting freebee theater tickets."

Polly started to object, but Tim cut her off. "We haven't got all day, Mother. In fact, I'm calling Detective Archer this minute and you're going to charm him into getting you in to see Dana." Tim flipped open his cell phone and punched in the numbers on the detective's business card. The line rang and Detective Archer answered with a curt, "Yes?"

Tim said, "One moment for Miss Polly Pepper, please," and tried to hand the mobile to Polly who waved it away as if she were shooing a swarm of flying termites. He pushed the device into Polly's hands and whispered, "Your boyfriend's on the line. Charm the man the way you did on the set!"

With a petulant look that she usually displayed after reading a bad review of her work, she accepted the phone. It took her a moment, but eventually, as if flipping a toggle that blasted a sports stadium playing field with effulgent light, Polly beamed and spoke superlatives into the mouthpiece. "Detective Archer! How are you? I'm calling to congratulate you on cracking this nasty case. You're brilliant, simply amazing! How you deduced that Dana Pointer was your mystery killer is beyond my comprehension. You're a sharp one! But I guess that's why you're assigned to protect us all from the monsters in Hollywood. Where were you when I was stuck on a dais next to Oliver Stone? Ha, ha, ha. Of course, I'm absolutely devastated to find that someone I actually knew and admired and cared for deeply, a colleague no less, is in jail for murder!"

Polly stopped and listened for a moment. "Don't be silly. The world won't stop revolving if you're wrong," she offered, hearing his misgivings about a lack of evidence. "Don't think twice about what I said before . . . the rumors I heard, etcetera! You'll find tons of proof, I'm sure of it. In fact, that's one of the reasons I'm calling, aside from needing to hear your warm, thoughtful, intelligent voice."

Polly listened and seemed to melt from whatever Archer had said. "Well of course, I'd love that very much," she replied. "I was going to ask you if you didn't pop the question first."

Tim and Placenta both looked at Polly with exasperation.

Polly saw the frustration on their faces and reeled herself in. "There's one other thing, Randy," she cooed. "I'm all yours. To help with the investigation, I mean." She giggled again and turned away from Tim and Placenta. "It's a little crowded here at the moment. Call me later and we'll discuss the particulars. Lovely. Ta . . ."

Polly was just about to disconnect the line when Tim and Placenta called out in unison, "Dana! You want to see Dana!"

"Oh, one more thing, Randy! Would you be an even greater dear . . . as if that's possible . . . and arrange for me to visit Dana in her cell today? Oh, please? It would mean so much to her to know that someone on the outside cares. She was a colleague, even if it was only for a short while. She must be extremely frightened and lonely."

Polly smiled. "Oh, I'm not really that much like Mother Teresa. Maybe Oprah. But thank you. I do try only to find the good in everybody." She looked at Tim and Placenta and ignored their smirks. "Two o'clock?" Polly said to Detective Archer. "Lovely! I'll be there. We'll chat again tonight, shall we? Lovely," she said again. And then Polly signed off.

"Satisfied?" she said with a hard edge to her voice as she slapped the phone into the palm of Tim's hand. "You've both put me in the most untenable position. Not only do I have to go to that scummy jail house, but Detective Archer misunderstood my views on the case and now even he is having second thoughts about Dana's guilt. Damn! Who ever listened to me before?"

Chapter 15

A polished Rolls-Royce parked in front of the Beverly Hills police station is no more unusual than finding cocaine powder dusting a supermodel's nose. When Polly Pepper and her entourage swept through the doors at the station on Santa Monica Boulevard, however, even the policewoman with the baritone voice and Adam's apple was impressed. "Miss Polly Pepper, as I live and breathe!" said the recently minted woman from behind the reception desk.

"Surprise!" Polly called out, taking on the persona from one of her favorite sketch characters: a sarcastic bouncer at The Voodoo Room.

"We've been expecting you," the policewoman said without a smile.

"It must be a surprise to receive a celebrity who's not here for fingerprinting and a mug shot," Polly said. "I suppose I'm a novelty."

"But it's such fun to see what they look like on a bad hair and make-up day," said the policewoman. "Too bad we didn't get Glen Campbell. Love that mug shot they took for his DUI. Looked like that Wichita Lineman got sparked by a lightning bolt shot up his hiney! I live for the day Paris Hilton drops in with her little mutt."

Then she pushed a buzzer next to her desk to unlock a re-inforced steel plate door at the far end of the room. "The sergeant will take you back to the prisoner," she said.

Polly whispered to Tim, "Reminds me of Sylvester Stallone in an Eva Gabor wig."

Polly and her tribe strode confidently through the open doorway, and a Rob Lowe lookalike in the requisite BHPD blue uniform met the trio. The officer smiled and nodded at Polly, knowing full well who she was. Then his green eyes locked with Tim's and his smile grew wider with delight. He scanned the locally famous party planner from head to toe. "I've seen you in *213*," he said, referring to a freebee gossip paper in Beverly Hills. Tim was equal parts embarrassed and flattered by the obvious cruising. He returned the flirt and looked at the policeman's name badge. "Sergeant Walker," he said, smiling devilishly. "Is it my imagination, or is the Beverly Hills Police Department cast by the Abercrombie and Fitch advertising department?"

Sergeant Walker raised an eyebrow and in his barely beyond choirboy voice said, "Rich people pay for pretty things 'round here."

Tim agreed. "We are kind of fussy about who arrests us for being under the influence of too much money." He forced a laugh.

Polly and her troupe arrived outside an interrogation room. Walker unlocked the door and ushered the VIPs inside. There, seated forlornly at a long metal table, with her wrists in cuffs, and wearing an orange jailhouse uniform that nearly matched her red eyes, was Dana Pointer. Her once oft-copied hairstyle was now pulled into a ponytail. It looked as greasy as Brett Butler's when she was on a five-day bender. Her eyes were puffy and swollen from crying.

"You'd never catch me or any of the other officers looking

like *that*," Sergeant Walker sniped, especially for Tim's benefit. When Tim didn't respond, Walker figured correctly that he just lost points for his lack of tact. He backed out of the room and closed the door.

Dana looked up, and for a moment she appeared dazed and uncertain about whom her visitors were. Then a small smile crossed her lips. "Polly? Tim?" she said. Dana acknowledged Placenta too but couldn't remember her name. "Thank God you're here! Get me out of this Wes Craven movie! I don't know what I'm doing in this scene in the first place!"

"Darling, girl," Polly cooed, spritzing the atmosphere with concern. "This is absolutely the most horrid misunderstanding. I'm sure of it. I can't even bring myself to speak aloud the words that the press has used to discredit you. It's appalling. I mean, geeze Louise . . . Crack whore. Slut. Harlot. *Murderer*! All in the same sentence. It's too rude!"

Dana wailed, "No! I'm none of those things. I didn't do anything wrong! I'm innocent! I've never harmed a fly! All those stories of misbehavior were created by my stupid publicist to make me look tough. I would never have touched a synthetic black hair on Sedra's wigged head. I swear it! I'm innocent!"

Tim gazed at Dana with more pity than he'd ever looked at anyone—other than John Goodman for whom he had once felt incredibly sorry for having to work with Roseanne. Dana was definitely pathetic. If she was indeed guilty, Tim thought she'd obviously been studying Susan Hayward's Oscar-winning performance in *I Want to Live!* He stood next to Dana and said, "The papers report that the police have evidence against you. The corpse—er, Sedra, I mean—even had strands of your hair in her hands. If you didn't commit the crime, who do you think did it? And why would the police think that you're responsible for such a monstrous act?"

"They haven't got anything on me!" Dana bawled. "They can't because I'm not guilty! I loved Sedra. Okay, not loved. Not even liked. But we had a special bond. And just 'cause you think someone is a conniving wicked bitch who deserves to die in a shark infested bathtub doesn't mean you necessarily want them dead. Well, usually it does, but you'd never do it yourself! Christ, I'm not Robert Blake! Do I even look like a Menendez brother? You've gotta help me!"

"That's exactly what we're here to do," Polly said, sounding as confident as Alex Trebek gleefully telling a "Jeopardy!" contestant that their answer wasn't in the form of a question and it was dead wrong anyway. "But you're going to have to help *us* in order for us to help you. Tell us why we should believe that you're innocent."

Dana began to weep. "Because I am!" She sniffled and wiped her nose with the sleeve of her jumpsuit. "You've just got to trust me," she said. "Shoot! I'm going to end up a forgotten nobody, like that old woman who played a mystery writer on television every Sunday night for like . . . forever!"

Polly thought for a moment and was then taken aback. "'Murder, She Wrote'? Angela Lansbury?'"

"Whatever," Dana said. "Grandma got a TV gig, big deal. I'm in the movies! The big screen. I don't want to end up like her!"

"Trust me, you won't," Polly said. "Miss Lansbury's a living icon! The greatest star ever! Four Tony Awards! Three Oscar nominations! Sixteen Emmy nominations! This is the problem with you young so-called modern movie stars, you have no background in the theatre. You don't know anything about the business you're in. Hell, you didn't even know that I'm a big star in this town. Once. Yeah, sweetie, I've got a closet full of Emmys to prove it! If you ever beat this rap I'll let you caress one of them."

Placenta had to calm her down. "Deep breaths," Placenta instructed. "Take a seat. Go to your quiet place. Think of Lake Como. It's springtime and you're on vacation in Switzerland. That's right. Everything is tranquil. Deep breaths."

Tim took over. "Dana, I'll be honest, things look really bad for you. You were overheard arguing with Sedra in her trailer the night she died. You're quoted saying you'd see her buried in Forest Lawn."

"That was very late," Dana said. "I thought that the rest of the cast had gone home. I didn't think anyone was around to hear us. Not that I ever really said those words." She thought for another moment. "It was that weasel of a security guard, wasn't it? That Duane. He never liked me."

"You didn't like him either," Tim said.

"And he sure as hell hated Sedra. I know the type. She publicly insulted him and he vowed revenge. These wussy types are all the same. He's the one who should be arrested!"

"What about the fact that you found Sedra having an affair with Jack? Did you, in a jealous rage, do something you now regret?"

For a long moment, Dana sat in silence while the gears in her brain were grinding. She finally conceded, "All right, it's true. I was angry with Sedra. But not because she and Jack were an item. That's just too weird to even think about!"

All eyes were suddenly riveted to Dana. "Sedra wasn't Jack's type. Hell, I'm not Jack's type either. Go figure."

The room was silent for a long moment as Polly, Tim, and Placenta tried to fathom what Dana was telling them. "Everybody knows that Jack's going to be a big star soon, and everybody wants to hitch a ride. When Jack told us all to step aside, that's when someone started spreading rumors that he was sleeping with all the grips and carpenters."

"As if that's anything unusual in this town," Polly added.

"Exactly," Dana agreed. "Like who isn't bi these days?

Actually, Jack's rather proud of the fact that he hooked up with Alan Cummings. Who wouldn't brag about that! Oh, and that screenwriter Ben Tyler, too. But that was mainly because the dude wrote an awesome role that Jack thinks he's perfect for." Dana looked at Tim. "Sorry honey," she said. "In your case you'd better stick to the Beverly Hills Police Department. You'll have better success of scoring here than in Jack's world. No offense. You're a cutie and all, but . . ."

"Drats! I knew it was too good to be true about Jack. Damn that silly rumor!" Then Tim returned to the subject. "What about your fight that night with Sedra? What was that all about? 'Cause she died just a short while later, so someone was pretty angry with her. Enough to make her go away permanently."

All ears waited impatiently for shocking news, something that they wouldn't even find in Ted Casablanca's "E! Online" gossip column.

Dana looked at the trio as if they were cannibals at a feast tying napkins around their necks and holding knives and forks in their fists.

Placenta, who until now had remained a silent observer, said, "You haven't satisfied me that you didn't murder Sedra. You talk a lot but make me believe you."

"I swear to God, I didn't do anything!" Dana yelled back.

"But you threatened her," Polly added. "There are witnesses."

Dana became contrite. "I'm scared," she said, tears streaking her famous face. "Please get me out of here." She sighed loudly and tried to remember the details of her last evening with Sedra. "That was the night that Sedra told me she'd booked a major film role. She asked me to come to her trailer before I left the location. When I arrived she was still in her costume. She put her hand on my shoulder and thanked me for helping to reignite her career. She said that the fact that I'd gotten her into *Detention* was the best thing that happened to her in years. Apparently Woody Allen had heard great things about her work—after only one day—and offered her the lead in whatever secret project he's doing."

"Woody Allen!" gasped Polly.

Tim and Placenta glared at her.

Dana groaned with frustration. "Of course I wasn't gullible enough to totally believe her," she said. "But when I asked if maybe she could put in a good word for me, that's when she got all bent out of shape. 'Trying to steal my role?'" Dana mimicked Sedra's affected voice. "I never even considered that, until she mentioned it. 'Gonna run along to Mr. Allen and offer your body in exchange for a few dumb ass lines?'" By now, Dana was yelling. "I told her that I had no such plans and that she was being ridiculous. She said that I probably thought that she owed me something because I had given her a break. I sort of agreed that she did. But then she said that by making my movie better with her iconic screen presence that was the best payback I could get. Well, I sort of agreed with that, too. But then I said something I guess I shouldn't have."

Polly, Tim, and Placenta stopped breathing.

"Since I knew someone who was actually in a Woody Allen movie once, I was aware that he never lets any of the cast, even the leads, read the whole script. They just get the pages on which they have dialogue. That is unless you're like a Mia Farrow, and you're raising his future bride. So I told her what I'd heard about his scripts being secret, and I called her bluff about getting a lead in Woody's film. I told her that unless you're Diane Wiest, who can actually act, all of Woody's actresses have to be young enough to be his great-granddaughter, like a Mira Sorvino, who's not all that young, but she's got the bazongas that he likes.

"That's when Sedra flew into a rage. If anybody heard us fighting, that's what it was all about. I was pissed because she wouldn't even think about helping me go legit by getting into Woody Allen's Fall Project. Then she was mad as hell because I accused her of being a big fat liar. I said that any role offered by Woody Allen would have to be a cameo, a one day job, and that she'd be playing another grandmother."

Polly came back from her *quiet place* and asked, "Did you call Mr. Allen after Sedra's unfortunate demise? You're just his type, although at eighteen, you're on the cusp of being too old."

Dana made a face that said, *Doh!* "There wasn't any Woody Allen film. She made it up. Then Sedra walked up to me and gave me a hard slap on the face. Like we were in some stupid daytime drama. I wasn't going to stand there and take a beating, so I slapped her back. I think she was used to fake slaps from her 'Monarchy' niece because she was really shocked by what I did. Her eyes grew wild with anger and she made a rather feeble lunge for me. I stepped aside just in time and she crashed into the minibar."

"No broken bottles?" Polly asked.

"Just a plate that she threw at me," Dana said. "And no broken bones either, I don't think, 'cause she got to her feet and started after me again. I decided to get the hell out of there before I really got mad and kicked her butt. So I dashed to the trailer door. I got out, but not before she grabbed a fistful of my hair. When I was safely outside, I told her she was a pathetic old thing, and how dare she treat me like a dog after all I'd done for her. I said I wasn't afraid of her, like everybody else in Hollywood, and that if it came to a showdown, she'd be dead meat."

Polly piped in, "And that's what the witness says they heard. You threatened Sedra."

"But I didn't really," Dana begged. "We were fighting over a stupid hypothetical role. And that's when she screamed at the top of her voice, 'You're killing me! I love you and you're trying to kill me!' I know she meant killing her career, but if someone heard us I could see how they'd think I was seriously trying to harm her."

Placenta leaned forward and said, "But she *was* murdered, and shortly thereafter."

"Yeah. Coincidence, eh?" Dana said without much enthusiasm. "Yes, I was angry. After the fight, I went back to my trailer to check my hair and to see what damage Sedra had done. My scalp hurt like hell where she'd yanked me so hard. I stopped long enough to look in the mirror. Then I got my purse and car keys and left the school campus. I only found out that Sedra was dead when I got a call from Adam. He didn't want me to hear it over the news. I was as shocked as anybody. I swear it!"

Tim tried to imagine the scene between Dana and Sedra. He'd seen Sedra angry often enough, and certainly watched her throw a tantrum on every rerun episode of "Monarchy," so he could easily visualize the altercation. "So when you left your trailer and went to your car, did you see anything unusual?" Tim asked.

"Like what?" Dana asked in a sarcastic tone. "A swimming instructor coming to give Sedra a lesson on how to dive? No. There wasn't anything particularly unusual. I rushed to my car because first of all it was a chilly night, but also I was afraid that Sedra might come out of her trailer and start up again with me. I just wanted to go home and read my lines for the scene we were supposed to do the next morning."

Polly asked, "Were there any other cars in the lot?"

"Yeah, there are always cars around," Dana confirmed. "I noticed Missie's, and Adam's, they hadn't left the parking lot. The cleaning people were there, too, and security. And that's the whole story," Dana said, exhausted from talking. "But I didn't see anything unusual. You've gotta believe me."

Placenta asked, "So Sedra was in her trailer and still alive when you left?"

Dana thought for a moment. "Absolutely. The lights were on, and I could still hear her yelling."

Chapter 16

Evening descended on Pepper Plantation, and the residents convened in the dining room beneath the halo of a Waterford crystal chandelier. They noshed on Placenta's Welsh rabbit appetizer while waiting for her famous blackened salmon. The trio sipped champagne as they mulled over their jailhouse meeting with Dana Pointer.

"I'm still in shock," Polly said.

"Yeah," Tim agreed. "I get the feeling that Dana may not be guilty."

"No, I'm shocked that the Beverly Hills Police Department doesn't employ a full-time hair and make-up expert!" Polly snapped. "What are they thinking? With all the celebrities facing the camera in that joint, a proper application of lipstick and hairspray is *de rigueur*!"

Tim shook his head. "Still, I get the feeling that Dana is telling the truth."

"Her eyes aren't as killerlike as I remembered," Placenta agreed. "It's possible that she's not a homicidal nymphomaniac after all. Maybe ol' Sedra was knocked off by someone else. D'ya think? Face it, Dana's not really an actress. So the sympathy performance that she gave this afternoon had to be genuine."

Polly took another sip of champagne and then rose from her seat at the head of the table. She walked out of the dining room and retrieved her cell phone from its recharging station in the kitchen, then returned to the dining room table. "We'll find out," she said, and flipped open the telephone. She scrolled down the directory of numbers. When she reached the one she wanted she pushed the send key.

Tim and Placenta stared at Polly, whose somber demeanor instantly flashed to sunshine when she said, "Missie? It's Polly!" After a moment's pause, and a trace of annoyance in her voice she added, "Pepper." A fake smile reilluminated her face and she launched into a conversation. "How are you, my dear? And your sweet mother? Coping with all the tragedy? Rotten timing, eh?"

Polly listed for a moment. "Absolutely. And to cheer us all up just a tad, you and your mother are dining with me tomorrow evening. Here, of course. Pepper Plantation. You practically groveled for an invitation. And I've wanted an opportunity to reciprocate your sweet hospitality. At the same time we can commiserate about our dear Dana."

Polly continued, "'Round seven o'clock? Just the family, dear. Is there anything that you or your mother don't eat? Mmm. Nothing with a face." Polly looked up at Placenta and made her own face of irritation. "Not to worry, I gave up cannibalism years ago." Polly laughed at her own bit of levity. "Lovely. Tomorrow." And then Polly flipped the telephone shut. "We've hooked another live one on the line," Polly declared. "We'll serve veal."

"You're starting to get into this," Tim added with approval. "Dana thinks that Missie's the one who should be behind bars. Maybe we can wrangle a confession from her. You're looking at your Dr. Watson and Barney Fife," he said proudly as his mother picked up her champagne flute.

"They make it look so complicated on television," Polly insisted. "In reality, all we have to do is round up the usual suspects and let 'em hang themselves by their own tongues. Actors love to chatter and gossip about everybody else. Surely one of them will spill their guts—with a little help from Dom Perignon."

"Break out a chilled bottle of *Chateau Grand Inquisitor*, nineteen forty-nine," Placenta chided. "We'll find out what, if anything, Missie has to implicate Dana—or anyone else."

"Every bird has a song to sing," Polly insisted. "I'm betting that after a few drinks, Missie's a parrot. And it really is high time we had the Millers slash Stembourgs over for a light repast," she agreed. "Then we'll make dinner dates with all of our new friends from *Detention Rules!* and ferret out the real killer. That is, if it's not Dana."

"Finally, a bit of excitement 'round here that doesn't include reruns of your old TV movie, *Dog is My Copilot,*" Tim said.

"Exactly," said Polly. Then she thought for a moment, and her eyes rolled up into her head as she considered all the work ahead. "I'd rather have hemorrhoids than live through an entire evening with the security blimp Duane. Lunch on the patio will suffice for him. Shall we say day after tomorrow? Then we can cram Adam and Judith in for the evening. Within a week we should have statements from all the major players."

Placenta gave Polly a defiant look. "You'd better be thinking of catering, 'cause I sure as hell won't be cooking lunch *and* dinner for folks who might be ruthless killers," she said.

Polly pursed her lips and closed her eyes. "Duane'll be fine with a dozen frozen pizzas," she said. "As for dinner with Adam and Judith, call up Gelson's. Tell 'em to deliver surf 'n turf for five. Just don't let me see those damn lobsters crawling around the kitchen floor. I swear that the last time the herd was plotting a *coup d'état* against me!"

* * *

After a full day of preparation and attention to every detail for a flawless and memorable evening with Missie and her mother, Polly retired to her bedroom suite for a bath before dressing to meet her guests. It was nearly six o'clock when Placenta ambled into her bathroom. She sat down on the side of the tub and immersed her hand in the warm sudsy water. She swirled it around contemplatively. "We haven't discussed our game plan," she said. "What exactly are we trying to wring out of Missie?"

Polly made a sound of complete satisfaction as she drained half the glass. "Leave it to me," she said. "I'll draw information out of Missie like a big ol' hypodermic. Remember, she's a toady. They're such the easy touch, it's almost pathetic. And her insufferable mother's goo-goo for me, too, I can tell."

"Ol' Battleaxe Elizabeth thought you were a brother and sister duo singing act, for crying out loud. So don't expect an obsequious bootlicker like Duane," Placenta said. "What should I wear to dinner." She changed the subject as she stood up to examine Polly's bottles of perfumes neatly arranged on the sideboard. "And don't say my uniform! We're all in this together. We're sharing the duties tonight! I'll be at the table with you and Tim."

Soon Tim appeared in the bathroom doorway. "Mom," he said, avoiding looking directly at the tub, "Detective Archer just called. He wanted to know if you were free for dinner on Friday night. He's miffed that you haven't called since he got you in to see Dana, so I lied, told him that in hopeful anticipation of his call, you'd already made reservations at The Ivy for eight o'clock."

"Hell, I meant to call him!" Polly frowned and splashed the water with annoyance. "On his salary, I'll be footing the bill."

Polly looked at the hand-painted antique clock on the

vanity. "I'd better get made up before Tweedle-Dee and -Dum arrive. Of course, I want to make an entrance, so you'll start with cocktails in the front living room. Or should you usher them into the Great Room so they can envy my Emmys? What about music?"

"The living room is a fine place to start," Tim said. "And I've already got the CD carousel loaded. A little Natalie Cole, some Rosemary Clooney, Sinatra, Doris Day, Michael Feinstein. Placenta and I will give them a guided tour and when you hear us return to the front entrance hall, that's your cue to descend from the heavens down the Scarlett O'Hara Memorial Staircase. They'll be in awe. Guaranteed."

Placenta dragged a beach blanket-size terry cloth towel from the warming rack and held it up to both shield Polly's modesty, and to gesture that she'd better get started on her dressing preparations. "We'll begin with champers, naturally, and nibbles I had sent over from Crustacean."

"Make sure they know where the eats have come from," Polly said, insisting that her company be impressed by her spare-no-expense extravagance. "Any faces in the appetizers?"

Placenta made a "Pfft" sound. "The lengths to which we're going to make them feel comfortable better yield us a murder confession," she said.

As Polly stepped out of the tub, Tim backed out of the bathroom. "By the time they've heard all your old showbiz stories they'll be charmed nearly to death by our hospitality. They'll feel like old confidants," Tim predicted. "By then even Missie's butch New England mother will be divulging all the dish that she probably picks up with her extra-sensitive semi-blind person's hearing."

And then Tim was out the door and headed down the hall to his own room. Earlier, he'd selected one of his sexiest but casual outfits to wear for the evening: Givenchy slacks with an untucked Armani purple tuxedo stripe shirt. The tailored cuts of both accented his toned body, and never failed to receive a double glance from men as well as women. He wouldn't shave—he liked the two-day beard stubble—but his ablutions would take as long as his mother's.

Time raced by, and he and Placenta were soon dividing their attention between the kitchen and the front living room, making last minute adjustments to floral arrangements as well as the tune stack on the CD player. They set out coffee table books of riotously colorful fall foliage in Vermont, to give the guests the impression that the famous Polly Pepper had paid close personal attention and recalled their New England roots.

Just as Placenta had finished changing the potpourri dish in the entrance hall, chimes rang out in the house. It was the security signal from the call box at the main gates. Although she was immediately next to the intercom and button for the automatic gate opener, Placenta was momentarily flummoxed and quickly walked away. "You answer it," she called out to Tim as she hastily retreated to the kitchen to dispose of the empty potpourri bag in her hand.

Masterful host that he was, Tim took a deep breath, squared his shoulders and exhaled all of his anxiety. Then he pressed the intercom button and said, "Come on down." He then pushed another button to open the gates.

"Battle stations," Tim called out loudly enough for Polly to hear on the second floor of the residence. "All hands on deck!" Then, just as Missie had done when the Pepper clan had visited her in Fryman Canyon, Tim opened the front door and stepped out into the evening to welcome their guests personally.

Missie maneuvered her black Mercedes along the driveway and came to a stop next to Polly's Rolls. When Missie opened her car door and stepped out, Tim called, "You found us!" He walked over and hugged the young star. She sounded out of breath as she half complained and half laughed that

the streets in Bel Air were very confusing. Tim quickly moved
to the passenger side of the vehicle to lend a hand to Missie's
mother. "Hope you didn't have a problem finding us," Tim
said to her. "I should have given you better directions. I always presume that everybody knows where Pepper Plantation is located. Heck, there are enough tour coaches that drive
by every day."

Tim started to chuckle at his bit of humor, but was interrupted by Mrs. Stembourg who declared, "We may be from
out of town, but we're not tourists."

And the evening is off to a fine start, Tim said to himself
as he deftly guided Missie and her mother up the steps and
into the house.

Missie was immediately struck by the thought that she
was actually standing in the fabled Hollywood home of Polly
Pepper. With the expected "Ooh's" and "Ahh's" and "Oh, my
God's" tripping over themselves to reach Missie's lips, she
admitted that she had saved the issue of *Architectural Digest*
in which Pepper Plantation had been the cover feature several years ago. "What's it like to actually live here?" she
asked in awe and reverence.

"It's a house for God's sake," Mrs. Stembourg said. "People just live here like anybody else."

Missie appeared embarrassed. "Obviously, I'm unsophis-
ticated and overwhelmed."

Just then, Placenta came into the front living room acting
as nonchalant as Wal-Mart employees avoiding customer assistance. "And we're overwhelmed to have you," she said,
having caught the last of Missie's comment. "Welcome! I'm
pouring drinks. We'll all have champagne, unless you'd like
something different."

"Then we'll give you the ten-cent tour," Tim promised,
winking at Placenta.

Both Missie and her mother agreed that would be a lovely
way to start the evening. As Placenta departed for the kit-

chen to retrieve the drinks, Tim made small talk about the easiest route to get to the house and he hoped that traffic wasn't too terrible. "Sunset Boulevard's a bitch this time of night," he said. "Especially around the UCLA campus. Of course, rush hour is twenty-four seven in this town, isn't it? I mean you have to plan well in advance just to go to the beach," he laughed.

Missie agreed wholeheartedly and said what everyone in Los Angeles says, that traffic was getting worse. "It's that damn Pasadena Rose Parade," she laid blame. "On New Year's Day, as the rest of the country is freezing their buns off, they're tuned in to the floats and see nothing but blue skies and those mountains that we never see in summer because of all the smog that's probably giving us black lung and emphysema."

"I don't count us among the throngs," Elizabeth said. "We're just here to become a star," she spoke as though Missie's celebrity was her own. "We're cashing in and too bad for the poor folks back home."

Tim was slightly taken aback. "With production closed down on *Detention Rules!*—and who knows when you'll resume—maybe your time's finally up," Tim tried to joke. Missie gave a weak smile and remained silent. Tim was suddenly uncomfortable, and looked around hoping to spot Placenta.

In the next moment, she came into the room with a silver tray on which she carried the aperitifs. She set the tray down on the coffee table and made the gesture of carefully handing a glass to Missie's mother. "Mrs. Stembourg, I'm handing you a glass," she said, a bit louder than was necessary. Placenta reached for Elizabeth's hand and guided it to the cold glass. When she was certain that Elizabeth had a hold of the flute she let go. Then she offered one to Missie and to Tim. They all took sips and acknowledged that after their respective rotten days, this was their just desserts.

Tim looked at his wristwatch and made a show of craning his neck in search of his mother. "So sorry that Mom's a bit tardy," Tim confided. "She rushed home from wrestling with Bruckheimer. Then she had a long phoner with *The Peeper*. It may take her a while to put her face on."

Placenta stood up. "In the meantime, while we're waiting, if you'd like to see the rest of the house, we'd be delighted to show you around," she said, as a prelude to ushering the guests out of the room.

Missie was overjoyed, but Elizabeth said, "I'll just sit here and play with myself. Don't know why I came in the first place since I can't see the damn place."

Immediately, the gracious host that emerged from Tim whenever a guest had even the slightest problem, came to the fore. "I'm so inconsiderate," he said. "Placenta can show Missie around. You and I will sit here and chat. Okay?"

Elizabeth harrumphed and took another sip of champagne. "Never mind," she said. "I'm used to being alone. I'll just sit here and wait for the mistress of the manor to put in an appearance. Don't worry that I might get bored out of my skull, or that I'll have to use the bathroom and have no idea where it is."

Missie sighed heavily. "Mother," she said as patiently as possible, "I don't have to have a private tour of Pepper Plantation. It's not that important. I can look at the magazine pictures in my scrapbook when we get home."

"Don't play martyr!" Mrs. Stembourg snapped. "Go! You too Mr. Docent. I'll sit here quietly and listen to . . . it sounds like Peggy Lee."

As Tim and Placenta led Missie out of the room, they could hear Elizabeth make a long sigh of resentment, as if she were a spoiled child being forced to sit in a corner as punishment. "She's in a mood," Missie whispered an apology to her hosts.

Tim dismissed the problem. "She'll be cool once Polly arrives and takes over."

Alone in the living room, Elizabeth became aware of how vast the area was. For a moment she concentrated on Peggy Lee's voice emanating from hidden speakers and vibrating throughout the room. From the distance she could distinguish the giddy sound of her daughter and her escorts moving off to a farther area of the house. She could hear ambient sounds coming from the second floor, presumably from Polly's boudoir. After a moment, already bored from sitting alone, she stood up, removed her dark glasses, and moved around the room. Elizabeth closely examined the paintings, framed autographed pictures of Roddy MacDowell, Virginia O'Brien, and Valerie Harper, and other *object d'art*. She drained her glass with one swift swallow and set it on the sofa table among a heard of antique elephants collected from the many locations around the world to which Polly had traveled.

Elizabeth stealthily prowled around, opening the drawers in the side lamp tables, and then the tall hutch. She sniggered at the mess she found inside the cabinet—a stark contrast to the everything-in-its-place order of the rest of the room. She let her fingers wade through a pewter plate, that seemed to be a catchall for coins, keys, mismatched earrings, an assortment of pins, and several small gold ornaments for a charm bracelet. She came across one, which was the icon of the Academy Award. "Oscar," she said in a whisper. "In your dreams!" she spat. "Missie will have hers by the time she's twenty-one if it kills me."

As her mind flashed on a recurring image of seeing Missie accepting an Academy Award and thanking her mother for making her life possible, Elizabeth was startled back to reality by a sound at the top of the stairs. Then the sound of Missie's distinctive laugh approaching from the opposite direction down the corridor toward the living room made her quickly close the cabinet door and hurry back to her place on the sofa. When Tim, Placenta, and Missie returned, she tried to appear annoyed that she'd been left alone for the ten minutes that it took to tour the first floor of the mansion.

Tim immediately noticed that not only was Elizabeth's drink glass empty, it was on the sofa table among Polly's collection of pachyderms. "More champagne, ladies," he said, which was Placenta's cue to return to the kitchen, open another bottle, and signal for Polly to make her entrance.

Placenta collected Missie's and Tim's glasses before spotting Elizabeth's. Without a word, Placenta moved out of the room to fulfill her duties. She returned with a tray of five filled flutes and passed them about. Then, just as the guests took a single sip of their champagne, Polly Pepper appeared in the doorway, as if conjured up by a magician.

With her hands on her hips and displaying her radiant smile Polly bellowed, "I'm completely ashamed of myself! Do forgive me, please! You can ask anybody and they'll tell you that I'm never tardy! After years of starring on television every week, it's simply not in my nature to keep even the lowliest production assistant waiting just for little ol' me! Please! Accept my sincere apologies!"

Polly swirled into the room, wearing a form fitting, magenta-colored ruched taffeta top with turned back cuffs, and a black column skirt, cut and darted with an off-center slit along the left leg. This flattered her still amazingly well-preserved figure. "I should have greeted you at the gate! But I'm confident that my darlings Tim and Placenta have made you both feel right at home. Yes?"

Polly then made the rounds of kissing Missie and Elizabeth on their cheeks. "Heavenly scent," she said to Elizabeth as she grazed the air next to her face. "Lilac?" And in the same rhythm she swiped a glass of champagne from the tray. Polly raised her glass and said, "To reunions and long-lasting friendships. We're so delighted that you could join us for the evening at Pepper Plantation." With that she drained her glass and the evening officially began.

Chapter 17

"... and that's the last time that Mother Theresa ever appeared on a musical/comedy variety show," Polly said triumphantly telling one of her favorite behind-the-scenes show business stories. "I guess after starring as my special guest that week, and having such a blast playing Bedpan Bertha's unlucky patient, she knew she'd never have more fun in Hollywood. So she skipped town. Back to Calcutta. Poor dear!"

"Too bad, 'cause after those incredible ratings she could have booked Merv and Johnny and Dinah Shore," Tim added to the story he'd heard a gazillion times. "The network suits wanted her to host a fashion awards special. She could have healed NBC!"

Polly sighed. "Mother Teri had a mean streak though. She really irritated dear Bob Mackie. Something wasn't right about the bugle-beaded life-size crucifix designed especially for her to drag in the sketch about the virgin birth of Liberace."

After a half hour of anecdotes and noshing on hors d'oeuvres, Polly looked at her watch, stood up and trilled, "Ding-dong! Soup's on. Follow the leader to the dining car, please."

As Polly led the conga line, Missie walked beside Tim, still chatting about the new Pavarotti documentary, "Belly and the Beast." Placenta held Elizabeth's arm and carefully guided her behind the others.

From the moment Missie arrived at Pepper Plantation, she was wide-eyed with wonder at every amenity in the big house. As she entered the formal dining room, she was completely overwhelmed when she spied the genuine Rembrandt around which the entire room had been decorated. She examined it closely before Polly pooh-poohed the period in which it had been painted and criticized brush strokes that prevented it from being acquired by the Getty. Then she called out, "You sit here. You sit there," speaking to her guests and pointing out the seating arrangement.

The long mahogany table could easily accommodate twenty, but tonight it was set for five and only at the near end, closest to the kitchen door. "This is like a state dinner at the White House," Missie marveled. "Or high tea at Buckingham Palace!"

"You'll get to Buckingham Palace eventually," Elizabeth said.

"In my dreams," Missie smiled. "I'll probably have to be a tourist standing in a long line. But this is darned close. And Miss Pepper is the queen."

Polly agreed, then took her seat at the head of the table. To her left and right her two guests took their assigned seats. Tim sat next to Missie, and Placenta sat down for a brief moment beside Elizabeth before realizing that someone had to serve the dinner and Polly was not about to share the agreed upon duties. Placenta graciously excused herself from the table and glared at Polly as she picked up the plates at each setting and left the room. She returned with the dinners on a serving cart.

"You sit," said Tim, "I'll serve." He rose and set the meals before the guests, then served Polly and Placenta, before finally laying a plate at his table setting and returning to his chair.

"What have we here?" Polly beamed, pretending to be surprised and impressed, as Tim praised Placenta for outdoing herself in the kitchen (although the food was delivered).

"Same thing we always have on Wednesday nights," Placenta bluffed, "Kofta balls in tomato sauce and spicy vegetable pilaf."

"And nary a face in the crowd," Polly added, touching Missie's forearm as a subtle knock to her vegan friend. She looked up at Placenta. "I see you've garnished with a few prunes to give it a sort of Middle Eastern flavor," Polly said and turned up her nose.

"Fiber," Placenta said, ignoring Polly's obvious dissatisfaction with the meal. "You need the extra push."

Once Placenta had seated herself and draped a napkin across her lap she called out "Dig in, folks!"

But just as Polly, Tim, and Placenta's forks were simultaneously poised at their lips, Missie asked in a small voice, "Shall I say grace?" Three pairs of eyes looked at her in momentary bewilderment before Tim said, "We nearly forgot."

Missie cleared her throat and reached for Tim's and Polly's hands. Polly intuitively knew to take Elizabeth's hand, then Missie began her prayer. And when Missie finally got to the last "bless this, and thank you for that," the five voices joined in with a simultaneous, "Ah-men."

"Allah, be praised," Placenta added as a tease. "Hey, I'm just practicing . . . in case," she justified her comment. "You read *Daily Variety*, and I'll scan the *Qur'an*. The way things are going with Washington's foreign policy I'm expecting a pop quiz from an Ayatollah one of these Ramadans."

Polly sighed with a tone of dissatisfaction then turned and complimented Missie on how lovely she performed her prayer ritual, and that she completely agreed that they were all inordinately blessed people. "And blessed to have you both at our table," she added, raising her glass.

After the initial, nonverbal expressions of satisfaction with their meals, Polly skillfully launched into the topic for which she'd summoned her guests. "And speaking of being blessed," she said, "glory be that Sedra's killer has been apprehended. Believe me, I sleep better. But I would never in a gazillion years have guessed that the lovely and talented Dana Pointer was the sinister henchwoman behind such an atrocity. What do you suppose got into her pretty head?"

Missie shrugged her shoulders and said, "Pride. Envy. Lust. Greed. You name the sin and Dana has transgressed."

For the first time since being seated, Elizabeth spoke out. "I warned my Missie to stay away from Dana Pointer, and that Lohan girl, too. Trouble! But did she listen to me? No! I can spot a bad seed a mile away, and the moment I laid my eyes on that kid, I said to myself, there's Jezebel. She'll be eating rats in hell."

Shocked by Elizabeth's medieval thinking, but not wanting to jeopardize her evening's plan of action, Polly simply said, "It's a mother's duty to protect her little darlings from ruining their reputations and getting engraved invitations to an eternal vacation at the lake of fire. You've done an amazing job of raising a perfectly delightful and talented daughter. Just as I've raised the ideal son. More prunes, dear?"

Elizabeth waved away Polly's offer. "The way that Dana dressed—wearing such revealing outfits that showed her navel!" Elizabeth looked at Polly, as if finally becoming comfortable and taking her into her confidence. "Did you see her hideous tattoo of a tongue? Like the logo of that satanic group, The Rolling Stones."

"Mick still has that indefinable sex appeal, doesn't he?" Placenta beamed. "He can still light my fire. Oh, I'm getting him confused with Jim Morrison. Now there was a real rocker."

Elizabeth was now nearly maniacal. "As a Christian woman, such sinful body decorations naturally made me rebuke that unsaved creature."

"Mick, or Dana?" Polly asked. "Or Jim?"

Elizabeth had to think for a moment. "She's certainly being punished now, in the constant company of Satan," Elizabeth said, making clear that it was Dana Pointer about whom she was speaking.

With a large and completely forced smile and an exaggerated lilt in her voice, Polly said, "What I adore about organized religions is that they're all so perfect and tolerant and forgiving! Every last one of them. And which practice do you follow? Catholicism? Protestantism? Nepotism? Have another ball," she said removing a Kofta from her plate and passing it over to Elizabeth.

"I was born again the day Missie's father died and finally left us alone," Elizabeth said.

As Tim sniggered softly at his mother's own intolerance for the intolerant, Missie diplomatically agreed with both Elizabeth and Polly. She added, "Mom has had a difficult time, but she definitely knows what's best for me. Thank you, Mommy dearest," she said, reaching across the table to take Elizabeth's hand in a show of support and affection. She held her mother's four fingers for a moment while slowly giving them a bone-crushing viselike squeeze, which brought tears to Elizabeth's eyes.

Tim chased a bite of Kofta ball with another sip of champagne before musing, "Indeed, Dana is certainly being punished. In a Beverly Hills gulag, no less! I wonder if they let her have video privileges?" He waited a beat then turned to Missie. "We're completely out of the loop," he lied, dabbing his lips on his linen napkin. "We haven't a clue about what's going on with this case and it's driving us nuts. All we know is what Anderson Cooper is saying about the crime, not much more. What have you heard? Have you talked to Dana, or anyone else on the crew? Are they saying anything about this?"

Missie, now comfortably filled with champagne and camaraderie, nodded her head. "Of course, it's all anyone's talking about," she said of the other cast members and the film crew. "They're all furious. Poor Ben the screenwriter is trying to figure out a way to rework the ending *without* Dana and me."

Polly, attempting to sound optimistic said, "I'm sure they'll figure something out and we'll all be back on set in a few days."

"I rather hope not," said Missie, sending a sudden wave of distraction through the room. "I'm too busy now."

Elizabeth smiled with satisfaction. "Missie's going into a new film, starting on Monday."

A stream of guarded "Congratulations," and "Marvelouses," and "Awesomes," filled the room as Missie lowered her head in false embarrassed appreciation. "Oh, it's a tailor-made role," she said. "But we were stuck in *Detention* and we thought I'd miss the start date. And if the studio makes us go back to work . . ."

"I'll be damned if I let that happen," Elizabeth said with a serrated edge to her voice.

Polly sat silently for a moment, thinking about the possibility that if Missie and Dana were both out of the film, production could be held up for months—if not permanently. Where would that leave her and the rest of the cast and crew, she wondered. "But we've got a job to finish," Polly said. "Can't your director hold off until you're out of *Detention*?"

"Not a chance," Missie said. "The start date is firm. Anyway, I don't care if I never go back to that crummy teen movie. I have another role and it's everything an actress could want. Comedy, tragedy, music, dance . . ."

"I have a role, too," Polly said, trying to make sense of the fact that one way or another, even if by some Hollywood miracle the production got back underway again, she was screwed out of a job because all of her scenes were with either Dana or Missie. "Perhaps they can shoot without you two. If Adam positions the camera just right, I can play to the stand-ins."

Missie didn't give more than a moment's thought to Polly's idea. "Fine with me," she said. "You'd be playing right into Lauren Whatshername's hand," she said. "You know Lauren. She's that crazy stand-in who's always hanging around the star. If Dana hadn't killed Sedra, I would have suspected Lauren."

Then Missie went on about her own new film assignment. "We've got John Cusack! I've been in love with him ever since I was a little girl. Is he married? Haven't heard that he's gay or anything. Doesn't matter. He's totally cuddly, don't you think so, Tim?" Missie's mouth was running like a radio commercial announcer stating the rules of a free checking account and that certain restrictions may apply. "I've kissed him so many times in my dreams, I know exactly what he tastes like."

Tim shrugged his shoulders and said, "Frankly, I never thought about him one way or another. Sure, I guess John Cusack's 'cuddly,' but he's not hot like Jack Wesley. Wouldn't you prefer to be working with an up-and-coming sex symbol? You two looked perfect together."

"I hate window shopping," Missie said, almost petulantly. "If I can't have something, I don't even want to look at it. And I can't have Jack."

"A lovely girl like you can have practically any man she wants," Placenta suggested.

"Right now Missie's too busy to think about boys. She's got a thriving career. After this new film project, she's booked as the voice of the cute mutant virus Sal Monella in the Disney animated musical comedy feature, *Guess Who's Coming With Dinner?* And there are tons of other offers on the table."

"John Cusack's a good actor," Tim backtracked, siding with Missie.

"He's a star," Elizabeth shot back. "He can make Missie a bigger star! I've already had my talk with that Jack Wesley loser. His fifteen minutes are just about up. Ding! There goes the timer on his career."

"Mother, you said the same thing about Matthew Mc-Conaughey," Missie politely reminded. "He seems to be doing just fine."

"And what's the film about?" Polly asked.

Missie smiled apologetically. "I've been asked not to discuss it with anyone. You understand."

Although neither Polly, Tim, nor Placenta did understand they agreed it was nobody's business.

As Placenta finished her dinner she poured another round of drinks for all. "From what I've heard, Jack dumped Dana," she said baiting Missie. "In fact, rumor has it that Jack and Sedra were fooling around."

Missie laughed. "No way!" she said, trying to stifle her amusement. "He spreads himself around," Missie declared. "I doubt that he has long-term plans for anyone except . . ."

"But he was about to elope with Dana," Polly lied, interrupting to plant a kernel of doubt in Missie's mind. "I have it on the best authority."

"Must have been Sedra who told you that," Missie said. "She spread tons of rumors. Made herself believe that she was young enough to attract him, if she simply removed all other obstacles.

"Sedra was the big obstacle, if you ask me," Elizabeth said. "She was especially difficult on the set and holding up production just to wreck Missie's chances to start this new film. But of course I was desperate for it to be over because Missie had this other gig."

"Then Sedra died. Lucky me," Missie said. "Oh, I didn't mean to sound . . ."

Polly, Tim, and Placenta were simultaneously aghast.

"So I'm baffled," Polly said. "What motive would Dana have to knock off Sedra, if you were the one who wanted out of the movie?"

Missie shrugged her shoulders. "Still, if you want my opinion, Dana is guilty. I heard their fight the night of Sedra's death."

"I suspect that she'll be released for lack of evidence," Tim said. "From what I've heard, that overzealous police detective moved too quickly. He apparently believed a lot of baloney from someone on the set."

Polly made a loud involuntary intake of breath. "I can't believe that the BHPD would make a mistake when it comes to a high profile celebrity murder case. I swear, this entire town should have learned their lesson with Simpson and Blake and Jackson, and the list goes on!"

Elizabeth, having consumed more champagne than she was used to, began pontificating about why she felt that Dana was guilty and should rot in jail. "She doesn't have a legitimate alibi. And everyone overheard Dana threaten Sedra. But trust me, all the police have to do is interrogate that stand-in who Missie mentioned, Whatshername, Lauren Somebody. She's a wacko. But she knew what was going on around the set. A stand-in's got to be the same height and hair color as the person she's standing in for, and this weirdo insisted that the costume and makeup department make her look exactly like Sedra. She was constantly mistaken for Sedra, which I'm sure is just what she wanted. She's clearly a frustrated actor. They're not supposed to let fans be stand-ins. This one slipped through the psycho testing phase, I suppose. She has motives, like getting Sedra's role, simply because they were at the end of production and she figured that no one else could have stepped in."

Polly pondered the theory for a moment then said, "Did

Sedra do something to this Lauren woman to make her vengeful? I can't make sense of your hypothesis."

Missie placed her fork on her plate and in an almost condescending voice said, "She wanted to take Sedra's place, as Mother suggested. These stand-ins are wannabe actors. She saw herself as taking over for the star, since she looked enough like Sedra, at least from a distance. It makes perfect sense that she would have wanted Sedra dead."

Although Elizabeth and Missie's idea sounded farfetched, Polly, Tim, and Placenta each made mental notes of this new potential suspect.

"Be sure to ask Duane about it when he comes by tomorrow," Elizabeth spoke up.

"Duane?" Polly asked, feigning bewilderment, and pretending to try and recall who that might be.

Elizabeth said, "Sterling Studios? Security? You've invited him to lunch. He's so excited he's calling everybody to tell them that you're his new best friend."

"*That* Duane! Of course!" Polly smiled while thinking, "*Damn! The Hollywood grapevine is getting shorter every day.*"

Chapter 18

"You better believe you're cleaning up," Placenta stated as they retreated into the house after waving good-bye to their guests and watching the automatic gates close.

"Elizabeth needs an enema, if you ask me," Polly said. "And she's not exactly blind when it comes to a vision for her daughter's career. It wouldn't surprise me to find that Mrs. Piety was seducing a Weinstein."

Placenta heaved a heavy sigh. "I've had enough of Holly-wood scandal for one night," she said. "If I hurry I can catch Jon Stewart."

As Tim and Polly moved to the kitchen they busied them-selves with the tasks of scraping food from plates, throwing lipstick smeared napkins into the laundry chute, and wrap-ping leftovers in plastic food storage containers. In the midst of putting away unused stemware, Polly stopped long enough to retrieve a split of champagne from the stainless steel re-frigerated wine cooler. She filled two flutes, as she and Tim began verbally replaying the events of the evening. They came to the same conclusion, that Missie had a motive for making sure that production shut down.

When the last Fitz & Floyd plate had been stacked in the dishwasher, and the soap tray filled with Rinse n' Shine, and the machine dial turned to the Stubborn Crud selection, Polly heaved a heavy sigh. "How could you have come to the conclusion that Dana Pointer was a killer? She was too obvious."

Tim was nonplussed. "I've maintained all along that she probably *didn't* do it, Mother," he said. "You're the one . . ."

"I, on the other hand, have always been on Dana's side, never for an instant have I wavered from my conviction that she was incapable of killing Sedra, or anyone for that matter."

Bordering on being drunk, Tim was exhausted and didn't want to argue with Polly, which was a lost cause even when he was completely sober. "Check this space after lunch with Duane tomorrow." He placed a wet dishtowel on the rack and spilled the remains of his champagne into the sink. "If he agrees with you about Dana's innocence, we'll consider alternative suspects." As Tim began heading out of the kitchen he said, "We'll see what security thinks of the situation." Then he turned around and gave Polly a peck on the cheek good-night.

"Pleasant dreams, Sweetums," Polly called as she dropped three empty champagne bottles into the trashcan. "This stuff was totally wasted on that Elizabeth creature," she added. "If I had served André, she wouldn't have known the difference."

"You would never let André pass your lips," Tim said. "Johnson & Johnson household cleaning products aren't nearly as lethal!"

Polly looked at her wristwatch. "I'm on my way, too," she decided, considering the dire fact that Duane was coming for an early lunch, and she had to look her celebrity best.

With only the swooshing sound from the dishwasher to invade the tranquility of the house, Polly left the kitchen, turned off lamps and wobbled down the corridor and into the living room. There, she checked to see that the security alarm system was activated, then began turning off the lights. She made her way toward the Scarlet O'Hara Memorial Staircase, and ascended to her suite.

Morning arrived way too quickly for Polly Pepper. And after Placenta spent an hour and a half trying to summon her mistress awake with everything from an *a cappella* rendition of "Oh, What a Beautiful Morning," to a Bloody Mary on a tray, there was just enough time for Polly to comb out her hair, and put on her sunglasses before Duane arrived. "You're the one who wanted to have the geek over for an early tête à tête," Placenta said as Polly whined about wishing she'd died in her sleep. Placenta poured two Advil and a Xanax tablet out of a prescription medicine bottle and pressed them into Polly's hand. "These'll work while you're splashing water on your puffy eyes. And for God's sake—moisturize!" she said, then turned to leave the room.

At the doorway Placenta added, "Gotta be especially nice to this one. The fan, I mean," she said. "They're scary when they're as devoted as he seems to be. Any adult who still takes his official Polly Pepper lunch box to work—one of the early ones that were recalled because all those school kids got lead poisoning—is a wacko in my book. Give these celebrity seekers the smallest reason to think you're not who they want you to be, and they go nuts. They can shred you to pieces on their Internet blogs and chat sites and message boards. So be as nice as Mary Tyler Moore. By the way, I've laid out an outfit from one of your old shows. He'll wet his pants when he sees you wearing it."

Polly moaned and slowly untangled herself from the sheets. She pushed away the covers and sat unsteadily on the side of her bed with her eyes closed. "I'm not drinking as much tonight," she vowed to herself before stepping onto the carpeted floor and stumbling to the bathroom. She looked in the vanity mirror and said, "My God. I'm turning into Bruce Jenner."

By the time Polly completed her ablutions and lethargically dressed herself in the clothes that Placenta had selected, she was almost sober and ready to start the day. But as she made her way down the staircase en route to the kitchen for coffee and another Bloody Mary she heard the security chimes from the front gate. Polly looked at her watch. "Damn, he's a half hour early," she wailed loudly enough for the rest of the household to hear her.

Tim met his mother at the bottom of the staircase. "You'd better greet Duane yourself," he said. "You'll score major points if he sees you as the down to earth star that everybody thinks you are. Answer the intercom before he gets all flustered and thinks it's the wrong day or worse, that you've forgotten about him."

"This sucks!" Polly lamented as she walked through the living room to the intercom station. At the security system keypad and intercom on the wall beside the front door she jabbed the talk button. She summoned what little energy she had and in her famous singsong voice called out, "Is that you, dear?"

The response came quickly and enthusiastically. "Yes, Miss Pepper. I got an early start because I didn't want to be late and keep you waiting."

Polly rolled her eyes then pushed the talk button again. "How refreshing to find the virtue of punctuality in one so young," she trilled, and then ground her thumb onto the button that automatically opened the gates. She turned to Tim. "I've gotta put on my interview smile and pretend to be interested in his life. You'd better not leave my side for one moment, mister. We're all in this together."

Tim stood before his mother and brushed a few strands of

hair off her forehead. He then reached out and adjusted the collar on her blouse before assessing her entire look. "A little out of date, isn't it?" he asked, not disapproving, but curious. "Oh, I get it," he quickly guessed. "A freeze-frame from 'The Polly Pepper Playhouse.' Good thinking. I'll give him thirty seconds to tell you on which show you wore this freakish thing, as well as who your guests were, the titles of the songs you sang, and the Procter and Gamble products that aired during the station breaks."

Polly gave her son a wearied look that said he was probably right. "Just make sure he's out by three," she said. "We've got more fish to fry tonight." Then there was a knock on the door.

"Catch you later, Mother," Tim said then disappeared down the hall corridor leaving Polly alone and flustered.

Polly took a deep breath and plastered a wide smile on her face. She opened the door and was nearly blinded by the daylight. She adjusted as quickly as possible and took in the sight of Duane dressed in jeans and a white shirt and striped tie. "How nice of you to pay a little visit to Pepper Plantation," she chirped. "Welcome!"

The moment Duane stepped into the foyer he pushed a dozen yellow roses and baby's breath wrapped in cellophane into Polly's hands.

"Oh you sweet man," she said. "You certainly shouldn't have gone to the expense just for *moi*!" She put her nose to the petals and inhaled deeply. "Ahh," she sighed, pretending there was a discernable scent to hothouse flowers. She looked at Duane and sighed. She looked at another proffered gift. "And what's this?"

Duane presented Polly with a white plastic bag on which the Sav-Smart drug store name was written in bold fading blue letters. "Just a token," he said proudly as he eagerly waited for her to accept the offer. Polly temporarily placed the bouquet of roses on the hall table and accepted the plastic bag. She looked inside and retrieved an ancient copy of *TV Guide*. Her image (as a blundering psychoanalyst character she occasionally played on her show) graced the cover, which was faded with time and had come away from the staples on the binding. Perplexed, but pretending to marvel at his thoughtfulness, she gave Duane a peck on both cheeks.

"It's from my personal collection," Duane announced, satisfied that he'd selected the perfect present. "I have almost every issue of *TV Guide* ever printed," he boasted. "I hope you don't have this edition."

Dozens! Polly wanted to scream. Instead she gave a noncommittal, "I remember the day the reporter came to interview me for this issue. Such marvelous memories! How can I thank you enough for thinking to give me such a treasure?" She dropped the magazine back into the bag and picked up the flowers. "Now, let's get Placenta to put your lovely posies into water." As she dragged Duane along toward the kitchen she asked, "What would you like to drink? Join me for a BM?"

Before Duane had a chance to understand what Polly was offering, she was strides ahead of him, practically barreling down the hall corridor, which opened into the kitchen. She wanted that Bloody Mary badly.

Duane gazed around in amazement. Not only was he in a real, live, movie star's Bel Air home, but the star was his all-time favorite. He tried to act as if this waking dream didn't faze him in the least; however, he desperately wished that his family and those who had placed him at the top of their loser list could see him now. *If they could see me now, that little gang of mine . . .* He wanted to sing and dance.

In the kitchen, Placenta was putting the final touches on a tuna salad luncheon. A pitcher of lemonade had been fresh squeezed and spiked with champagne. When Polly and Duane stepped into Placenta's domain she greeted them both warmly and made a pleasant fuss about the gift of roses. "I have the perfect vase," she said, untying the red ribbon that bound the stems together, and placing them on the kitchen's center island. "You two go outside. Here's your drinkie," she said to Polly. "I'll take care of the flowers, and Tim will bring refreshments for Duane."

The early afternoon had turned comfortably warm and Polly was delighted to see that without exception her landscape workers were shirtless. "Don't mind the help," Polly said to Duane, who now seemed more interested in the perspiration glistening Latino pushing a wheelbarrow than in his hostess. "They're unobtrusive, and should be breaking for lunch soon," Polly said. "Appearance is so important, don't you think so?" she asked trying to redirect Duane's attention to her garden. "These lovely men do an extraordinary job of spilling their seeds and fertilizing the tender buds? Tim insists they have an extraordinary way with a thallus. And he should know. Oh, a thallus is the early flat leaf of a fern," she said to a dumbfounded Duane.

Remembering where he was and with whom he was speaking, Duane brought himself back to the moment and mumbled, "Yes. Well maintained," he said, stealing another glance at the muscled workers. "The garden and lawns, I mean." Then he actually took a good look at the acreage. "This is awesome!" he said. "I've heard so much about the famous parties you've had here. It's so cool that I get to be where all the action is!"

Just then Tim appeared bearing a tray with the pitcher of lemonade and four tumblers. "Heya, Duane!" he called out as he set the tray down on the patio table. He wiped his wet hands on his jeans and reached out to shake Duane's. "So glad you could make it, man. Have a seat."

The trio pulled out chairs from around the table and sat down. Tim reached for the pitcher and without asking if Polly or Duane wanted a drink, he poured them each a tall one over crushed ice. "Has Polly given you the grand tour?" he asked, knowing full well that she had not.

Grinning from one splotchy red check to the other, Duane said, "Gee, if I could really see Pepper Plantation, that would be so neat!"

Polly looked at her wristwatch, trying to calculate the amount of time she would require to serve lunch, get Duane to open up about who murdered Sedra, and discreetly send him back to wherever he lived. If Tim gave Duane a tour, that was less time she'd have to spend trying to act as though she was interested in whatever hobbies kept him busy when he wasn't guarding movie studio's location sets. She trusted Tim to gather whatever gossip he could from Duane. "You two run along," Polly said, standing up from her seat and practically sweeping Duane away. "Just be back within a half hour. Placenta's serving lunch, and I want to really get to know all about your Polly Pepper collections!"

"Follow me, sport," Tim said, "and take your drink." He led Duane back into the house. They began in the Great Room where Polly's most treasured mementos where on display.

As Duane drooled over the Emmy Awards, and the large oil painting of Polly that hung over the fireplace mantle, he began to offer anecdotes about how he had come to worship Polly. "There was just something unique about your mother," he tried to explain. "On her show, which I only saw in reruns, she wasn't a goodie-goodie like some stars of the era pretended to be. She had a naughty side. Oh, I don't mean to be disrespectful," he amended. "I mean, she was a regular person. She could use curse words, but coming from her they sounded tame and got huge laughs. Can I hold an Emmy?"

Tim reached out and picked up one of the awards. He read the engraved plate. "Second season," he said as he handed the statuette to Duane.

Cradling the treasure in the crook of his arm, as if he'd just been handed the last offspring of an otherwise extinct species of animal, Duane began caressing the statuette. He stood in a trance, not wanting the dream-come-true to end. "Polly Pepper's Emmy Award," he sighed, "I memorized each of your mother's acceptance speeches," he said, which made Tim cringe. Duane continued, "She had tears in her eyes by the time she reached the podium. Then she screamed out, 'Mama! I won!'"

Duane fell into a trance as he recited Polly Pepper's acceptance speech. "'When I was eighteen, my lovely and talented mother said that I needed to learn to face rejection . . . as if I didn't get enough of it at home. Mama pushed me out of the house to an audition, expecting me to come home crying. I got the role and it took me to Broadway. I never had to look back.'"

Tim interrupted what he could tell was going to be a verbatim recitation of Polly's speech. "Let's continue the tour," Tim suggested and carefully pried Duane's fingers from around the torso of the golden woman with lightning bolt wings who held the world in her hands. He gently reclaimed the statuette and placed it back onto the bookshelf. Then he cocked his head for Duane to follow him out of the room. "No one ever gets to go upstairs, but come on, I'll show you Polly's bedroom."

Duane's eyes grew wide with gleeful anticipation. "Are you sure it's okay?" he asked not wanting to do anything that might displease Polly.

"Of course. You're with me," Tim said, making his guest feel as though they were buddies. As they entered the foyer and began to ascend to the second floor Tim said, "This is what we euphemistically call 'The Scarlett O'Hara . . .'"

"Memorial Staircase," Duane interrupted. "I know. Isn't it great? It's sorta modeled after the one in *Gone With the Wind*. When Polly was a little girl she dreamed of living at

Tara. So when she got rich and famous she had one built to her specifications."

"Between you and me, I think she built the staircase just to make a grand entrance when company arrives," Tim said with a conspiratorial wink of his eye.

In the upstairs corridor, Duane stopped at every painting and photograph. When they came to an autographed picture from Mel Torme, Duane said, "He was on 'The Polly Pepper Playhouse' eighteen times. The most of any guest. Way past Phyllis Diller. She was only on nine times."

Tim truly marveled at Duane's encyclopedic knowledge of his mother's career. "I can tell that Mom is flattered by your interest in her," Tim said. "She definitely appreciates her fans, and I'll bet that you'd do just about anything for her."

"Darned tootin', I would," Duane pledged. "I'm very loyal when it comes to my devotion to Polly Pepper. She could ask me to do anything, and I wouldn't question her. Anything at all. Is there something?"

Tim waited a few silent moments before softly saying, "As a matter of fact there is something. But Polly doesn't have the nerve to ask you herself."

Duane looked surprised. "She shouldn't feel that way at all," he declared. "Her wish is my command."

Tim put a hand on Duane's thick shoulder and said, "Mom doesn't want to get you into any trouble, that's why she feels she can't talk to you as one dear friend to another about something this important."

"What could possibly get me in trouble?" Duane said.

Tim hesitated for a moment. He felt that he had to straddle a very fine line between asking a direct question about Sedra's death and getting Duane to volunteer information on his own. As if drawing Duane further into his confidence, he said, "Polly feels sure that you're a man with a great deal of dignity and integrity . . . and that you of all people would probably have some very wise thoughts about the current situation on *Detention Rules!* Like when the cast might return to work. Or whom she should talk to about keeping one of her costumes for her museum. Or, um, who really murdered Sedra Stone . . ."

Duane stared at Tim for a moment. His silence gave the impression that he was either trying to think of what gossip to repeat, or that he was insulted by an obvious attempt at manipulation. When Duane came out of his daze, he looked around as if to search for eavesdroppers. He stepped closer to Tim, and in hushed tones said, "I'm just the man to help answer all of those questions. And, I can even get her marijuana if she needs a score."

Tim smiled, relieved. "That won't be necessary. We've got plenty. It's just that Polly hasn't worked on a film location in such a long time, and it seems that protocol is different in features than in television, especially when it's her own show. She really could use your guidance."

"Never fear," Duane said. "As for the person who wacked ol' Sedra? It's not who everybody thinks. Although I did hear every word of the fight between Dana Pointer and Sedra Stone that last night. They were downright nasty to one another."

"Did you see Dana leave the set?" Tim asked.

"Not exactly. When the fight ended my shift was over. Don't tell anyone at Sterling, 'cause we're supposed to punch the time clock right at eleven o'clock, but I hung out just long enough to see Sedra throw Dana out of her trailer. I didn't see the murder, but I know Dana's not the killer. Too many other people were around."

"If you weren't there yourself, how can you be so certain," Tim asked as casually as possible, as if he were simply shooting the breeze. He was surprised by Duane's response and wanted to make sure he had his facts straight. "Why do you think Dana's innocent?" he said.

Duane scoffed. "Don't get me wrong. Dana's got a killer's

instinct, just like every actor. And maybe she really did the deed. That's what makes this crime almost perfect. There was tons of competition to see who could knock Sedra off first."

"Motives?" Tim asked, knowing full well that there were as many reasons for wanting Sedra eliminated from the planet as there were people on Earth.

"See, it's like this," Duane said, as if explaining quantum physics to a three-year-old. "Connect the dots. Up-and-Coming Star—Dana—helps Has Been—Sedra Stone—get a job. When Has Been gets famous again, she thanks Up-and-Coming by dragging out an old autobiographical screenplay she's been working on for half a century. She serves up a heaping plate of stinking garbage about her own past sins, as well as those of everyone in Hollywood, especially the new generation of stars. Up-and-Coming gets hold of a copy of said screenplay and when she finds that she's the centerpiece, she goes berserk and puts a quick end to the possibility that Has Been is going to make a big chunk of taxable change off her sorry ass."

Tim was intrigued. "A memoir?" he mumbled, trusting that no producer would think the public might be interested in the life story of Sedra Stone. "My God," he said, "is there really a screenplay? Does it contain anything that's shocking and slanderous? If it's truly a vengeful story there must be plenty of other people besides Dana who would have reason to silence Sedra. And how do you know about the script?"

"Everybody in town has one, don't they? A script, I mean. Plus, I'm in security," Duane said, matter-of-factly. "Sterling Studios is pretty notorious for being a Peeping Tom when it comes to knowing everything about everybody who works for them. One of my jobs is to find out in advance if any of the talent is breaking the morals clause in their contracts—like surfing the net for porn on company time and property—so the studio publicity department can do damage control before anything gets out to the press."

"Big Brother is watching, eh?" Tim said, taken aback. "So how did you find out about the script?" he asked again.

"Simple," Duane shrugged. "I read parts of it on her laptop while she was filming scenes. It worked out great that Missie and Dana are such lame actresses that they had to shoot those scenes over and over, so I didn't have to rush."

Tim took a deep and dramatic inhale of breath. "Why were you reading her personal information in the first place?" he asked.

"Like I said, looking for stuff that Sterling might need to know about," Duane smiled. "It's part of my job. We check employees' computers all the time."

"But that's private," Tim said, trying his best not to sound judgmental.

"No," Duane insisted, "not at all because the laptop belonged to Sterling. It was just a loaner. So everything she had in there actually belonged to the studio."

"Splitting hairs," Tim said. "Who has the computer and all of Sedra's files now?"

"The killer, I guess," Duane said. "Boy did I get in a ton of trouble. After they found the body, my boss wanted me to retrieve the computer. But, um, it wasn't in Sedra's trailer. And it wasn't in her rented limo. Sterling sent someone to her house, but they couldn't find it there, either."

"Oh, Christ," Tim said. "This sounds like something out of a Tom Clancy novel! What if you're in danger? Aren't you afraid that you might be the man who knows too much?"

Duane stopped, dumbfounded. "You're the only one I've told," he said.

"Why trust me?" Tim asked.

"Because you're Polly Pepper's flesh and blood. And I'm your friend."

Just as Tim was about to suggest that others might know about the screenplay, such as Sedra's agent, Placenta called out from the bottom of the staircase. "Mister Tim! Mister

Duane! Polly's hypoglycemia's kicking in. She's starved. You guys finish your tour and beat it on down to the patio. Hurry up!"

Duane looked at Tim and looked down the few feet of corridor before Polly's bedroom door. "Darn. I won't see where Polly Pepper sleeps." Then he smiled. "No biggie," he said. "I can see it the next time I come over. Let's not keep the great Polly Pepper waiting. I don't want to make a bad impression."

Tim was far from ready to end his conversation about Sedra's bio pic, but conceded that they'd better hustle down to lunch. "Just tell me one more thing," he said. "What did Sedra say in her screenplay about Polly?"

Duane turned and faced his host. He looked deep into Tim's eyes and said, "I did a global search for the name Polly and/or Pepper and they came up five hundred and seventy-seven times. But I only read as far as the beginning of a story that started off with the time Sedra and Polly were dating Burt Reynolds . . ."

"Are you two coming down?" the voice of Placenta rang out again. "I know that Polly is eager to chat with Duane."

"We're coming," Duane responded. Then to Tim he said, "I'll tell you the rest later."

"Tell me now," Tim said, eager for news. "Am I mentioned?"

"You only had three entries," Duane said.

"Doesn't matter," Tim said. "Dana's probably going to fry in the electric chair, or get a massive dose of some lethal injection, or hang from a gallows, 'cause I'll bet they find the computer in her house, even if she's not really guilty. I mean who really cares about a movie star anyway, right?" He gave a lascivious wink to Tim.

"It's not at Dana's house," Duane said as Placenta came to fetch them.

To Tim's surprise, Duane stopped at the top of the stairs and said, "I've been in this business long enough to know that nothing is ever as it appears to be. God knows people in high places usually get off scot-free. It's the people below them who end up taking the blame. I think that some people are born to get away with murder all their lives. If they're pretty or rich or both, people fall all over themselves to protect those who project a little star shine. Maybe Dana will walk."

As the two men descended the stairs, Tim asked sotto voce, "Was Sedra surfing for porn?"

Chapter 19

Lunch with Duane was not the Tower of Terror that Polly had anticipated. Tim and Placenta guided her to reveal dozens of inside show business anecdotes—which she exaggerated out of all proportion—giving Duane the lowdown on her meteoric rise to fame and fortune. Although she covered well-known territory about how poor and deprived she'd been as a child, and that she had to clean the tarantula cages at the L.A. County Zoo to earn extra money to feed her bipolar, alcoholic single mother, she mesmerized Duane by offering a few details that she'd kept from all but her earliest interviews. When three o'clock arrived, Duane was sated and willing to leave without too much of a fuss.

As Polly, Tim, and Placenta escorted Duane to the front door, and all exchanged expressions of appreciation for the other's hospitality or generosity, it was Placenta who finally asked the question that Polly seemed to have forgotten during an afternoon of self-involved pontification. "Such a sweet boy," she said to Duane. "I don't suppose you personally had anything to do with Sedra's death?"

"Talk about a marksman's point-blank, between the eyes,

direct hit," Polly said, apologizing for Placenta's blunt remark.

Duane's smile had turned to a look of horror.

"Don't look so startled," Placenta said. "Hell, I'll tell you a little secret. Years ago, I thought about having Polly bumped off. Yeah, I actually got on the phone with The Queen Mum, and she gave me a schedule of fees for taking out princesses and former nannies with tell-all books. The rates for hitting a Hollywood TV icon weren't all that bad, considering. But in the end I decided she wasn't worth it. Was Sedra worth it to you?"

"My Placenta's not a well person," Polly said, putting her arm around her maid's waist. "She has a condition of the tongue. Something like Tourette's."

Duane collected himself and said, "As I was explaining to Tim earlier, it wasn't Dana Pointer who did the deed to Sedra Stone. I'm almost positive."

"Almost?" Polly said.

Duane shrugged his thick shoulders. "Even though they were in Sedra's trailer, fighting like Krystle and Alexis."

"But you didn't actually *see* Dana and Sedra together?" Placenta said.

"Sterling's notorious when it comes to not allowing overtime," Duane said. "I had to clock out precisely at eleven when my shift was over. So no, I didn't actually see Dana push Sedra off the diving platform, if that's what you mean. As far as my involvement, the fact that my mother is still alive proves I'm pretty harmless."

The others offered uncomfortable laughs, as Duane quickly changed the subject and tried to make plans for another lunch or dinner at Pepper Plantation.

He was subtly thwarted by Polly who saw no further need at the moment for his services. "I'll check my schedule and let you pick a date that's mutually convenient," Polly said as she ushered him out the door. "We'll definitely make it soon, dear! And thank you again for the posies and the *TV Guide*. I'll cherish them as I do your adoration of me." Then she waved good-bye in tandem with Tim and Placenta.

As she closed the door, Polly pouted. "That was a waste of my time. The little pisher didn't give us any new material to work with."

"Maybe if you hadn't talked so much," Placenta shot back.

As the trio made their way back to the patio to collect their drinks, Placenta roiled. "If you hadn't gone on about how much you hated working with Vickie Lawrence when she was a guest on the show, or how Steve McQueen was a bully, and Jimmy Stewart wrote lousy poetry, maybe we could have grilled him. Lady, he was ripe for pumping."

"I did the pumping for you," Tim said with a smug smile.

"Oh, my poor Timmy," Polly said, genuinely sympathetic. "You could do so much better than Duane!"

Tim stopped and folded his arms over his chest. "Mother, you're a freakin' nut job. I pumped Duane's brain for information about Sedra's death."

"Don't mind your mama," Placenta said. "She's on the right track, but taking the wrong train."

Tim continued. "He's a big ol' vending machine. Drop in the right amount of coins, or in this case, let him fondle one of Polly Pepper's Emmys, and the treats come sliding down the chute. Barbara Walters could learn a thing or two from me!"

As they reclaimed their seats at the patio table Tim continued to entertain his mother and their maid. "I couldn't very well talk about it while he was still here, but as I was showing him around the house he said that Dana didn't kill Sedra, even though she's pretty much a main feature in Sedra's tell-all autobiographical screenplay."

"Screenplay?" Placenta remarked.

"She was writing a movie?" Polly said, startled.

Tim continued, "Sedra apparently has some big secrets to

reveal. So I think that someone killed the messenger. So-to-speak. At least according to Duane."

Polly thought about the idea of Sedra writing a script about her life. "Everybody says that I should write a book," she said. "I would set the record straight and refute all those horrid tabloid stories. The tales that I could tell would make Sedra turn over in her grave! That is, if her bones weren't all broken and she could move 'n stuff." She considered Sedra and her screenplay for another moment. "You don't suppose she had anything interesting to say about me, do you? She wreaked so much hell in my life, I'll have to devote more than a chapter to her in my own bio," Polly said, already out-lining her tome.

Tim said nothing of the number of entries that Duane claimed to have found for Polly. Instead he focused on whether or not Duane was telling the truth about the script. "He can't even be sure that the screenplay exists anymore. It was on Sedra's computer, which has gone missing."

"Missing evidence!" Placenta said. "Listen, if Duane had come across anything in which Polly's name was mentioned he would have downloaded the files. I'm sure of it."

"As if anybody would be interested in anything written by Sedra Stone," Polly said. "Hell, she was a national joke even when she was famous. Who would spend more than a nickel to see a movie about a washed-up star?"

Tim defended the idea. "Hell, it's a classic story. Especially when the lead character climbs back on top again. As Sedra was starting to do."

"You've answered your own question about whether or not you should write your own story," Placenta said to Polly. Then she gave the idea of Sedra's screenplay more consideration and suggested that if such a thing existed and was on the verge of being produced, it shouldn't be that difficult to find out. "Wouldn't J. J. have represented her in a film sale?"

she asked. "I think he's someone to add to our list of people to invite to dinner."

Polly made a face. "Ach!" she said. "Let's first see how it goes with Adam and his main squeeze this evening. I'm getting tired of riff-raff coming in and out of this house. It used to be so quiet here. Perhaps after tonight there won't be a need to investigate any further."

"Until we can prove that you didn't get Dana Pointer locked up by mistake, then we're on this case," Tim said. "A few dinner parties with people you dislike is the price you have to pay for wanting to sleep with a police detective who was dumb enough to take your word that Dana was a killer."

Polly stood up from the patio table. "Perhaps I made a teensy mistake. Who's to say? Matlock was thrown off the trail now and then. I need a nap if I'm going to put on a performance tonight for Adam and Judith." She began to wander into the house. "Wake me by five, please," she called out and then spotted their gardener, Hector, in all his shirtless glory. "I think I've changed my mind. About the menu for dinner, I mean. Instead of the surf 'n turf, let's do a Mexican theme. I could use a burrito. And a pitcher of sangria. *Por favor.*"

While Polly was comfortably snuggled under her comforter, dreaming of Hector turning the garden hose on his perspiration-soaked torso, Tim decided to pay another visit to Dana. At the Beverly Hills jail, he again met Sergeant Walker who complained about Tim's obvious lack of interest in dating a cop. "Guess I'll have to write you a citation to get your attention," he pouted. Tim promised Walker that as soon he got to the truth about Dana's guilt or innocence, he'd take him up on his invitation for a night out of twirling on the dance floor.

As Tim waited in the interrogation room for Dana to be brought from her cell, he considered what evidence there was against her. It was all circumstantial. Missie and Duane had only *heard* Sedra fighting with Dana. The fact that strands of Dana's hair had been found clutched in Sedra's fist was not proof that she was present in the final moments of Sedra's life. Tim wasn't even certain that he accepted Duane's story of a missing computer containing the script of a Hollywood bio potboiler in which Dana's private life was to be publicly trashed. As he considered the lack of quality in the information, the steel door to the room opened, and Dana Pointer was ushered inside.

Tim stood up as Dana entered. He held out a metal chair for her and when they were both seated at the table, Tim broke the ice with standard innocuous questions about her health and mental attitude. "I hear that The Garden Bistro caters the meals here. True?" he asked. "Personally, I'd prefer California Pizza Kitchen," he tried to joke, but was met with an icy stare. "I'm sorry. I shouldn't try to be humorous when you're going through hell. Are you being treated okay?"

Dana shrugged her shoulders in resignation. "One of the hardest lessons I'm learning is that a lot of the people who I thought were my friends have abandoned me. As a matter of fact, except for my attorney, you and Polly and your maid are the only ones who've come to visit. I take that back. Paris was here, but she only wanted to see if perhaps there might be a reality show idea about movie stars in prison."

Tim snorted in agreement. There was silence while Tim mustered the courage to bring up the touchy subject of Sedra's death. He decided to simply rip the bandage off the wound. "Sedra was writing a screenplay and you were a prominent character, right?"

Dana shrugged her shoulders. "That was the rumor," she said, shaking her head. "A stand-in told me that she'd heard from the make-up artist, who heard from that security guy

Duane, who was apparently acting as an undercover opera-
tive for Sterling Studio's parent company. They get sued so
often by mommies and daddies who think their little brats
are being corrupted by Hollywood that he was charged with
making sure we were good boys and girls. Rumor has it that
he got into Sedra's laptop and discovered a folder stupidly
labeled, 'My Life.' I'm supposed to be so important to Sedra
and I have to find out about this biopic from a freakin' stand-
in."

"You killed Sedra over a screenplay that may or may not
really exist?"

"Oh, it exists, all right. But no!" Dana yelled and slammed the palm of her hand on the table. "I didn't do anything
to Sedra! I swear it! Sure, I wanted to kill her, but she was
alive when I left the location! So alive in fact, that I could
still hear her throwing a tantrum when I got to my car."

"How did Duane access the file without a password?"

"You don't need a password if you're working off-line on
a floppy disk," Dana said.

Tim took a deep breath. "You never saw Sedra's screenplay, so you don't know if she was really writing a memoir.
Even if she was on the verge of producing a movie about her
own life, what were you afraid she would reveal about you?
God, you're too young to have anything so big to hide. I
mean, you're not anywhere near as famous as Tom Cruise
for crying out loud! He doesn't kill people who spread rumors, he just sues their asses off."

"I can't talk about it," Dana said in an adamant tone. "We
all have skeletons that are best kept locked away in the
closet."

Tim was more skeptical than when he first entered the interrogation room. "If you didn't read the screenplay, why do
you think that someone's dark secrets were going to be exposed? More rumors?"

Dana was silent.

"You don't want to be a fink, is that it?" Tim said. "Let's play twenty questions. Tell me if I'm hot or cold. Sedra was involved with your boyfriend, Jack."

Dana uttered, "Sheesh!" and rolled her eyes. "Below zero!"

"Duane took revenge on Sedra by killing her off?"

"I pity your partners at a party game," Dana scowled and examined her fingernails.

Tim finally became exasperated. "Goddamn it, Dana! I'm only trying to help. Everyone claims innocence when there are necks on the chopping block. I wanted to believe you're innocent. However, you've gotta help! Stand up for yourself, for crying out loud. What are you trying to prove by not talking?"

For the next few moments, there was silence in the room. Then Sergeant Walker knocked on the door and entered. "You guys finished?" he said, meaning that visiting hours were over, but giving them the courtesy of wrapping things up.

Tim looked at Dana and said, "We're having dinner with Adam tonight. I'll tell him you said hi."

Before Dana got to the door she said, "Crappy director, sloppy in bed, and I'll bet he knows a lot about Sedra's script. Ask him."

And with that comment, she was escorted out of the room and down the hall to her cell.

Chapter 20

Adam and Judith simultaneously stood to greet Polly when she made her long-overdue entrance down the Scarlet O'Hara Memorial Staircase and into the cavernous living room.

"La, what a day!" Polly lamented as she wafted to their sides and presented a cheek for the obligatory Hollywood-style air kiss greeting. "Adam, you're a dream," she said as his beard-stubbled face grazed her skin. "That you tolerate legends who can't be on time is a miracle," she added and accepted his dismissal of any appearance that she might be tardy for her own dinner party. "And Judith, you seductive thing. Looking as bright as always," she raved without paying attention to what her guest was wearing.

"So sweet of you both to clear your calendars to join us for a quiet family evening at Pepper Plantation," Polly insisted.

"Now, about my being a bit off the clock!" Polly lied an unnecessary apology. "As you know from first-hand experience, I'm never late. This is practically the first time in the history of the universe! It's mostly the fault of that pesky reporter from *The Peeper* who would not stop asking inane questions! Honestly, how many ways are there to explain that I'm new to the young circle of talent in *Detention* and that as far as I know Dana Pointer and Sedra Stone were just dear girlfriends? That so-called journalist had all these crazy no-tions—which I won't bore you with. Then there was a meet-ing for a new play—which of course I turned down flat. But nicely. Honey," she said, looking at Adam, "those hacks over at The Majestic need your clever take on contemporary the-atre if they're ever going to succeed in turning that depressing-as-hell Sylvia Plath collection into another *Vagina Monologues*!

"After that I was shackled to a booth at the Polo Lounge—I swear it was almost white slavery—for a meeting with Whatshisname, that director. You know the one, tallish, sort of cute, but not really. Well maybe a decade or two ago. Ego the size of the *Titanic*. Thinks he's king of the world just be-cause he made a movie about a big ol' jagged chunk of the arctic floating around in the middle of the ocean sinking per-fectly lovely boats. From the way he heaped praise on him-self and his one movie, you'd think that practically everyone on the planet had turned out to see it. Jerry Bruckheimer he's not! My lack of familiarity with his little opus didn't go over too well, I'm afraid. But frankly, I'm fine with that because all of his ex-wives are dear friends of mine and I wouldn't jeopardize the friendships I've established by working with their mutual *bete noir*. I'm as loyal as Lassie. Ask anyone."

Polly finally came up for a breath of air.

Tim and Placenta pretended to be as intrigued by Polly's eventful day as Adam and Judith were. It was a testament to her talent as an actress, or as a liar, that nobody ever ques-tioned the veracity of her tall stories.

"But enough about me and my tales of a wasted day," Polly continued, practically trembling with a need for cham-pagne. "I see that Tim and Placenta have you set up with drinkies and nibbles. Excellent. I'll join you for a wee nip. Timmy?"

Tim was handing her a chilled flute even before she completed her request. Polly took a long pull of what was for her a rejuvenating tonic. "Ah, yes!" she sighed, almost smacking her lips, while simultaneously taking a seat on the Le Corbusier chair that Placenta had guarded in the center of the seating area. "When I go to my final reward, it won't be any better than this," she said, looking around the room. "Cheers, everyone!" Polly raised her glass. "Now, whose jugulars did you rip into before I arrived? Arnold and Maria? Warren and Annette?"

Tim recapped highlights of the small talk that had been ricocheting among the gathered while Polly was upstairs putting final touches to her make-up and eavesdropping over the intercom, stalling for the precise moment to make her entrance. "We jabbered about Dana, of course. Did you know that she was an orphan? Yeah, Adam says . . ."

". . . Abandoned the day she was born, poor thing," Judith interrupted. "Her mother was apparently too busy with a career and made arrangements with an Amish charities home in Pennsylvania."

"I'm surprised we never read about that in *The Peeper*— or heard it on Anderson Cooper," Placenta said.

Polly looked astonished. "Poor baby. No wonder Dana's such an angry and sullen little thing. Curious though. This is the second time today I've heard that rumor," she lied.

"Adam does his homework when it comes to knowing as much as possible about the stars with whom he works," Tim said. "Ammunition to keep 'em in line, I suppose. Right Adam? Oh, and then we talked about the rumor of Sedra's secret screenplay," Tim continued. "Wouldn't you know it, Adam and Judith were shocked that such a rumor was running rampant. They don't believe that such a thing exists."

"I'll bet you've got a hot book on the burner," Adam smiled at Polly trying to redirect the subject.

"*Moi*?" Polly said. "Hardly! I'm too busy *living* my life! I don't have time to write about it! Anyway I don't dwell on the past." She looked at Placenta and gave her a nonverbal warning to not contradict her statement. "But if and when I eventually do sit down and put pen to paper, I'll have only lovely things to say about you and what a divine time I had being in *Detention*—however brief. Alas."

Adam waved away Polly's suggestion that their time working together was over. "We'll soon be back on location," he said. "So much depends on the D.A. Thank God we're in Los Angeles, where *stars in stripes* are as common as girls who've serviced Charlie Sheen."

"Bail's been denied for Dana so she can't finish the film," Judith said. "We only had six more pages of script to shoot, for cryin' out loud! Hell, even Robert Downey, Jr., gets to work between trials!"

Judith patted Adam's leg soothingly then said to Polly, "Of course, you'll have to include a flock of naughty nuggets in *your* tell-all. Something shocking that nobody would ever have guessed about you and your amazing life. Quote a lot of dead stars saying things that can't be corroborated. The way that Sedra did. The dead can't sue for libel," she chuckled.

Tim contributed his own analysis. "I've known Sedra for as far back as I can remember," he said. "Yeah, she was a mediocre actress all right. But *she* didn't think so. Sedra Stone believed that Hollywood was damn lucky to have her working in the industry. I'll bet her story would have been huge fun, as well as a box office hit, simply because it probably would have been filled with her own revisionist history on all the gossip we've heard about her over the years."

"God, I hope so," Adam replied. Tim and Placenta shot each other a quick, pointed glance.

"But we may never know," Polly said, holding out her flute expecting it to be refilled by whoever was nearest the bottle.

"Because it doesn't exist except in myth, is that it?" Adam said.

Polly sat up straight and squared her shoulders. "Not at all. The screenplay definitely does exist," she said. "That darling security guard Duane says that he actually saw it. But the computer on which the script was being written has gone missing. Can you imagine? No one can find it. He said that studio security teams have searched high and low."

Judith interrupted. "Duane? He can't be trusted with anything more important than checking off names on a set visitor's list. And he gets that wrong. You believe him? I wouldn't," she said. "He's a star struck wimp who bawled his head off the day that Sedra jumped down his throat for not knowing who she was, and for trying to make her wait for a silly security clearance pass."

Polly reached for a puff pastry ball hors d'oeuvre and played devil's advocate. "Duane's a sympathetic and harmless young man," she said. "He's been blinded by pixie dust. He only has eyes for one star—me. I know how he feels. I still have the hots for Tom Selleck. Never missed an episode of 'Magnum, P.I.' Duane is a by-the-book guy who didn't know to allow Sedra Stone on the location set because she registers in his mind with about as much clarity as John Vivyan does for all of you."

"Who?" everyone in the room asked at once.

"My point, precisely," Polly said. "John Vivyan. Look him up in IMDb. You can't expect anyone to know every celebrity who ever had their picture plastered on the cover of a fan magazine. Duane's no different. Stars come and go so quickly in this town. And if he says that he saw a script in which I'm featured, I trust him."

Adam spoke up. "Actually, just between us, I heard that

he's being let go from the studio. They have a three strikes policy and he just racked up his third demerit. I don't know all the details," Adam said in a solemn tone. "Something about bothering too many stars for autographs, and not punching his time card at the end of his shift. Stupid stuff, I'm sure. But I'm told he's getting the boot on Friday. To-morrow."

Tim was dumbfounded. "That's really too bad. Sure he was a fan, but he wasn't a nuisance or anything."

"Duane swears that he saw Sedra's script in a desktop folder on a computer that she borrowed from the studio," Placenta said, defending the guard. "If Sterling's security force, an entity that picked up where the Gestapo left off when it comes to spying on their employees, can't keep track of a laptop, then maybe it was taken by someone who didn't like what Sedra was writing. Any idea who else knew that Sedra was cooking up a potboiler?" Placenta thought for a moment then turned and said, "Judith?"

Judith was slightly startled. "Yeah, sure," Judith responded dryly. "Inside job. Betcha ten to one that as the studio's secu-rity representative on location, Duane snooped around, found Sedra's screenplay, then sold the story to *The Peeper*. And that's why he's being fired."

Polly made a sound that indicated she found the theory intriguing. "If one is writing a tell-all, they certainly wouldn't leave the material out for wandering eyes. Wouldn't want anyone getting wind that they may be in for the full Kitty Kelley treatment. Especially if, as you say, she had to throw in a lot of stuff about her friends—the dead ones as well as the living. No doubt I made the soiled pages."

"I wonder if she mentioned the affair with Lawrence Welk?" Tim asked. "That was while she was still married to Dad! And we all love Nancy Sinatra, but you know how nasty Sedra was to her over the years. Hated everything but her boots. D'ya think she opened up about Kaye Ballard and their special relationship?"

"She certainly had a 'special relationship' with enough of my husbands!" Polly grumped.

"Join the club," Judith said, then immediately regretted her declaration. All eyes turned to her.

"You're not going to bring that up again, are you?" Adam asked petulantly.

"Oh, do!" Placenta said.

"Forget it," Judith said. "I'm starved. When do we eat?"

It was nearly midnight by the time Adam and Judith practically stumbled out of the house and down the steps to their Jaguar. Giggling and fumbling for the car door lock with his key, Adam called back, "You guys are amazing! Thanks again for a swell evening. I'll replace the tureen first thing tomorrow."

"Don't be silly," Polly said. "It wasn't Ming! Are sure you're able to drive?"

"And if Placenta can't get the bisque out of the table cloth, please let me know," Adam said, ignoring the query about his suitability for driving. "Love you all. Bye." Then they slipped into their respective car seats, and swiftly drove down the lane and out through the open gates.

Polly, Tim, and Placenta stepped back into the house and closed the door. "Jesus, Joseph, and Mary," Polly snapped. "Thank God that's over with."

Tim set the gate alarm and Polly kicked off her shoes as she unclasped her earrings. She went to the antique hutch and dropped them into the pewter bowl. "Oh, by the way," she called, "has anyone seen my Joan Crawford Oscar? I swear I put it here a couple of weeks ago."

Both Tim and Placenta responded nonverbally with as

much apathy as if Polly had asked, "Whatever happened to Peggy Lipton?"

Tim began helping Placenta in the dining room, carrying coffee cups and dessert plates into the kitchen. He bundled up the hand-crocheted lace tablecloth.

Polly looked at the once-ecru colored heirloom and sighed. "It really is your fault," she said to Tim.

Tim shrugged his shoulders and gave in to Polly's accusation. "I thought we were all having fun and getting along so well. I didn't think that bringing up Dana's jailhouse suggestion that Adam had had an affair with Sedra would cause such a reaction," he said.

Polly said, "Oh, sweetie, it's nothing. I probably would have done the same thing. But the next time you decided to regurgitate scuttlebutt don't do it in front of the cuckolded girlfriend, especially while she's passing a tureen of tomato bisque. Oh, this is simply a mess!" she added and walked into the kitchen.

"Placenta, dear," Polly said. "What did you think of Judith's cryptic comment about Sedra's script? Remember she said that I should write a book, but to put in a lot of dirt 'like Sedra.' How would she know what Sedra had written about?"

Placenta continued stacking the dishwasher as she contemplated the question. As she carefully placed the silverware in the utensils basket, and with her back to Polly, she said, "Maybe the folks at our table this evening know more about Sedra's life—and death and a missing screenplay—than the police do."

With a guttural sound, Polly clearly agreed that Placenta had a valid point. "Tim," Polly called from the kitchen to the laundry room where he had taken the tablecloth. "We've got to go back and visit Dana before my dinner with Detective Archer tomorrow night. Take me first thing, will you, please?"

Tim came into the kitchen and leaned against the center

island. He folded his arms across his chest. "I didn't want to say anything at dinner, but I saw Dana again today."

Polly and Placenta both stopped what they were doing and looked at Tim. "She didn't confess, did she?" Polly asked, hopefully.

"Of course not. And it's your fault that she's in the slammer in the first place. Sure, we can pay Dana another visit tomorrow, but you'd better be prepared to tell your dinner date that you and he have made a horrible mistake. Dana may have had motive and opportunity and no alibi, but she's innocent."

Polly growled. "Okay, smarty pants," she said pouring the dregs of the last bottle into a flute, "if you had to take a wild guess about who killed Sedra Stone, who would you point your finger at?"

"You tell me, Miss Marple. If we rule out Dana Pointer, who's left?"

"Everybody," Placenta answered the question for Polly, as she reached for a bag of coffee filters. She set the clock on the Mr. Coffee machine to begin brewing at seven o'clock in the morning.

"Sure, everybody had a death wish for Sedra, but who's the most logical in terms of actually carrying out the crime?" Polly said. "After tonight, I'm ready to vote for Adam Berg."

"Not Judith?" Tim asked. "She alluded to thinking that Adam slept with Sedra."

Placenta crossed her arms over her bosom. "When did they have the time to screw? Sedra was only on location for a day, and during that time, she was being a pain in the neck to everyone, including Adam."

"Could have been a charade, to throw everybody off," Polly thought aloud. "It's practically common knowledge that Sedra always 'auditioned' directors for her television series."

"But that's when she was young," Tim said. "She wasn't

in any position to help Adam. In fact, it was the other way around. No, I'd vote for Judith before Adam. But I'm not saying I'm sold on her as the killer either. There are too many other possibilities. The thing you've gotta remember about your date tomorrow night, is to shake the detective down for whatever he knows about the case. Flirt with the man until he can't stand it anymore and gives you anything you want."

Polly looked at Tim with trepidation in her eyes. "I'd better bring along the deluxe collector's edition of 'The Polly Pepper Playhouse' DVD. That'll get any fan's juices flowing."

Chapter 21

Friday morning. Nine o'clock. To Tim's way of thinking this was still considered predawn. But he was awake and from his still-warm and comfortable bed making a telephone call to Duane.

With pre-Java lethargy, Tim dialed the Sterling Studio's main switchboard. Speaking in a voice that belied his sleepiness he asked for Duane Dunham, and nearly fell asleep again listening to the classic songs from the Studio's film score catalogue while waiting to be connected. The fact that Duane was still on the studio's payroll was a good sign that perhaps Adam Berg had been wrong, Tim thought. Then it occurred to him that most employers, especially the notorious Sterling Studios, generally wait until late Friday afternoon, after they'd gotten another full week of work from their soon-to-be-axed employee, before hauling them into the human resources office and giving them the heave-ho.

When Duane finally and gleefully picked up the line he said he had exactly one hour for lunch but that he'd be thrilled to see Tim at precisely noon. And thus, Tim was set to plow full steam ahead—without his mother's interference—

and fleece Duane of every scrap of information he had about Sedra Stone's murder.

It was eleven forty-five when Tim drove up to the guard kiosk at the studio's main gate.

Soon, Tim was walking past ancient soundstages garnished with plaques that gave a thumbnail history of the structures' famous pasts, listing the most noteworthy movies that had been filmed on each stage. Bronze stars, with the names of legends from Hollywood's Golden Era were embedded in the stucco walls. Greta Garbo had worked here. As had Lana Turner, Greer Garson, Audrey Hepburn, John Wayne, Peter Lorre, and Julie Andrews. Tim silently admitted that it still gave him a thrill to be on a movie studio lot. He continued smiling as he approached the main avenue. Then he caught sight of Duane in the distance, taking up much of the space on the patio steps. Duane instantly recognized Tim and waved both arms over his head as if to signal an S.O.S.

Tim waved back, and when they were finally together, they shook hands and Duane ushered his guest into the restaurant. They picked up lunch trays and while Tim went to the salad bar, Duane headed to the pizza station. They reconnected at the soft drinks dispenser where Tim filled a large Styrofoam cup with water. Duane filled a larger-sized cup with a Coca-Cola.

"By the way, it's my treat," Tim declared as they moved on toward a bank of cashiers. "I insist," he fought Duane's weak objection. "I invited myself to lunch," Tim said and handed the cashier a twenty dollar bill. All the while he was thinking, "You'd better save your dough, boy. You won't be working here much longer."

As they searched for an empty table, Tim and Duane wended their way past costumed film extras, necktie wearing low-level executives, and denim-clad office assistants. "Let's take that one," Duane suggested, nodding his head toward the far corner of the dining room where they could talk in relative privacy. Finally seated, the two exhaled loudly, as if they were settling in for a leisurely, friendly lunch.

The small talk didn't last long before Tim got to the point. "Polly needs your help," he said.

Immediately Duane put down his first slice of pizza and looked as eager as a puppy who knows he's going out for a walk. "When I said that I'd do anything for Polly, I meant it," Duane said, nodding his head.

"And Mom appreciates your kindness to her," Tim said, slathering false praise on top of his preparation to interrogate Duane. "Here's the thing. Word is starting to get out about Sedra Stone's script, the one you said you found on her computer."

Duane suddenly looked nervous. His enthusiastic smile disappeared. He took a long slug of his Coke.

Tim continued. "Of course I haven't told a soul that you read the screenplay . . ."

Duane interrupted in a whisper. "I told you that I just counted how many times Polly was mentioned."

Tim nodded. "Absolutely. You're a man of principle and integrity. Those are the aspects of a person's character that Polly values most. She recognizes that about you."

Duane relaxed and smiled again before consuming half a slice of pizza in one bite.

"We had Adam Berg and his girlfriend over for dinner last night and they talked as though they knew all about the script," Tim said.

"Bitch," Duane said, almost under his breath.

"And considering the stormy relationship that always existed between Polly and Sedra, Mom's really worried about how her rival may have depicted her. If the script gets produced it could ruin her reputation."

"Sedra wrote all lies," Duane said, siding with his favorite celebrity.

"Polly's so insecure that she was crying all morning," Tim lied. "She's sick to death about the possibilities."

Duane picked up a second slice of pizza and considered what Tim had just said. He ate the whole piece then chased the crust with another large gulp from his drink. He was contemplating.

"In between Polly's tears, she kept repeating, 'Do you think dear darling Duane can help us? He's so smart and adorable. What would we do without Duane?'" Tim established. "I'm becoming jealous of how much she likes you." He chuckled.

Duane beamed. The fact that his idol had apparently come to rely on him gave him enormous satisfaction. "Judith and Adam claiming that they know of Sedra's screenplay is true. But they're beasts," Duane spat. "Judith was mean to me. Mean like Sedra. Mean like Adam and Dana and Missie and Missie's mother, and that costume lady."

Tim maintained a poker face, as Duane revealed himself.

"They know about Sedra's script because Judith sneaked into the trailer one afternoon when she didn't know I was already there. She caught me. Using Sedra's computer, I mean."

Duane motioned for Tim to lean in closer. "Truth be told, the chief of Sterling security makes all of us write detailed reports of everything we find in each trailer. We're supposed to snoop. It's gotta be illegal. But I need my job."

Tim was aghast. He whispered, "Why is Sterling interested in the private lives of the stars they hire? They can pick up *The Peeper* and find out almost anything they could ever want to know." A thought occurred to Tim. "Is it possible that the tabloids get *their* information directly from someone in security at Sterling?"

Duane lifted an eyebrow. Without saying a word, he assented. "But I was protecting Polly!" Duane declared. "That's why I was reading Sedra's script." He stopped himself. "Um, okay, I did read the script. But only because I wouldn't let that awful Sedra write anything negative about my Polly Pepper! But I wouldn't go as far as to kill her, if that's what you're thinking."

Tim nodded. "No, no, not for a moment. But whatever Sedra wrote about Polly could still come out because Judith read the script, too. What was she doing in the trailer in the first place?"

Duane recounted the incident. "When she came in she pretended that Sedra had left her script in the trailer and that she'd been told to retrieve it. That was a lie. You can tell when someone's been thrown off. She was surprised to find me in the trailer. I know that she was really looking for material. She sells gossip to 'E! Online.' Anyway, she saw me at the computer and insisted that I explain why I was there and what I was up to. Then she leaned over my shoulder and started reading the text. She didn't get far before she gasped and her eyes went wild. Like in the movies when someone finds a dead body. That's when she told me to get out of the trailer or she'd call Sedra. I ran."

Tim pressed on. "What was so startling to Judith?"

Duane waited a beat. "Probably the part where Sedra admits that she gave her baby up for adoption."

Tim didn't remember that Sedra was ever pregnant. "That happens every day. Why the fuss?"

"It was your father's."

At that moment, Tim froze. His mind reeled. With great effort he said, "Oh! My! God! I have a half sister somewhere?"

Duane stalled. He looked around to confirm that there were no eavesdroppers. "Um, somewhere closer than you think. Sedra's script was titled *DNA*. I figured that's an anagram for . . ."

Tim slowly came to a realization: "Dana."

"A John and Mary Pointer adopted her. You do the math."

Tim cupped a hand over his mouth. When the information finally settled in he said, "Dana? Sedra? Love child? Dana Pointer is my . . ."

"Blood kin!"

"The tabloids will have a field day with this," Tim said. "What did Judith say when she read that news?"

"She looked just the way you do right now. Utter shock," Duane said.

"So why hasn't this appeared in the gossip papers yet?" Tim asked, suddenly wanting all the lurid information that only *The Peeper* would sink so low to provide.

Duane grinned with satisfaction. "Because. I'm not as stupid as I pretend to be." Duane leaned back in his chair, and stretched. "I immediately had one of the production assistants page Judith to the set. I watched and waited until she left the trailer. As soon as she was out of sight I got back in and removed the floppy disk from the computer."

"It wasn't on the hard drive?" Tim said, amazed.

Duane froze. "Um, I don't know."

"Sedra wasn't that stupid," Tim said. "No way was she going to download her screenplay onto a borrowed laptop."

"I've stashed the disk someplace where no one will ever find it. Polly's secrets are safe with me."

"You're such a good friend to my mother," Tim said. "She'll be so relieved to know that her indiscretions—however mild—won't end up in a screenplay. But Polly's such a pessimist sometimes. Even though she completely trusts you, I know that she's going to grill me until I can prove to her that the story of her bitch fight with Elton John all those years ago isn't going to be rekindled." He faked an uncomfortable laugh.

"I mean for crying out loud, *The Peeper* is on to this story, I'm sure of it," Tim continued. "A reporter called Polly yesterday. Those gossipmongers definitely have a nose for news. I'll bet they smell blood at Polly's door."

Duane gave a look of consternation. "What did the reporter say?" he asked, putting down his half-eaten second slice of pizza. "I'm the only one on the planet who knows the full extent of what Sedra was writing. I think."

"You think?" Tim tried to act as calm as possible. "At least you have the disk. But it's too bad that Judith had to read what was probably the most shocking part of the story." He tried to recall what Polly had said was the nature of the reporter's interview. "*The Peeper* people were interested in the relationship between Dana and Sedra," Tim said. "Polly thought they were trying to get a story about an affair between the two. Now it all makes sense. They want to surprise Polly, or at least get a statement from her acknowledging that she knows the truth of Dana's lineage. Hell, readers will think this is why she and Sedra have been enemies all these years."

Tim noticed a pained expression on Duane's face. "What?" he asked.

"Do you think that Sedra may have had a production deal in place? If so, then her agent would probably have a copy of the script, or at the very least, an outline. Every old star thinks they should write a memoir and most of 'em write terrible books. This time, one of 'em wrote a good screenplay . . ."

Tim interrupted Duane and, reading his thoughts said, "A ghost. What if there's a ghostwriter who knows all about this screenplay? Jeeze, maybe you don't have the only copy? Maybe the leak to *The Peeper* didn't come from Judith but rather a ghost or an assistant at a studio."

Duane suddenly looked ready to cry. "I hadn't thought about that," he said. Then as if seeing a silver lining he said, "If another copy exists, then it should be evidence that Dana is innocent. She wouldn't kill her own mother."

"How's that?" Tim asked. "Maybe she was so angry with Sedra that she actually did knock her off. I'd be pretty upset if I found out that Polly wasn't my real mother. If I were Dana, I'd probably be doubly pissed off because she could have saved a ton of time and rejection breaking into the business if she knew she had a famous mother who could open doors for her. On the other hand, she should be proud that she achieved her minor stardom all on her own. I'm beginning to be more impressed with her. My sister. Do you see a resemblance?"

Duane ignored Tim and thought back to the night of Sedra's death. "Dana was upset alright. And so was Sedra. They fought so hard I thought they'd destroy Sedra's trailer. But at the time I didn't think it was about the mother-daughter connection. I do remember for sure that when Dana left Sedra's trailer, she went straight to her car and drove away. I watched her leave. And Sedra was still yelling. So Dana didn't kill her."

"Doesn't mean she didn't come back," Tim said.

Duane nodded. "I hung out for another ten minutes before I punched my time card. Sedra was still yelling—maybe at someone else—when I passed by her trailer. I got to my car and could still hear her bitching all the way from the parking lot."

Tim's curiosity was aroused. "Who else was still on the location when you left?"

Duane thought for a moment. "Um, Missie's car was still there. So was Adam's. Judith came to the set with him, so she was probably still there, too. It was late. I had the feeling that Adam and Judith were probably making out in his trailer. And Missie was more than likely going over her lines with the screenwriter. Missie's mother had him suckered into helping her in exchange for a promise to put in a good word with the studio so he'd get his next script read. A couple of the other cars probably belonged to extras and the stand-ins. I think everybody else was gone."

Tim made a mental note that most of the principals from the cast were still at the location well after Dana left. The exception was Jack. Tim asked about the film's hunky co-star.

"Jack walked with the others to their respective trailers the moment Adam called 'cut!' and wrapped up production for the day," Duane recalled. "He was eager to leave. Jack's got a double life. The studio knows where he's going and whom he's dating. But as long as he keeps a low profile, they won't bother him."

Tim was intrigued. "Can you give me a hint who he's seeing?"

Duane took another long pull from his cup and smiled. "Let's just say that his box office ranking would probably plummet if teen girls and their mothers ever knew what their heartthrob's extracurricular activities included. Others would be crowing, "I knew it! I told you so!" Duane sniggered and Tim joined in knowingly. "I know you still hate Dana, but if she's innocent we've gotta do something to get her out of jail. After all, she's my sister!"

"There isn't enough proof to keep her locked up," Duane said. "She should sue Sterling for every penny in their bank."

Chapter 22

Tim's mind was reeling as he drove off the studio lot and headed toward Mulholland Drive for the trek home. He was terrified of how he'd break the news to his mother that Dana was his half sister. This new wrench in the grinding gears of life was far too disturbing. But, he had to talk to someone about the situation. Tim picked up his cell phone and dialed Placenta's number. They agreed to meet in the parking lot of the Hollywood Bowl overlook.

It was an unusually clear afternoon. Santa Ana winds had swept away the smog. As Tim sat in his car staring out at the spectacular view of the city below, his thoughts tumbled in summersaults. "I have a sister," he said aloud. "Dana Pointer. She's famous. And we almost made out at a party!" His thoughts quickly jumped to seeing Dana on the set of *Detention Rules!* and then flashed on her wearing an orange uniform in her jail cell. "I can't let her spend another night behind bars!" He was startled back to full consciousness by knuckles rapping on the passenger side window. Placenta had arrived. Tim pushed the button to unlock the door and Placenta slipped into the bucket seat beside him.

After a half-hour of conveying his conversation with Duane, Tim pounded the steering wheel. "Polly's gotten herself into deep doo-doo again, and we're in the middle of the mess as usual," he said.

Placenta sat in silence for a few moments. Then she sighed and said, "First of all, don't mention these developments to your mother just yet. She's nervous enough about her date with Detective Archer tonight. All day long she's been rehearsing how she's going to weasel classified information from him."

Tim vehemently disagreed. "She needs a huge kick in the pants! And, I think she should have as much information as possible. The more she knows, the better prepared she'll be to ask Detective Archer the right questions."

Placenta relented with a deep sigh of resignation. "Do me one favor? Don't mention that Dana is Sedra's and your daddy's kid. That's too much information to take in."

"Why, 'cause she's always wanted a daughter?"

Placenta snorted. "You come close enough for that. Kidding of course. Sort of."

Polly sat in The Great Room tinkering at the keyboard of the Yamaha grand piano and was seriously thinking about calling her accompanist to discuss putting her old nightclub act together again. She hummed a little then started singing, "Leading lady, a leading lady, I've always wanted to be a Broadway leading lady . . ." It was a song that she had ripped off from an old Diana Ross television special and used in the "Showstoppers" medley in her own act. Polly thought about the last time she performed in a live venue. She saw herself dressed in black, with a choker of pearls. In this reverie, she was leaning against a shiny grand piano, and telling jokes in between her musical numbers. "I was so excited about seeing you all tonight that I nearly broke my leg as I rushed to the club," she remembered her between-songs patter. "Yeah, they would've had to rename the show, 'Saturday Night *Femur*!'" Burump-bump!

"Ach!" she now moaned. "That joke didn't go over the first time I used it and it still sinks like a bag of puppies down a well."

As Polly was about to launch into her old arrangement of "Edelweiss," Tim knocked on the door. "Got a sec?" he asked, walking into the room with Placenta trailing behind.

"Just barely," Polly said, closing the lid on the keyboard. "I've gotta get gussied up for the big night. Not that this is an actual real-life man meets woman, woman gets kissed, kind of date. Or is it? Placenta, would you be a dear and add those new lilac crystals to my bath? And take the tags off my new Chetta B. I'll look sensational in that red ruffled top with the black velvet pants. A little showy, but I want this to be a night the ol' Sarge will remember."

"He's a detective," Tim said and held out his hand to guide Polly to the sofa.

Polly was suddenly aware that this was a summit meeting, not just idle chitchat. She pushed away her son's outstretched hand and stood with her arms folded across her chest. "No more bad news, please!" she insisted. "Every time we're in this room together one of my nearest and dearest drops dead on a movie set. I don't want to hear about any crummy role that I may be up for by default. Those days are over. From here on out I'm only accepting roles that come *to* me, *for* me! No more cast-offs." She thought for a moment. "No pun intended."

Tim looked into his mother's eyes and said, "I don't mean to say I told you so, but Dana Pointer is not Sedra Stone's killer. I'm sure of it. And you've got to let go of your false idea about Dana's guilt."

"Give me a break," Polly said. "You know that I lost interest in Dana as a suspect ages ago. In fact, I'm going to spring the poor egomaniac from the slammer over dinner tonight."

Tim's look of disbelief encouraged Polly to explain her change of mind. "Early on my arm may have been slightly twisted by you two."

"We never . . ." Placenta protested.

"For the sake of family peace I may have gone along with the suggestion that Dana was a *possible* suspect," Polly continued. "Hell everyone who ever crossed Sedra's path represents a possible suspect with motive. But if you've been paying attention as I have to the latest developments, then you'd completely drop your obsession with finding that pathetic soon-to-be has-been guilty of such an odious crime."

Placenta made an "Mmm, mmm" sound. Polly accepted this to mean that her maid agreed that it was totally lame to keep Dana on the list of suspects.

"Actually, I'm betting on Duane or Missie or Judith or Adam as the perp," Polly continued. "After tonight with Detective Archer, I'll have a better idea of course." With a self-satisfied tone she smiled and said, "I'm getting rather good at this sleuthing thing, don't you think so too? It seems to come naturally to me. Like singing. The vibes are kicking in and I'm single-handedly paring down the list of whackos to a mere half-dozen dubious characters."

Tim said, "The list hasn't changed, Mother. You've just listed the usual suspects."

"Didn't I add the screenwriter?" Polly said, dismissing Tim's observation. "Maybe this Ben Tyler hack couldn't bear to have his perfectly awful script made more odorous by the way Sedra delivered his lines, so he done her in. It happened to Jennifer Tilly in 'Bullet's Over Broadway.'"

Placenta weighed in. "Mister Tim had a power lunch with your biggest fan today. Seems that Sedra Stone's screenplay has a character that more than resembles you," Placenta said. "Even her name . . . it's Molly Schlepper!"

"We went through this with Adam last night," Polly said waving away the very idea of Sedra having written a screenplay. "He said that the script was only a rumor. Anyway, it's impossible because Sedra was practically illiterate."

"Have you been to a movie lately?" Placenta said. "When has literacy been a prerequisite for screenwriting?"

"Seems Adam was lying," Tim said, "Duane found the text on Sedra's computer. And Adam knew the screenplay existed because his little gold-digging gopher Judith saw it, too."

"I didn't think that Sedra had the brains to work a computer," Polly sniped. "But why would Adam be untruthful with me? Why would he care if Sedra wrote a movie? What's the big deal? By the way, how am I treated in the screenplay?" Polly perked up. "That's it! Adam was trying to spare me some horrible heartache, which is why he lied. What did Duane say?"

Tim and Placenta exchanged looks. "Picture an overwrought, attention grabbing, media whore. She has an overactive sex life, which is why the lead character, who is so thinly disguised as Sedra herself, easily plucked your husbands out of Pepper Plantation in the dead of night."

Polly turned to stone. She was catatonic with disbelief.

"Here's an idea," Placenta said. "What if Adam read the script and thought it had potential as a vehicle for him to direct? He may be a lousy director, but he's no dummy. Perhaps he sensed that it was a hot property. *Citizen Kane* meets *Mommie Dearest,* and he wanted to direct it. It's just a guess, but from what I hear scripts aren't exactly flying over his backyard fence. He needs a new project to follow up *Detention Rules!*"

Polly threw up her hands. "Whatever happened to the Hollywood code of moral principles?" she said. "Stealing someone else's script. Indeed!"

Tim looked at his mother and said, "More interesting than

what's in the screenplay, is who was left on the film location the night of Sedra's death. According to Duane, the major players were all there: Missie, Elizabeth, Adam, Judith, etcetera. Only Dana and Jack were missing. So Dana couldn't have done the deed."

"Tonight, you've gotta get more details about the crime from your boyfriend," Placenta said.

Polly smiled. "He's not my boyfriend, silly."

"You'd better make him think he's your boyfriend," Placenta demanded. "You're an actor. Or so you've seduced the world into believing. Get out there and prove you deserve your reputation."

Polly put her fingertips to her forehead and whined, "Too much pressure! You're all giving me a headache. How about a little more credit for my intelligence and ability to manipulate fans? I'll handle Detective Archer. By the time he's spoon feeding me crème brûlée, I'll know more about the murder of Sedra Stone than Michael Jackson did about the consequences of combining sleepovers with Jesus Juice.

"Now, don't you all have things to do?" Polly concluded the meeting. "Placenta? My bath, please. Tim, call up Duane. He was blubbering all over the machine. Sterling canned his tushie today. Adam was right about that."

As Polly rose from her seat on the sofa and swept out of the room she ascended the stairs to her bedroom suite. Placenta harrumphed but dutifully followed behind to prep her mistress for a night on the town.

In the meantime, Tim reached for the cordless phone and pressed the menu button. He scrolled down to Duane's name and selected his home number then pressed the telephone icon to make the connection. "Guess I can delete the office number," he said as he heard the ring tone on the other end of the line. Duane picked up.

"Heya, buddy," Tim said somberly. "What's this I hear about Sterling letting you go? Jerks."

Duane made a sniffling sound, then croaked out a hard to understand series of sentences that sounded like, "They think I stole Sedra's laptop. Accused me of cheating on my time card. Said if I tried to sue them for wrongful termination that they'd bring out all my Match.com e-mails. And the websites I visited on company time using the studio's computers. That witch in HR said they have a thick file of infractions to use against me."

Tim tried to offer words of comfort. "Gosh, Duane, do you want to meet for a drink? Would it make you feel better if you came to the house to talk? How can an employer just decide you're no longer needed?"

"It's not fair," Duane sniffled again. "Jobs are tough to find. I never stole anything in my life. I'll never get another job unless I clear my name of their false charges. Hell, I know a lot about Sterling that the company wouldn't like the world to know. I just might have to call up 'Access Hollywood.' Yeah, that's what I'll do. And Liz Smith, too."

Tim reiterated his offer to take Duane out for a drink and to talk about the situation. "Rest for a couple of hours," he said. "Give me your address and I'll be over at six. Polly's going out for the evening, so I've got some time." When he'd collected the information, Tim hung up the phone and went to his computer to print out driving instructions to the West Hollywood street on which Duane lived.

In a short while the house was suddenly in turmoil as Placenta came rushing in to The Great Room, excitedly calling, "Mister Tim! Detective Archer's car is coming through the gate! Come and greet the man, for crying out loud. Polly'll make her appearance as soon as you've plied him with a drink."

Tim rushed to the foyer, checked his hair in the hall mirror, and waited for the doorbell. He looked at Placenta who was wringing her hands in anticipation. "Shouldn't you be the one to let him in?" Tim asked. "You know how Polly likes people to get the impression that she's got a staff of ob-sequious toadies."

Placenta folded her arms across her chest. "Your al-lowance is bigger than my salary. You can play the boot-licker for once."

The doorbell rang. Placenta ducked out of sight.

"One, one-thousand. Two, one-thousand," Tim began counting and maintaining the appearance that whoever was at the door was of little consequence. "Nine, one-thousand. Ten." He stomped his feet for the sound effects of one who had just arrived at this place, then he opened the door. "De-tective Archer!" Tim said with a burst of false enthusiasm. Both men simultaneously offered a hand to shake. "Great to see you again. Come on in. You were in the paper last night. You're becoming famous!" Tim didn't know what else to say other than, "Please come this way." He cocked his head and led Detective Archer into Pepper Plantation. "How about a drink?"

As Tim escorted the detective into The Great Room, Pla-centa arrived with a tray of champagne flutes. "Just in time! You remember Placenta? Of course, you interrogated, um, *interviewed* her about Sedra Stone's death. By the way, you're doing a heck of a job on the case."

Tim then began an exhausting and hopefully surreptitious cross-examination of his own. The words tumbled out in a near stream of conscious chain. "With all due respect, I have a hunch you've got the wrong person in jail . . . Dana Pointer, I mean . . . she's hardly the killer type . . . absolutely not a killer . . . oh, I know witnesses heard a screaming match be-tween them the night of the murder . . . and Sedra had some of Dana's tresses clutched in her hand as if there was a strug-gle, and they seemed to hate each other, but then who didn't hate Sedra . . . it all looks horrible for Dana, but . . ."

At that moment, the scent of Chanel No. 5 filled the air, and all eyes simultaneously turned to see Polly Pepper, standing in the doorway, and looking every inch a *Vogue* cover model for still attractive over-the-hill TV stars. Tim and Detective Archer both stood up to give the lady the attention she deserved, and both were speechless with admiration.

Polly floated into the room and went directly to Detective Archer. She leaned in to receive a kiss to her cheek and said, "What did I do to deserve such a handsome escort for the evening?"

Detective Archer blushed and simply said, "You look awesome, Miss Pepper."

In that moment, Polly wanted to scream, "Lord, not another 'Miss Pepper' sycophant! I thought he was straight. Tim and his damn broken gaydar!" Instead she smiled and said, "Now detective, we promised that you'd call me Polly."

"And I'm just Randy," Archer smiled back. "Shall we head out? Traffic's a bear and we'll just about make our reservation."

"I'm all yours," Polly chirped, not letting on that she was desperate for one of the champagnes on Placenta's tray, and that she made it a general rule to never be on time for a dinner reservation. She liked the celebrity perk of getting the best table in the house whenever it was convenient for *her*. "Would you drive?" she asked, handing Detective Archer the keys to her Rolls. When he appeared a little flustered she said, "Never driven a Park Ward Rolls-Royce?" she said in response to his look of trepidation. "Trust me, it's just a Ford—with a ridiculous sticker price."

And then they were off.

Chapter 23

As Detective Archer exchanged the Rolls for a valet ticket and followed three paces behind Polly up the steps of The Ivy, he felt as uncomfortable as he did during his recurring nightmare of being naked in a public place. He asked himself if he was simply paranoid, or had indeed every diner on the restaurant's patio turned to stare at Polly Pepper, and to judge her escort.

"Adorable Kevin!" Polly cooed to the waiter who warmly greeted them. "Don't they ever give you a night off? Lucky for me of course, but I worry about your love life. FYI," she whispered, "Tim isn't dating anyone—that I know of." She smiled and accepted a quick hug from her favorite member of the waitstaff. "Would you be an absolute dream and seat us inside?" Polly said. "This is more than a tête-à-tête, and we've got a potentially gargantuan deal to discuss," she smiled, intimating that she was at The Ivy for business rather than recreation.

"Way ahead of you, Miss Pepper," Kevin said, as he led the way to what he knew was Polly's favorite table. "I just booted out Sarah Jessica. And, as you can see, the Veuve's chilling. If you're ready, may I pop the cork?" he said, nodding to the bottle already in an ice bucket beside the table.

"I've been ready since New Year's!" Polly feigned a reprimand as she accepted the chair that Kevin had pulled out for her. "It's well past Lush Hour and this darling man was afraid we'd miss our reservation if we dallied over a quickie. Drinkie, that is. Oh, and I'm forgetting my manners. Kevin do you know Randy Archer?" she said introducing the detective as though the paths of the waiter and police detective surely must have intersected at one time or another.

Randy and Kevin exchanged greetings and shook hands. Kevin uncorked the bottle, filled two flutes half-way, and asked, "A basket of calamari to start?"

"This is why Kevin gets the big tips," Polly said loudly enough for other diners in the room to hear her. "He remembers the tiniest details of all his guests' culinary fetishes. Oh, did that sound too lascivious, dear? So sorry," Polly said, smiling playfully at Kevin.

Polly took her first sip of champagne. "Yum!" she declared. "Calamari, of course! That is if Randy will share. Yes?" She looked at her date who nodded in agreement but secretly couldn't imagine eating squid any more than he'd ever allow a calf's pancreas to pass over his lips.

"Back in a jiff," Kevin said and retreated to the kitchen to get Polly's order started.

Polly looked at Randy and smiled. "It was very nice of you to suggest dinner," she said, blinking like a coquette and staring into the detective's brown eyes. "I confess," she looked down for effect, "that I've been quite eager to spend a little time with you. I'm absolutely fascinated by police work. I never miss any of the plethora of "CSI" shows. You must tell me every detail of your exciting career in law enforcement. Is it as exciting as we see in the movies?" From this moment on, as predicted, Detective Archer was putty in Polly's hands.

The warm summer afternoon had dissolved into a cool but pleasant evening as Polly gave Randy Archer a thumb-nail biographical sketch of the ups and downs of her own career. That he claimed never to have seen her legendary musical variety television show and did not know the lyrics to her hit record "For New Kate" made her feel certain that he wasn't dining out with her just for the sport of dating a star and adding another notch to his list of conquests. On one hand she was thrilled that he was a potential paramour, but on the other hand—the one that tightly clutched her ego—she was slightly perturbed that she had to explain all that she had accomplished in show business and who was someone named Martha Raye, whom she credited with being her inspiration.

In a short while Kevin was dividing the dregs of the first bottle of champagne between Polly and Randy, collecting their appetizer plates, and bringing a second bottle to the table along with their entrees. That's when Polly began to ramp up her charm and furtively skim the surface of the Sedra Stone murder case.

Polly tilted a flute to her lips with one hand and reached out and placed the other hand on Randy's. "It's time that I confessed something to you," she said. "Something dreadful. I hope that you won't think less of me as a result of my stupidity and lack of cleverness," Polly said, preparing to launch into the real purpose for their date. "I've done some-thing so appalling . . . so untenable . . ."

Randy gave a reassuring smile and said, "I'm not going to have to arrest you, am I?"

Polly looked at him and hoped he was joking. With Randy's dry sense of humor, she wasn't completely certain how to read him. "If I'm ever arrested, you're just the man I'd want to do the job, you gentle beast, you," she said, trust-ing that her famous seductive charm would disarm him. "What I have to say is that I've changed my mind about

Dana Pointer being the assassin. She couldn't have knocked off Sedra Stone."

Detective Archer nodded his head. "Yeah, that seems to be the general consensus. Tim said the same thing. But honestly, I'd already come to that conclusion. In fact, Dana was released this afternoon."

Polly made a show of enormous gratitude and raised her glass to the detective. "Oh, you smart man! What made you change your mind about her lack of guilt? Was it the fact that she wasn't even on the location set when Sedra was killed? Or do you have evidence pinning the crime on Missie? Or Adam? Or his flirty squeeze, Judith? Or that Boy Scout masquerading as a studio security guard? I wouldn't be surprised if the killer was the screenwriter."

Detective Archer shook his head and took a small sip from his champagne flute. "I was never completely sold on Dana Pointer's guilt anyway. But I had to take someone into custody, if only to be able to work on a high-profile Hollywood scandal and prove to *The Peeper* that with all our sophisticated techniques, the LAPD is damn serious about finding the killers of movie stars. You actually made a reasonable case for her guilt. Or at least reasonable enough to convince the judge who issued the warrant—who said that Polly Pepper's word was good enough for him. Oh, and he asked me to bring him back an autographed eight by ten."

Polly clasped her hands together and said, "Dear Lord, forgive me for my false judgment."

Detective Archer waved away Polly's apology. "Hell, we're always making false arrests. It's good for the community. Makes the law-abiding citizens aware that if they hang out with the wrong sorts, their lives and careers could be ruined in an instant."

Polly was equally dismissive of Dana's plight. "She'll be fine in a few years. The public tends to forget arrests as long as the offender is attractive. I wouldn't worry about that kid. But let's put on our thinking caps about this case. If we were writing a made-for-television movie, would our killer be Ted Danson, Barbara Eden in a comeback role, Joe Pesci in another comeback role, Goldie Hawn in a career-saving role, or Mark Harmon cast against type. Let's go back to Ted. I never trusted those deep set eyes of his."

Polly seductively touched her date's hand once again. "Was I ever a suspect?"

Detective Archer swallowed hard. "As a matter of fact, when it was rumored that Sedra Stone had written a screenplay, and that all the characters were thinly veiled depictions of real-life celebrities, and that you were one of the more prominent, and not well represented, then yeah, a few signs pointed to Pepper Plantation. But we can't find any script."

Polly was flabbergasted. "Maybe," she said, "if it was incendiary as you suggest, that might be motive enough for someone to get rid of both the script and its author."

Archer shrugged his shoulders as he fed himself the last of his crab cakes. "If we find it, I'll wager it leads to the killer."

When the bill arrived, Polly placed her hand over the plate on which the check rested. "My treat," she insisted. "No arguments, please. I'm rich and famous. Next time we can go someplace that you suggest."

Detective Archer smiled and looked deep into Polly's eyes.

"What?" she asked, trying to read his thoughts.

Randy tilted his head slightly and grinned. His eyes appeared to be filming Polly for future reference. "I like you. That's all," he said. "You're fun, and generous, and quite nice. Everybody said you would be."

Polly smiled back and nodded her head. "I like you, too, Randy. Why aren't you already taken by some gorgeous meter maid half my age?"

Randy inhaled. "All the usual excuses," he said. "Married to my job. Selfish with my free time. Genital herpes."

Polly's eyes grew wide with shock.

"Kidding!" Randy quickly laughed. "Maybe I'm too much of a kidder for anyone to take me seriously."

Polly laughed too. "I've been accused of the same thing. But at least I made a fortune getting the last laugh. And speaking of the last laugh, if Sedra Stone were alive today and saw us together, she'd be so jealous that she'd try her damndest to get you to go out with her." Polly raised her glass. "I'm certainly not laughing at Sedra's terrible misfortune, but I am laughing on the inside as I think about how she tried to ruin my life. Yet, I'm still here and she's not. So who do you think pushed her into the empty pool?"

Detective Archer suggested they take a drive to his office where they could talk more openly.

"You're not taking me in for interrogation, are you?" Polly said, wide-eyed with sudden excitement.

"Not unless you want me to," he said, impishly, making her quiver with excitement. "I thought we could go over evidence."

"You show me yours, and I'll show you mine, eh?"

Detective Archer smiled mischievously as he pushed back his chair then helped Polly out from behind the table. "We could just as easily discuss the case at my apartment."

"I'll ask Kevin to put a bottle of Veuve into a doggie bag," Polly said then corralled her waiter who raised an eyebrow along with a dimpled smile, and said he'd meet her at her car. As Polly led the way out of the restaurant she was forced by etiquette to stop at various tables and accept air kisses and bits of chatter from various friends and acquaintances. "I've got all your episodes on DVD," she said to Jerry Seinfeld. "Ellen, I watch you every afternoon. Keep dancing, girl. Wish I had your rhythm!"

But just as she reached the steps of the patio and was about to accept Detective Archer's hand to guide her to the sidewalk, she automatically exclaimed, "Missie! Adam! J. J.! Sweethearts," before realizing she was face to face with Missie Miller seated with their mutual agent, and Adam Berg. "Working out the details of getting us all back to *Detention*?" she said. "I'm ready when you are. Oh, but I forgot about your new project," she said, looking at Missie. "You start filming on Monday, right?"

Missie forced a smile, but she didn't say a word. No one at the table was particularly effusive in their greeting of Polly. "Well, then, I'm off," Polly faked a warm smile. "My best to your mother," she looked first to Missie. "And say hello to Judith," she blew a kiss to Adam. "Love to Jackie," she addressed J. J. "Vickie? Whatever."

By the time Polly's Rolls was delivered curbside, Kevin her waiter had arrived with a bottle of champagne protectively covered in bubble wrap and placed in a colorful party bag. As he placed the handles over Polly's fingers he asked, "Want me to mess with their food?"

Polly smiled and affectionately touched Kevin's cheek. "Don't get into trouble on my account," she said. "But if you happen to overhear what they're scheming, I'd love a report."

"Done," Kevin smiled and returned to the patio dining area. As Detective Archer began to ease the Rolls away from the curb and into traffic, Polly watched as Kevin started to clear away the plates at Missie's table. Then they were down to Third Street and turning left.

Detective Archer was the first to break the silence and to wonder aloud what two of the other suspects in his investigation were doing together. "Who was the third wheel?" he asked.

"My idiot agent, J. J. Norton. He's Missie's agent, too. And he represented Sedra," Polly clicked off the list. "What's weird is that Adam is still speaking to Missie. Now that Dana's out of jail, production can resume on our film, but Missie's taking off to do another project. You'd think that Adam would be so furious that he'd not only be ready to kill her but he would be bringing her up on SAG union charges."

"I hear that his career isn't going too well, so maybe he's trying to play nice," Detective Archer said. "Maybe they're all having dinner to try to convince Missie to change her mind."

"That's unlikely," Polly said. "We had Missie and her mother to dinner the other night. That old woman runs the show. She's determined that her little girl will become a star. Trust me, Elizabeth makes Mama Rose look like The Flying Nun."

As the car glided to Crescent Heights Boulevard, Detective Archer make a left hand turn and drove north to Fountain Avenue. "I'm a little embarrassed to have you see my place," he said, making excuses for the condition of his living arrangement. "It's just a small condo. But there's a nice view of the city."

With those words, Polly set the exchange between Missie and Adam and J. J. to the back of her mind. All she could see was the man driving her car, and her thoughts turned toward touching what she hoped was a firm hairy body.

Chapter 24

The marine layer had inched its way inland overnight from the ocean and settled deep into the Los Angeles Basin. Although the morning sky was overcast, Polly couldn't have felt any sunnier had she been strolling on a romantic beach in Tahiti.

After a night of easy conversation with Detective Archer, as well as a serious discussion about the Sedra Stone murder investigation, followed by long-overdue intimacy with a man to whom she was genuinely attracted, Polly felt younger and more optimistic than she had in ages. "Lip-to-lip combat can work miracles on a girl's self-esteem," she cooed as she stepped from the shower stall and allowed herself to be enfolded in a bath towel gallantly held out for her by Detective Archer.

"You'd be a star in any man's life," Archer whispered as he kissed Polly's wet shoulder.

After dressing and consuming a light breakfast of toaster waffles and four Advil tablets chased with a cup of Folgers's instant coffee crystals, Polly promised to reserve the following Saturday for another dinner date with Randy. She kissed her host/lover and reluctantly said good-bye. She then stepped into her Rolls, and in a trance, drove herself home to Bel Air.

It was nearly ten o'clock when Polly entered the estate grounds and parked her car. When she unlocked the front doors and walked through her quiet home, she found Tim and Placenta at the poolside patio table each reading a script and arguing about the way in which familiar people and events—themselves included—were portrayed in the screen drama. They both looked up and jostled for her immediate and undivided attention. Polly joined them and settled herself into her usual chair.

Tim won. "I hate to bring you down so quickly," Tim said. "You're obviously on a sex high. But . . ."

"Then don't," Polly interrupted. "Pretend I'm not here. Pretend it's not quite midnight and I'm still wearing glass slippers and a Do Not Disturb sign instead of my pearls. Let me first change my clothes, then I'll return to you and reality, and my everyday monotony."

"This is urgent," Tim said. "Read this. Duane printed out a couple of copies of Sedra's so-called lost script." He held up his copy. "It's called *DNA*, and it's a damn good screenplay. We're all characters in the story! If Adam Berg chose to kill for a script, I don't blame him for this one. Who would have guessed that Sedra Stone could write such a compelling movie?"

"Enough!" Polly begged. "Now that Dana's been released from jail—I presume you've heard that news—we no longer have to be involved in this true-crime drama. We can all go back to our usual activities of dissing Bea Arthur and Teri Hatcher. Leave the crime solving to our overcompensated men in Beverly Hills blue. Speaking of our fine public servants, you haven't asked about my date. Thanks for being so supportive," she said in a derisive tone.

"Of course we're dying to hear all about your night on the town—and your dessert between the sheets," Tim feigned remorse for his lack of giddy teenagerlike curiosity about his mother's love life. "Would you believe that we wanted you to enjoy your ecstasy in private for a while?"

"Since when do we not reveal every juicy detail of each other's sex dates?" Polly said. "We're supposed to be a liberal Left Coast progressive family unit. The very model of everything Focus on the Family wants to throw into the lake of fire—or worse: an eternity of having to watch reruns of 'Highway to Heaven.' I endure all the nauseating chatter about the Mr. Rights you both drag in from God knows where every now and then. But I go five years without so much as a tongue in my ear, and when I finally reel in a decent size fish, I don't even get a 'way to go' thumbs up from either of you!"

Placenta picked up her coffee mug and took a tentative sip. "Okay, Cleopatra. We're all ears," she said. "Did he wear a condom?"

Polly skewered them both with a look. "We used an entire box!" she snapped; however, she quickly eased up on her displeasure. "As a matter of fact," she said, "we had a marvelous time together. Dinner was divine. After I checked in to tell you that I hadn't been abducted, but wouldn't be home, things heated up for Randy and me. That's Detective Archer, to you." Polly went on to provide more detail than necessary about her night of adventurous lovemaking. "Hell, I almost got snatched up in the rapture and shook hands with Jesus," she sighed. "Hallelujah and Amen!

"The only dissonant note came when Randy said that they're closing in on Sedra's killer," Polly continued. "That's a good thing, of course. But, although he wouldn't tell me who they're about to finger, I got the impression it was Duane. It doesn't make sense to me."

"It's absolutely not Duane!" Tim charged. "I had drinks with Duane last night. In fact, he's fairly sure it was Adam Berg who killed Sedra."

"Why on earth would Adam kill off one of his actors?" Polly said as if the idea was absurd. "He's a limited talent who needs all the help he can get making this movie. Scorsese, he's not!"

"Precisely the point!" Tim said. "Here's what Duane thinks: Wunderkind choreographer slash rap music video director gets a shot at a Hollywood feature film. But he finds he's not the talent everybody expected. He's been handed full rein of a big movie and it's gone way over budget and dragged miles behind schedule. The guy's drowning in career disaster and he desperately needs a lifesaver. Then, unexpectedly, the showbiz Gods throw him a rope when he happens to come across a highly marketable screenplay. And, he's got the perfect actress for the lead role. Think Missie Miller. But there's a catch. The screenwriter has already precast herself in the film. Think Sedra Stone. She insists on playing the main character. After all, it's a movie she apparently wrote herself."

Once again Tim held up his copy of the script, which claimed in bold typeface: A SCREENPLAY BY SEDRA STONE.

Polly snorted. "Oh, brother. You've got a wilder imagination than Mary Higgins Clark enjoying an LSD aromatherapy," she said.

Placenta spoke up. "If we're counting killers, I'm putting my money on Judith or the *real* screenwriter—'cause I don't believe for one moment that Sedra Stone had the mental capacity to write a thank you note all by herself, let alone a screenplay as stunning as this one. If Duane is right about Adam's culpability, I'll bet it was Judith who told Adam about the screenplay in the first place. I mean the other night at dinner she did say that she saw the script on Sedra's computer. Duane corroborated that. Perhaps Judith realized that if Adam made this sure-fire hit, he'd owe her big time, and she'd finally have the Sugar Daddy she's been trawling for. So let's suppose that *Judith* bumped off Sedra to insure that Adam got his next project before his lack of talent and the disaster of *Detention Rules!* was discovered and ended up in the pages of *Rolling Stone* or *Premiere*."

Polly slapped her knee and pretended that she hadn't heard a funnier joke since Rodney Dangerfield's last benefit at the Actors and Others for Animals annual charity banquet. "Where's the laugh track to this farce?" Polly cracked. "Your ideas are positively insane. If you tell me that you guys write those lame sitcoms on CBS to earn extra income, I'll totally believe it."

Tim stood up and began to pace the patio. "I think that Placenta's onto something," he said, moving to the bar to mix Polly a Bloody Mary. "What if Sedra didn't write the screenplay? I agree she couldn't write a check let alone a movie. This may seem like a farfetched guess, but what if . . . what if someone—let's say Ben Tyler 'cause I can't think of another screenwriter at the moment—wrote the script, and gave a disk copy to Sedra to read on her computer. She liked it and told him she'd do his film, but only if she got her name on it as a credited co-writer. Ben's no different than everyone else in Hollywood, desperate to succeed. Especially after his crappy *Detention Rules!* so he agrees to Sedra's extortion demands. In the meantime, Sedra goes into the computer and erases Ben's name from the script altogether."

"That's absurd!" Polly wailed. "She'd know that she could never get away with stealing intellectual property."

Placenta added to the mystery. "Then along come Duane and Judith. They read the script in Sedra's trailer and think it's her solo work. Judith tells Adam, who then approaches Sedra and asks to read the completed screenplay. She gives him a printout, which the real writer eventually sees and is psychologically destroyed to find his name is missing from the title page. Sedra's an easy target for a hit man—what with so many enemies—so Judith, along with the screenwriter, gets one of Adam's rap stars' entourage to send Sedra to her next life."

Tim said, "The screenwriter—Ben, or whoever—can't come forward and scream 'thief' because he'd be the logical primary suspect in Sedra's murder. He'd be seen as just another disgruntled writer who discovers that someone plagiarized his work."

Tim was wild-eyed with melodrama. "For Adam then to come along and usurp Sedra's name after she eliminated someone else's—well it's ironic and almost a perfect crime for Adam."

"There's no such thing as a perfect crime," Polly poohpoohed the scenario. "Everybody pays the piper eventually. Chickens come home to roost."

"Every crime is perfect until someone gets caught," Placenta agreed with Tim. "This one could have worked, if it wasn't for . . ."

Tim set Polly's Bloody Mary before his mother on the glass tabletop. "If it wasn't for what? I'm stumped."

"I haven't figured out the next step," Placenta said and then turned her attention to Polly. "First a wee drink, then a lovely soak in the tub. Then you've gotta read this script! If you don't play the role of Molly—which has you written in invisible ink all the way through it—then Laura Linney or Meryl Streep will grab it. And face it, they're better actors than you so you've gotta book this one fast. This script has Miramax, Merchant Ivory, Fox Searchlight, and Lion's Gate written all over it! Spacey should direct."

Polly set her Bloody Mary aside without taking a sip, a gesture not lost on either Tim or Placenta. "Too many flaws in your cockamamie theories," she said with a dismissive wave of her hand. "You suggest that Sedra took the original screenwriter's name off the script. For what purpose? Why would she do such a thing? To see how her name looked on a title page? No, she's seen her name on the big screen! To dupe others into thinking she's a writer? No. She used to get co-writing credit on 'Monarchy.' If she so much as contributed one line to the week's episode, her name went on the crawl. Next you'll be suggesting it wasn't an act of malice, but rather to give the living a clue into her death. As if she knew someone wanted her dead and this is her way of communicating from the grave!

"Then you'd have us believe that after Sedra's convenient demise, Adam took *her* name off the script, the easier to claim credit all to himself," Polly continued. "But don't you see, Sedra's death removes any obstacle for the real screenwriter—if there is another—to claim the work as his own. Sedra's out of the way and he now has a case against Adam. It's like money laundering. In this case, the writer is no longer linked to Sedra, so it's a simple matter of siccing the WGA on Adam. In all likelihood the script was registered with the Writers Guild anyway. And since Adam has a zero track record as a writer, they won't even get to an arbitration. He'd be busted."

Tim and Placenta thought about Polly's surprisingly cogent analytical skills. They looked at each other and telegraphed agreement with Polly's assessment.

"Not so fast," Tim suddenly said. "Sedra would *have* to be the sole author of *DNA* because all the characters are based on real people she knew and worked with, including you," Tim challenged. "It's a guess, but that screenwriter guy, Ben, wouldn't have known Sedra's history, or yours for that matter. So he's probably not part of the equation. Did you notice how young he is? I'll wager that not only doesn't he shave yet, but he also doesn't even remember a world in which Cher's first and middle names were Sonny And. Therefore, I wouldn't be surprised—although it pains me to say this, Mommie Dearest—that he probably never even heard of Sedra Stone, 'Monarchy,' or 'The Polly Pepper Playhouse.' Stupid though he would be, of course."

"Of course," Polly agreed. "But everything can be researched on the Internet. Google me and you'll find my cholesterol count. Anyone could have written about Sedra and her peccadilloes without ever doing an honest-to-God interview."

"But who would spend so much time writing a spec bio script?" Tim said. "Sedra's life may have had its interesting chapters, but she was never a big enough star to warrant a movie about her life." Tim paused. "Only a fan would take the time to write a movie about Sedra Stone and her nemesis Polly Pepper," he said. "And the fan is . . ." Tim caught himself midthought.

"Duane's a walking encyclopedia about *Polly's* life," Placenta said, patting an understanding hand on his forearm. "Polly is his idol. He insists that he had no interest whatsoever in Sedra Stone."

"Maybe that was to throw us off track," Polly said. "Could Duane really be the writer *and* the killer?" she mused.

Placenta's lack of a response said that she was thinking the same thing.

"I refuse to consider the possibility," Tim said. "What about Missie Miller? The part that Sedra would have played in her movie is really meant for a much younger actress. Missie's perfect for the part. And playing it would alter her goodie-goodie image. Working against type is what gets Oscar notice. Think of Heath Ledger in *Brokeback Mountain*."

"Here's an idea," Placenta offered. "Perhaps Missie signed to do Adam's production of *DNA*. Suppose she and Adam knew what a piece of crapola picture *Detention* was and they were stuck with it on their resumes. They might kill to get out of doing that film. Maybe they *did* kill. Maybe Trixie

Wilder was a victim of a crime, too, rather than just old age. Perhaps they figured the *Detention Rules!* production would be shut down if a cast member died under suspicious circumstances and they'd be able to escape the career-wrecking reviews that were sure to follow. I can only imagine what Joel Siegel would have said. They didn't count on a dumb coroner who pronounced Trixie's death natural. Too soon everyone returned to work."

"Production resumes and they're more desperate than ever because Trixie's replacement is a terror," Polly said.

Tim added, "But then a silver lining appears in the form of *DNA*. Adam and Missie know that film could be a hit. But they need Sedra out of the way because supposedly she's the writer and she won't let anyone else be the star. Another on-set death would surely shut down production indefinitely. It's a simple matter of killing two birds with one stone. Or one Stone being killed by two birds."

"By eliminating Sedra, it paves the way for Missie to get the role, and for Adam to get 'written and directed by' credit," Placenta said.

Polly thought for a moment. "This is so preposterous that I'm starting to think you two may have a brilliant idea after all," she said. "Here's a bit of a curiosity. I saw Missie and Adam and J. J. at The Ivy last night. I even mentioned to Missie that I thought it odd that she wasn't in New York yet, since she's supposed to start a film project the day after tomorrow. She ignored my comment."

"The plot thickens," Tim said stroking his chin. "I've got a proposal."

"It'll have to wait until after my bath," Polly said, tired of playing V. I. Warshawski. She rose from her chair and snatched up her Bloody Mary. She took a long pull. "Your bizarre-o theories have made me dizzy and exhausted."

"You'll like this idea. I promise," Tim declared. "You're throwing a party."

Polly smiled for the first time since waking up next to Detective Archer that morning. "What are we celebrating? New love?" she asked. "Randy and I have only had one date. I don't want to jinx the affair by introducing him to all the eccentrics in our lives."

Tim huffed. "He'll fit in perfectly because the theme is Jail House Rocks!" he said. "Or rather, being released from the big house. We'll bill it as a Welcome Back to Freedom party for Dana. She'll be our guest of honor, and we'll invite the cast and crew from *Detention Rules!* as well as all the big names from the police blotter. Robert Blake, of course. Macaulay Culkin, Nick Nolte, Kim Delaney, Vince Vaughn, Tonya Harding, Paul Reubens. Do you think your new salami could spring a Menendez—doesn't matter which one—just for the evening? My God, Hollywood is such a mess that we need a bigger estate to hold all the cons!"

"Is that just a wee bit crass?" Placenta shook her head trying to imagine Pepper Plantation being turned into a lockdown cellblock.

"You don't get it," Tim said. "We're bringing all the possible killers on our list together. Like a real-life game of 'Clue.' But here's our spin. In our version we'll put on a little staged reading. Can't have a real Hollywood party without entertainment. This will be the world premiere, opening night, cold reading of *DNA*, written by Sedra Stone—as performed by the Off-Off-Off-Broadway troupe, *The Usual Suspects Ensemble*."

Polly looked at Tim as if he'd lost his mind. "Dear, for the first time ever, I think one of your party ideas sucks. *Major* sucks. What would anyone trying to solve a murder mystery learn by having a group of Hollywood misfits read Sedra's screenplay aloud in front of their peers?"

"I'm not completely sure, but I'm dying to find out," Tim said. "Here's our cast of stars . . . no supporting players: Dana Pointer, Missie Miller, Missie's mother, Adam Berg, Jack

Wesley, Duane Dunham, Judith, Ben Tyler, and we'll get that stand-in Lauren Gaul to read the part of Sedra since they look alike. All of this in front of your police detective," Tim smiled evilly. "Just go read the script," he said practically shoving Polly into the house. "I don't want to give away all the surprises, but here's a big ol' teaser: Dana Pointer is Sedra Stone's love child. I have a sister. Now see if you can soak in a tub!"

Polly drained her glass and pushed it into Tim's hands and said, "Make it a double."

Chapter 25

The bell tone from the intercom at the front gate sounded and Placenta moved from her baking chores to the speaker next to the kitchen door. "Who the hell . . . ?" she asked herself, as she looked at the clock. It was 11:15. She pressed the speaker button and changed her voice to a honeyed, "Good morning. May I help you?"

The response was from a familiar voice. "Hi, um, this is Kevin. Kevin Cartwright. From The Ivy? Miss Pepper left her reading glasses at the restaurant last night and I thought I'd return them in person."

Placenta smiled. "Oh, heya, Kevin. It's Placenta. Haven't seen you in ages. Come on in." Placenta pushed the button to release the estate gates automatically. She removed her apron, left the kitchen, and headed toward the front entrance hall. She checked her hair and make-up in the mirror before opening the door and stepping outside onto the front steps to greet Polly's favorite waiter. When his Honda Civic came to a stop next to the Rolls, he switched off the ignition and stepped out of the car.

"Those cheap old glasses?" Placenta called as Kevin approached. "You're a dear to bring them by, but Polly's got dozens more. They all look alike. She'd never have noticed one missing." When Kevin reached the steps, Placenta accepted a chaste hug hello.

Kevin smiled and looked at the leatherette eyeglass case he held in his hand. "I got the impression that Miss Pepper had more on her mind last night than whether or not she could read the menu," he said, chuckling lightly.

Placenta snorted. "Let's just say she finally scored. Do you have time to say hi to Polly yourself?"

Kevin's smile widened. As a waiter in one of the trendiest restaurants in Los Angeles, he was far from starstruck. It wasn't in his mindset to meet celebrities just for the sake of meeting them. He found most of them to be arrogant, impatient, and way too fussy for him to care much about anything more than doing his job and earning a sizable tip. But several had become more than just customers. Polly Pepper was one of them. Because he was always professional and genuinely friendly to her, she in turn, treated him with much graciousness. During the two years that Kevin had been employed at The Ivy, he and Polly had developed a mutual fondness for each other. He sincerely liked her and Tim and Placenta. And they very much liked him, too.

"Actually, there is something I'd like to tell her, if she's available," Kevin replied.

Placenta took his hand and guided him into the house. "Wait outside by the pool. I'll bring some lemonade. Tim'll be glad that you're here, too," Placenta added with a wink of her eye, as she escorted Kevin through the living room, kitchen and finally to the backyard. She pointed to the patio table. "Make yourself comfortable. They'll be out in a sec."

In only a moment, Tim was vaulting through the doorway that lead from the kitchen to the outdoors living area. "Kev!" he called out, moving toward the guest. "Polly wasn't embarrassingly provocative last night, was she?" he asked conspiratorially and with a knowing grin as he sidled up to Kevin and gave him a hug. "You're here to warn us that the town is buzzing about Polly Pepper's night on the town with a secret male admirer, right?"

Kevin smiled, first because he was glad for the hug, and because he enjoyed Tim's camaraderie. "Wait'll you see the shocking photos in *The Peeper*!" Kevin chuckled. "But hey, who can tame wild and rapacious love? And the dude she was with was sort of almost bordering on semi-attractive."

"Like you," Tim gave Kevin's shoulder a mischievous shove. "Bordering."

Kevin parried and gave Tim a slightly harder shove and stared for a long moment into Tim's eyes. He was about to say something, when their cavorting was interrupted by Polly emerging from the house, closely followed by Placenta who was bearing a tray of glasses filled with lemonade.

Dressed in a youthful outfit of blue jeans and ruffled floral V-neck blouse, Polly wore a wide smile and insinuated herself between Tim and Kevin. "You sweetest of men," she said to Kevin and planted a kiss to his cheek. "I've been looking for these glasses all day. You've saved not only my eyes, but my fashion statement!" she gushed.

Kevin obliquely looked at Placenta who rolled her eyes in a "don't believe the drama" shake of her head.

"Not a problem," Kevin assured Polly. "Service with a smile. And since you're not an ex-wife of O. J. I figured I'd be fairly safe personally returning them directly to you. Oh, and I also wanted to rat out your stingy so-called friends from Table 43 last night. To heck with ethics. A measly ten percent tip does not warrant my loyalty. You asked me to keep my ears open. I heard some stuff. I have no idea what it means, but maybe you will."

Polly gave Kevin another hug and said, "They're hardly friends, dear," she said. "The decent looking guy with the goatee was my director on a lousy piece of film I did a few days ago. Missie Miller you have the dubious pleasure of already being familiar with. And the other guy is my so-called agent. A motley crew! Let's sit."

The group settled into the heavy wrought iron chairs around the patio table. After Placenta served the glasses of lemonade, she, too, pulled out a chair and sat down. All eyes were focused on Kevin.

He began, "So after you and your date left—by the way, you guys look cute together—I hung around their table as much as possible. When I heard your name and Sedra Stone mentioned in the same sentence, I was intrigued. Anyway, they were talking softly. But, having to work outside on that busy boulevard, I've somehow developed pretty good hearing in order to understand what my customers are ordering. So this trio had no idea that I could pretty much hear their entire conversation. Better yet . . ." Kevin paused.

Polly knitted her penciled eyebrows and looked deeply into Kevin's eyes. She could tell that Kevin was embarrassed by something, but waited for him to continue the conversation on his own.

"I'm not proud of this Miss Pepper. I swear, I would never, ever do this to *you* . . . or anyone that I liked . . ."

Tim took a sip of lemonade. "We know that you're not one of those horrible waiters who feeds the tabloid papers with the gossip you overhear at work."

Kevin, too, took a sip of his lemonade. "As a matter of fact, as much as I hate that gossipmonger Tiffany Jones and her stupid 'Dirty Dishes' segment on 'The Peeper P.M.' show, where she talks about what *she* supposedly overhears at restaurants, she pays me five grand a month to keep an ear open for anything anyone might say about a certain celebrity. I can't name names because she made me sign a confidentially agreement. Let's just say he's—um, rather, *the* nongender-specific star—is sort of the biggest on the planet. Tiffany got me this incredibly expensive recorder and microphone that picks up every syllable from a conversation, even in a noisy restaurant."

Kevin removed a business card size tape recorder from his pants pocket and laid it on the table. "It's feather light, but God it picks up everything!"

Polly frowned. "Kevin. Sweetie. How on earth did you get caught up with that horrid Tiffany Jones? She's got the biggest mouth in town. She's the first to report all of the most vile and private stories of the rich and famous."

Kevin scratched the back of his neck and lowered his head. "I'm ashamed of myself," he admitted. "But on a waiter's salary, I need the bucks to live in L.A., and it's only one actor. Um, one nongender-specific *celebrity*, that is. And frankly, he . . . um, the *celebrity* . . . has never even been to The Ivy. Probably never will be. He, um, the *star*, is too famous. So I figured my chances of ever having to fink on the nongender-specific *star* were almost nil. But this dandy recording device certainly came in handy last night. After you left, Missie Miller and your director had a lot to say. And I've got it all on tape. I brought it over to give to you. As a matter of fact, your reading glasses aren't in that case. You didn't bring glasses with you last night."

Now that the conversation was suddenly about how Kevin's covert work was somehow a benefit to Polly, she changed her attitude. "Just so you know that I'm not a one hundred percent moron, I knew these weren't mine the moment I saw leatherette! Everybody knows that I'm strictly a Coach girl! But I played along. I figured you had an ulterior motive for dropping over."

"Yada, yada," Tim said. "What's on the tape that's so important?"

Placenta picked up the tape recorder. "This is smaller than a Nano!" she exclaimed. "I want one! There's so much dirt that goes on in this house. For five grand, I'm willing to sell my best material to that foul mouthed, crazy-haired, collagen bloated bimbo Tiffany! I can't stand showbiz news, but I may as well make a profit from what I know!"

Kevin looked at Placenta, and in a show of his earnestness, told her to be his guest and keep the spy equipment. "I haven't any use for it now. Let me show you how to work this thing so you don't accidentally erase what's on the tape."

"Push play and let's find out what Missie and Adam and J. J. were up to," Polly said.

"Just don't shoot the messenger," Kevin pleaded. "That Missie must have taken vocabulary lessons from David Mamet. She plays pious, but the mouth on that woman is utterly obscene. And what she says about you and Sedra and Tim and Placenta . . ."

"Placenta?" Tim said.

"Tim?" Placenta asked simultaneously.

Kevin picked up the recording device. "This is the 'play' button, he said and pushed it. Missie's voice began tumbling from the speaker.

After twenty minutes of listening to the tape, Kevin reached over and turned off the machine. "This is where it ends," he said. "They get up and make the rounds of other tables before leaving the restaurant." Kevin faced blank stares of Polly, Tim, and Placenta who were stupefied by what they'd heard. "Hard to believe, isn't it?"

Polly shook her head in despair. "As a matter of fact, it's not such a stretch, now that I see more clearly," she said. "What's hard to comprehend is that we didn't recognize all the signs sooner. I mean, the lengths that fans and social climbers and money grabbing ne'er-do-wells will go to achieve their undeserved end never fails to astound me."

Placenta's adrenaline rush from what her ears had absorbed began to fade and she realized aloud that murder has always been part of the divide between the haves and have nots.

Tim, too, finally recovered from the shock and looked at Polly. "You're right. Now it all seems so obvious . . . and downright pathetic. Are you going to call Detective Archer and share the news?"

Polly thought for a moment, then abruptly stood up. She walked to the poolside bar with her half-full lemonade glass and poured two fingers of vodka. She stirred the mixture before taking a long pull. "I think the good detective is still in trouble with the District Attorney for paying attention to my suggestion that Dana might be the killer they were after. It would be better if we let Randy come to the right conclusion by himself. He does have a healthy ego about his ability to sniff out criminals."

Polly returned to her place at the table. She took another pull from her drink and looked intently at Kevin. Then she reached out and placed her hand on his. "Can you get next Saturday off, dear? We need you to work at Pepper Plantation. Tim is organizing one of my marvelous soirees."

"I am?" Tim said.

"This is a very special event," Polly continued. "We're welcoming the entire cast and crew from that movie I was working on, *Detention Rules!*, the one on which Sedra gives her second to last performance."

"Second to last?" Tim blanched. "I know you wield a lot of clout in this town, but a resurrection is a bit much, even if you called up Oprah for help."

"Oh, Sedra will be here, alright. Well, at least a part of her . . . the dialogue and stage direction that she left behind in a screenplay called *DNA*."

Tim smiled. "Ah! So you liked my idea of giving a staged reading of her movie script," he brayed. And then he caught up to Polly's thinking and his jaw dropped. "You're smarter than the average bear!" he practically shrieked. "Sedra's script actually reveals the killer! And Kevin's cassette tape corroborates it. You're brilliant!"

Placenta smiled too. "If you're going about this the way I think you are, then you'd better warn Detective Archer to have his handcuffs ready." Placenta cackled loudly as she imagined the forthcoming party and the melee that would surely follow. "The party is one week from today!" she exclaimed. "Let's get going. There's tons to do!"

Chapter 26

The Hollywood cognoscenti know that an opportunity to visit Pepper Plantation, especially if it's for a blow-out planned by Tim Pepper, is more prestigious than being invited to wear silk PJs for dining with Hugh Hefner and his bunnies at the Playboy Mansion. With the help of the cast and crew telephone contact list that had been provided to Polly on her first day of work on *Detention Rules!*, Tim and Placenta began inviting everyone who was even remotely involved with the film to the party. The response was immediate and positive.

Pepper Plantation was decidedly not like the child-friendly Neverland Ranch. Under Tim's direction, his mother's parties never failed to offer jaded Tinseltown adults with a fantasyland of superb cuisine, a startling array of colorful martinis, and unique entertainment—give or take a hyperbaric chamber—or a troupe of dancing bears.

With only a few days in which to pull together the affair, Tim quickly settled on a theme. "I'm calling it 'The Black Cat Ball,'" he announced.

"Don't offend Bill Cosby!" Polly protested. "I don't want to be on his list. Let Wanda Sykes have all that fun!"

With a roll of his eyes Tim said, "Um, I was thinking more along the lines of Edgar Allan Poe."

Polly looked quizzical.

"Too obscure? The symbolism, I mean," Tim said, looking first to Polly, then to Placenta who shrugged her shoulders.

Over the years of having Tim around to single-handedly raise awareness of his famous mother as a great hostess, Polly had learned not to second-guess his party theme ideas. As deathly afraid as she was that Tim might become too bold in his avant-garde themes, the reality was that the more outrageous his parties became, the more celebrated and admired Polly emerged.

"How much is a kilo of catnip on the black market these days?" Polly asked facetiously as she studied Tim's presentation of how he planned to transform the house into a combination Skull and Bones hazing and Hollywood feature film casting cattle call.

Ignoring his mother's subtle attempt to put a cap on the household treasury, Tim merely continued to present his party design sketches. "We'll have the back yard tented, and a stage will be built over the pool," he said, showing his handiwork as a sketch artist. "The closed circuit large screen televisions will be strategically placed throughout the great room and in the library. The better to view the killer being apprehended."

"This could all blow up in our faces, and we'll be the laughingstock of the Beverly Hills party circuit," Polly whined. "Not to mention that Randy could be in more trouble with the D.A.'s office." Alarm filled her voice. "What if we're sued for libel, or slander, or party malpractice?"

"Failure is never a possibility at Pepper Plantation," Tim

insisted. "In fact, I think that your reputation will reach greater heights when the CNN headlines shock the world with news of how you, iconic Polly Pepper, comedienne extraordinaire, personally brought a killer to justice. Think of the publicity you'll get! And the job offers. And maybe hosting 'Saturday Night Live.'"

Polly smiled. She was easily seduced into thinking that her son's plan was almost foolproof, and that after this party she would be an even greater toast-of-the-town. Her only job was to play the gracious hostess, and allow Sedra Stone's murderer magically to appear. "You're usually right," she finally agreed. "Today, Placenta and I will run down to Kinko's and have copies of *DNA* printed and bound. One for the director—you," she said, looking at Tim, "one for me, and eight for our principal cast. I can't wait for opening night!"

It was a frantic week at Pepper Plantation. Although life at the mansion always got a little crazier before an important party, nerves this time frayed faster than sales associates at Tiffany when Dr. Laura and her entourage filled the store. Polly, Tim, and Placenta realized that for once the success of a Polly Pepper party really was a matter of life and death. They each knew that this was their one and only chance to prove who killed Sedra Stone. Their own lives, and the lives of their invited guests, could be jeopardized if anything went wrong.

Finally the big night arrived.

As valet attendants collected cars at the main gate, a contingent of hired security guards checked off names from lists on clipboards. Guests walked down the long cobbled drive, ooh-ing and ah-ing at the vast illuminated grounds, in the midst of which sat the mammoth and mythical Pepper Plantation mansion. Through her bathroom window on the second story of the house, where Polly was still making up at the time the affair was scheduled to begin, fragments of conversation drifted up to her like little bubbles.

"Must be nice . . ." a woman's voice dripped with sarcasm. Polly presumed she was referring to the house. Other comments weren't as generous or concealed. "Who'd she have to screw to get this place," said another, her voice oozing resentment. "Think the old woman needs another husband? I'll volunteer," said a male voice, laughing at his own lame joke.

Placenta stepped into the bathroom. She was dressed in a black cocktail sheath, her hair coiffed and frosted and several of Polly's diamonds were clipped to her ear lobes and pinned to a shoulder strap on her dress. She carried two flutes of champagne and handed one to Polly, who gratefully accepted the glass and took a long sip. "This is just until the exorcist gets here to cast out the unclean spirits—which, since this is Hollywood, should take like forever," Placenta said. She made the sign of the cross. "Honestly, I didn't think I was going to be this nervous. How are you holding up?"

Polly uttered a sound that was somewhere between "Don't ask," and "How the hell did we get into this mess in the first place?" She busily touched up her eyebrows with a Clinique pencil, while simultaneously examining herself in the floor to ceiling mirrored wall. The look on her face showed that she accepted what she saw: a face that bordered on attractive, but with a still killer body swathed in a dark ivory colored shirred bodice Vera Wang dress. The V-neckline and seamed bust accentuated her still great figure. The gold sequined sleeves and gathered skirt provided all the glamour expected of a star. Then she examined her nose in the lighted vanity mirror and checked her teeth for lipstick smudges.

"I must have been out of my freakin' mind to have wanted

that stupid role in *Detention Rules!*" she whined to Placenta. She knocked back the rest of her flute of champagne and set the glass on the marble-top sideboard. "If I hadn't been so desperate for the ego stroking of getting a film role, I'd be relaxed and probably hosting an intimate dinner party tonight. Instead, I'm lording over this massive variation on the theme of *The Last Supper*! I feel like I'm going to my execution. Someone certainly better face a judge after tonight, for all the work we've put into this event!"

"Now hush yourself," Placenta insisted. "We're all nervous, but we've got to act as calm as a corpse."

"That's the best analogy I've heard all day, considering the reason for this affair." The voice came from Tim who had arrived to check on the lady of the manor and to once again go over their much-rehearsed plans. "Let's get ourselves downstairs and start to mingle. Kevin's staff is hardly an appropriate substitute for the hosts."

Polly sighed in resignation to her fate. "Remind me again that I'm not a complete moron for throwing this party for a million people I don't even know." Then, as she used to do in the stage wings before facing her television audiences each week, Polly closed her eyes and passed a hand in front of her face. She changed from mask of tragedy to mask of comedy. With a brilliant smile she said, "Showtime!"

As the trio made their way out of the bedroom suite and into the second floor corridor, Tim whispered last-minute instructions. "Okay. The caterers know to keep the hors d'oeuvres circulating, but they're not to serve dinner. We don't want anyone starving, but we don't want them to eat and run before the main event either. As soon as we know that all our principals are here, I'll give the signal and we'll begin the program. Got it?" He looked at Polly for a response. "You take the microphone and make all the banal introductions. 'Dana this. Sedra that. Blah, blah, blah.' Then I'll pretend to select our cast of readers arbitrarily."

"I know we can pull this off," Placenta insisted. "Now, 'Smile Baby!'"

Polly, Tim, and Placenta linked arms and descended the Scarlett O'Hara Memorial Staircase together. When they reached the last step, they involuntarily reached for each other's hands and squeezed tight before disengaging and going off in different directions. They immersed themselves in the crowd.

Because Polly knew only a handful of the guests now milling about in her home, she went out of her way to stop at each clique and introduce herself. She accepted with sincerity every carpenter's' "Thank you for inviting us," and craft service worker's "Gosh, I've been a fan of yours ever since I was little," and production assistant's "Do you know Brad Pitt?" As Polly found herself enveloped by genuine affection, her nervousness melted away and she began to enjoy herself.

"Darling Dana!" she cooed when the quasi guest of honor arrived. "Your first time out after wallowing in jail should be with friends," she said as if Dana had just lost a spouse. "I hope this isn't too overwhelming. We just want you to feel our love."

Dana offered a weak smile of acknowledgment. Then the crowd parted for security guard Duane who wobbled through the masses and arrived at Polly's side. He hugged her too hard and then offered another bouquet of roses.

"Aren't you the sweet one," Polly said, not exactly knowing what to do with the flowers. "Can you hand them over to one of the caterers to put in water? Lovely, dear. Do say hi to Dana."

"Hi."

When Missie walked in she looked every inch a rising star, seductively wearing a dress from Neiman's. Her mother, Elizabeth wore wrap-around black glasses and held onto her daughter's arm. As Polly kissed the old woman's cheek, she noticed the distinctive smell of Lithium on her breath. Polly simply smiled and said, "Lovely scent. White Diamonds?"

Judith and Adam were also arm-in-arm as they entered the house, and each planted kisses on Polly's cheek when they greeted her.

Jack Wesley wore jeans and a T-shirt with a cashmere jacket. He introduced his date as the screenwriter Ben Tyler. "I'm so impressed by your work," Polly gushed to Tyler. "*Detention* rules!" she made a joke of the title and did a MacCauly Culkin *Home Alone* fist pull-down to express her approval. "I certainly hope we get to finish the shoot soon," she said. "You're in for a treat tonight because some very talented people are going to be giving a staged reading of a brilliant new screenplay. I know you'll adore it."

At that moment, Tim sidled up to his mother, and put his hand on the small of her back. "My mother is the epitome of modesty," he said, flashing a playful smile at Jack and Ben. "But I agree. *Polly* has written a fantastic movie!"

A large fake smile crossed Ben's lips. "Awesome," he said. "She sings, dances, tells amazing jokes. Are there any limits to your talents?" he asked facetiously.

"We'll soon find out," Tim teased. He whispered into his mother's ear. "*Imetay orfay unfay*," he said in code. "Most of the principals are now in the tented theatre."

"What's up?" Ben asked. "Colonel Mustard, in the library, with the candlestick?" Polly grimaced uncomfortably. She looked at Tim with unease, then returned to Jack and Ben. "Something like that," she said. "You two must come along as well. The treat is about to unfold," she said, extricating herself from the conversation. Together with Tim, they all moved toward the Great Room, which led to the tent, which was attached to the house.

When she finally arrived at the stage she picked up a microphone that was set on a barstool. She tapped the ball of the instrument. "Testing! Testing!" she said. "Is this thing on?" she groused, looking around for confirmation. When she was assured that indeed the microphone was live and that her voice could be clearly heard, Polly went into her well-rehearsed speech.

"Welcome, everybody!" Polly squealed, and for the moment she had slipped back in time to every Friday night taping of her variety series before a live audience. "You're all so lovely and well behaved! Hi, Candice! Hi, Tom! Jane, you look fab! Divorce suits you! Susan. Sweet of you and Tim to come!"

After a few moments of smiling and waving to various people in the crowd seated before her, Polly asked, "There, now. Are we all settled? Lovely!"

"Dear friends," she said in her most endearing hostess voice, "thank you all so much for coming to my little evening of free food and booze. We're here especially to welcome back from the brink of hell the lovely and talented Dana Pointer."

Applause filled the air in the large tent. All eyes scanned the crowd looking for Dana who was found to be sitting alone in a corner sipping a whisky from a rocks glass. She looked startled and morose when her name was called, but soon surrendered and reluctantly stood up to accept the acknowledgment.

Polly drew attention back to herself. "I hear that the Beverly Hills jail system is a veritable Tower of London horror!" Polly lamented. "Am I right, honey?" She looked at Dana. "Poor baby. No Starbucks? No iPods? No copies of *The Peeper* to keep you apprised of whom Jennifer Aniston is sleeping with? You'll have to write a book!"

The crowd murmured and looked at Dana with pity.

When her guests once again faced the stage, Polly said, "Dana has returned to us safe and sound. And, as a special treat, we've got a bit of entertainment planned for the occasion."

Again, whispers circulated throughout the crowd. "Now, my darling son, Tim, the man who makes all of my parties glorious events, is going to select eight lucky guests to join me on stage to read my magnum opus to you. And the most fun part of all is that if it turns out as well as I know it will, Sterling Studios will demand to make my marvelous film. Sundance will flip. HBO will get all the Emmys. Now, who will volunteer? Don't everybody rush the stage all at the same time!" she joked.

No one raised his or her hand. Then, on cue, Tim appeared from the house and picked up a microphone of his own. "Hi, y'all," he said. "I'm Polly's *brilliant* son, Tim." He laughed and the room of now sedate guests politely groaned. "I've read this script and it's really good. I promise," he said, holding a copy high above his head. "Of course I'm slightly biased. My allowance money depends on how brown my nose gets! But I really like Hollywood mysteries," he continued. "This one is all about this actress—a diva really . . . and there's murder and plot twists and . . ."

Polly called out, "Honey, don't give away the story! You'll spoil it like Disney does in their coming attractions film trailers!"

"Not only am I brilliant at throwing parties," Tim continued, I've got a knack for casting too." Tim wended his way through the crowd. "I know exactly who should play these rich roles," he said. "Oh, hey, we've got two huge stars right in our midst. Dana Pointer and Missie Miller!" He made his way first to Dana and handed her a copy of the script. Then to Missie. "We won't take *no* for an answer," he joked good-naturedly. "Get up on that stage, you two. You'll both be playing young actresses, so you won't have to stretch at all."

As the two girls reluctantly accepted the scripts it was clear they were silently thinking, "This is one lame party!"

Tim continued, "There's a really meaty role for a strong male figure. Someone to play a film director. Let's see . . . Oh!" Tim exclaimed again as though he'd just thought of another brilliant choice. "Mother's most recent director, the handsome and talented Adam Berg! Adam, where are you?" Tim looked around and found Adam trying to make himself invisible. "Oh, you must join our troupe!" Tim pleaded as he squeezed down an aisle of seated guests to reach Adam. "You'll be brilliant, I'm certain! Oh!" Tim exclaimed again. "Your lovely girlfriend Judith would be great too! You'll do it, won't you, Judith?" Tim begged. "You're star material. I know this! You can be the girlfriend. Again, not a stretch."

Glumly, they both took copies of the screenplay proffered by Tim and headed for the stage.

Polly spoke into her microphone. "Darling," she called to Tim, "if Dana and Missie are reading, don't you think that the gorgeous and hunky Jack Wesley should be too? Sort of old home week. And Duane! Sweet Duane! You'll do anything for Polly, won't you? Of course you will! Wonderful! That's so precious. You'll be amazing in the role. I promise!"

Tim handed Duane a script. "You can play the security guard," Tim said. "That leaves, um, let's see, oh, the role of a screenwriter. Any screenwriters here?" He laughed. "I guess that's a little like asking if there are any tummy tucks present. Ha! How about Ben Tyler? Is he here? Sure. We chatted a little bit ago. Oh, Ben?" he sang. "Where are you mister sexy and talented screenwriter?" He looked around and found Placenta pushing the reluctant Ben toward Tim. "Please come and read this awesome script," Tim cajoled, handing a copy of *DNA* to Ben who looked flabbergasted.

"You're forgetting the most important role, dear," Polly called from the stage.

"The role of the actress who's not supposed to be Polly Pepper, but happens to be a mirror image of someone just like you?" Tim joked.

"No, silly. That's my role. I mean the one who's not sup-posed to be Sedra Stone, but with my limited imagination I wrote a character that just happens to slightly resemble my dear dead friend."

"Right. Of course," Tim pretended to be thinking about who would be ideal to read for this role. "I need someone to play the lovely and talented Sedra Stone—but not really Sedra. I think Sedra's real-life stand-in is here. Yes? Stand-in? Are you here?" He looked around the tent until a woman finally stood up. "There you are! Your name again?" Tim asked.

"Lauren. Lauren Gaul."

"Great! Come on up. Here's your chance to finally step into Sedra's shoes. Or an actress who's supposed to be some-thing like Sedra," Tim chuckled.

By now, all of the scripts had been handed out, and the cast was assembled on the stage. Each was seated on barstools set before microphones and music stands on which to set their scripts. Polly initiated a round of applause and thanked them for being such good sports on such a special night.

Then, as if forgetting her manners she exclaimed, "I'm not being a very polite hostess! Missie Miller's lovely mother Elizabeth, who has an eyesight problem—she can't see worth a damn—should be with her daughter. Where is she?" Polly scanned the room with her hand held against her fore-head like a visor. When she spotted Elizabeth trying to walk out of the tent and back into the house she called, "Placenta! Be a dear and escort Elizabeth to the stage, would you please?"

The audience tittered at the sight of the old woman trying unsuccessfully to swat away Placenta, as if the maid was an annoying Pterodactyl. Embarrassed and caught off guard, Elizabeth wended her way through the center aisle of chairs and was helped by Polly up the three steps to the stage where she took her place next to Missie. Presently, Tim and his waiter friend Kevin carried a chair onto the stage, and set it down for Elizabeth to be seated in comfort.

Polly said, "Now that we're all comfy, I'd like everyone to please sit back and enjoy the show! Lights, please," she called out.

Chapter 27

The lights inside the tent faded to black. The room became deadly silent. Pin spotlights suddenly illuminated the stage and the eight people seated there on barstools. With the exception of Polly, they all looked confused and irritated, as though they'd been unceremoniously dumped off in the middle of Detroit after an intergalactic tour aboard the Mother Ship.

Tim stepped onto the stage and faced the audience. He began in an exuberant carnival barker voice. "Ladies and gentlemen. Welcome. And may I present to you, *DNA*, a new screenplay by Polly Pepper!" He slipped his copy of the script under an arm and led a chorus of applause, which was only politely echoed by the audience. Sensing that a pall of indifference had already settled over the crowd, Tim became less animated. "This is a story," he continued, "a tale of an irritable little girl who grew up to be an equally obstreperous and cunning adult. A shrew, if you want to put a face on her," he said. "But she wasn't your run-of-the-mill *Kiss Me Kate* all-singing, all dancing sort of shrew. She became a celebrity shrew, not unlike Ann Coulter. Her name was Sedra."

Adam Berg immediately erupted and spoke out. "With all due respect to your lovely opus," he said, sarcastically addressing Polly in an imperious tone, "I think that's rather a tad in poor taste. I mean, using your dead colleague as a joke in your screenplay. Not a good move."

Tim intercepted. "Please note. This story is a work of fiction. The writer, Polly Pepper, assures that no dead people were harmed in the writing of her screenplay."

All eyes turned to Polly for her rebuttal to Berg. "Pumpkin," she said sounding perplexed, "I haven't even gotten to the jokes yet. Tim is merely providing backstory to enable the audience to know who the players are. Still, you bring up a good point about using real names. And this is precisely the sort of constructive feedback that I need as I rewrite my masterpiece. That's the only reason, aside from wishing Dana well, that we're all here tonight—to work out the kinks, so-to-speak. Thank you, dear Adam. You're a true and talented director."

Polly looked at Tim and gave a nod of her head, signaling for him to continue his introduction.

Tim said, "For the sake of brevity, and the grumbling stomachs I hear and that need to be fed, we're going to jump forward in our story. You can use your imaginations to fill in the obligatory charity hospital breach birth, wrong-side-of-the-tracks lineage, and typical rotten childhood latch-key kid routine, along with the usual ruthless cutting a swath through bodies that are in-the-way to reach the pinnacle of professional success. We flash cut to the present year. In fact, we begin in a time not too long ago. Two weeks ago, to be exact."

Tim turned to his assembled cast on the stage. "People," he said, serving as their director, "would you please turn to page ninety-one of your scripts."

The troupe complied, albeit with obvious reluctance. Adam Berg and the others looked at the title page, exchanged questioning glances at each other, then quickly flipped through the text. Adam said, "This looks familiar."

Polly teased, "Genius is easy to recognize. I channeled Orson Welles and The Brontës."

When the players had settled down, Tim said, "Mmm. I smell HoneyBaked Ham. So let's begin because I'm starved and know you are, too. Lights!" he called out. For dramatic effect, the tent once again faded to black. In the darkness Tim's voice began reading stage directions.

"IT WAS A DARK AND STORMY NIGHT."

Everyone chuckled.

"EXTERIOR. SCHOOL CAMPUS MOVIE SET LOCATION."

Lighting slowly enveloped the stage, enabling the cast to finally see their scripts and find their dialogue.

Tim continued. "A security guard STANDS beside a dressing room TRAILER. He is eavesdropping. WHAT HE HEARS is a caustic verbal confrontation between two WOMEN. Their quarrel crescendos until we hear the sound of a plate or a vase meeting a wall and shattering into thousands of shards."

On cue, the sounds he described blasted through the audio system, startling the cast and audience alike.

Tim continued. "WHAT THE SECURITY GUARD SEES: Shadows through a curtained window. And then the door to the trailer violently flies open."

Again the audio system speakers issued exaggerated sound effects of a door opening and banging against aluminum siding.

"The security guard RETREATS just out of sight as a

FIGURE exits the trailer in haste. This FIGURE turns to the WOMAN standing in the doorway and YELLS . . ." Tim stopped and waited a beat for Dana. "Line," he called out.

"Oh, um," Dana fumbled, confused. In a monotone and bored voice she read as if she were an audio-animatronic figure from "Great Moments with Mr. Lincoln" at Disneyland.

You are a dead woman. You will pay dearly for this outrage.

As an aside to the audience, Dana added the word, "Yawn," and patted her lips with her long fingers, while glaring at the audience who chuckled in agreement.

Tim ignored the response and prompted the next actor. "Line, please."

When the stand-in Lauren Gaul realized it was her turn to read, she shifted uneasily on her barstool; however, she recited her dialogue with an ease and naturalness that displayed an innate gift for acting. With a scowl, she replied to Dana's character.

Ahem, Honey, I survived four impotent husbands, two weeks as Mrs. Strakosh in a Kansas City production of Funny Girl opposite Pia Zadora, and a year of split weeks on the road in Love Letters with Jerry Lewis. Ya think anything scares me now? Ha! I'm Teflon, baby!

Tim prompted Dana again.
Dana mumbled:

Just because you claim that we share something special between us does not mean that I owe you anything. You can be disposed of as easily as that old actress Trixie Wilder.

Adam Berg spoke out again. "Polly, really, what's the point of dragging the dead into your screenplay? If you expect this piece to be taken seriously, and to appeal to the next generation of moviegoers, I strongly recommend that you excise all references to these stars."

Polly made a notation on her script. "Eliminate names," she said aloud as she wrote down Adam's suggestion. "Thank you, dear. I'll remember that bit of professional advice. Names are easily changed on the computer program."

Tim cleared his throat and continued his narration. "CAMERA SMASH CUTS TO THE INTERIOR OF A NEIGHBORING DRESSING ROOM TRAILER. The caravan is immersed in darkness, but soft ambient lighting filtering in through a window allows us to make out the SILHOUETTES of TWO people. They are EAVESDROPPING on the disturbance next door."

Again there was a moment of silence until Missie Miller realized that she had the next line. "MISSIE GASPS," Missie said before realizing that she was reading stage direction. "Cut! Sorry," she blushed. "Um. Take two, please?" Then Missie inhaled sharply to affect an exaggerated gasp.

Mother! Did you hear that? I think that a body is about to be killed. Should I call nine-one-one? Or that handsome and talented director who is doing such a rad job on my new movie? Do you think he is straight?

With that line the audience burst into laughter.

Polly feigned slight indignation for her supposed serious work being mocked.

Eager to continue and be done with this portion of the party, Tim spoke up and said, "I'll read the role of Missie's character's mother." He cleared his throat and in a voice that clearly caricatured Elizabeth Stembourg, he said,

*Gimme a pill. One-a-dem red ones. An' a bottle-a Scotch,
too. Now, when will you get it into yer brain-dead skull
dat there ain't nothin' that spineless worm of a director—or anyone else—can do fer you dat I cain't? I'm
yer eyes an' ears in da biz, kid. As for yer career, jus'
leave everything t'me!*

Elizabeth slapped her thighs in fierce contempt at the
recognition that she was being personally mimicked. "A
young star's sight-challenged mother is not fiction!" Elizabeth nearly wept with indignation. "It's not in the least bit
amusing." Missie tried to comfort her mother by leaning
over for a hug.

Polly waved away Elizabeth's comment as a presumption.
"All writers create characters combining elements of interesting people they know, but that doesn't mean I've written
about anyone in particular," she said. "That character is
nothing like you, my dear, Elizabeth. If you want the truth,
it's really Dakota Fanning's mother. Mixed with a little of
Ginger Rogers's mother. Now, that's certainly not *you*, Elizabeth!" Polly declared triumphantly.

Again, the audience erupted into laughter. They were now
paying closer attention as if watching the behind-the-scenes
of a reality drama in trouble, rather than simply a staged
reading.

Tim resumed reading the script's exposition and brought
the audience up to the minute. He described how in the
story, an ensemble of actors was making a film about misfits
in the Spring talent show at the Manhattan School for the
Performing Arts; however, in addition to death stalking the
production—one player had died—the actors were caught
up in webs of intrigue, personal relationships, and vendettas.
And the actress who replaced the dead one now feared for
her own life.

"The police have uncovered clues implicating several

members of the cast," Tim said, and then pressed on. "Adam, it's your line," he said.

But Adam threw up his hands and railed, "I won't read this ridiculous drivel." His British accent was becoming less noticeable. "Polly, you cannot incriminate famous people by writing falsehoods about them with such . . . such . . . ignominious dialogue!"

"Ignom . . . what?" Polly said to Adam. "Oh, hon, I can tell that you're tired. You're jumping to conclusions. Who do you think I'm lambasting in my lovely screenplay?"

Adam continued his diatribe. "For one thing, you have the director character, who I presume is a reasonable facsimile of me, saying—he looked down at his script—'Now that the bitch is dead, I claim her unknown and forgotten screenplay for my own.'"

"Fiction sometimes reflects reality,' Polly said. "Why Sedra Stone herself used to pull writers off her series then take credit for their work. They seldom complained because they didn't want to jeopardize possible future work."

Adam continued. "And you make one of the leading actresses very Dana Pointer–like, and spewing such venomous prattle as, 'Someone had to do the dirty deed. Thank God that someone saved me the time and energy, and the hassle of a trial.'"

"Ach!" said Polly dismissively. "When I was writing this I was thinking of what I'd do to Nick Lachey if I were Jessica Simpson. That's all. Beautiful women get away with murder all the time!"

Adam's diatribe went on. "Polly, with all due respect, you're a comedienne, not a writer. You've wasted your time on a screenplay that purports to accuse a member of the *Detention Rule!* cast of a crime."

Polly acted dumbfounded, the way her Bedpan Bertha character responded when a patient went missing a liver when he was only supposed to be sent for chest x-rays. "But this is fiction, dear." She turned to Tim. "I think we made a grave mistake . . ."

"Damn right you've made a mistake!" Judith interrupted. "Do you think that just because you were once a star you can thinly veil me in your story? I don't deny that I'm the upwardly mobile girlfriend of a movie director, but I have had no part in helping him plan a murder the way this character is written!"

Missie Miller spoke out. "Can we please stop this farce and have dinner? I read a ton of scripts and this one is the most ridiculous black comedies of all time." She looked at Tim. "Chalk it up to the first party disaster at Pepper Plantation. Sorry hon," she said, looking pleased with herself.

At that moment, Ben Tyler stood up and in a daze he said to Polly, "Excuse me, but I know this screenplay. At least the early pages that I've skimmed through."

Polly shrugged her shoulders and smiled. "You're a smart one. I was going for a *Richard III* sort of storyline," she said.

"I don't mean to cast aspersions," Tyler said, "but I've been flipping through the early parts of the script and it's certainly not Shakespeare, it's the one that Adam Berg and Missie Miller asked me to punch up for them. This *DNA*, is their new project." Ben looked at Adam. "You start shooting this thing on Monday."

Adam and Missie looked at each other and simultaneously stood up off their barstools. They glared at the screenwriter. "Don't be an idiot!" Missie declared. "Polly's *DNA* is nothing like Sedra's *DNA*. I mean . . ." She caught herself. "Nothing like the screenplay with a Sedra-like character that Adam wrote expressly for me. There may be some similarities. I mean, how many different plot types are there. Anyway, my new role is about a famous lady opera singer, not some old half-forgotten TV star, for cryin' out loud."

Adam Berg agreed. "Not an actress. A diva!" Then he softened his defense. "But I can see how you might be confused." He tried to chuckle. "Our opera singer is sort of like Kathleen Battle. I mean a big ol' soprano who eats conductors and tenors alive, and has the girth of a whale to show for it. Sedra Stone was like that, too."

Ben didn't back down. "It's the same script, Adam. The same title, too." He looked at Polly. "Couldn't you have at least changed the name?" he said.

At that moment Duane, too, stood up. "Polly, I'm very upset," he whispered. All eyes on the stage and in the audience were now fixed on Duane. "You know that I'd do anything for you, but how can you stand there and claim that you wrote this screenplay?"

Polly pretended not to know what on earth Duane was chattering about. "Duane, darling," she tried to coo, "whatever are you suggesting of your favorite living legend?"

Duane hung his head, and then spoke in just above a whisper. "I don't blame you."

Polly walked over to Duane. In an affectionate voice, she spoke into her mic, "Don't blame me for what, dear?"

Slowly, Duane raised his head. His eyes met Polly's. Then in a stronger voice he said, "I don't blame you for wanting to take Sedra Stone's mean old screenplay and change it because she said terrible things in it about you, and about all your friends. I know, because I found this screenplay on her computer while doing a routine security check of Sedra's trailer and her laptop. She left the floppy with the script on it, in the disk drive."

The audience took a collective intake of breath.

Polly placed an affectionate hand on Duane's shoulder. She said, "Darling, have you considered that perhaps Sedra loved *my* screenplay so much that she wanted to claim it as her own, and that she deleted my name from the byline? She *was* a thief you know."

Duane thought about it for a moment. Then a look of relief and a smile crossed his face. "Of course! That's what happened! You wrote a brilliant screenplay and *she* stole it from you! You said she was famous for pilfering other writers' work."

Polly trilled. "In this town, nobody has an original idea. That's why we have so many damn remakes and sequels to *Superman*, and *King Kong* and *The Pirates of the Caribbean*. But when something original comes along like "The Dukes of Hazzard," everybody jumps on the new bandwagon. *Daily Variety* says they're going into production with a feature film version of "The Price is Right.""

Adam Berg once again attacked Polly. "Sorry to be the bearer of bad news, but Sedra wouldn't have written anything as trite and derivative as what we've had the dubious pleasure of hearing recited tonight."

Polly countered. "You're so right, Adam dear. As a matter of fact, what you're hearing tonight is new and raw text. I haven't had an opportunity to polish it. I assure you that the first ninety pages are golden!"

"Yes, they are," Ben Tyler agreed, "because I rewrote them. I saw it in its dreadful original state. The story was sensational, with terrific possibilities for drama and tears, like a Lifetime cable channel made-for-television movie. But there wasn't any structure. And the dialogue sucked, big time. It was obviously written by a rank amateur. But I fixed it."

Lauren Gaul brought her microphone to her lips and cleared her throat. "Excuse me," she began. "Guess I'm out of the loop. I don't quite follow. Tell me again who is the real author of this screenplay? Polly Pepper? Sedra Stone? Ben Tyler? Or Adam Berg?"

"Yes!" Three voices simultaneously shouted, claiming ownership.

As the audience collectively tried to fathom what was happening before their eyes, Dana Pointer slowly stood up from her barstool. With her microphone in hand, she stared out at the invited guests and waited until they recognized that she had something to say. When she had their attention, Dana said, simply, "Sedra Stone wrote *DNA*. And she got herself killed for it."

Chapter 28

In that instant, the tent was thrust into silence. Everyone waited for the next explosive words to vault from Dana Pointer's lips. Detective Archer, too, was poised along with a half dozen plainclothes policemen pretending to be caterers and wannabe actors, waiting for the right moment to make an arrest. From the invited audience, eyes furiously darted from Polly to Tim to Adam to Missie to Dana to Ben to Duane to Elizabeth and to Lauren. Those on stage viewed each other with the skepticism of good apples suspecting that a rotten one was in their midst.

Dana looked around at her colleagues and smiled evilly. "Cheaters never prosper," she said quietly into her microphone, shaking her head and chuckling with disgust. Each of the other eight people on the stage feigned affront and made nonverbal noises to express their resentment at being lumped collectively with the others. She continued, "Polly, you're as transparent as an open window. No one believes that you actually wrote *DNA*."

Polly swallowed hard and was about to interrupt, but she was cut off by Adam Berg. From across the small stage he called out, "Desperate times call for desperate measures, eh, Miss Polly Pepper?" He looked at the star with a bird-eating grin. "Aside from plagiarism, what else might you be guilty of?"

"I have air-tight alibis," Polly wailed.

Dana broke in with a small laugh. "Plagiarism?" she sniggered at Adam. "Even an illiterate would know better than to steal those lame lines." She turned to Ben. "After page ninety it's Polly Pepper all the way. Yes? It reeks of television melodrama."

Ben nodded in agreement.

For a moment, Polly smiled with satisfaction. Then she realized she was being insulted.

"She put her name on someone else's work and tried to deceive us all into thinking this was her own screenplay. Pure and simple," Adam said with a snide grin.

Dana looked at Adam, "As you'll see, nothing's 'pure and simple,' " she said. "Polly didn't try to sell the work as her own, as you did. However, the act of appropriating the literary work of another—lousy writing though it may be—and passing the material off as one's own, *is* the definition of plagiarism. And that's what you did with the script that Duane and Judith found in Sedra's laptop. Fess up. Missie's agent J. J. promised to get you a small fortune for the screenplay, didn't he? Judith, who seems to know everything, has a mouth as big as her phony tits."

Berg looked at Dana and was suddenly at a loss for words. He sputtered, "I'll see to it that you're back in the slammer by the time Leno finishes his monologue tonight."

"I'm so scared," Dana mocked Adam. "And it's Saturday. Leno's off. Even before finishing *Detention* you knew that you'd squandered what little capital you brought to Hollywood," Dana said. "You're already considered a has-been in this town. Word travels faster than a Google search. You tried to blame Missie and me for your incompetence. I know it was you and Judith who planted those stories with *The Peeper*. We weren't being difficult and unprofessional. Trust me, Missie and I were only trying to save our careers from your inept filmmaking."

Security guard Duane Dunham suddenly offered an opinion. "A murder on the set of *Detention Rules!* should have done the trick for getting you off the film—at least during the few weeks that the police conducted an investigation," he said, knowingly. "After Trixie Wilder died, you expected to be shut down for a while. Her death—her murder—was in vain because you and Missie and the rest of the cast and production team had to return to work when her death was ruled natural. Bummer."

Polly spoke up. "Ah, but then the movie gods smiled on you, Adam. It was a red letter day when Judith and Duane found Sedra's unfinished screenplay. You realized it was something surefire for you to jump right into, something that you couldn't possibly screw up, at least not once it was polished by Ben—whose name you inadvertently forgot to put on the title page. Sedra Stone's autobiographical script was the perfect vehicle to relaunch your career. The script had everything that appeals to audiences and critics alike. A maniacal star is born. The star falls. The star rises again. It's the Diana Ross story—without that last part."

Missie Miller lifted herself off her barstool and stood to face Dana. "Who are you to accuse us, and Adam in particular, of doing something not only unethical but illegal? Next you'll be trying to convince us that Sedra was killed for her lousy screenplay—one that even Ben Tyler said sucked when he first read it. Gimme a break."

"I'll do more than give you a break," Dana said. "I'll give the police a break and testify that you and Adam were working together to sabotage *Detention*. They might be interested to know that you were determined not only to extricate yourselves from that worthless movie, whatever the cost, but that

Sedra told you she'd die before letting you play the role she'd created for her long overdue return to features. I know because she told me. She told her daughter a lot of things."

Polly pretended to be floored. "Dana, dear," she said. "Are you prepared to publicly libel yourself in front of all these people, and accuse Adam and Missie of . . ."

"Can't say the word, *murder*?" Dana asked.

"Oh, I can say it," Polly said, "but I enjoy living here at Pepper Plantation, and don't want to risk being sent away to a concrete suite at *Maison de Prison* for slander."

"Which is where I'll be sending Dana her Christmas cards for the next twenty-five to life," Missie said.

The tented theatre instantly became filled with noisy arguments. The guests, and those on the stage, began pouring out their thoughts regarding the previously only whispered-about suggestion that the death of Sedra Stone may have been perpetrated by a member of the film's cast or production team. As the roil of words and accusations collided, Lauren Gaul slipped down from her barstool and stood center stage clutching her mic to her chest.

After years of kowtowing to stars, and ardently following the unwritten law on a movie set of never speaking to the on-screen talent unless they spoke first, Lauren boldly addressed Dana and Missie. She cleared her throat and demanded, "If I may. . . ." The clamor of an audience in heated discussion continued to obscure all that she said, until the sound technician, at Tim's direction, cranked up the volume on Lauren's microphone while she was in midsentence. Suddenly the audience's ears were blasted by Lauren's voice and they heard two words: "*Dead body*." All eyes and undivided attention were now focused on Lauren Gaul, who was startled by the abrupt silence that filled the tent.

She continued, "I mean. . . . I've never been on a more dysfunctional set. An Oliver Stone movie comes close, but *Detention Rules!* was a freak show. I'm as professional as they come," she said distancing herself from others. "I even dress exactly like the star for whom I'm standing in. I've heard some say it's an ego thing, or that I want to take the star's place. But trust me, I have no delusions about my career. I never made it as an actor. Big deal. Now I just do what I do, and do the job well. By making up to look like the star it expedites the process of setting the lighting for the DOP. And usually one day's the same as another. But not the day that Trixie Wilder died. Now that was a strange and surreal day."

The audience watched as she became still, and stared off into the replay in her mind's eye. "It was so weird," she repeated in a voice that sounded distracted. "It was dark outside by the time that Adam Berg got all huffy because he couldn't decide which abysmal take to make as his master shot. As I left the set and headed toward the make-up trailer, I had the sense that I was being followed. You know the feeling," she said, shivering at the memory. "It's creepy, and you think you're being watched, but you're probably being silly and paranoid because what can possibly happen on a film set with so many people around? I just wanted to get to where I was going as quickly as possible. Then, from out of nowhere someone came up behind me and pushed me to the ground. I fell on my hands and knees.

"Then the attacker straddled my back and pushed my face into the wet grass. Here's where it gets weirder. Whoever was accosting me, grabbed my hair and . . . and when my wig came off, she . . . it was definitely a woman's voice . . . said, 'Who? What the . . . ? Oh, Christ!' Then she got off of me and disappeared back into the darkness. I didn't see who it was, and she didn't seem all that big—but she was pretty strong.

Lauren loudly exhaled. "You can check with the production nurse, if you want to. I went for Band-Aids because my knees and the palms of my hands were scraped and bleeding.

I said I tripped in the dark. I was too tired and shook up to file a formal report with security. I know I should have told someone. It might have saved Trixie's life because I'm convinced it was a case of mistaken identity since I was dressed exactly as she was. Someone wanted to hurt Trixie. She died and I still think—despite what the coroner says—that she was murdered. I feel horribly guilty. Then I became Sedra Stone's stand-in . . . and I dressed exactly as she did . . . and then she was . . ." Lauren's voice trailed off but everyone knew what she was thinking.

Polly walked over to Lauren and put a comforting arm around her. "Poor baby," she cooed. "I know how you feel. I was once attacked. Yes! Joel Siegel said that my last MOW was aptly titled *Bite the Bullet* because it was what he had to do to sit through the film past the opening credits. Oh, the pain!"

As Polly enfolded Lauren in a protective motherly embrace, she tried to assure her that even had she reported the incident to the Sterling Studios security department there was no guarantee that the same attacker had killed Trixie and Sedra. "You're not responsible for the fate of others," Polly said. "Now, if it had happened again, when you were dressed as Sedra's character, then I would have certainly been freaked out and taken action," she said.

Lauren looked at Polly and the color in her face drained. She reached into her bra and withdrew a piece of paper. "A note—from Sedra's killer, maybe," she said.

Lauren continued in an embarrassed and halting voice. "The day that Sedra was murdered I was minding my own business and simply walking around the school campus between scene changes. I wasn't needed on set for an hour, so while still wearing my costume I did what I always do when there's a break. I go exploring. Gary High has some great old buildings. At one point I had to use the bathroom, so I went inside the school to find the lavatory. And that's when it happened.

"I was walking down a deserted corridor, and again I felt as though I was being watched. Of course, by now I'm sort of paranoid all the time. I heard noises . . . just sounds, like a steel locker door being opened and closed—even though school is out for summer vacation—and a custodian's floor polishing machine whirring in the distance."

Polly had returned to the comfort of her barstool seat to hear the tale as all eyes continued to focus on the stand-in, who, for the moment at least, was suddenly the star attraction.

Lauren looked at Polly and continued her story. "I found the restroom, and while I was in the stall I heard the door to the lavatory creak open. Then there was silence. Nothing. I didn't hear footsteps or anyone running the tap to wash their hands, or entering another stall. But I remember there was a scent of perfume. Something icky and pungent, like lilac. Then suddenly an arm reached under my stall door and shoved this note on the floor at my feet. I was totally startled." Lauren handed the paper to Polly and said, " Please read it."

With a look of apprehension, Polly accepted the paper and unfolded the plain white sheet and silently read what was on the page. She grimaced as she read the words. When she finished, she looked up at Lauren. "Have you talked to Detective Archer? This is evidence."

"Evidence of what?" Lauren asked. "There's no way to tell who wrote it."

"Don't you watch 'CSI?' Crime labs can detect a gazillion things; from the brand of ink used on the paper to microscopic traces of hand lotion that may have rubbed off on the page. Start watching the tube, girl!"

A hubbub ensued. "Read it to us!" the audience demanded. "Does it say who killed Sedra?"

Polly nodded her head. She cleared her throat and brought the microphone to her lips. "Okay. It's typed and addressed to Miss Sedra Stone." Polly looked at Lauren. "Someone obviously doesn't see so well. They keep mistaking you for other actors." Polly returned to the printed page. "It's double spaced. No salutation. 'This movie production has gone on way too long. We have bigger fish to fry. Time for you to go bye-bye. Leave on your own. Or in a body bag. The choice is yours.' Period. Hell they didn't even have the social etiquette to sign their name," Polly griped.

Adam Berg now looked intrigued. "Let me see, please," he said reaching out to Polly to retrieve the note. He read in silence and passed it to Judith. When she was through she handed it over to Missie. Adam said, "This doesn't mean squat." He looked at Lauren. "You could have written this yourself and then killed Sedra Stone, and made it look like your mystery person. I still wouldn't have cast you in her role."

Lauren was aghast. "Sedra Stone was an evil bitch," Lauren admitted. "She fired me from my first stand-in job. But that was twenty years ago. I hold grudges, but not that long. I'd say the people who would benefit most from Sedra being eliminated are you and Missie and Ben. Your careers were in the toilet with *Detention Rules!* You needed out of this film project and you wanted her screenplay."

Pandemonium ensued on stage and Polly stepped in to referee. "Here's what we know for sure," she began. "Duane, although you should have kept your resentment of Sedra to yourself—you're in a very large anti-fan club. Your time card shows that you punched out at ten o'clock. The police say there are witnesses who saw you drive off the location shortly thereafter. No one saw you return. So unless you changed cars and returned under a cloak of invisibility, you had nothing to do with Sedra's death, except maybe wishful thinking.

"Lauren Gaul was at Micky's in West Hollywood, having

beers with the *Detention Rules!* unit publicist," Polly said, raising an eyebrow.

"I have more fun at gay clubs than boring old cocktail lounges," Lauren said. "And you know how film publicists are," she smiled coyly. "They're like butch chorus boys."

"Oh, and Jack Wesley has an airtight alibi too," Tim said. "Sorry to do this to you, man, but unless you want to be a suspect in a murder investigation—I talked to Ben Tyler's landlady, whose apartment is right next to his. She said that she saw you arrive at his place at ten-twenty that night."

Jack simply shrugged as though he trusted Tim and that being publicly outed was a load off his mind.

"She's a nosey one, isn't she?" Tim said to Jack and Ben. "Claimed that you two made whoopee noises all night long. Then she watched you leave at six-thirty the next morning. She'll testify—in graphic detail—that you and Ben were home during the time that Sedra is believed to have been killed."

Then, from the back of the tent, Placenta's voice called out. "Oh, Mister Tim!" she said. "Mister Tim! Don't forget that Adam and Judith were seen at The Four Seasons Hotel having drinks with Whitney and Bobby at eleven o'clock. Detective Archer said so on the news the other night."

"Right. And Dana's home security company show that she punched in her secret code at the house long before the time Sedra died," Tim said. "Of course that doesn't prove that she personally punched in, but it's a good bet that she wouldn't give that code to anyone. So none of you were around the set at the time it's estimated that dear old Sedra fell in the empty pool. Who's left without an alibi for their whereabouts?"

The audience and the players on stage began to tote up the scores. Only one name was unaccounted for. Missie Miller.

Almost simultaneously, all eyes turned to the young star. "So what if I might have still been on location when Sedra died? Sure, it's possible," she said fumbling for excuses. "And okay, I admit that I wanted out of *Detention*, mostly 'cause Adam cast me in his new movie which, until tonight, I totally believed he'd written expressly for me." She turned to Adam. "Did you tell Whitney it was for her? Anyway, I wouldn't have killed anyone just to stop production. I don't care if you believe me or not. Oh, and my mother's my alibi."

Now it was Polly's turn to pressure Missie. "Hon, you're the only one here who was still in close proximity to Sedra when she got whacked. In fact, Detective Archer said that Sedra's chauffeur, in his statement to the police, claimed that he went looking for his client at midnight, and bumped into you and Elizabeth as you were running toward the parking lot."

Missie looked at Elizabeth, then squared her shoulders and raised her head. "Mother can't run. But so what if we left the location later than everybody else? Mother wasn't feeling well, so we stayed in the trailer until she felt up to traveling home."

"Can you prove that you were there the whole time?" Polly asked.

Missie sighed. "To be honest, our bathroom in that crummy trailer stopped functioning, so we had to use one of the johns in the gymnasium. We left the trailer and I had to wait a long time for Mother to finish. Okay?"

"Poor Elizabeth," Polly said. "Nothing contagious I hope. Haven't been kissing any Asian birds lately, have you?"

Elizabeth's sour expression became more so, as she deflected Polly's lame question. "I had ladies' problems," she said. "Not that it's anyone's business."

Polly feigned sympathy. "Oh honey, I know how you feel! One would think that after menopause we'd be finished with all that icky nonsense. But it never seems to end, does it? The depression. The mood swings. Hot flashes. Ach! I can't tell you how many times after I've forgotten to take my pill I end up wanting to kick the dog."

Then, turning back to Missie, Polly smiled and said, "You're such a good girl, just like Billy Bush says you are when he reports on how film crews adore you and the way you smile for the paparazzi. Taking care of your poor, nearly blind mother, while you're trying to be a star, is to be commended. I'm sure she appreciates your love and support."

Suddenly, Duane's hand shot up into the air, like an A student who wants to show off that he knows the answer to $Y=mx+b$. "Um, Polly?" he said. "What Missie says is sort of strange."

"What's that dear?" Polly asked.

"Well, um, I made my final rounds and turned off the lights and locked all the gymnasium doors before I punched out at ten o'clock," he continued.

"You're such a dedicated worker. I can't imagine why Sterling fired you," Polly said.

She turned back to Elizabeth. "Of course you're used to finding your way around with limited vision, so the lack of lights wouldn't have been an obstacle to answering the call of nature, would it?" She changed her tone to one of reflection. "Since Duane locked the gymnasium door, how did you get in? I don't suppose they leave a key under the front doormat?"

Missie gave out a sigh of defeat. "Okay. You're right. Again. The doors *were* locked," she admitted. "I let Mother into *Dana's* trailer."

Dana shrieked, "*Eww!*"

"I didn't say this before because Dana's so damn fussy about who comes and goes in there," Missie said.

"If I'd known your mother was using my bathroom to be sick I would have called in a fumigation service. You should've asked first! What else did you do in my trailer after I left? I suppose you made out with that gaffer's assistant you're seeing? Oh, I know all about him. Who doesn't. They don't call 'em 'Best Boy' for nothing."

Then a previously unheard voice from the crowed spoke up. "Your trailer's a pig sty so we did it on Missie's convertible sofa."

Everyone in the room turned to connect the voice with the person who had spoken. When a blonde, blue-eyed, broad-shouldered, soap star-handsome Adonis stepped forward, all eyes appreciated his Versace magazine ad face and cock-of-the-walk self-assurance. "Sorry to kiss and tell, Missie," he said, "but other than your mother, I'm your only alibi." He ascended to the stage and took Missie's microphone. "It's true," he said to the crowd. "I'm Mike. Missie and I had been trying to be together all day and it wasn't working out. Then, Adam sent everybody home and we figured we'd be safe from lookie-loos. The only problem was what to do with Elizabeth."

"Sight-challenged mothers can be such a nuisance, can't they," Polly said.

"My mother's not a nuisance," Missie brayed. "But Mike and I were desperate. It was the last night I'd planned to be on the set and we didn't know when we'd have another chance to be together. I can never do it at home because *she's* always there," Missie pointed to Elizabeth. "And Mike's girlfriend keeps him on a tight leash."

Polly looked at Elizabeth and said, "Don't you just hate it when your kids say you're in their way? After all that we do for them? Changing their little nappies when they're babies, and the heartache of shipping them away to boarding school, and all that other maternal stuff. They grow up to be so ungrateful! You must have been totally upset knowing that Missie didn't want you around that night."

Elizabeth shrugged. "She sent me off to Dana's trailer. That's what really made me sick. Mike's right. It's filthy!"

Polly smiled. "Thank God for the cure-all of champagne,

eh? I just hope it was a decent bottle. Never drink from any-thing with a plastic cork!"

"As a matter of fact, I had my usual. Veuve," Elizabeth said proudly.

Tim interjected, "Such a coincidence! Sedra loved cham-pagne too! In fact she must have had a little too much the night she died. Detective Archer said there was a champagne cork at the bottom of the pool with her. I guess you guys have similar tastes 'cause the cork was from a Veuve Clic-quot bottle. Isn't that a fluke? Of course, nobody doesn't like Veuve. At least if they can't get their hands on Dom or Cristal." Tim chuckled. "A whole bottle all to yourself?" he said. "Way to go! Glad you didn't have to share with anyone. Although Sedra would have loved it. You two could have commiserated about your rotten kids."

"I loathed Sedra," Elizabeth growled. "She was standing in the way of Missie's career!"

Polly switched on her charm. "Tell me, what did you do the whole time that Missie was enjoying her, shall we say, 'gentleman caller?' I'm ashamed to admit this to anyone, but when my Timmy has a sleepover, I find myself rather jeal-ous. Mostly because the men he dates are far better looking than anything that appears in *Boinked* magazine. It's hardly fair. Don't you feel that way, too? You should have called me to commiserate. Or at least called Sedra. She would have been so pleased to have the company, I'm sure. By the way, that ring on your finger is to die for!"

Polly made a loud purring noise as she picked up Eliza-beth's hand and held it to examine the stone and its unique setting. "As a matter of fact, I've been drooling over this ring ever since first laying eyes on it at your lovely party. Look everybody," she called more attention to Elizabeth. "It's a Mexican opal! About ten carats, I'd say. Stunning. And a gold granulation setting . . ." Polly tsk-tsked, to express her covetousness.

"After all that Mom had done for me, I thought it fitting to spend my first big paycheck buying her something I knew she'd treasure," Missie proudly boasted.

Then Lauren Gaul suddenly leaped from her chair and rushed to Elizabeth's side. "That's the ring!" she wailed.

Elizabeth instantly tried to pull her hand out of Polly's but Polly was too fast and her grip too tight. She held on firmly, keeping the hand and ring on public display.

Again Lauren shouted, "That's the ring! The hand that reached under the stall door . . . was wearing that exact ring. I'll never forget it!"

Chapter 29

Polly let go of Elizabeth's hand and eyed her with renewed curiosity. She held firmly to her microphone as she slowly circled the chair on which Elizabeth sat.

Elizabeth displayed a mean, curled lip sneer, like an angry pit bull ready to sink its jaws into someone's throat. If she hadn't been wearing her wrap-around dark glasses, everyone would have seen the rage in her eyes as well.

"My, my, my," Polly sang. Then she looked out into the audience and called, "Placenta, darling, would you bring me a lovely glass of champies, please?" Then Tim sidled up to his mother. Polly looked at him and said, "Hon, have you been keeping score this evening?"

Tim shook his head and said, "Poor Elizabeth, she's forever being left alone. I felt bad the night she and Missie came to dinner. I was such an ungracious host leaving her to sit and drink by herself while Placenta and I gave Missie the grand tour of Pepper Plantation. Sorry again, Elizabeth," he said.

Polly patted her son on the back. "Nonsense, dear," she excused his behavior. "Elizabeth has learned to make her own kind of music. In fact, that evening she took a self-guided tour of our little home. Well, at least a tour of the drawers and cabinets in the living room. It's where she picked up that little Oscar charm she's wearing tonight."

All eyes in the room moved in unison to catch Elizabeth's response to being called a thief.

"I happened to be watching from the balustrade of the second floor," Polly said. "I wasn't spying, I promise. I'm not Homeland Security, for crying out loud. I was simply pacing about waiting to make my entrance."

Elizabeth was crestfallen. "I'm so very sorry, Polly," she said with deep contrition. "It's true that I was snooping around. But I didn't take it on purpose, I swear. It was in my hand when I heard everybody coming back to the room. I closed the cabinet and hurried back to my chair. I didn't notice that I still had your little Oscar until it was too late to put it back. I was going to put it back the next time you had us over. Here," she said, unclasping the gold chain from around her neck, and offering to return the item.

Ever the gracious hostess, Polly waved away Elizabeth's offer. "Nonsense, dear. In civilized cultures, if someone admires something of yours, it's considered rude not to make them a gift of it," she said. "By all means, please keep the little sucker. It belonged to a great star. Not much of an actress, but a star nonetheless. And obviously whatever star shine it once possessed hasn't rubbed off on me. It wasn't doing any good just sitting around taking up space. But, speaking of taking up space," she said, "I still have to ask myself, what else may you have accidentally absconded with? I don't mean from my home, dear. But you seem to be the only one here without a real alibi for the time frame in which Sedra Stone was supposedly killed. Did you take . . . um, Sedra's *life*?"

Missie jumped to her feet. "Polly!" she bellowed. "How

could you . . . ? How dare you insinuate . . . !" "Mother wouldn't harm a . . . she was with me the whole evening!"

Tim turned and said, "Actually, you were wrecking the sheets with Mike for forty minutes that night. Remember?"

Adam Berg stepped into the fray. "Now you've gone way too far," he said. "What you're implying is insane. This is an old blind woman, for crying out loud. She couldn't have possibly done anything . . ."

"Semi-blind. Or so we're told. And she's Polly's age, which is *not* old," Tim contradicted Adam.

"Thank you, dear!" Polly exuberantly praised Tim. "I'm putting you back in my will."

Lauren followed Adam's tirade with one of her own. "I was threatened by this woman. It was her, I know it from the ring! Missie bragged that it's a one-of-a-kind! The ring proves that Elizabeth passed that note under the stall door! Now that I think of it, she looks strong enough to be the one who attacked me on the night of Trixie's death, too. And her letter threatened that Sedra would leave in a body bag, and she did. Isn't that enough to get the police involved?"

Polly spoke into her microphone again and said, "Placenta! A star is parched. Where the hell's my drinkie?" Then she returned to the melee in progress on the stage and spoke to Lauren. "I know how upset you are sweetheart, but your suggestion that dear Elizabeth may have been involved in Sedra Stone's demise is circumstantial at best. Surely that fabulous detective Archer interrogated everyone at the scene of the crime. Didn't you detective?" Polly looked out into the audience and spied Archer walking toward the stage.

A murmur swept through the audience as the guests watched Archer, a man previously little noticed, wend his way through the crowd. When he reached the stage, he ascended the three steps and walked to Polly's side.

To the crowd Polly said, "Detective Archer is becoming

so famous on the television these days, he's more familiar to the masses than I am. It wouldn't be a true Hollywood murder investigation without this precious man giving us regular updates on the eleven o'clock news!" Then she looked into the detective's eyes. "I'm delighted that you accepted my invitation. Now, be a love and clear up a few things up for us—from a seasoned detective's point of view. I'm just as curious as Lauren, and I think I speak for everybody else, when I ask, who killed Sedra Stone?"

Detective Archer was silent for a moment. Then he took Polly's microphone. He looked at Elizabeth Stembourg and held out his hand. "Pleased to meet you ma'am," he said. "I apologize for not having spoken with you before."

Polly's voice was loud enough not to require any amplification from the mic she'd given to Archer. "But surely you spoke to Elizabeth during the investigation. You interviewed everybody who worked on the movie."

"Oops," Archer confessed. "I didn't think an old blind woman could have had anything to do with taking out a faded television star—especially in the particular fashion of her demise. But now that you've brought her to my attention, and the fact that relatives don't make the best alibis, and that she's been accused of writing a death threat, well I think there's some explaining to be done." He returned his attention to Elizabeth. "Now, Mrs. Stembourg, no one's insinuating anything, but please tell us where you were at the time of Sedra's death?"

Elizabeth became flustered. She stuttered, "I, I was alone."

"And what were you doing while you were alone?"

"Watching 'Animal Planet.' In Dana's trailer. Yeah, and there was a documentary on about bird eating spiders in New Zealand. Check the listing, I'm sure that was the program."

Detective Archer pushed the red button on his micro cassette recorder and made a note to himself to check the *TV Guide* listing. He knelt beside Elizabeth and as gently as possible said, "Mrs. Stembourg, would you do me a big favor? Would you think back to that night and try to recall if you saw or heard anything unusual that might lead us to whoever perpetrated the crime of killing Sedra Stone? I'm just thinking that since you were all alone in that trailer, maybe you can recall something . . . anything . . . even something that made no sense to you at the time. Think back, would you?"

Elizabeth folded her arms across her chest and looked at Missie. Both women seemed to be reading the other's thoughts as they shrugged their shoulders in unison. "You mean after the big blow up between Sedra and Dana?"

"Anything," Archer pressed.

Elizabeth shook her head. "I kept the sound up on the television so I wouldn't have to hear Missie carrying on next door."

"And you've got great hearing," I suppose, Archer suggested.

"As a matter of fact, even with the volume up high, I heard more than I wanted to. And before I knew it, Sedra was pounding on my door."

Polly shot to attention. "Sedra came over? So you were probably the last one to see her alive! What time was that?"

Elizabeth said, "I don't remember. Ten. Ten-thirty."

"What did Sedra say?" Polly persisted. "Did she talk about her fight with Dana? Did she seem overly agitated about anything? Did she say why she was still on the location?"

Elizabeth paused. "Oh, yeah," she said. "Now I remember. She did appear very upset. Like she was particularly worried about something. I asked her what was wrong and she told me that she was writing and that the noise from the television was distracting her. She came in herself and actually turned the show off. I was furious because now I had absolutely nothing to do until Missie had her little *organism*."

"You let her get away with that?" Polly said.

"I said some things that I maybe shouldn't have. Things that made her more upset," Elizabeth said. "Then she left, so I just sat there for a while. I was lonely. So after a few minutes I decided to go next door to Sedra's to apologize and borrow a bottle of champagne. Plus I guess I wanted some company, even if it was Sedra."

Tim considered the time of night and the state of inebriation that Elizabeth claimed to have been in. He tried to sound as concerned as possible when he asked, "How'd did you manage to maneuver the trailer steps and find your way to Sedra's in the dark? You could have fallen and hurt yourself."

She made a "Pfft" sound.

"I knocked on Sedra's door and she told me to beat it, that she was busy. She dismissed me, the way she always has. No matter how many times we've met she still doesn't know who the hell I am. Oh, she knows that I'm with Missie, but I could be Missie's maid for as much recognition as Sedra ever pays to me. But I plopped myself down on her steps and wouldn't leave until she gave me another drink. I guess just to get rid of me, she gave me a bottle. Then she told me to scram. The bottle hadn't been refrigerated. I'm like Polly, my champagne has to be ice cold."

"What else did she say?" Polly asked.

"Before Sedra closed the door she warned me not to get sick all over the grass in front of her trailer. Said if she stepped in anything, she'd find me and rub my nose in the mess as if I were a dog."

Again, Polly cut in. "Darling, from the way you put away the champagne at my dinner, I thought you had a hollow leg. You weren't even drunk."

"I never get drunk," Elizabeth agreed, then caught herself. "Um, but that night I hadn't had so much as a peanut to eat."

Detective Archer spoke into his tape recorder and recapped all that Elizabeth had stated. Then he asked, "Some time between ten o'clock, and when her body was found at around midnight, Sedra Stone threatened you. Is that correct?"

"Yeah, I guess so," Elizabeth said, as if the concept of Sedra threatening her had somehow never actually computed.

"How did that make you feel?" Polly asked in the way that Freudian analysts pry their patients into digging for deeper understanding of why they want to kill their mothers.

"I wasn't surprised. She didn't have a gracious bone in her body."

Placenta finally arrived with Polly's champagne. "Sorry it took so long, she apologized. "I TiVO'd 'Fear Factor' and got caught up with Danny Bonaducci being stripped half naked, drizzled with honey, and hog-tied over a fire ant hill. Not a complete turn-off, for a redhead." She looked at Elizabeth. "You were telling us about clobbering Sedra Stone with a bottle or something?"

Elizabeth huffed in frustration. "Never! I was saying, Sedra berated me and told me to jump in the pool. I figured she meant that would make me sober up. Now I think she probably knew the pool was empty and wanted me to break my neck. So I said she had a good idea and that I was going to the pool. But first I told her off."

"What about?" Polly asked.

"About how my Missie had another film job she had to start, and that *Detention Rules!* better wrap on time, or else. Sedra laughed in my face and said she intended to milk the job for all the overtime she could get. Then she baited me. She said, 'Careful you don't drown.' But she didn't say it like she had the least bit of genuine concern. It was more like there was a punchline of a joke waiting for me. But off I went to the pool building."

Polly confidently said, "But the door to the pool building was locked, right? Duane is so careful about these things."

"I don't lock up the school," Duane conceded. "Just the gym where the sets and camera equipment are kept."

Elizabeth nodded her head. "The door was unlocked. So I went inside. Of course I saw right away that the pool was empty. But I didn't know if Sedra knew, or if she possessed the slightest bit of concern for anyone other than herself. Still, I hoped that she might be worried about a supposed drunk woman taking a swim by herself or falling in a cement pit, and come and check up on me, 'cause I sure as hell wasn't finished telling her off. But I climbed up the stairs to the ten meter platform and waited anyway."

"For?" Detective Archer asked.

"For Missie to find me and feel bad about leaving me alone. Or, the unlikely chance that Sedra might check on me and I could continue trying to convince her to stop wasting time on the set and just finish the show so that Missie could move on. Then, lo and behold, Sedra actually opened the door and came inside. Maybe she had a second thought about telling me to take a swim. She looked around and when she saw where I was, so high up, she said I was totally stupid and tried to coax me down. I pretended to be terrified of heights and needed help. She said she'd call 911. I said it would look terrible in *The Peeper* if a story was printed that said Missie Miller's mother was found drunk. So she reluctantly agreed to come up and help me down herself. Good, I thought, 'cause I wanted to bargain with her and maybe share the champagne, if she was rational about the work situation. While Sedra was on her way up the steps I removed the foil wrapper from around the champagne bottle cork and untwisted the wire. Not all the way. I didn't want the cork popping out before I was ready.

"When Sedra finally reached the top, all huffing and puffing, and looking every minute her sixty-something years, saying she hated heights, I asked her if she was going to finally act like a professional and follow orders to do the work and get the film in the can by Saturday."

Tim exclaimed, "You *were* Laura's phantom! You put the threatening letter under the stall door!"

"Alright!" Elizabeth exclaimed. "But it was harmless. If this freakin' film kept on falling farther and farther behind schedule, Missie'd never be able to start her new movie. I wanted Sedra to wrap it up. I didn't want to hurt her. Just scare her a little."

Polly and the others had gathered around Elizabeth like a village of peasants ready to stone the Laird's tax collector. "You'd do anything to make Missie a star," Polly said, repeating the exact words that Elizabeth had spoken the night of the dinner party. "Anything," she reiterated. "You've said as much. So tell us, Elizabeth, are you a cold-blooded killer? Did you push Sedra Stone to her death?"

Elizabeth cried out, "No way! I said I only wanted to scare the bitch! Honestly, I *never* touched her!"

Missie forced her way through the circle of accusers and calmly said, "Mother, don't say another word. You don't remember anything because you were drunk. Remember!"

Polly handed her own flute of champagne to Elizabeth and said, "I think you need this more than I do. Drink up, honey. Placenta will bring a bottle and we can all relax. So what happened next?"

Elizabeth put the rim of the glass to her lips and emptied it with one long swallow. Ignoring Missie's command, she resumed her story. "I realized that I'd given that note to the wrong person because I believed Sedra when she claimed not to have any idea about what I was talking about when I said she had been warned in writing to finish her job and get out," Elizabeth said. "Sedra reiterated that this was her chance to return to the limelight and she didn't care about any threat, that she'd had plenty of those during her lifetime. We argued back and forth until she finally gave in and agreed that she should complete her last scene then move on. But I knew it was only a ploy so I'd come down from the platform. I suspected that she wasn't going to budge in the way of quitting the movie anytime before she absolutely had to. And I hated her for thinking I was dumb enough to believe her. I didn't know what to do. And just then, Missie arrived on the platform. I hadn't heard her come in. Sedra was surprised, too, and almost lost her balance and fell right then."

Suddenly, all eyes on the room were focused on Missie Miller. "What a place to find your mother, way up on a diving pool platform. It was dangerous. So I quietly climbed up the stairs so I wouldn't startle her or Sedra. Yeah they were surprised to see me all right, but grateful, too, I think. Sedra especially because she didn't want to have to somehow get Mother down on her own."

"Missie to the rescue!" Polly cheered. "Thank God you finished your business with Mike when you did and, that you thought to check the pool for your missing mother. Brava! Saved the day."

"I noticed the lights were on in the pool building so it's the first place I checked, after Dana's trailer," Missie said, proud of her ability to deduce the most likely place to find Elizabeth.

Then Polly turned to Mike. "Did ya have a swell time together?" she asked, smiling with envy for the easy intimacy the young seem to find wherever and whenever they want it.

"Never enough time," Mike beamed with satisfaction.

"We didn't want to keep Elizabeth waiting, so we were in and out, so to speak," he said, chuckling.

Polly returned her attention to Missie and said, "Not to worry, dearest, you're young. You and your beau will have longer and more encounters, I'm sure. As long as the girl-friend doesn't find out." Polly gave a weak laugh. "Well, the brevity of your visit with Mike made it possible to collect your mother before anything happened to her or Sedra. Were you surprised to find them together?"

"Totally," Missie proclaimed. "Sedra was far from the nurturing kind—just ask Dana—and to hear her actually try to help Mother down from the platform was pretty amazing."

"So you were in the building long enough to hear dear Elizabeth plead her case for Sedra to step aside and let you move on to your next project. When she refused, how did that make you feel?" Again she was playing analyst.

"Like shit, of course!" Missie snapped. "Look, lady, I know that you're trying to connect Mother to Sedra's death, like it was premeditated, or something. Well that ain't gonna wash. Sedra died, and it was a horrible mess, but it wasn't anybody's fault."

Detective Archer came around to Missie's side and scratched his neck. "I gotta tell ya, I make mistakes all the time on my job. And when I do, my first thought is how to cover my butt so that nobody finds out I goofed big time. Usually I'm pretty good at covering my tracks. Sometimes, not so good. I have to say, I think your mom, Elizabeth, has done a damn good job of covering her butt. Until now. But I think she pushed Sedra off the platform and almost got away with it because nobody would suspect a nearly blind woman of get-ting up that high in the first place. And you covered for her."

The crowd was almost unanimous in their agreement that Elizabeth Stembourg had pushed Sedra Stone to her death.

But she protested with loud sobbing tears. "I never touched Sedra! This isn't how my Hollywood dream was supposed to turn out! Missie was supposed to become rich and famous and take care of me!"

Elizabeth stood up and removed her dark wrap-around glasses. She looked first at Dana with eyes that seemed to see perfectly well. "This is all your fault. I told Missie not to hang out with you. And look what happens. The bad girls always win." Next she focused on Adam Berg. "If you had an ounce of talent in your creepy little brain, you would have finished this picture long ago, and I wouldn't have had to take care of things on my own."

Tim asked, "What 'things,' Elizabeth?"

For a long moment there was silence in the tent. All eyes were glued to Elizabeth Stembourg as they watched her contemplate how to answer Tim's question.

"Yeah, Missie overheard what Sedra said about her being nothing more than a pretty face, but with no more talent for acting than Kathie Lee Gifford has for singing," Elizabeth said. "Missie was justifiably furious. When Missie arrived on the platform it was pretty crowded and I just wanted to get down. So I took the first tentative steps toward the stairs. And then . . ."

"And then nothing," Missie spoke sharply to her mother.

"Tell 'em what happened. Or I will," Elizabeth said. "Fine. Okay. Have it your way." Elizabeth thought back to that moment. "I decided we should have a toast to Missie's new film because come hell or high water I was going to make sure she was on the set of *DNA* bright and early on the first day of production. And that's when it happened. The bottle of champagne was still on the platform so I picked it up."

At that moment Missie yelled, "Stop it, Mother! There aren't any witnesses. You don't have to say another word!"

But Elizabeth continued, as if on autopilot headed for impact against the face of an Andes peak she said, "I picked up the bottle and told Sedra that Missie was going into a new film project right away, regardless of whether or not *Detention* had wrapped. I started blabbering about the new film, and Sedra said that the story was exactly like a screenplay she'd written herself, but that the floppy disk it was on had gone missing. That's when I realized that Adam had screwed my Missie and Sedra. That the screenplay was probably Sedra's after all. But the role was too good for Missie not to play. It would win her an Oscar. I was sure of it."

Suddenly determined to make certain that everybody understood that her mother was not in her right mind that evening, Missie finished the story. "I could practically tell what Mother was thinking as Sedra began demanding to know more about Adam and the screenplay he'd supposedly written. I looked over at Mother and saw her shaking the bottle. Then she pointed it at Sedra. I yelled at her to put the bottle down. Then suddenly . . . POW! You'd think a cannon had gone off for all the noise it made in the emptiness of the building! The cork hit Sedra square in the forehead and she reeled. She automatically tried to dodge the cork and stepped backward. She was right on the very edge of the platform. She wobbled, then . . ."

Missie's eyes took on a glassy stare. "I see everything in slow motion now," she said. "Sedra didn't say anything. No scream, or sound came from her. But the look on her face was complete and utter shock. In a split second she reached out in vain for anything to grab on to in order to stop her from going over the edge of the platform. But there was nothing to grab hold of. For an instant she flailed, like she thought she could flap her arms and fly to safety. And I couldn't move fast enough to stop her falling. I would have gone over the edge, too. And then she belly-flopped . . . into nothingness."

As the audience listened in horror, Elizabeth suddenly

stood up from her chair. She faced Polly and glared at her with a look that was filled with anger and hatred. Then, with the swiftness of a slight-of-hand card sharp she simultaneously struck the fluted part of the champagne glass she was holding onto the metal arms of her chair and wielded the sharp jagged stem. With the swiftness of a rabid pit bull she lunged at Polly. A stronger woman than she appeared to be, Elizabeth easily wrestled Polly to the stage floor and held the sharp weapon to her throat.

Instantly, Tim, Placenta, Detective Archer, and everyone except Missie raced to Polly's rescue; however, Elizabeth screamed for everybody to back off and threatened to make it nearly impossible for even the best plastic surgeon in Beverly Hills to do repair work after she was finished with Polly's famous face.

"Let her go!" Tim begged. "Polly never did anything to you!"

"She's ruined my chances! She's taken away my dream! I've settled up with the others who stood in my way, and I'll do it again!"

Polly laid perfectly still, her mind reeling and trying to figure out a way to save her life. The weight of Elizabeth sitting on her chest, and the sting of sharp glass pressing against her throat made it difficult to breath, and she dared not try to speak and talk reason with her assailant.

Tim yelled out again, "Just let her go, Elizabeth! I promise we won't press charges! You and Missie can leave and go back to Boston. I promise!"

"We can't go anywhere now," Elizabeth spat back. "All my plans are over! And it's all Polly Pepper's fault! If she hadn't gotten in the way with her snooping around and getting Dana off the hook . . ."

Suddenly a voice came over the speaker system. "Everything is always about you, isn't it Mother?" All eyes turned to Missie Miller who was walking toward Elizabeth. "*Your* chances? *Your* dreams? *Your* plans? What about what I want?"

"You don't know what the hell you want!" Elizabeth shrieked. "Your problem is that you dream too small. You would have been content to stay in Boston. But I'm not about to let all your potential just shrivel up and go unnoticed!"

"Mother," Missie pleaded, "let Polly go. They said we could leave. But if you hurt this woman you'll never see me in another film. I'll be completely washed up. And then where will *your* dreams be? Let her go, Mama."

With Missie serving as a distraction, Tim and Detective Archer gave each other a look and simultaneously rushed Elizabeth and dragged her off of Polly. In an instant she was handcuffed and being led away by Archer's contingent of plainclothes police officers. Before leaving the tent she yelled out, "You're nothing without me, Missie Miller! You have no ambition! Go ahead and have Mike's babies and see how happy you are without being in the spotlight. You'll be a miserable nobody! I promise!"

And then she was gone.

Chapter 30

As guests made their way off of the Pepper Plantation property, more than a few stopped to tell Polly, Tim, and Placenta that the drama of the evening exceeded their expectations for what they'd heard made a Polly Pepper party so spectacular. "No wonder this place is world famous!" said one of the *Detention Rules!* location assistants. "Wasn't this like the most awesomely fun event ever? Is it like this every night?"

"Every night, dear," Polly said.

"It was like being in a Hitchcock movie," said the sound effects editor to Polly.

"With a touch of *The Texas Chainsaw Massacre*, eh?" Polly trumpeted.

"By the time we get home everyone who was here tonight will have started writing their own script about it," said a Stedicam operator.

"Hell, I may as well jump on the bandwagon," the sound effects editor retorted. "I'll call it, *Set for Murder.*"

"Or *Put a Cork in It,*" said the Stedicam guy, who laughed as he tried to concoct different titles.

"Never a dull moment at a Polly Pepper event," said Candice Bergen with her trademarked sly and sardonic phrasing. As she kissed her hosts good-bye she added, "Leave it to adorable Tim to plan another winner. If the networks ever get around to buying your life story, or starring you in an updated version of 'Murder, She Wrote,' you'll add a ton more Emmys to your trophy room. Call me in the A.M. You should guest on 'Boston Legal.'"

Polly gleamed at the accolades, and the idea that television might come beckoning again. When Ellen DeGeneres sidled up to Polly and gave Polly a hug she whispered, "Portia and I loved your performance tonight. What about producing *DNA* as a feature for Lifetime? I could play Sedra and Portia could play you. What do you think about Shirley Jones for Placenta? Oh, and Neil Patrick Harris would be ideal to play Tim! Let's do lunch to discuss. Ta!"

When the house was in relative peace again, with only the distant sounds from the caterers who were cleaning up in the kitchen, the family gathered in the Great Room together with Dana Pointer, Detective Archer, and Kevin Cartwright. "Geeze, what a night!" Polly exclaimed to no one in particular, as she flopped down on one of the sofas. "I swear I'll never be able to open another bottle of champagne again as long as I live! I'll always be reminded of the way Missie's mother killed poor old Sedra!" She looked around. "Placenta, dear, would you break out the Cristal? We all deserve the good stuff."

Placenta looked at Polly and wryly said, "So you'll start your new sobriety the day after never?"

Polly looked momentarily confused. "Oh, hell," she waved away Placenta's suggestion. "I said I'd never be able to *open* a bottle of champagne. I never said I wouldn't *drink* the stuff! Lord, are you insane?"

With Detective Archer seated beside Polly, and Tim next to Kevin, the room took on a more romantic vibration than usual. Observing the arrangement, Placenta decided to add to the atmosphere by lighting the gas fireplace and slipping a Michael Feinstein disk onto the CD carousel. As the crooner's plaintive "My Romance" tenderly filled the air, Placenta poured champagne and began distributing the flutes. When she got to Dana, the teen screen queen was holding one of Polly's Emmy Awards and examining it carefully. Dana accepted the flute and said, "Hell, this 'Polly Pepper Playhouse' show must've been popular. I guess I should see what all the fuss was about. Maybe there's a Polly Pepper section on Netflix." She then returned the award to its place on the bookcase shelf and wandered over to where her hosts were gathered.

Dana sat down beside Placenta and raised her glass. "I'd like to propose a toast to both Trixie Wilder and Sedra Stone," she said. "You were both so different yet you had a couple of things in common. You both died before your time. But at least you'll forever be in the chapter of the celebrity history books reserved for the likes of Bob Crane and Sal Mineo. I guess sometimes murder can be good for a career."

Everyone sipped from their respective glasses and murmured agreement with Dana that Sedra and Trixie were now immortalized because of the way they had died. Tim leaned back and stretched out his arm behind Kevin on the sofa. He said to Dana, "So, what's up now? I mean, with *Detention*, and your career?"

Dana took another long pull from her glass. "Well, first of all, Sterling will probably make Adam finish the film, so I'll be going back to work. Of course, I'm going to sue his ass for selling Sedra's screenplay under his own name." She stopped to think for a moment. "I mean, now that Sedra's dead, and I'm her only living relative, her estate becomes mine. That means intellectual property, too." Then she gave Tim a quizzical look. "The fact that we're somehow related, does that mean we'll fight over the estate?"

Tim made a motor noise over his lips that implied that

Dana was being absurd. "Honey, I'm not the least bit interested in anything from the woman who done my mama
wrong—twice. I won't lay claim to a red cent of Sedra's estate. But don't expect there to be very much. Remember, she
hadn't worked during the past two decades. She lived lav-
ishly, but the house is bound to be mortgaged to the hilt. I
think she wrote the screenplay because she knew it was a
potboiler and would be a quick sale to one of the studios.
Despite hurting a ton of people, which she was used to
doing, it was probably going to be her annuity."

Dana simply nodded.

"But now that it's going to be common knowledge that
you were Sedra's blood relative, what do you think *The
Peeper* will say and do?" Tim asked.

Dana smiled and for the first time that evening seemed
genuinely delighted. "It should place me squarely on the
cover of every issue for a year," she said. "And with the right
PR spin, I can be the sad and long-lost orphan forever
searching for her mother, then finding her just when it was
too late." Dana faked a sniffle. "Hell, if I play my cards right
I'll be able to shed my bad girl image! And now that Missie
Miller is considered an accomplice, however unwitting, to
her mother murdering Sedra, the tables will be completely
turned. I'll get all the sympathy, and maybe a couple of
Kiera Knightly roles! Missie'll join Tonya Harding in the
'Whatever Happened To . . .' game."

Polly snuggled a little closer to Detective Archer and
asked, "What about you? Now that you've solved this case?"

Archer made a sound similar to the one Tim used to dis-
miss Dana's concern about her estate. "You and Tim and Placenta solved this case, not me!" Archer said. "I royally
screwed up right from the beginning. I'll be lucky if I get to
keep my job. If Dana is litigious enough to whoop Berg's
butt, I can only pray that she takes pity on mine, and my otherwise long and distinguished career."

Dana's silence was inscrutable, as she raised an eyebrow and sipped daintily from her flute.

Polly preened. "We did solve the case, didn't we," she said with complete satisfaction. "We're crusaders for truth and justice, and the Hollywood way! This town is a safer place tonight because Robert Blake has had his firearms permit revoked, and Elizabeth Stembourg is behind bars with Phil Spector."

"Yeah, you guys set out to prove Dana's *innocence* and in the process discovered not only Sedra's killer but got a confession that Trixie Wilder was the recipient of Elizabeth's murderous hand, too."

Polly thought about Trixie's death for a moment then said, "For Elizabeth to have strategically placed that brick on the floor, and determine ahead of time from where and how hard to push so that poor creature would fall just right, she's gotta have a background in mathematics. Or she's just lucky."

"She'll be lucky if our illustrious governor doesn't personally flip the switch that fries her wrinkled hiney," Placenta said. "And on that note, I think I'll call it a day. A very long day."

"Us, too," Tim said, looking at Kevin, who blushed his acceptance to the unspoken invitation to sleep over. He gave a sly grin and soft exhalation of breath.

Polly placed her lips on her glass and surreptitiously looked over at Detective Archer, who instantly picked up on her body language. "We're cool," Archer said to Placenta.

Placenta wanted to say, "You're about to be hot," but she held her thoughts to herself. Instead she looked at Dana and said, "Hmm. Looks like we're the only ones in the house who aren't paired off for the night. And there's no way we're letting you drive home at this hour. I'll be upstairs fluffing your pillow in the guest room when you're ready."

"Lead the way," Dana said as she leaned over to give Polly a goodnight peck on the cheek. Then she tousled the hair on Tim's head and gave him a wink that said, "Way to go, bro."

As Placenta stood to exit the room she made one final comment, "The next time we stumble over a dead body or unmask a killer let it be while watching reruns of 'The Avengers,' or 'Perry Mason.' This sleuthing work is exhausting . . . and we drink way more champagne than usual. Our bill from the Liquor Locker this month is into five figures!"

Polly sighed. "I'm with you kiddo. From now on I'm leaving detective work to the specialists." She looked at Detective Archer and smiled. "If you promise not to get a television show, I promise not to poke my nose around people who mysteriously and unexpectedly turn up dead. Deal? Or no deal?"

Polly Pepper, the legendary superstar of television's golden age, is finally back in the entertainment headlines. She's landed the title role in a new production of the musical *Mame,* and though it's off-off-off-off Broadway (Glendale, California, actually), Polly's bank account—and her ego—need the job. And if all goes well, the show just might go to New York! There's one minor detour, though: On the second day of rehearsals, wünderkind director Karen Richards turns up dead.

Of course Polly's nose for news needs to know, and though Karen was well liked, it seems some last-minute casting changes from artistic director/megalomaniac Gerold Goss did her in. Sadly, Polly's suspect #1 is her new friend and co-star Sharon Fletcher, who also plays a deliciously sultry bad girl on the popular daytime soap "It's *Never* Fair Weather." Sharon was the last person seen with the deceased director . . . and her Emmy matches the dent in Karen's head.

But as Gerold takes over the director's chair, Polly finds her cast-member-suspect-list reaching epic proportions. Could it be Charlotte Bunch, who Karen politely corrected until she got her Irish brogue right? Everyone knows actresses can be *very* touchy. Or Gerold's sweetly innocent girlfriend Mag Ryan, who drunkenly revealed that she wouldn't let anything stand in the way of her landing a part in the possibly Broadway-bound musical? Or maybe even Karen's young assistant Jamie, who Polly discovered was promised a role in the play . . . after Karen's untimely demise?

The more Polly sniffs, the surer she is that Sharon didn't haul off and bash Karen with her Emmy. But the evidence is mounting, and it'll take all of Polly's wits—and some help back at Pepper Plantation from her ever-dependable son Tim and their perpetually wisecracking maid Placenta—to save the jailed soap star from a murder rap . . . and a starring role in a real-life drama tentatively entitled *Framed*!

Please turn the page for an exciting sneak peek of
FINAL CURTAIN,
coming next month in hardcover!

"I'm just a Broadway baby," television musical/comedy legend Polly Pepper began to sing in a strong, cheerful voice as she pressed the OFF button on her cordless telephone and placed the handset on her concert-grand piano. She performed an impromptu soft-shoe across the carpeted floor of the great room at Pepper Plantation, her Bel Air mansion. With a smile as wide as the Wal-Mart happy face on a price-busting day, Polly skipped and twirled and finished the song, belting out, "In a great . . . big . . . Broadway . . . show-oh." She held the last note for a long moment, long enough to grab the attention of her still-living-at-home adult son, Tim, who rushed into the room.

"Did I hear 'Broadway'? You got a show?"

"Yep!" Polly opened her arms and hugged the light of her life. "But I'm more of a Broadway *maybe*," she amended.

"Out-of-town tryout?" Tim pressed.

Polly nodded. "Sorta."

Polly's maid and best friend, Placenta, had also heard the commotion, and rushed to her employer's side just in time to hear the words "Broadway" and "maybe." Her brown eyes locked with Polly's blue ones. "Let me guess. Your smart-ass agent J. J. booked your usual summer gig and says there's a *chance* this one may crawl into New York?"

Polly waited for Placenta's other accusatory shoe to drop.

"Sure. And there's a *chance* that Harry Connick Jr. will let me iron his underpants."

Polly made a face and whined, "For once in your life, try to practice positive thinking. Be happy for me. For you, too. These summer tours pay your salary. Musical revivals are all the rage on Broadway; and J. J. says that he's heard through the grapevine that if this production is half as good as expected, I can end up on a billboard over Times Square!"

Tim folded his arms across his chest. "A revival? What moth-eaten show are they *dragging* out this season? *La Cage Au Folles*?"

"Getting warm," Polly said.

"*Hello, Dolly!*? *Mame*?"

"Bingo." Polly clapped her hands. "Four solid weeks in one of my all-time favorite roles! You're too young to remember, but I was a sensation as the Belle of Beekman Place when I played the Music Tent in Manassas."

"A quarter century ago," Placenta reminded her.

"The critics stumbled all over their typewriter keys to find superlatives to describe my performance," Polly countered.

"What's a typewriter?" Tim teased.

"And don't forget that split week in Little Rock. Audiences cried when I was suddenly widowed by John Davidson."

"Because they were stuck with you and Rita Moreno on-stage for the rest of the night," Placenta said. "And where, pray tell, does New York fit into this improbable dream?"

Polly hesitated. "All I know is that the new Sondheim show is apparently so depressing, it's actually scaring away the Broadway tourist trade. They need a fun and familiar placeholder at the Palace Theatre until *Snakes on a Plane— The Musical* opens in February. The producers are looking at

Mame. Please, dear Lord, let me get to Broadway before God brings down the curtain on my life."

For reasons beyond her control, starring on the Great White Way eluded Polly. Over the years, four musicals had been written expressly for her, but they either closed in Boston or fell apart while in rehearsal.

Now, as Tim watched his mother's joy turn to self-doubt, he decided to act as if she were a Tony Award winner. "Another op'ning, another show" he sang and faked a wild and crazy Steve Martin–esque tap dance over to the wine cooler.

"Hold your hats and hallelujahs, Polly's gonna show it to you," Placenta sang, quoting a lyric from "Rose's Turn." "Broadway, here we come," she announced, helping to cheer the atmosphere. "By way of . . ."

"Em, Glendale," Polly reluctantly admitted. "We're at the Galaxy Theatre for the summer."

Tim and Placenta both stared at Polly.

Glendale, California had only one thing to recommend it: Forest Lawn Cemetery, which boasted the remains of more stars than there were on the devil's rotisserie spit. After one had seen the celebrity homes in Beverly Hills, and found their favorite stars' names embedded on the Hollywood Boulevard Walk of Fame, the natural progression was to visit the plots and vaults where their famous bodies or ashes were dumped. Forest Lawn was a tranquil plot of acreage where, among the sweeping lawns and clusters of evergreen trees, headstones served as reminders that Clark Gable, Carole Lombard, Humphrey Bogart, Jimmy Stewart, and even Walt Disney—who everyone knew was collecting freezer burn somewhere in the bowels of Disneyland—all had expiration dates on their passports to Earth. Otherwise, Glendale was the sort of town where the residents considered the Olive Garden fine dining.

"I know it's not Boston or Chicago, or San Francisco," Polly said. "But it's a job."

Despite the grim prospect of having to spend his summer shuttling Polly to and from work each day, Tim tried to sound enthusiastic. "You'll kill the audiences," he said as he pulled out a cold bottle of Veuve Cliquot from the cooler. "Placenta," he said, "call Wolfy and reserve our usual table. We need to celebrate." Tim was actually pleased for his mother, but was also delighted that he wouldn't have to spend the hottest part of the year sweltering in St. Louis or Kansas City, where Polly usually toured during the summer.

Polly smiled as she once again began to feel that her career was on the upswing. "My personal psychic at Future tense.com recently emailed me and said that after all the dark shadows and negative energy that have stalked *moi* during the past few months—what with dead movie stars cluttering up my last film location—it's definitely time for a big shift in my planetary fortunes."

"Famous people die just like run-of-the-mill folk." Tim popped the cork from the champagne bottle. "This is Hollywood. Everyone knows a killer or two."

"But they're usually agents and personal publicists," Placenta said.

As Tim poured three flutes of champagne he added, "You've had your once-in-a-lifetime encounter with real-life blood and guts—if you don't count that week on your show working with Vicki Lawrence—and you lived to tell about it. The fact that you're now the main topic of conversation at every cocktail crush in town is publicity you could never afford to buy. The notoriety is money at the theater box office."

"I admit there were moments when tracking down the killer was actually fun," Polly said. "But it was scary, too. Like Faye Dunaway's new face. Still, I've promised that I'd never interfere with police work again."

Polly was suddenly quiet as she considered her pledge to the new man in her life, Detective Randal Archer. After years of self-imposed exile from romance, Polly met Detective Archer during the investigation into the murder of her archrival, television legend Sedra Stone.

Tim raised his glass, and the trio simultaneously clinked their Waterford crystal flutes together. "To the legendary Polly Pepper, the best Auntie Mame ever," he began. "As you descend on Glendale, may all the bodies you encounter be breathing . . . and holding tickets to see Polly Pepper live on stage!"

Polly gave her son a playful shove. "Slaughtering an audience is what I do best, dear. It's why I get the big bucks." She paused. "Although they certainly are tight with a dollar at the theater. J. J. said that with the exception of a piano and a couple of strings and percussion, the orchestra is canned. The sets are mere suggestions for the imagination. There's no budget for new costumes either. I'm stuck with Kathie Lee Gifford's stinky wardrobe from the road company of *The Vagina Monologues.*"

Placenta took a long sip of her drink and asked, "Who else is in the cast?"

Polly furrowed her eyebrows as she tried to recall. "A couple of soap opera stars, I think. Never heard of 'em, but apparently they're dying to work with me."

"You can recall entire paragraphs from old reviews verbatim, but you can't remember what J. J. said about your cast just a few moments ago?" Tim complained. "For the role of the adult Patrick Dennis, please tell me it's Trent Dawson from 'As the World Turns'! Or better yet, Don Diamont from 'The Young and the Restless'! Ooh! Make that Paul Satterfield from 'One Life to Live'! I think I'm going to love working in the theater again."

Polly and Placenta looked at each other and nodded, knowing that Tim would be in love before the first week of rehearsal was over.

Tim giggled. "It's about time that Andy Hardy found romance again, or at least a summer fling. You have a sexy police detective. I'll settle for a 'Days of our Lives' soapstud."

As had become her custom before leaving home to go to work, Polly Pepper stood in the center of the great room of her mansion and took a nostalgic look at the awards displayed on lighted glass shelves. "Lord, forget about keeping your eye on the sparrow. Keep 'em both open wide on my Emmys," she prayed, as a wave of separation anxiety washed over her.

It was late June, and Polly was heading out for what she euphemistically called her "mortgage tour." Although this time she was only going a few miles to Glendale, she generally traveled to regions of the country where, thanks to perennial rebroadcasts of her classic '80s television variety show on local cable stations, Polly Pepper was still a star.

Beyond the age to believably play a virginal singing-nun-turned-nanny, and tired of working alongside smudgy and obnoxious little girls as moppet orphans, this year Polly would own the stage as Mame Dennis Burnside, one of theater's most enduring roles for a star of a certain age. She dismissed the denunciation of her few critics who, upon hearing that Polly Pepper had been cast in this classic, bellowed, "The role must be played by a great lady—like Angela Lansbury. Polly's a clown!"

But being a clown is what made Polly famous in the first place. No one made audiences laugh at everyday situations and the absurdities of life the way Polly Pepper did. Throngs of devoted fans would surely drop their barbeque briquettes on a hot summer's night and drive to the theater to see her cavorting on stage. At least that was the hope of the Glendale Civic Light Opera.

Polly looked at her wristwatch and sighed. In a few minutes, Tim would honk the horn of Polly's Park Ward Rolls-Royce and whisk her over the hill to the theater. She squared her shoulders and blew a kiss to the room. "Be good while Mommy's away," she whispered, and closed the door behind her.

The drive from Bel Air to Glendale was hardly a whisk. In Southern California, every hour is rush hour; and when Tim finally found the theater, the parking lot was full. He let his mother and Placenta out at the curb and he went in search of a space to park on the street. As Polly ascended the steps and walked into the forecourt of the old theater, she was reminded of being in an ancient Egyptian temple. "They don't make theaters like this one anymore," she said to Placenta, who walked slightly ahead of Polly and pulled open the entry door.

Entering the lobby, Polly stopped for a moment to look around and absorb the intoxicating scent and feeling that she always embraced when working in a theatrical shrine.

Polly's euphoria was abruptly shattered, however, when Gerold Goss, the theater's artistic director, appeared from the men's room. Upon suddenly seeing Polly, he began yelling. "You're four hours late! Just because you're the famous Polly Pepper doesn't give you the right to treat the rest of the cast with disrespect. Their time is just as valuable as yours!"

Polly was stunned. She looked at her wristwatch. "Honey, I'm five minutes *early*. It's only quarter to two!" she stuttered. "Everyone knows that I'm the most prompt star in Hollywood."

Gerold ground his teeth and the veins at his neck began to pulsate. "Rehearsal from *ten-to-two* does not mean *one-fifty*!"

Polly was mortified. "Ten to two. Ha!" she laughed. "I thought it meant starting at ten minutes to two."

"No one has your phone number!" Gerold growled.

"Your agent wouldn't return my calls! It occurred to me that at your age, you might be dead. Wishful thinking!"

"My *age*? I'm expressing my deep regret to you for the little misunderstanding, and promise that it will never happen again. But I'm a little concerned about your imperious attitude." She squared her shoulders. "Stars are people, too. Sometimes we make mistakes. I'm sorry and I won't be tardy again. *Mea culpa* already!"

Polly turned to leave. "If you'll kindly direct me to the rehearsal room, I'd like to express my apologies to the director and the rest of the cast."

"They're all on the stage," Gerold yelled as Polly began to rush away. "You and other over-the-hill stars should be on your knees giving thanks for another chance to be in a show. I didn't even want you for this role. Now you act like a diva! There's no place in the theater for ego!" He turned and stormed away. As he retreated, he nearly collided with Tim, who had just entered the theater lobby.

Polly was now in a panic and rushed for the double doors to the auditorium. "That damn J. J. gave us the wrong schedule," she called back to Tim, who, along with Placenta, was following at Polly's heels.

"Your momma's just been given thirty lashes from that schmo Gerold Goss," Placenta said. "Seems we were supposed to be here from ten this morning until two in the afternoon."

"I thought the call time was odd," Tim said, trying to catch up to his mother, who went barreling into the auditorium.

Polly rushed down the aisle and threw out her arms as she called out, "Everybody! Everybody! I'm mortified that I missed our first day! Please, please forgive me! I'm never ever late for anything, especially anything as important as work!" When she arrived at the stage, the entire cast stood to greet her. Now out of breath, Polly clutched her chest and walked up to Karen Richards, the director. "Ms. Richards," she panted, "this is a horrible way to begin our relationship. Please don't be harsh on me. You'll see that I'm the most professional artist with whom you'll ever work. I promise."

Karen smiled warmly and shook her head. "Not a problem, Miss Pepper. First of all, I'm your most ardent admirer." She reached out to shake Polly's hand. "In fact my college thesis was an examination of your amazing career. I even have the boxed CD collector's edition of the first season of 'The Polly Pepper Playhouse.' I'm dying for the next season to be released."

Polly exhaled a deep sigh of relief.

Karen continued. "You've played this role exactly three hundred and seventy-seven times over the years. All to rave reviews. You missed one little rehearsal today. I'm not at all concerned. Let me introduce you to your cast."

Karen knew precisely how to treat divas in order to induce mutual trust and respect. In Polly's case, however, Karen was a genuine fan. She had set out on her career path with the mission of one day working with Polly Pepper. This was her golden moment. "This is Emily Hutcherson, our Vera Charles and your 'bosom buddy,'" Karen said as she singled out Emily from the group.

Both actresses smiled and shook each other's hand. "Lovely to meet you, Emily," Polly said. "You know, you really have the best role in the show."

"It's not the lead," Emily said through gritted teeth.

"No, it's not, honey." Polly returned Emily's frosty greeting.

Karen continued. "Marshall Nash is our Beauregard. Sharon Fletcher is Gloria Upson. Charlotte Bunch will be playing Agnes Gooch. Hiroaki Goldfarb is Ito. And here's little Ward Stewart, your adorable nephew Patrick." As Karen introduced the entire principle cast, Polly was overwhelmed by their graciousness. No one other than Emily Hutcherson seemed to mind that the star had nearly missed the entire first day. However she again apologized to each of them for her untoward and totally out-of-character behavior.

Karen looked at her watch. "Okay, gang," she said. "Thanks for a terrific first day." She glanced at Polly. "I'll see all of you back here tomorrow at *ten* A.M."

As the cast collected their cell phones and car keys, they each welcomed Polly again with handshakes. Part of Tim's job was to pay attention to the people his mother met in business and social situations. She was notorious for her inability to remember the names of anyone who wasn't a star. However, as Polly made small talk with her cast, Tim's peripheral vision picked up something interesting. Instantly, his gaze was riveted to a muscled stud in a tank top leaning against the auditorium wall who seemed to be intently observing all the on-stage action. For Tim, the world instantly came to a freeze-frame stop. However, the planet abruptly began to spin again when director Karen Richards walked up the aisle, kissed the god, and left the theater with him linked in her arm. Tim's heart sank as deep as the *Titanic*.

When most of the other actors had left the stage, Sharon Fletcher, who was cast as bubblehead Gloria Upson, approached Polly. "Miss Pepper?" she said.

Polly looked up and smiled. "Please, dear, call me Polly. And you are . . . ?"

"We met a moment ago. I'm Sharon. Fletcher. I'm engaged to your nephew Patrick, but of course I'm the wrong woman for him, and you'll get rid of me." She laughed.

A light dawned on Polly. "Didn't I see you on 'Hygiene of the Stars'?"

Sharon blushed. "That's awfully sweet of you, I mean a great big star like you knowing about little ol' me and my unique flossing technique. I'm flattered. I just wanted to tell you how happy I am that I get to work on the same stage with you. Wait'll I email my dad, who thinks you walk on water. Oh, I hope I'm not being sacrilegious! I just mean that he worships you. I do too, of course."

Polly was instantly captivated by the pretty young actress. She assessed Sharon and instantly decided that her blond hair was natural, as were the two substantial breasts, which nested in her pink cashmere sweater. "Shelley," Polly said, "I feel terrible that I've never seen your daytime drama, 'One Life . . .'"

" 'Weather,' " she corrected. "And it's Sharon."

Polly looked puzzled.

"'It's *Never* Fair Weather,'" Tim translated for Polly, as he held out his hand to Sharon and gushed, "I'm Polly's son. Wow! I watch your show all the time. This is very cool. Where's your husband Troy?" He looked around.

Sharon sniggered. "That's just on the show, silly. But Heart—the real name of the guy who plays Troy—is one of my best friends. He'll be around, and I promise to introduce you," she said as she looked Tim up and down.

Now it was Tim's turn to blush. "I'm not usually starstruck but Troy, er, Heart, is . . ."

"Tell me about it," Sharon interrupted. "Even I'm in awe of his looks. As a matter of fact, *he's* in awe, too." She and Tim shared a laugh.

Polly chimed in. "Sharon, honey, if you're not booked for dinner this evening, why don't you come to our little place? You can fill me in on what I missed today. And give me a rundown on everybody else in the cast. I'm still feeling abominable for the screw-up. It was my agent's fault."

"Ach! Agents! You can't work without 'em and you can't kill 'em. I was negotiated out of the role of Lois Lane when my brilliant agent insisted on more money than Warner Brothers was willing to pay. I should have had Kate Bosworth's agent. Oh, and I'd be absolutely thrilled to have dinner with you!"

Polly acted as though she were the grateful one. "Everyone seems so darn nice around here," she said. "Except Gerold Goss, of course."

"Oh, him," Sharon said with a shake of her head. "He stormed in this morning and began cursing at poor Karen. What a temper! He backhanded a can of Coke on the table and sent it flying into Hiroaki's lap. Anyway, from the way Karen and Gerold were acting you'd think they were either lovers or mortal enemies. I figure one of them will eventually murder the other."

Thrilling Suspense From
Wendy Corsi Staub

__All the Way Home	0-7860-1092-4	$6.99US/$8.99CAN
__The Last to Know	0-7860-1196-3	$6.99US/$8.99CAN
__Fade to Black	0-7860-1488-1	$6.99US/$9.99CAN
__In the Blink of an Eye	0-7860-1423-7	$6.99US/$9.99CAN
__She Loves Me Not	0-7860-1768-6	$4.99US/$6.99CAN
__Dearly Beloved	0-7860-1489-X	$6.99US/$9.99CAN
__Kiss Her Goodbye	0-7860-1641-8	$6.99US/$9.99CAN
__Lullaby and Goodnight	0-7860-1642-6	$6.99US/$9.99CAN
__The Final Victim	0-8217-7971-0	$6.99US/$9.99CAN

Available Wherever Books Are Sold!

Visit our website at **www.kensingtonbooks.com**

Get Hooked on the
Mysteries of
Carola Dunn

Get More Mysteries by
Leslie Meier